To Alcuin,

"Happy Birthday."

Best wishes

[signature]
October 2005

# The President Is Down

## Colin. G. Poplett

*1663 Liberty Drive, Suite 200*
*Bloomington, Indiana 47403*
*(800) 839-8640*
*www.AuthorHouse.com*

*This book is a work of fiction. People, places, events, and situations are the product of the author's imagination. Any resemblance to actual persons, living or dead, or historical events, is purely coincidental.*

*© 2005 C. G. Poplett. All Rights Reserved.*

*No part of this book may be reproduced, stored in a retrieval system, or transmitted by any means without the written permission of the author.*

*First published by AuthorHouse 09/16/05*

*ISBN:1-4208-6126-3 (sc)*

*Printed in the United States of America*
*Bloomington, Indiana*

*This book is printed on acid-free paper.*

# Preface.

A fast moving bang up to date novel based on historic and current fact and events, George T Clayton the President of the United States of America, and Tony Salter the British Prime Minister, are embroiled in a terrorist attack outside of their wildest nightmare.

A plan to assassinate George "T" and possibly Tony Salter, whilst leaving Europe in total turmoil, and the USA potentially crippled for its life blood of "Oil". And thus held to ransom. Suspense on every page in this totally believable novel of the 21$^{st}$ Century.

Passion, love, hate, violence, greed, and humour are all experienced with a final twist in the tale. The suspects are Al Qaeda, Osama Bin Laden the Taliban, and the Russian Mafia.

Baghdad, England, Ireland, Belgium, Paris, Moscow, Poland, the holiday island of Kefalonia Greece, and finally The United States Of America are visited before all is concluded in this up to date novel.

## DATE LINE Wednesday August 18$^{th}$ 2004 London, England.
*As generally reported in the British Media. Television and Leading Newspaper's. .*

On Wednesday 18$^{th}$ August 2004 eight men were sensationally charged with terrorist activity, the charges relate to an allegedly planned Al Qaeda 'Dirty Bomb' attack on a prime London target such as Heathrow Airport or Buckingham Palace the residence of Queen Elizabeth the British Monarch. The men were among thirteen arrested in a series of dawn raids on houses and premises on the 3$^{rd}$ of August 2004. Security forces stated that had the attack/s taken place it would have been the deadliest terrorist outrage since the September 11$^{th}$ attacks in America. Osama Bin Laden's UK General a 32 year old man from North West London was believed to be amongst those arrested. One of the suspects was arrested in possession of a 'Terrorist Handbook'. Which gave instructions on how to manufacture explosives and bombs from chemicals?

*Book One*

# Chapter one

**Westbury Wiltshire. Wednesday 15th October 2003**

Since the end of the cold war, and the scaling down of operations in Northern Ireland, the SIS facility at Westbury in Wiltshire was now little used. Or that's what we are supposed to believe. In the 1960's 70's and 80's it was at its height of activity, much of the "training" of our agents, some of whom we now know were businessmen took place at Westbury.

The debriefing of the spy's we "turned" were all done there. A supposedly highly secure establishment and still having armed guards to let you in and out. Barbed razor wire and active camera's protect its perimeter.

The local's have long since got used to its presence and don't even see it.

Peter Henderson had spent the last four nights interrogating Abdullah Sugama a 35 year old Taliban who's family had been killed by the Taliban, a British Army Captain had effectively 'turned' him some 10 days before in Basra Iraq leading to his arrival by RAF Hercules at Lynham, Wiltshire, England 30 miles away some 5 days ago.

At first the Arab's heavily pockmarked face, thin and gaunt, and his way of not looking you in the eye when he spoke, plus his reluctance to talk about anything but his reward package for coming across had irritated Henderson, even though he was a top flight intelligence officer and heard it all before and should have been used to it.

They always thought they were the bloody first to come up with demands, demands that these days would not be met, and would be more realistic.

It was only at the end of the third day that he had made the breakthrough, the Taliban were planning something in Europe, and it was big. Beyond that he would not go until his 'package' was agreed. 'Worse than a bloody football star', thought Henderson.

Well not the sort of thing he could talk about over the phone, he would need a brief from Sir Bernard Hills the SIS Chief. And that meant a day back up in London, and a chance to sleep in his own bed for a night before his return to Westbury.

He had said his temporary goodbyes to Sugama the previous night and having had a full cooked breakfast in the mess, was packing his few belongings away prior to setting off for his 09.30 meeting at SIS headquarters in London. In went his socks, shirts, pants, and the pair of chino's he had spilt his coffee on. Martine would be at the washing as soon as he got in that evening.

He looked at his watch and decided to give Martine a quick call before he left for London. If she could get the next door neighbour to baby sit Jamie their 4 year old little terrorist, they could slip out and have an 'Italian meal' in Luigi's in the high street. It might make up for not being there for the last few days.

Particularly as she suffered a bit this time of the month and found Jamie even more of a trial beautiful and much loved as he was.

6.50am she would be up now grabbing a quick coffee before taking Jamie to pre-school at 7.45am. Should he ring her now or later? No he would wait until she had dropped Jamie off.

He would give her a quick ring before he got on the M3. A few minutes later he climbed into the 3.8 1960's Jaguar, his one indulgence in life, that's apart from his German born wife of some 5 years and 4 year old Jamie who he doted on. He turned the key and the starter; the car awoke with a steady growl and settled down to a satisfying exhaust note.

As he approached the security barrier the army corporal took a good look at him and raised the barrier lifting his left hand in a friendly goodbye as he did so. He drove the few meters to the main road, checked right and left and with a final glance turned right onto the A350 towards Salisbury.

The road was quiet and he did not expect to see much traffic until he hit the A303 prior to the M3. He drove out of Westbury and towards Warminster, his thoughts dwelled for a moment on the happy times he had had on the Army "Ranges", and the friends he had made along the way.

Fellow Captain Pat Harrison being one in particular. And reflected on the phone call with Pat only last night. How the hell had he known where to telephone him? And what was the photograph he said he was sending him.

He was now on the A36 Warminster bye-pass and opened the throttle a little nudging the speed up to 65mph coming ahead was a small roundabout with a right turn to Longleat, Lord Bath's famous safari park.

*The President Is Down*

He noticed a white Ford Transit slowly approaching the roundabout from the direction of Longleat and pressed the accelerator gently taking the Jag up to 80mph; he beat the transit on to the roundabout and accelerated away, then remembering the dreaded white police safety camera vans that sat at the side of the main road he pulled back to 60mph.

Glancing in the rear view mirror he was surprised to see the white transit 150m behind him and travelling at the same speed as him. As he approached the last roundabout on the bye-pass he eased up moved over to the centre of the road, checking his mirror as he did so.

The white transit was about 30m away now and he felt a little uneasy. He braked and dropped into second gear intending to take the roundabout and come out under power and blow off the transit.

One final check in the mirror, what the hell are the two Arab looking men in the van laughing at? *Arab looking men, Arab, Oh God NO!*

The world stood still for Peter Henderson as he watched the passenger pointing a long thin tube at him through the passenger door window and steady it on the mirror, a puff of smoke and as he screamed at the top of his voice he knew he was already dead.

The RPG hit the rear of the Jag dead centre, the car continued for a millisecond on fire, then reared up in the air, turned over and over, breaking up as it did so, finally coming to rest upside down on the roundabout, as the transit approached it, the Jag blew up and became an inferno.

The transit slowed and the occupants looked at its remains, and then gently drove round the wrong side of the roundabout, and headed towards the A303/M3 and the anonymity of London. The passenger spoke a few words into a mobile phone, and then replaced it on the dashboard.

**56, Westfield Gardens, Ealing, London.**
**9.30am Wednesday 15th October 2003**

He couldn't hear the bell so he knocked on the door using the brass knocker, a young fair haired woman, answered the door to the smallish dark skinned well dressed stranger who stood before her. He smiled. He looked like a door to door salesman, but it seemed a little early for that.

'Mrs Henderson'? She smiled back, 'Yes, how can I help you'? The stranger drew his hand from behind him, pointed the silenced berretta at her forehead and pulled the trigger twice. She fell over backwards, crashing into the hall table, and knocking the phone to the floor. The pale magnolia paintwork was splashed with her blood and a huge pool of blood began to collect behind what was left of her head. Seeping into the heavy twist pile carpet as it did so.

The stranger gently reached out and closed the door, wiped the knob with his handkerchief, turned and walked back down the path, closing the gate behind him. He failed to notice the curtains nearly opposite at number 38 twitch!

Mrs Parry confined to a wheelchair now for the last four years found people watching her greatest entertainment. Her high back chair came complete with kettle and teapot close to hand; opera glasses completed the ensemble.

She picked them up. She looked at the man who had just left young Mrs Henderson, he looked foreign, French maybe, and she wasn't good at placing where people came from.

Her late husband had been excellent at placing people, that's if he was telling the truth after all what was a small white lie? When the man lifted something in his left hand to his face she saw it was one of those new fangled mobile phone things? She saw the scar, which ran from just in front of his left ear, and down to the middle of his cheek. It was quite deep.

The man spoke on the phone and then put it back in his pocket and walked on towards the tube station at the end of the road.

## SIS (MI6) Headquarters London Wednesday 15th October 2003

9.30am exactly as Sir Bernard Hills entered his conference room at SIS headquarters on the Thames or the carbuncle as it's affectionately called. Glancing round and quickly taking in those present, he growled, 'Where the bloody hell is he then'? Has that blasted death trap of his broken down again? It was going to be a good day!

'We don't know where he is Sir'; this coming from John Barnes, his head of Security who somehow felt it was his fault that Henderson was not with them.

Sir Bernard had that effect on you. Recently taken over when his predecessor had been killed in a 'Hill Climb' event with his 1930's Austin 7, when he had slipped of the winding upwards track through the woods that was favouring the days event. The car had rolled over and over down the embankment, coming to rest up against a huge oak tree. He was dead before the car finally stopped, his neck being broken at the first roll over.

Sir Bernard, a favourite of the PM Tony Salter had been appointed very quickly, and had come in with a 'New Broom' He thought it a privilege to work in the security service, so should you if you worked for him, stop watching the bloody clock, early finishes on Fridays now a thing of the past. Expenses!! Forget it. Yes his broom was certainly visible.

When he had taken over two short months before, he had inherited John Parson's secretary of some 25 years. At first he couldn't get used to the bloody woman, interfering old bag, told him when he could have his tea, cut down on his coffee intake, telling him it made grumpy. Cheeky sod, but he had to admit cutting down to 4 cups of coffee a day, and a similar number of cups of tea, had made him less irritable.

The fact she knew where everything was, and gently guided him as to who he should take notice of, and who to sideline had been a big help. He could never replace her John Parsons who he thought she had carried a secret affection for years. She never married although spent a lot of her spare time and holidays with her married sister and family in Devon.

The door burst open, to reveal a totally distraught Mary Bishop, Sir Bernard's secretary. Tears streamed down her face, she stood shaking, and sobbing, Sir Bernard stood up.' Mary what on earths wrong'? She didn't answer, 'Mary tell me what is it'? 'It's Mr Henderson Sir, ---- he's had a road accident, and -- she started sobbing again, he's dead Sir.'

Sir Bernard visibly shocked, looked at Barnes and nodded towards the Sheraton drinks cabinet at the other end of the room. Barnes opened the cabinet and poured a stiff brandy into a Waterford crystal glass and handed it to Mary Bishop. Who gulped it down in one? She spluttered and coughed, and taking a handkerchief from the sleeve of her dress and dabbed her eyes. 'He crashed his car somewhere near Warminster some hours ago. A Superintendent Johnson of Wiltshire Police would like you to telephone him Sir Bernard.'

'Yes of course, you sit down, John look after Mary please.' Back in his office, he picked up his telephone and rang the number he had found on Mary's desk. Within seconds he was put through to Superintendent Johnson.

'Superintendent Johnson, Sir Bernard Hills here, what's happened Superintendent?'

'Good morning Sir Bernard, at about 7.15am today two of my traffic officers attended an RTA, sorry a road traffic accident on the A36 close to Warminster.'

'At first it looked like the driver had been driving far too fast on the bye-pass, as there would be little traffic on it at that time of day. They thought he might have miss-judged the distance to the roundabout. However, what did not stack up was there were no skid marks, and the vehicle itself was totally destroyed.'

'One of the officers is ex-Army and he thought the car had taken a missile strike. And unlikely though it may have been, we do have of course

Warminster Barracks literally 1 mile from the scene. So we asked the army to attend.'

'A Lieutenant Briggs of bomb disposal thinks it was an RPG. Before we start at our end filling out reports and so forth, I thought I had better ring you, you see we found a telephone number on his mobile that we know to be restricted and put two and two together sir and as result I have taken charge and restricted access to the site, until I could be advised by yourself'.'

'I have put diversions in place. There was one male occupant of the Jag, not a pretty sight I'm afraid.'

'Hmm, very astute of you Superintendent! I shall have Chief Superintendent Gardner of Special Branch contact you within the hour. In the meantime, thank you for your help and might I ask you to preserve as much of the accident site as you can until you have spoken with Gardner. I know it must be difficult for you but, it could be very important.'

# Chapter two

**GCHQ Cheltenham, England 11.00am Wednesday 15th October 2003**

Bradley Smith was an 'Intercept Interpreter'; he often laughed at this description of himself which sounded quite grand in a way. And for which he was paid the princely sum of £17,877 per year. Today Bradley was about to make a name for himself. On his desk sat 5 envelopes all contained tapes of part conversations that had been collected by one of his colleagues on 'listening'.

Not many people knew that GCHQ and Menwith Hill near Harrogate in North Yorkshire England between them snoop on every phone call made into and out of the UK.

Some very specialised software analyses all phone calls and picked out those of interest, today Bradley for his sins was about to listen to all 5 tapes, and report on each, this would take him about an hour, then in would come another five.

He had the tapes recorded up to 0800 that morning. As luck would have it, the third tape made him sit up, although in Arabic the word Taliban was used three times in 4 minutes, and the word Westbury just once, but once was enough.

He had heard about the road accident that had crippled the roads around Warminster, and the fact that the man involved was believed to have left a defence establishment at Westbury shortly before.

He picked up the phone and spoke to his boss; some 12 minutes later both of them were listening to an Arabic-speaking member of GCHQ translate the tape for them.

'Basically, what he is saying is that they have executed the infidel as instructed and are returning to London. Also that he did not have our friend with him. Whatever that means. The person they were speaking with told them they had done well and that Allah would reward them'.

'Would you have that transcribed please as a matter of urgency, we have some phone calls to make, come on young Bradley you may as well see this through with me. See that we get the transcript in the Directors office within the next 15 minutes please.'

At 11.30am that same morning a white transit van was seen by two dropouts having their breakfast of McEwans lager to roll into the Thames at Wapping. Behind the derelict Hovis warehouse.

Just prior to that a well-dressed dark skinned man who had been driving it was seen to throw two objects into the river. He saw both men watching him and started to walk towards them and then changed his mind and walked away.

The more coherent of the two drop outs said to his partner, 'See I blame the fucking politicians, you have to pay the fucking council now for getting rid of your car, that's why they push um in the river, with a loud belch, he broke wind noisily, rolled on his side and went to sleep again.'

# Chapter three

**M3 Motorway 10.45am Wednesday 8th October**

The 4.2litre Jaguar was cruising at 125mph in the outside lane of the M3 out of London and just passing Farnborough. 'I'll go a bit quicker when I lose this traffic Sir,' said Police constable Lowe who was driving.

Chief Superintendent Gardner sat in the back and his sergeant Tommy Tucker sat in the front. 'No that's OK Constable this is just fine, we will be there soon enough and I need some time to collect my thoughts.' Lying sod, thought Tommy to himself, he's shit scared, and I'm having a great time this is the fastest I have ever gone. It's fantastic. 'Sierra Control to Cobra 96'. 'Go ahead 'said the police driver. 'We have an up date for you; a Wiltshire car will meet with you where the A303 / M3 junction is. He will sit on the shoulder drive straight past and he will catch you up Cobra 96, do you copy.' He'll have to put his foot down thought Tommy. 'Yes I copy Sierra control thank you.'

The Jag took the run off from the M3 at a mere 100mph, and sure enough the Wiltshire Police Volvo was already picking up speed on the hard shoulder, they went past it, and a short time after it took the lead.

Both cars were now doing about 100 mph in the outside lane of the two lane undulating A303 The cars swept on past ' Porton Down' and 'Stonehenge' and onto the A36 at Deptford.

'Not far now Sir,' said PC Lowe his driver.

**Warminster Wiltshire 11.45am**

In less than 10 minutes they came upon the scene. PC Lowe wound his way through the police fire and ambulance vehicles and stopped 50m from the roundabout.

It was once pretty with a raised bed of flowers welcoming you to Warminster, it wasn't now! What was left of the old Jaguar was upside down in an undignified manner, scorched and barely identifiable as the classic that it had been.

The area was roped off with blue and white chequered tape; there was no traffic on any of the approach roads, only emergency service vehicles, and one Army bomb disposal vehicle.

A tall thin man dressed in police uniform broke away from a gathering of people and walked towards Gardner and his sergeant. 'I'm Tom Johnson Sir, sorry to meet in such bloody awful circumstances.' 'Yes, I'm Bill Gardner and this is my sergeant Tommy Tucker,' seeing the look on Johnson's face, he said 'it's for real I promise you.' Tucker merely smiled he had heard it all before. Johnson said, 'I am sorry about your chap, he didn't stand a chance, nowhere to go you see, he had to slow for the roundabout.'

'If it's any conciliation, it would have been instantaneous.'

'How the fucking hell do you know that'? Bellowed Gardner, even Tucker jumped back. Superintendent Johnson looked shocked, 'I'm sorry ', said Gardner I was thinking of his wife and the young boy I think they have. His wife doesn't even know about this yet.'

'She is probably preparing him something special for his dinner when he gets home, he's been away for a few days you see, Oh hell, I'm making a balls of this, I am sorry lets get on.'

They approached the car, and now they were nearer they could see a short curled up lump under a grey sheet. Johnson very carefully pulled one corner back, and they could see the tightly stretched face of Peter Henderson grinning back at them, his teeth bigger than normal. How does a fire do that to your teeth thought Tucker? Then the penny dropped.

'It's a bit of a shock seeing him like this Superintendent, he was 6 foot 3 inches, a big lad and now he's only 4 foot and a shrivelled lump of charcoal. I can tell it's him though. It would not be a good idea to ask his wife to identify that mass of charred flesh. Whoever did this are dead men, I promise you.' Said Gardner quietly, and turned away.

'This is Lieutenant Briggs of Army Bomb Disposal, Superintendent Gardner.' The men shook hands, 'and this is Sergeant Tommy Tucker.' Briggs took the lead, 'I have had plenty of time to examine the vehicle, and I can confirm it is a Russian built shoulder launch RPG. We found some bits, very effective over 200m more in the right hands. The device hit the petrol tank, which as you will know is pretty low down on these older cars.'

'The petrol tank wasn't full but sometimes a nearly empty tank can be more devastating than a full one. This simply ruptured caught fire and exploded. The weapon itself would have caused all the primary damages and killed the driver.'

'The petrol exploding simply finished things off. It has the hallmarks of an IRA or terrorist attack; I have seen plenty of this in Northern Ireland and during Desert Storm in Iraq.'

'If I could go now gentlemen? You know where to get me if you need me.'

'Yes, that's OK lieutenant thanks for your help, and please let us has your observation in writing, it would be a big help.' With that Gardener turned away.

Constable Lowe approached the two senior police officers. 'Excuse me Sir,' he said directing his comments to Gardner. 'You are wanted on the car radio. I am told its private Sir.'

3 minutes later Gardner was back'.

'How far is Cheltenham?' 'About an hour or less if you are lucky replied Superintendent Johnson. We can get you on to the M4 at Tormarton in 20 minutes tops from here. Then it's straight down the M4 past the Bristol turn-off and on to the M5 Heading North. Come of at Cheltenham junction 11 turn off straight into Cheltenham.'

'Can I ask you where you are going?'

'Yes, sorry GCHQ, they have picked something up.'

'That changes things a little, still take the second turn off for Cheltenham, that's junction 11, I'll get you a map. GCHQ is about a mile down the road on your left. I will ask for a Gloucestershire car to pick you up before you leave the M5. Good hunting Bill.'

The Wiltshire police Volvo followed by Gardner's Jaguar headed off towards Bath and the A36, they skirted the historic City of Bath with its World famous Roman Baths, flew down the London road, and up the winding A46 to Tormarton. Less than 20 minutes after leaving Warminster the police jaguar dropped down the slip road and on to the M4.

PC Lowe moved straight across into the outside lane and up behind a Porsche doing 90mph. The Porsche driver sat there until he realised the car behind was a police car, and sheepishly moved over, wondering why he hadn't been pulled over.

PC Lowe eased up to a 100mph and held it there, he swept up and over the M4 and on to the M5 with barely a change of speed. A few minutes later a police Volvo shot out of Michael Wood services and on to his tail, he moved over to the centre lane to allow the Volvo past and then kept station 100m behind the Volvo in close convoy.

# Chapter four

**SIS Headquarters London 11.00am Wednesday 15th October**

Sir Bernard Hills picked up his secure line to the Prime Minister. The PM answered almost immediately.

'What can I do for you Sir Bernard?'

'I need to talk to you Sir, preferably right now.'

'Come on over Sir Bernard, I shall expect you shortly.' 20 minutes later he was sat in front of the PM. A life long friend and one whom he had a lot of time for.

Sir Bernard led off; 'You will recall Sir, that 2 weeks ago we received intelligence from Saudi Arabia that Al Qaeda was planning something big in Europe, and possibly in the USA as well.'

'We were told two Al Qaeda planners were in Iraq. Our intelligence people in Iraq had picked up a freedom fighter who wanted to change sides, he gave us certain intelligence which was absolutely spot on, and in fact we picked up the two planners and one other most wanted.'

'He must have created some problem for himself as he was 'arrested' by his own lot; seemingly they were going to give him some grief. It was only the bombing by the Americans of one of the Old Palaces that he was being held in that allowed us to get him out and over to the UK. He has an elderly father and a younger brother still in Iraq there is some concern for their safety. The probability is that they are both dead by now, paying the penalty for him as it were.'

'We thought the body we left behind would have led them to believe he had been killed in the air raid. This is a bloody mess!!! Sorry Sir.'

'That's quite all right Sir Bernard 'I quite understand. Going back to chummy, after we had whisked him over to Westbury, he refused to talk to anybody the ungrateful sod, that is any body but Peter Henderson. Well young Peter Henderson went over to Westbury to meet with the Taliban.'

'He was there from Sunday night until around 7.00 this morning, there is no easy way to say this Prime Minister, but he was blown to bits or as near as is possible.'

'Until we read Henderson encrypted interviews we won't know what this is all about. That's being worked on as we speak. I should get the first ones later today hopefully.'

'We now have a positive identification of Henderson, Superintendent Gardner knew him well. I shall have to go round to break the news to his wife, something I am dreading doing. As I was saying Sir, this incident would seem to indicate otherwise. We now have good reason to believe they know he is at Westbury in Wiltshire.'

'You will recall Sir, this is the place where the de-briefings used to take place with the Uri Penkofski's and the like some years ago'.

'A Russian built RPG has been identified as the weapon used. We have a positive 'ident' on that from an army bomb disposal lieutenant based at Warminster. He says it was fired at close range possibly from a vehicle following Henderson, as the initial impact was from the rear'.

'That stacks up because Henderson would have been driving reasonably quickly I would have thought. There were also no skid marks indicating that he did not have any warning of events, probably as well poor sod'.

'We don't yet know why the Taliban at Westbury insisted on speaking only to Henderson. I have run a check on Henderson as he came to us quite recently from Army Intelligence just to see if we can pin point any link between them'.

The PM looked decidedly unhappy, 'I have just been speaking with US President George Clayton, you know he is thinking visiting Europe this Autumn, at the moment its pretty hush hush, so I would be obliged if you would keep it to yourself at this stage.'

'The last thing we want is him involved in anything whilst he is here'.

'We need to get this thing cleared up and pretty damn quick. Do you think there is any link to this intelligence brief from the CIA yesterday, or was it last week? We seem to get so many false titbits of information recently. Everybody seems to be running scared. Since 9/11.'

'Who have we got going over to Warminster Sir Bernard? I presume somebody will be seeing our Taliban pretty quickly?'

'I have sent Chief Superintendent Gardener of Special branch up to Warminster he should be there about now. He will then go on to Westbury.'

'Have words with Tom Franks at the American embassy, I saw him at a dinner only last night so I know he is not going to Washington until this coming weekend.'

Tom Frank's ex-Brigadier General US Army, and now CIA liaison officer in London. Sir Bernard knew him well, about 220lbs of pure muscle, lean tall, and with iron-grey hair cut short in the army fashion. His piercing steel blue eyes could be a little menacing at times. Certainly one who would not put up with any nonsense, liked by his men for his unstinting loyalty to them and the Army.---- He expected, and got the same back.

When he left the Army at the request of the President some two years and moved over to the CIA and White House liaison he had felt lost at Langley. That was until the bombing of a school bus in Miami, which turned out to be a car bomb being transported on a motor cycle, which exploded at a set of traffic lights. Wiping out 11 children between the ages of 9 and 11, and seriously injuring another six.

The school bus driver was killed outright. Initially it was thought to be a terrorist attack gone wrong, but in the event it was a drug "Turf" war bombing. DNA showed the motorcyclist to the son of a Mafia soldier trying to earn his stripes. The Everglades had two new visitors three nights later; that never came back, the alligators no doubt dined well that night.

Sir Bernard left the PM, promising to give him a progress report later in the day. His car and driver were waiting for him and drove him straight round to the American Embassy in Grosvenor Square. Whilst on the way he spoke with Tom Franks on his secure car phone.

Signing him in past the Marine on duty, and hurrying him into a meeting room known to be swept and secure. The room had no windows and it did not have a straight line of sight to it from the open area at the front of the embassy.

When the coffee arrived, and the pleasantries were over, and with typical American frankness, which initially Sir Bernard found irritating to say the least, but by now found quite refreshing, although he would be appalled if any one but an American had spoken to him so directly.

Franks said, 'What the hell is eating your arse Sir Bernard?' Over the next 10 minutes Sir Bernard told him. Franks listened, occasionally breaking in to clarify a point. When Sir Bernard had finished, Franks looked him in the eye, and said,' You may, or may not know that Peter Henderson and I met up during Desert Storm he was attached to your Guards Regiment as Intel Officer, and a bloody good one too.' ---'He spoke near perfect Arabic. '

'Did he now said Sir Bernard, now that's something I didn't know it may just shed some light on why this Taliban chap at Westbury wanted to speak to Henderson, and only Henderson.'

'We will know more when Chief Superintendent Gardner reports in. He went on up to Cheltenham to GCHQ, and is going to drop in and have a few words with Mr Abdullah Sugama, at Westbury afterwards.'

'In the meantime can you do your bit and see if we can get anything on this incident from your guy's, on the other side of the water.' With that Sir Bernard left for SIS Headquarters.

# Chapter five

**GCHQ Cheltenham 1630 hours Wednesday 15th October.**

The new circular stone/brick and glass GCHQ building, with its shell proof glass roof, and armoured glass double windows, meant to resist bullets and light shells, is an incredible structure, in the centre is an internal road way, with mature trees growing at a height 15m or more within the building. Called the doughnut simply because from the air it is.

GCHQ is the nerve centre for information gathering from telephones and satellite communication systems in the UK, some would argue it's the best in the world. Specialists of all types inhabit its very exclusive being, and far more goes on there than we would like to admit. Or ever would admit to.

Menwith Hill near the spa town of Harrogate in North Yorkshire provides a similar function. And is manned by an American army contingent, on what is a British military base.

Between them every single phone call made out of and in to the UK is monitored and eaves dropped on.

In a specially set aside conference room sat Chief Superintendent Gardner, Tommy Tucker, a very nervous Bradley Smith, the GCHQ Director Peter Wilson, and Assistant Director Alan Price.

'Well Mr Smith, or can I call you Bradley, tell us in your own words, what you heard.' Said Chief Superintendent Gardner.

'It was about 10.00am this morning Sir; I usually do all my paperwork and reports from the previous day when I first come in on the next morning. And that's what I was doing this morning; I heard a news item on the radio in the staff restaurant whilst having my coffee break. It mentioned Warminster and an explosion or something and the traffic problems around the immediate area. At 11.00am I was listening to a tape that had been triggered the previous day in it there were references to the Taliban and Westbury. I knew something was wrong and told my superior Mr Higgins.'

'We listened to it again and took it our Director who called his contact at New Scotland Yard in London. One of our Arabic speaking linguists listened to it, and said they were discussing if it was possible to get into the Westbury MOD site, and there was some mention of the Taliban guy that's there.'

'However Sir, a few minutes ago, and whilst you were on your way here I received another tape which had been selected because it seemed to relate to first tape.'

'Mr Wood our Arabic language expert listened to it also he said' 'basically, what he is saying: is that they have executed the infidel as instructed and are returning to London. Also that he did not have our friend with him. Whatever that means. The person they were speaking with told them they had done well and that Allah would reward them. This was recorded at about 7.15 this morning.'

'We are now tracking this phone in real time, and it's been moving around a bit at about 9.30am it was used for a short call of 15 seconds in Ealing London, the caller simply said 'It is done' and rang off. It was used again at 11.37 in Wapping London. The signal was weak and we could not get any of the conversation this time. Since the last call it's been turned off.'

'You see what people don't realise is that we can target any given mobile phone number and get its location if it's turned on. It's all done via satellite. Did you say Ealing?' Said Gardner nearly jumping down young Bradley's throat.

Tommy Tucker's heart missed a beat and he suddenly felt sick. 'Do we know if Mrs Henderson's been told yet Sir?' Said Tucker looking directly at Superintendent Gardner.

Gardner's voice was very strained and quiet, 'No the Met were sending a Police councillor around with Sue Hedges from SIS to break the news just after lunch. Go and give one of them a quick ring Tommy.'

Back at Ealing police station Sue Hedges and WPC Atkins a Police councillor were trying the door bell for the second time that day, it was quite a warm afternoon, and when Sue couldn't get an answer she looked through the letterbox. The smell made her pull back from the door.

WPC Atkins seeing the look on Sue Hedges face said,' what's wrong?' 'I can smell blood, I think she has probably hurt herself and she didn't go shopping after all I think she is behind the door lying injured! We need to break in. If we can't find a key.'

Under the doormat, under the plant pot, top of the door casing, under the stone birdbath, they were running out of options, when she spotted it a child's plastic sand bucket and spade. There was sand in the bucket and she dug her fingers in and pulled out a latchkey and a mortise key. Gingerly she inserted the mortise key first and unlocked that lock, then turned her attention to the latchkey and opened the door.

The pool of blood under and around Mrs Henderson's shattered head was now turning black and the sweet cloying smell coming from the drying blood made her fell sick.

The only thing that stopped her was the whimpering coming from upstairs, she stepped over the body and climbed the carpeted stairway to the landing, and being guided by the ever-increasing volume of the whimper entered the front bedroom.

The child was curled up in a foetal position with blood on his pyjama's he faced away from the door and just laid there whimpering and in a trance like state. She touched his head gently and he moved away, she laid her hand on his body and spoke to him quietly.

He seemed to calm down, and stopped his whimpering; he got hold of her hand and gripped it with suprising strength. She picked him up and called for WPC Atkins to come upstairs to the front bedroom.

WPC Atkins carefully entered the room and approached the king size bed with Sue Hedges sitting on the edge, and cuddling the boy whilst gently rocking backwards and forwards. He was nearly asleep now, and in a few minutes dropped off into a fitful slumber, she laid him on the bed and tucked a duvet around him. He put his right thumb in his mouth and began to suck on it.

Sergeant Tuckers mobile rang he stood and walked away from the others and answered the phone, he stopped mid pace and slowly turned towards Chief Superintendent Gardner, he couldn't speak, when it came it was all in a rush, ' They have killed her Sir.'

'Killed Mrs Henderson, oh my God, who the hell has killed her and why?'

The five men sat round the oak boardroom table it was a sombre gathering, they had just heard from Superintendent Gardner about Martine Henderson. Everybody was looking at Superintendent Gardner. After what seemed to be hours, but was in fact a mere 20 seconds, he spoke!

'Well it would appear somebody is a bit pissed off that we have 'Chummy' your local Taliban. So I would ask you three gentlemen to put your bits together for me and courier it up to London. I would like it all

*The President Is Down*

there when I get back tonight. Thanks for some sterling work, particular thanks to you Mr Bradley you were very sharp and quick of the mark, well done.'

'Director, I wonder if we may ask for your indulgence, we need to speak with this fellow at Westbury, we desperately need someone who can speak Arabic. If we could borrow Mr Wood for this evening it would be a big help. I want to get at this chap quickly?'

The Director looked at Wood who nodded his head; he was on duty until 6.00am the next morning so this would be an interesting diversion. He went to get his jacket.

'I will get you dropped back here Mr Wood or have you taken home afterwards if you will help.'

'I would be delighted Chief Superintendent,' said Wood...

With that Gardner stood up, shook hands all round and left the boardroom with Tucker and Wood. Outside in he corridor, he stopped looked at Tucker and said, 'When we get back to the car set up a meet for 9.00pm at Westbury tonight. That should give us chance to get something to eat before we get there.'

Ten minutes later back in the Jaguar and on the M5 Motorway Sergeant Tucker was talking to Westbury and setting up the meeting. They came off the motorway at the A46 Bath turnoff, travelling less than a mile they pulled in to the Crown Pub. At just after 8.20pm they left the pub having had a good meal all round, and now felt ready for anything.

PC Lowe pulled up at the MOD facility at Westbury just before 8.45pm. The duty officer a young Army Lieutenant Rees-Jones met them. He looked a little flushed'. I couldn't get in touch with you Sir, but Mr Sugama says he is tired and would be happy to see you tomorrow morning around 9.00am.'

Gardner went very quiet, and spoke with immense control, which Rees-Jones took for compliance until he realised what Gardner was saying to him 'Lieutenant if you wish to keep those very shiny new pips on your shoulder, you will have us in front of Mr Bloody Sugama within the next 2 minutes.'

'If you doubt my words then the clock is ticking .'

A very red faced Rees-Jones took them to a locked room at the rear of an accommodation block. He opened the door and the four of them entered the room. Sugama sat in a comfortable armchair watching television.

Gardner walked over to the TV turned it off and said. 'Get up, my name is Gardner I am a Chief Superintendent of Police, this is Sergeant Tucker, and this is Mr Wood who is an official interpreter for the British Government. We wish to ask you some questions.'

Sugama said something in Arabic, Wood said after a little hesitation, 'he would prefer to talk to us tomorrow he is feeling very tired, he says he told the Army man this.'

'Thank you Mr Wood, now as politely as you wish, tell him to get his bloody arse in gear and follow us, or there may not be a tomorrow.' With that he turned on his heal and walked the two doors down to the interview room allocated to them.

The room was cold looking, with very shiny polished vinyl flooring, four upright chairs, a table, a tape deck sat to one side of the table. It wasn't meant to look attractive or feel inviting and in that respect it was spot-on. There was an ashtray looking like an afterthought which Gardner consigned to the waste bin. Lieutenant Rees-Jones entered followed by Sugama, Woods and Tucker.

Gardner pointed to one of the chairs at the other side of the table, smiled at Sugama and said, 'Sit, he turned to Lieutenant Rees-Jones and smiled again. 'Thank you Lieutenant you may go.' Rees-Jones face turned brick red, he turned on his heals and left. Tucker shut the door quietly and firmly.

'Please sit down gentlemen, sergeant please sit between the table and the door, Mr Wood please sit next to me.' When they had settled in their positions he looked directly at Sugama and spoke to Wood.

'Please tell Mr Sugama, that I have had a long day, I have had a senior intelligence officer Mr Henderson killed, and I want some answers.'

Wood did as he was asked, he looked a little uncomfortable,' he says he will most happy to help when he has confirmation of the British Governments settlement package; at least I think that what he means.'

'Tell him there will be no settlement package if he does not answer my questions, and answers them fully and honestly.'

Again Wood told Sugama what had been said. 'He says it is important to him that we understand his position, and confirm his "compensation" or package promised him.'

Tucker flew across the room, banged on the table and with obvious rage, slammed his wristwatch onto the table in front of Sugama. 'Listen you bloody wop and listen good, you have five, holding, holding five fingers up in front of Sugama, minutes to start making sense or you are back on the next RAF Hercules from Lynham tomorrow morning.'

He took his mobile out of his pocket. Pressed a couple of buttons, and spoke into the phone. 'This is Sergeant Tucker Squadron leader, regarding the conversation we had earlier. Please have your aircraft available for 0600 in the morning. That is unless you hear from me within the next hour. Yes—thanks, just the one passenger. Baghdad that's right .or what's convenient, thank you.'

The other person could be heard to be still speaking when he rang off.

Wood spoke up, 'he got the message sergeant, and says he is offended that we thought he would not talk to you, of course he will.' Gardner looked at Tucker with a new respect as he carefully picked his wrist watch up off the table and placed it back on his wrist.

Somewhere in Essex when Fred Cousins got back from his nightly visit to the pub Doris Cousins his fifty eight year old wife would be telling him of the strange lunatic phone call from somebody arranging to send him to Baghdad wherever that was!! He would tell her not to be so bloody daft and that some idiot was having a laugh, and make her a cup of tea.

'Now Mr Sugama why did you ask to speak to Mr Henderson?' Sugama looked from Gardner to Wood the latter translated the Superintendents question.

'He was good to me during what you call Desert Storm.' God this is going to be long night thought Sergeant Tucker.

'Lets try another tack Mr Wood said Gardner; ask him to describe exactly how he met Henderson? What Henderson did for him?' Sugama started to answer Gardner's questions in broken English.

'Mr Henderson was Army officer; he was having soldiers going in my house, and my friend's house. My friend a bad man, he go to stab with knife a soldier who go in his house. Mr Henderson shoot him, but not dead just leg! I in my friend's house and soldiers go to shoot me.'

'Mr Henderson say no, and have big how you say, row/shout!! with other officer. He take me home to my family. My wife she sick and need medicine, but Baghdad no medicine. Mr Henderson bringing medicine and my wife get better.'

Superintendent Gardner cut in, 'I thought you only had a father and brother in Iraq'!!

'My wife killed by helicopter with rockets three weeks later. My father and brother still in Baghdad.'

Superintendent Gardner jumped straight back at him and changed course completely. 'Where did you do your Taliban training ?'

Sugama's eyes flickered and he looked away 'I do not understand' he said.

'You are a Taliban; Mr Henderson told us so when he spoke with us this morning. (Sugama would not know this was untrue). So I say again, and if you do not understand then Mr Wood will ask you. Where did you do your Taliban training?'

Sugama haltingly replied, 'Afghanistan, we fight the Russians, I do not fight British and American!!'

'Why do you not fight British and American troops? They occupy your Country blow up your power stations and offices and shops and homes, and kill your people.' He was being deliberately provocative to elicit a reaction.

Sugama did not reply. Superintendent Gardner repeated the question.

'I want Saddam Hussein dead; he killed my Mother, my two sisters, my uncles and my little brother who was baby of 2 years. I can not kill Saddam, British and American can. British and American they kill some of my people who are bad, some who are good. Allah looks after them all they are all martyrs.'

Superintendent Gardner had no reply, and was silent for a few seconds, 'I am sorry I did not know.'

Sugama started to speak, ' I was going to be doctor, I was in Baghdad hospital for two years training when American bomb blow it up, I was injured, he held up his right arm and pulled up his loose and baggy sleeve. His arm was slightly twisted, and showed lighter and darker lumps of skin on the forearm, the result of poor skin grafting. I was sent by my uncle to Saudi Arabia for my arm.'

'Where did you get involved with the Taliban?' Asked Superintendent Gardner.

'When in hospital I with some men who injured, they are Taliban. They tell me many stories of fighting the Russians who rape Afghan women and kill women children and old men. I go back with them to Afghanistan, and learn to fight the Russians. When the women catch a Russian they cut off, ---- he stood up and pointed to his penis, and put in mouth, he take long time to die and scream all time.'

'When did you go back to Baghdad?' Asked Superintendent Gardner.

Sugama thought for moment! 'I go back to Baghdad when Saddam's men kill my Mother and my baby brother. I take 4 months to walk home. When I get home Saddam he killed my uncles. Then I start to find people to help me kill Saddam. Then War it start again. Americans in Baghdad and British soldiers some too.'

'When you were in Baghdad you were still in Taliban!' Superintendent Gardner said, not exactly a question, more a statement as he thought of fact.

He was surprised be the vehemence of Sugama's response.

'No I give up Taliban, Taliban want all western people dead and only Taliban live, this is wrong. Koran not say that. I leave Taliban. But they

## The President Is Down

come to me and say I have to help or die. They tell of many things they will do to Americans, with bombs and rockets and mines.'

Sugama continued, Superintendent Gardner did not interrupt, as Sugama stumbled along speaking with passion and seeming sincerity.

'When Americans pull down Saddam statue, I watch with glad heart, and I see Mr Henderson with two American officers. I am afraid to speak to him and never see him again in Baghdad. One week after they pull down statue, Ali Halakim, he big man in Taliban in Afghanistan. I see him in Baghdad and follow him. He goes to old part of Baghdad which is many bombs. He speaks with many men in old Saddam Palace. One of the men I know he was friend of my dead uncle.'

'I go to his house after two days and he tells me of how we are getting rid of Americans. And how they going to kill the American President in England.'

Superintendent Gardner, kept a straight face, 'yes of course, said Gardner when was that? When he is here next year perhaps?'

'No-No!! Said Sugama some time now. I tell Mr Henderson last night before he goes.'

'This sounds rubbish to me', said Superintendent Gardner, how exactly are they going to kill him?'

Sugama, looked at Gardner and said, 'they shoot down his plane!!' As if it should have pretty obvious that that's what would happen.

'What exactly did you do to warrant the British Army in Basra sending you to England for Mr Henderson to speak to?'

Sugama looked at the floor, his shoulders slumped obviously is some distress, in a way Gardner felt sorry for him, a feeling he soon dismissed.

'Mr Wood repeat the question please,' Wood did so, and Sugama looked up.

He said very quietly, 'I gave 50 of my people to the British Army; they had just finished learning bombs, and tank rockets. They were in a camp near Afghan border, big fight and most killed. Ali Halakim was not with them. Three days I was picked up with eight other men and taken to Old Saddam Palace. One by one they torture us, no food just water for three days. 'They Palace wall blow up and many Americans and British Soldiers; one hit me with rifle and drag me outside. I see the Army Officer I told of my people. He shoots me twice very close but no bullet hit me. He drag me in little tank and take me to Air force plane send me here.'

Mr Sugama said Gardner looking at him with a mix of understanding/ passion and disgust. 'I have listened to your story and if it can be substantiated that what you say you have done is true, and then I will be visiting you again with somebody from what is called the Home Office. In the meantime thank you for your help.'

Sugama for the first time looked Superintendent Gardner in the face; he said 'I am so sorry Mr Henderson has died.

I did not know they could do this. Then after some hesitation he said.----- Can they do this to me?'

Superintendent Gardner stood up, 'I wouldn't worry about that you are in a pretty secure place and we were not expecting Mr Henderson to be attacked.' He made no mention of the horrific end to Henderson's wife Martine.

'Sergeant, go and find' our Army chap please tell him we are going.'

A little later in the car park, he spoke on his mobile to the Wiltshire Police control room at Devizes; he spoke with Chief Inspector Price. 'Chief Inspector we have finished at Westbury could you have a car take Mr Wood back to Gloucester please as previously arranged. Thank you.

Superintendent Gardner turned to Mr Wood; 'I am ever so grateful for your help and do hope we haven't inconvenienced you too much. I know that you have signed the Official Secrets Act, but in view of what you heard in there, he nodded towards the main building please do not say a word to anybody about tonight's events and conversations.'

Back in the car he spoke to Sir Bernard on the secure car phone, 'he spoke about our American friend visiting us shortly and that he might have an accident.' There was no reply for a couple of seconds.

'Bill I know it's late, and you have had a hell of a day, but could you be at No10 tomorrow morning at 8.30?'

A little surprised Gardner replied, 'Yes of course I can, see you there Sir.' and rang off.

PC Lowe dropped Chief Superintendent Gardner and Sergeant Tucker of at Paddington Green police station, central London around 1.00am in the morning. Gardner had a flat above a row of shops, with a very pleasant roof garden. 'You had better get off home Tommy see you around 10.00am in the office.' Both shared an office at New Scotland Yard.

Gardner said his goodbyes to PC Lowe and thanked him for his support and efforts.

# Chapter six

**10 Downing Street, London. 8.30am Thursday 16th October 2003
The home and office of the British Prime Minister.**

Tony Salter sat in a comfortable wing backed chair opposite two other similar in which Chief Superintendent Gardner and Sir Bernard Hills were sat. A low highly polished oak coffee table separated them, and a Georgian silver coffee pot, silver milk jug and silver sugar bowl adorned it.

The British Prime Minister looked relaxed and comfortable; his youthful face had a slight smile on it. He was dressed in a mid-blue oxford shirt with open necked button down collar pair of beige chino's and dark brown loafers.

He looks far too young to be the PM thought Sir Bernard, not for the first time as he looked at his friend Tony Salter.

In contrast, Sir Bernard wore a dark blue Grieves and Hawkes double breasted light pin stripe suit, a crisp white shirt, and a maroon Brigade of Guards tie. His black oxford shoes were well worn, comfortable, and you could see your face in the shine on them.

Chief Superintendent Bill Gardner, looked slightly uncomfortable in his obviously off the peg dark grey business suit, his white shirt and matching dark blue tie, and well polished black shoes pegged him for what he was a successful businessman or a senior police officer.

Tony Salter finished pouring the coffee and handing them both a cup, sat back in his chair, put his arms on the arms and said. 'Well Chief Superintendent, Sir Bernard told me you mentioned George Clayton and a potential visit to the UK and that our Taliban chap said there would be an attempt on his life. Oh, by the way may I call you Bill?'

'Yes of course Sir,' (I don't get to call you Tony though I notice thought Bill Gardner).

'Well Bill, would you like to tell us what happened from you leaving New Scotland Yard yesterday morning until you finished interviewing this Taliban chap!'

Bill Gardner related the whole of the day's events, leaving nothing out, the state of Peter Henderson body, the murder of his wife, and finally the interview with Abdullah Sugama.

Tony Slater and Sir Bernard interrupted little, and then only to clarify a point.

'That's about it Sir, for what its worth chummy seems genuine, and most definitely could not go back, he wouldn't last a day.'

Tony Salter looked at Chief Superintendent Gardner, glanced at Sir Bernard, and then back to Gardner, 'You see Bill, what's a little disturbing about your interview last night. Is that George Clayton is coming to the UK and will be visiting London and Brussels. He is to be a surprise visitor To the European Parliament, only four people this side of the pond are supposed to know that, now five people with you.'

The PM looked at Sir Bernard, 'Is Franks still here? Glancing towards Gardner he explained', Tom Franks is CIA liaison in London, but his main job is liaison with the CIA at Langley for the White House. He is a George T appointee. Franks has ruffled some feathers in the last two years over there. You will like him he calls a spade a shovel as my Dad used to say in the North of England.'

Sir Bernard said, 'he should be he told me his flight was this coming Saturday evening.'

'I suggest you speak with Franks this morning and set up a meeting in your offices Sir Bernard, ask him what he makes of it. At the same start to put some feelers out it looks like there are at the very least a couple of Taliban or Al Qaeda here. I want them taking out Sir Bernard, you know an eye for and eye, they believe in it so do I.'

'Whilst we are talking what's the latest on your house to house in Ealing? Anybody see anything'? Said the PM.

'My people are knocking on doors right now Sir,' said Superintendent Gardner.

Both men left the PM, and agreed to speak to each other later in the evening, the encrypted tapes had arrived, and told them little they did not now know.

**SIS headquarters that same afternoon.**

In Sir Bernard's office the four men sat around the conference table at the end of the room, near the windows and facing the Thames. Special screening and microwave interference backed up by a variable acoustics limiter passed across the windows to stop any body eaves dropping on conversation.

Sir Bernard sat opposite Chief Superintendent Gardner, and Sergeant Tucker sat opposite Tom Franks. 'Right Gentlemen thank you coming over Tom', directing his comment to Franks. Franks nodded!! 'I think we ought to discuss this business of George 'T's visit but before we do. Bill, I have been looking at your firearms record, you haven't had a session on the "Butts" for over twelve months, I know you have this idea of not being armed is safer, but these bastards will shoot you dead as soon as look at you.'

'Also young Tucker here has a wife and family so he needs to be looked after too, he's up to scratch with his small arms, and Tom as for you, I won't even ask.'

'Before you leave today both of you pick up side arms, Sergeant Daley is expecting you both, and Bill find an hour for the range please.'

"Right, Bill will you go over where we are for Tom, sorry it's a repeat of this morning.'

Chief Superintendent Gardner repeated the verbal report he had made to the PM, he left nothing out and as Franks was "operational" he put a little in. This did not escape the notice of Sir Bernard.

Franks, leant forward on the table as though trying to speak in confidence to each of them, his voice was not loud but very clear. 'The Boss is coming over it will be in about 4 weeks. The usual checks are being made along his route; he is keeping security down to 40 personnel. And his total entourage to 150, which will include ten Marines, his personal doctor, a trauma surgeon, and his own chef.'

'There will be two aircraft Airforce 1, his Boeing. 747 and another identical 747 of the presidential flight. Normally there would be around 400 people involved, but he has kept it down to around 150 as I said. .Incidentally Air force One, is whichever the President flies in.'

'He has a number of options, and I will take your advice, Lakenheath between Thetford in Norfolk and Cambridge is a US Air Force base. He can drop in there and helicopter down to London."

'He could land in the grounds of Buckingham Palace as the Queen suggested on his last visit when he and his wife stayed with The Queen and Prince Phillip.'

'RAF Northolt just the Oxford side of Ealing on the A40 and only 20 minutes or so out of central London Then there is Heathrow- Gatwick and Luton.'

'I like the idea of Northolt, said Sir Bernard. Not too visible, short time out of town, and a straight run in. by car or Helicopter.'

'Excuse me Sir, said Tommy Tucker, Why don't we arrange all of them, and then let the pilot choose when he is an hour away.'

Sir Bernard looked at him,' sounds like a good idea to me, what do you all say?' All agreed.

Tom Franks spoke up, 'I have been in touch with Langley, apart from the normal whispers and rumours, and they have heard nothing to suggest that an attack on the Chief is imminent. 'They are not in the know about his proposed visit at this time. Too many loose tongues I am afraid.'

'If they have somebody in place feeding information on lets say Air Force 1, then although the flight plan is not filed until an hour before take-off, that still gives them over 8 hours to get units in place. Therefore I like the idea of multiple landing sites, and the pilot choosing at the last minute.'

'Why is he coming here do we know?' Asked Sir Bernard.

'Well he knows Tony Salter is taking a bit of stick, and wants to be seen to be supporting him. We Yanks think a lot of Salter you know; he's got some guts, and has proven to be a good friend of America, just like Margaret Thatcher was.'

'I think the reasoning behind the visit to the European Parliament is to show there are no hard feelings over the luke warm support from other member states during the Iraq war. He wants to be seen to be on the best of terms with Europe as a whole. Bear in mind most of Americans have European ancestry. It's a big vote.'

Sir Bernard brought the general meeting to a close, and promised to keep in touch with Franks, and update him before Saturday evening and his Washington flight.

Sir Bernard sat down again with Gardner and Tucker.

'We need to know where these guys are they might be locals, by that I mean here in the UK or they may be outsiders. Let's concentrate on the outsiders until we have any worthwhile Intel on our home grown ones'.

'Is it fair to assume Bill that if they have come in from abroad, it would have been within the last week say? In other words after chummy turned up?'

Gardner said 'it's a fair assumption if they are outsiders and it's a big if.'

'OK, so go over the usual, at ports of entry one again, we may have missed something, also remember that Iranian two years ago you were telling me about who came in through Ireland.Don't miss that one'. 'We need a daily update, lets say 2100 hours until further notice, give me a list of what resources you want and I'll get the PM to sanction them. He wants these bastards.'

'One final thing before you leave, what do you think of PC Lowe?'

'Well he's a terrific driver, never felt safer and never gone faster why Sir?' Said Gardner.

'I have decided to leave him with you during this investigation, the thought of you using a pool car and young Tucker here, who lets face it, is not the Worlds best driver.' (He was referring to the two accidents minor though they were that he had had in the last 6 months).

'Also Lowe is a bit special, he taught the SAS pursuit and evasive driving techniques for two years, he is also handy with a weapon, and can look after himself. A good bloke to have around as back up to the two of you.'

'He is due promotion, so I thought Area Commander Scott might be persuaded to promote him, also I think he should wear civvies, not a uniform. He should be waiting outside for you.'

Gardner and Tucker left, with Gardner going as promised to the indoor range under SIS and drawing a Browning Automatic, he expended 100 rounds. At the end he was quite confident in his renewed ability to use the weapon effectively. He chose an under the arm holster and signed for 50 rounds of ammunition. *"Fight a bloody war with that lot he thought.'*

Whilst he was there Tucker picked up and signed for his weapon also a browning automatic, and fired off a dozen rounds. Every one without exception overlapped each other; he had totally taken out the centre of the target, and at 50m that was good, --- bloody good.

PC Lowe was in fact outside waiting near the Jaguar.

'Well PC Lowe, welcome aboard, I understand we shall be in this together, I think that's splendid news, don't you Tommy'? 'Absolutely Sir, perhaps I can pick up some driving tips.'

Chief Superintendent Gardner looked at him as if the say that wouldn't be difficult.

'Get yourself a side arm Sergeant Lowe, and meet us back here in an hour in civvies.'

'Did you say Sergeant Sir?'

'I certainly did, official!!, ------------ he looked at his watch, about now, well done,' and shook his hand. Tucker also shook his hand in congratulation

# Chapter seven

**38, Westfield Gardens, Ealing, London    3.00pm Friday 17th October 2003.**

Mrs Parry sat in her high chair looking out of the window; this was the best entertainment she had had for years. The Police were down there; there were four police cars and a big caravan thing. The police had been in and out of the Hendersons all day; all those going into the house itself had white overalls on. But she could tell they were police.

Then there the people who were knocking on doors, they hadn't knocked on hers or rung her bell, or had they, she had very good eyesight for her age, but she was as deaf as a post. Her Charlie used to say it was 'convenient', she could hear when she wanted to. But that wasn't true her hearing had been going for years, and now it was a blessing in way.

She couldn't hear those noisy beggars next door with the loud music and banging around all night, coming in at all times of the night. Her son Colin had fitted a flashing light on the window ledge, when someone pressed the doorbell the light flashed. And it hadn't flashed in weeks now.

She wondered if that nice looking Frenchman she had seen leaving the Hendersons would be able to help the police, she hadn't seen either of the Hendersons since the other day. Mrs Parry did not have a TV, as she couldn't hear it there seemed no point. Instead she read two or three novels per week. That nice young man on the ground floor who worked in the library got them for her. She did not see the Hendersons on the TV news, and did not have a newspaper.

By Friday afternoon all the residents of the street had been spoken to apart from Mrs Parry, Mr James at 62 he was on holiday, Mr and Mrs

Rodney at 125 who were cat sitting for their son and his wife whilst they went up North to a wedding.

On Saturday afternoon the nice young man, his name was David he worked in the library with his friend Peter, she thought it funny how they always seemed to be touching each other, but maybe that's what young people did nowadays. Came to see her with five new books.

David wrote on a large pad:
PETER AND I ARE GOING TO ITALY ON HOLIDAY SO WE BROUGHT YOU 2 WEEKS OF BOOKS IS THAT ALL RIGHT?

She nodded and said 'I hope you both have lovely time, will send me a postcard please.'

David nodded, and mouthed 'yes of course'.

He said something to Peter which she couldn't hear, David said something back to him, and David reached for the pad, and wrote:
YOU MUST KEEP YOUR DOOR LOCKED THE
LADY ACROSS THE ROAD HAS BEEN KILLED.

She said, 'Is that why the police have been around for days?'
YES wrote David.

She looked at him and said, 'I wonder if that nice young man who went to see her on Wednesday morning would be able to help the police.'
WHAT YOUNG MAN wrote David?'

'Oh just a young man, he was French you know and probably selling things at the door. She looked confused, no that can't be right-- he didn't have a suitcase just a telephone like my Colin.'

'Oh shit shit shit, said Peter in an effeminate mincing voice, I bet she saw the fucking killer, now what do we do?'

'I don't know let me think,' said David.

'Right we have to tell the police and the sooner the better, as we are off tomorrow at 6.00am.'

David wrote on the pad:
WE THINK THAT MAN MIGHT BE ABLE TO HELP THE
POLICE. I SHALL HAVE TO TELL THEM. PETER WILL
STAY WITH YOU UNTIL I GET BACK. IS THAT ALL RIGHT?

Mrs Parry thought to herself, this is going to be good, better than looking through the curtains. David had not been gone more than 10 minutes when a police car with flashing lights on top slid to halt outside. And two policewomen shot out and ran for the front door the apartment and the stairs.

Peter met them at the door; 'you were quick he said trying to sound as manly as possible and failing miserably. Mrs Parry is through here, now she can't hear what you say so you will have to write everything down on this pad.' He handed the older WPC the pad. She read what David had previously written, and then spoke to Mrs Parry.

As with the deaf, and when some who do not speak a foreign language are on holiday. WPC Allen shouted and did so very slowly, 'Mrs Parry we are Police Officers' starting to write it down. Mrs Parry said,' I would never have guessed it!!' Peter nearly peed himself it was so funny. The look on WPC's face was a picture.

David came back through the door, 'who are you? Said WPC Allen, 'I rang you 'said David. Write your question down on the pad, and Mrs Parry will answer you. She's not daft only deaf.'

After a couple of questions it became apparent that Mrs Parry may well have seen the killer. She wrote: 'Mrs Parry, we need to bring our colleagues in to see you, as we think you might have seen the man that hurt Mrs Henderson.'

Half and hour later Chief Superintendent Gardner, and Sergeant Tucker were sat in Mrs Parry's sitting room. The Superintendent has introduced himself and Tucker, and was trying to be as gentle as he could in telling her what was what. In the event he need not have bothered she was made of sterner stuff.

'Mrs Parry, said Gardner, I am not sure what you know,' she looked at him in a strange way, and then it dawned on him she couldn't hear him. Seeing the A4 pad Peter and David had given her he started to write.

She stopped him. 'I can lip read Superintendent if you speak slowly and directly at me she said.' Thank God for that thought Gardner.

'Mrs Parry, I am not sure what you know. I think you might know the couple opposite they have a young baby or little boy about 4 years of age.'

She said, 'Yes I know them both, not to speak to you understand, they wave sometimes if they see me at the window. She looks nice, I don't see much of him apart from at weekends, and I think he must work in an office in the City or somewhere.'

'Can you remember two days ago in the morning, it would have been before lunch, said Gardner, somebody visited Mrs Henderson, that's the name of the lady opposite, when they were there they hurt her badly', he didn't want to say they had murdered her or how.

'The only people I saw was the postman, he's not very good you know he leaves letters sticking out of the letter box, my late husband worked for the post office for 43 years and he wouldn't have done that! That was about 9 o'clock they get later and later.'

Then at 9.30 exactly that door to door salesman came, only I don't know what he was selling as he didn't have a suitcase or anything really, and in any case she can't have wanted anything because he wasn't a minute before he went.'

Gardner looked at Tucker, who was writing down what Mrs Parry was saying in his pocket book. Tucker looked up and at Gardner; their joint looks said it all. She had seen the killer!

'Can you tell us what he looked like Mrs Parry?'

'Oh Yes, he was quite good looking I suppose, about as tall as my late husband.'

'How tall was that Mrs Parry?'

'He was just less than 6 foot, about six inches bigger than your Sergeant.'

Damn thought Gardner, Tucker was six foot to the inch. She wasn't good at height.

'What about his face?'

'Ah, now let me see, he had a mobile phone, that is what they call them isn't it? In his left hand and like this. She held her left hand up to her cheek. But I could still see it!'

'See what Mrs Parry?'

'This great big scar, it went from here, she pointed to just under her left ear, right down here, she drew her finger down her cheeks towards her mouth, and finished here, indicating about 2 inches from the mouth. It was quite deep; it must have hurt when he did it. And it was sort of brown even though he had a nice sort of tan look. You know like the French look at the cinema.'

'Mrs Parry, could this man have been an Arab?'

'Oh, I don't know do they look French?' She said.

'Mrs Parry, I have an idea, I would like to send one of my men to see you, he actually quite and interesting man, he will bring a box with different noses, chins, hair styles, things like that he will try to give your "Frenchman" a face. Would you help him to do that?'

'That sounds quite exciting Chief Inspector, he let it pass, she was looking out of the window and suddenly said, now there you are a Frenchman,' Gardner quickly got up.

Nearly opposite parked on the road was a UPS parcels delivery vehicle, the driver smartly dressed in his brown uniform was examining a clipboard, and comparing the details on it to the name on the gate, the man looked up at the window and saw Gardner looking, the driver was an Arab. Bloody bingo!!

He looked to the left and the end of the road and saw Sergeant Lowe talking to a lady traffic warden. Don't say she was trying to book a police car!! He turned back to Mrs Parry.

'You have been a big help Mrs Parry my man will come this afternoon if that's all right.'

'Oh Yes I shall look forward to it Superintendent', he smiled things were improving!

Together with Sergeant Tucker he walked towards the Jaguar and Sergeant Lowe, he was still talking to the traffic warden

'This is Mrs Pain, she works out of the local nick, as you can see Sir this side street is reserved for residents parking, most of them park overnight only, taking their car to work or whatever.'

'She gets to know those cars that would usually be here during the day. She checks at about 9.15am after doing a school crossing round the corner in the high street. This is because some people just drop their cars off here taking a chance when using the tube just off the High Street, and hope they don't get booked.'

'This Wednesday she was a bit late getting here because she had to change her shoes, they were new and hurting. As she was walking down the road here, she said good morning to a well-dressed man. He looked Arabic; the time was about 9.30am.'

Sergeant Lowe arranged for a statement to be taken, and they all drove back to SIS headquarters. Gardner was feeling a bit chirpy and it showed. Ten minutes later drinking his coffee and munching a ginger biscuit he had a phone call from Superintendent Tom Johnson of Wiltshire Constabulary.

'May have something for you Bill, do you remember coming off the A303 the other day, and onto the A36, you came in a sort of circle coming up from below round and up onto the A36?'

'Yes Said Gardner I remember it well that was the slowest bit of driving in over an hour.'

'Well you turned left, just imagine you are a cyclist and wanted to go straight across that dual carriageway at those lights, its quite a wide road, well we have a cyclist doing just that at about 7.30am on Wednesday give or take a minutes or two.

'As he was crossing he saw a white transit van coming from his left going a bit quick. It was coming from the direction of Warminster. He took particular notice because he thought it might not stop for the lights. And if he kept going it would hit him'.

'So he stopped, as did the van, which was just about to overshoot the slip road down to the A303. The van had the name Price Construction Ltd in Dark blue letters and a 02-telephone number'.

'How does he remember that Tom?'

'Because his name is Price, and you don't see many Arab construction workers in Wiltshire.'

'His statement is being faxed to you as we speak, and the hard copy is coming down by courier. I have got our artist seeing if he can come up with anything, but it's not promising at the moment. It was all over in seconds.'

'Tom, I am very much obliged to you, thanks ever so much.' He put the phone down

# Chapter eight

**Frystone-on-Sea, England Friday 6.30pm Friday 17th October 2003**

The seaside town Frystone-on-Sea has nothing special going for it lying on the rugged west coast of England 10 miles north of Maryport on the Solway Firth, its porcelain works had long gone, and its little fishing port was now the home to the pseudo rich with their 28 foot Marans that rarely went anywhere, apart from a few miles out to sea, under power on a nice day, with not an unfurled sail in sight.

The nearest large town was Carlisle some 56 miles away and just off the M6.The obligatory mix of Land and Range Rovers BMW and Merc 4 wheel drives sat comfortably with the shiny Mercs- BMW's and Jaguars that littered the narrow streets. The cottages that had housed the hard working fisherman of past, were now the weekend home to their part time occupants. The intrepid travellers had driven a mere 150 miles at the most from home.

The three local pubs, one having a superb fish restaurant, the Chinese take away, and Italian restaurant, catered for the new arrivals at the weekend more than the locals, and reverted to the local use during the week. Cribbage, darts and domino's pool and indoor bowls suddenly appeared. And mostly disappeared come Friday opening.

Not many of the locals could now afford a home here, not unless that is they were one of the local pseudo rich, and John Thompson was certainly rich.

He had "Old" money, Daddy's fortune in mining, and rubber of past, carefully looked after and wisely invested. A Former Mayor, a pillar of society, and one you turned to for that tricky advice from time to time. A supporter of the local hospital and school, *"No they bloody well were not going to close either if he could help it "*. And they didn't.

Well thought of and liked by most people, and unbeknown to all a staunch supporter of the IRA.

He had his table at the Ship and Anchor, and ate there two or three times a week since his wife was into W.I. Mothers Union, the local Drama Society, and anything that bloody moved.

The weekenders knew better than to take John's table, it had been tried two or three times. But the individual trying it suddenly found them selves unloved and unwanted.

He was there now quietly discussing the price of fish and the weather with the licensee. Arthur Wray, a big man in height and girth, one you did not argue with. He was however a gentle giant who's gruffness belied his kind nature.

The harbourmaster came in for his evening couple of pints now he had finished tucking up his toy's for the night. 'Hello John, have another?' He said catching sight of John sat at his table.

John looked up;' no you join me Dennis I want to talk to you.' Dennis went across and sat at the table, his pint of bitter appeared miraculously at his left side; He looked up and thanked Arthur Wray. 'It's about time I took my boat out,' he had a superb teak decked clinker built sailing barge, bought some years ago and retired from the River Rhine.

Fully restored it was beautiful, with sumptuous accommodation and spacious hold for light cargo. And made the weekenders craft look like Dinky toys.

'I am rather fancying a trip over to Ireland for a couple of days, thought you might come with me next Tuesday to Saturday.'

Today was Friday and the invasion was just starting, in came the scrap merchant from Dudley with his loud wife, rapidly followed by the dentist from Birmingham who ironically had bad breath.

Looking at them with a disdainful look Dennis said, 'life's a bitch John, there's nothing I would like better, but the wife's mother is coming for the week, in fact I am picking her up at Carlisle tomorrow morning. And after the last time she came there is no way I can be absent again.'

'Oh. That's a shame I'll have to get somebody else then,' (he already knew that Dennis's mother-in-law was coming his wife had told him) And Patrick was already lined up.

Monday he provisioned the boat, topped up the fuel tanks with diesel, checked over the engine and running gear, radios and navigation equipment, he finished late that afternoon put the stores on board, and topped off the water tanks. Time for pint he thought before Patrick arrives.

A quick steak with Patrick at the Ship and Anchor, and home to bed, Patrick would be sleeping on board, they would catch the tide at 0615 tomorrow.

11.00 on Tuesday morning saw them well on the way catching the wind in a strong westerly the sea was running and the waves a gentle two foot, which led to interesting but not uncomfortable sailing. Patrick was making the bacon sandwiches in the galley.

He soon appeared with bacon sandwiches and a strong mug of tea, the obligatory whisky was strong enough to make him cough as he took his first mouthful. *'Christ all Mighty you'll have us drunk Patrick'!!*

'How are we doing Patrick?'

'About 6 hours yet if we keep this up. That should put us off the coast in sight of the inlet by 1700 and with less than an hour of daylight. Perfect!! The sat-Nav puts us bang on course, don't forget the ferries. One coming at us at 1300 approx and one come from behind at 1530. That's if they are both on time.'

Their route took them south west, and north of the Isle of Man, and across the ferry routes to Dublin and Larne, not a problem when you knew what you were doing and Patrick knew these waters like the back of his hand.

He had run guns in the early days of the troubles, but that was some time back, today's trip could be more dangerous if patrols were still being made by the Royal Navy or less so because of the " Peace" protocol. He wasn't to know that there were no Royal Navy patrols, because of defence cut backs, and just two sweeps a day with a nimrod anti-submarine patrol.

You could forget the Irish Navy and Air Force; it had one but merely a couple of light gunboats, and very little more aircraft. At 1715 they dropped the sea anchors bow and stern and turned off the running lights. They were 3 miles up the coast from Larne in one of its many inlets, and just lying off shore and a shingle beach. The nearest houses were over a mile and a half from them.

'19.50 he's late said Patrick, we can't afford to be hanging about much longer,' in the half light they saw a shape appear and then they heard a muffled exhaust and Tom O'Leary little fishing boat hove into view.

As he closed to the starboard side of the boat, he shouted,' now there's a sight for sore eyes two of my most favourite people would you be having the Bushmills handy?'

'No we bloody wouldn't and you're late, said Thompson. Get the boxes on board and let get out of here. I wanted to be back before dawn that's not

*The President Is Down*

possible now.' He handed O'Leary an envelope, careful how you spend that now.'-------- He wasn't at all careful!!----- In fact he was bloody careless.

Ten minutes later he pulled up the stern anchor backed off from the bow anchor and brought the bow facing out to sea, he gently ran forward, released the bow sea anchor and reeled it in, and safely stowed they headed out into the Irish Sea.

The trip back to Frystone-on-Sea was without mishap; they arrived a little before dawn and quietly coasted on to the end of the sea wall furthest from the town.

He had parked his Toyota Landcruiser with a couple of other vehicles, and two trailers. As he had been doing now for six weeks whilst he had his drive widened. It was now a regular feature, everybody was used to seeing it parked there now, and Dennis Ward the harbour master bless him had issued the vehicle a harbour parking permit.

There were no lights showing as they quickly and without using a torch or any illumination put the three boxes on the floor of the Landcruiser. Thompson immediately drove away leaving Patrick Duffy to close the boat up. Duffy then walked alongside the harbour wall and out though the town. 10 minutes later he met up with John Thompson they changed seats and Duffy drove off.

A few minutes later Thompson was banging on the harbour master's door. 'What are you doing back,' said Duffy?

'Patrick's fathers been rushed into hospital, he's had a heart attack he barely survived the last one three years ago, he wanted to be with him. It was just as quick to turn round and come back as go on to Belfast and fly back. You'll be needing to check me in Dennis do you want to do it now.'

'Have you had anything to eat John?'

'Not since last night, well that's not true Patrick made us one of his door step sandwiches, which I have to admit I fed to the fishes,' he said.

'Pru, shouted Dennis would you put some bacon and eggs on for John he can join me for breakfast, sorry John is that OK?'

'Dennis, I am very happy to accept my stomach is rumbling just at the thought of it.'

The Harbour master's records showed the boat berthing at 0750 some 40 minutes after it actually had.

**Leeds General Infirmary. 8.30am Monday the 20th October 2003.**

Mr Pilcher was making his rounds of the 'heart' ward; he stopped by the bed nearest the door

'Mr Duffy, I have some good news and some bad news, he said smiling, which would you like first?'

The tired eyes of Patrick Seamus Duffy met his, 'I tink I'd loik the gud furst Sur ', he said in a very heavy Irish brogue.

'I am very pleased to tell you Mr Duffy, that you are perfectly alright, your ECG was acceptable, and your blood levels are OK all things considered. What you probably had was a very bad case of indigestion.'

'You were perfectly right to come in, with your history and at your age you must always err on the safe side.'

'Now for the bad new's, I don't think that your 6 pints of Guinness on an evening are helping. By all means have a drink but only, ----- let's say two pints, and see how we go.'

*'Mr Pilcher couldn't have drunk a pint of Guinness to save his life, bottle of Grande Cruz, chilled Chablis or a Sapphire Bombay Gin and Tonic yes.'*

'He'll be patting me on the bloody head in a minute Patrick senior said to himself.' Who only ever drank two pints a night anyway? The six was a figment of his very fertile imagination. He did hope his son Patrick was enjoying his drive to London!!

In fact Patrick wasn't quite going as far as London, now travelling at a steady 75MPH he was approaching his destination junction 7 Great Bar turn off on the M6 come and go over the top turn towards Walsall, join the dual carriage and immediately get into the right hand lane, turn right across the carriageway and into the Holiday Inn hotel car park, go to the far end and round the corner to avoid the CCTV camera's.

The time should be exactly 12.00 noon. His instructions from John Thompson were very precise.

As he came up the slip road of the M6 it was exactly 3 minutes to 12.00 noon. He drove into the car park straight across it and turned round the corner into cul-de-sac he looked for the cameras, there were none. In the far corner was a " Reasons" Bakery bread van with the back doors open although nobody could see that because of the way it as facing, he backed up to within two meters of the bread van. He got out and lifted the tailgate, within seconds the three boxes were in the bread van and the doors were shut.

He closed the tailgate, and got back into the Landcruiser, a rather plump, and cheery looking man sat in the passenger seat spoke to him. 'Mr Duffy I presume?'

'Yes that's me'.

'Sorry about the rush back there, I have something for you; he handed him a black leather briefcase. You will find £60,000 in used notes inside. Please count it if you wish.'

Patrick opened the briefcase, and looked at the bank notes inside. Each pile appeared to be a £1000 in £20 notes. 'No I was told it would be all right. After all we have done business before and you are trusted.'

The plump man got out of the landcruiser and into the bread van, and drove away.

Patrick put the briefcase and money behind his seat and drove out of the hotel, turned left, came off the main road onto the roundabout, he went right round and dropped back down on to the M6 and headed North.

A short while later he pulled of the motorway and came off at Sandbach services. Using the public telephone he spoke to John Thompson.

'Delivered and paid for', after which he put the telephone down.

Chief Superintendent Gardner looked at the sheet of paper that Sir Bernard Hills had given him. 'That's it then, he's coming and we have fifteen days to make some sense of this lot. He's gone along with the multiple landing sites and the pilot choosing which one to use.'

## The End of Book One

*Book Two*

# Chapter one

**SIS Headquarters London 7.00am Tuesday 22 October 2003**

Sir Bernard Hills, stood looking out over the River Thames from his office window, he was drinking his first coffee of the day, and contemplating his joint Intelligence meeting across the river at 8.30am. Hosted by his toffee nosed and close chested friends in MI5. Today it would include. New Scotland Yard's Anti-Terrorist squad's Chief, Commander Banes. Special Branch with Chief Superintendent Gardner, and himself for SIS. (MI6) It would achieve little.

He reflected on the massive cut backs each service had suffered over the past two decades, each retained jealously its hard won meagre funding, and were loath to impart valuable hard won knowledge and Intelligence to the other. They simply didn't want either of the other security services looking better as a result of their efforts. So what was new in that?

The French with their myriad security services, the Americans with their three, the Israelis with two the high profile Mossad being famous for kidnapping Adolph Eichmann from Argentina in 1960 and putting him on trial in Jerusalem, Israel in 1961. He was hanged in Jerusalem in 1962. Eichmann was the architect of the greatest terrorist outrage ever the extermination of over 6,000,000 Jews. But never referred to as such.

The Russians with the GRU and the KGB, now defunct, yet there still under more acceptable names, the high players from each having left and were capitalising on their knowledge-contacts and fear to produce the modern Russian Mafia. They didn't hide it driving around in their stolen BMW's Range Rovers, Mercedes and Jaguars. They were the new rich. And not forgetting our own MI5, MI6 (SIS), And a whole raft of other intelligence organisation within the services and now Industry.

Moscow now had more genuine millionaires than any other capital city in the World, and all since Perestroika and glasnost. The average Russian was still poor, had incredibly bad health services, social services and housing. The once all powerful Russian Baltic Fleet of warships and nuclear submarines, reduced to a mere handful now, mothballed old nuclear submarines lay rotting at anchor, bleeding their radio-activity into the sea, and killing or malforming the marine life. The Americans had offered to clean it up free, but it didn't happen.

The up and coming security services belonged to the Chinese, Japanese, the North and South Koreans, the middle and Far East spawned many more on nearly a daily basis. The Arab Nations and now terrorist organisations, freedom fighters all had their networks and sympathisers on an escalating basis.

Spying had always been there the Romans had their 'Spy network 'Lord Walsingham for the Elizabethans formed our first 'spy' network.

Napoleon, had his, the fictional Scarlet Pimpernel in the days of the French revolution, echoed the real spies on both side of the Channel and Marie Antoinette and her famous " Let them eat cake ", when told that the country as a whole had no bread.

The Abhwer, German military intelligence in the last war was responsible for many atrocities, and resulting in the fictional films, The Maltese Falcon, Casablanca with Rick and "Play it again Sam, The African Queen. Films all depicting spying, making famous, Sidney Greenstreet, Herbert Lom, Lauren Bacall, and of course Humphrey Borgart. Glamorising the seedy world of spying, espionage and counter espionage.

The 1960's saw a heightening of tension by the Two Super States, taking the World to within an ace of nuclear disaster. Was this terrorism at it worst, taking the planet to the brink?

In May 1960 the U2 Spy plane flown by US Air Force Captain Francis Gary Powers was shot down over central Russia. He was captured and put on trial for "Spying", subsequently freed two years later in 1962, in exchange for Colonel Rudolf Abel who had served 5 years of a 30 year sentence for running a Russian "Spy" ring in the USA. As they crossed a river bridge separating East and West Germany walking from opposite directions, an American student Frederic Pryor was also quietly released and walked the same route as Gary Powers.

1961, the ill-fated Cuban 'Bay of Pigs' a CIA sponsored invasion of Fidel Castro's Cuba, supporting the invading Cuban exiles. The following year in October 1962, John F. Kennedy the 35th President of the USA, and its youngest President ever faced up to Nikita Khrushchev's Russia, and demanded they remove the Nuclear Missiles they had sited in Cuba, a deadline was imposed.

The Russians removed the missiles. Some cynics say it was a political act to support Kennedy's own ends with the mid-term Presidential elections coming the next month. And a massive irresponsible gamble some would say. Whilst others would say an act of immense courage.

On the 22$^{nd}$ November 1963, in the very heart of Dallas Texas the 35$^{th}$ President John F Kennedy was shot and sustained head injuries from which he did not recover, dying some few hours later, his wife Jacqueline covered is his blood was by his side when he died.

Lee Harvey Oswald shot him with a cheap mail order rifle from the Texas School Book Depository. His accomplice was never caught. Was this retaliation for Cuba by the KGB that theory and others still abound today?

The USS 'Pueblo' a spy ship captured on its maiden voyage by the North Koreans in January 1968 whilst spying in the territorial water off North Korea, the ships captain Lloyd 'Pete' Bucher, had been told specifically by Rear Admiral Johnson before setting sail, 'You are not going out there to start a nuclear war', in the event he failed miserably and nearly did.

The thousands of people throughout Europe spying for their country, who also died for their Country when the likes of Burgess and MacLean 'came out' and went over to mother Russia. To become Colonels, given a low security desk jobs, and pensioned off. Virtually alone in a foreign land that didn't trust them, and never would.

What did any of it achieve, now technology was taking over? We were told we didn't need the human assets.

The spy in the sky now could pin point, a convoy of trucks from outer space and could read a number plate at the same distance. Fighter aircraft that didn't need pilots were being developed.

We were breeding nations of computer nerds, high on violence with their virtual reality games. Low on reading and writing skills, would these same people be fighting the next war, with a computer and little else, where the end game really was --- the end game?

What was it all about, was he really getting to old for this game? Where did spying, and reactive action cease, and terrorism begin?

Couldn't the actions he had thought of in the last few minutes. State induced, taking a nation and its people to the very brink of final disaster and total annihilation with no veto from the public at large, isn't that the height of terrorism?

Was it lack of education that turned people into terrorists, a feeling of being done down all the time by the have's of this World.

The so called 'Terrorists' now had the edge, no political masters other than themselves, no need for huge amounts of technology. Why spend £500,000 on couple of missiles, when 2 stolen vehicles, a couple of oil drums and fertiliser and rusty nails, and scrap metal would do just as well.

They could move fast and far, and because of the loose borders now in Europe in particular and the European Union allowing you to take jobs within the whole of Europe you could disappear in any City in Britain or Continental Europe. Swallowed up and invisible within the ethnic and cultural communities in hours.

Just how much they can disappear, or appear un-noticed by those around, was clearly demonstrated by the events leading up to the tragedy of September 11th 2001, he thought. How many warnings had gone unheeded, how many clues not investigated... Easy now to think this, impossible to forget the cost.

On 11th September 2001, now the second most infamous day in America history, at 0848 EDT and 0903 EDT 2 aircraft were deliberately crashed into the North and South Towers of the World Trade Centre in New York, killing 175 people on one, and 92 on the other plus many hundreds in the towers, many hundreds, firemen, police, ambulance and *'Joe Public'* gave their lives trying to save people in the towers that day.

0937 EDT American Airlines flt 77 crashed into the Pentagon killing 64 on board and 125 in the pentagon. At 1003 EDT United Airlines Flt 93 crashed in a field Nr Pittsburgh, the passengers causing it to crash to avoid the loss of life if it flew on.

Arab terrorists to a man, including three believed to be brothers, why would they choose to throw away most of the male lives in a family, how can we understand, and if we can't then we have little chance.

No, we were in danger of losing this one, at best we could destroy them for a while, but more of the same would spring up. It was a depressing thought.

Mary his secretary came in and interrupted his thoughts, 'good morning Sir Bernard.'

'Good morning Mary,' he replied and smiled his thanks for stopping his thoughts.

'Your driver will be here in ten minutes Sir Bernard, is there anything I can get you?'

'No I'm fine Mary I've had my coffee, and ready for the fray,' he smiled at her.

We have to give some thought to the Taliban at Westbury this afternoon. Could you ask Sir John at the Home Office to give me a bell some time this afternoon, you can tell that I would like discuss Mr Sugama. Apologise for my not telephoning direct and explain that I am at a meeting and wished to give him as much time as I could before our conversation this afternoon'.

'I have no doubt he will need to take it upstairs.'

Mary left the room, and as he took one last glance out of the window, watching the ambulance below being skilfully driven weaving in out of the traffic, now down the wrong side of the road, and finally turning onto Westminster bridge. A lot like life he pondered as he walked away from the window and on to his meeting.

In spite of the traffic, which was getting worse he arrived at his meeting at 8.20am just in time to be next to last.

It went as envisaged with all factions after his Taliban, well they could sod off 'Put your questions in writing and what SIS cannot answer from our interviews with him, we will try and obtain the answers I will put them out in a 'round robin' general security brief.' That wasn't liked. Well to hell with them that's all they would get.

# Chapter two

**Army Western Command Headquarters. Wilton, Salisbury, Wilts. 0700 Tuesday 22nd October 2003**

General Sir Peter De Large had just finished talking to Colonel Chippy Lane. So called for hacking his way out of the Malayan jungle with a machete and almost single handedly saving his troop when their supplied were air dropped into hands of the enemy!

'So when exactly will our surprise be arriving at Westbury, said Sir Peter?'

'About an hour from now Sir,' Chippy Lane said looking at his wristwatch.

**MOD Facility Westbury Wiltshire   0815 Tuesday 22nd October 2003**

The dark blue Range Rover pulled in to the entrance to the facility at Westbury directly Outside of the guardhouse, it was a being a little obstructive the way it was parked. The driver leapt out and approached the sliding window on the front of guardhouse, just as the corporal on duty was sliding it back. More fool him thought corporal Hemming, it was raining, and he wasn't the one getting wet.

'How can I help you Sir?' He said.

'Ah – Yes good morning, I'm looking for Mr, oh damn, excuse me, as he started to go through his pockets - ah here we are'------ then he dropped his glasses, as he bent down to pick them up an old battered Ford Fiesta turned into the gate driven by the lovely Dianne from the kitchen.

She was drop dead gorgeous, and he was plucking up courage to ask her out, she was a bit of a man-eater by all accounts. He smiled at her, raised the barrier and let her through, just as the man was getting up and examining his glasses. 'Yes they look OK.' He found the letter he was seeking on an Official Western Command letterhead and handed it to Corporal Hemming, who read:

'If you are reading this you will have failed to protect the Westbury base from a potential terrorist attack. The man presenting this letter will provide full military identification to your satisfaction'.

'Follow his instructions and call your next in line.'
Signed
*Sir Peter De Large*
Sir Peter De Large.
Commander-in-Chief
Western Area Command.

The man produced his military identification; Hemming asked if he could check it at Warminster garrison, 'most certainly you can' said Staff Sergeant Pete Brook. Two minutes later, Staff Sergeant Brook was identified as 3 Para on detachment to MOD Westbury, Wiltshire. Corporal Hemming was devastated.

'Call your Sergeant please,' Corporal Hemming looked at his watch and phoned the mess, Sergeant Ellis 34 years of age, 6 foot three inches running a bit to fat over this last two years, not particularly helped by his eating habits. Waiting to be consumed on his plate were 3 rashers of smoked bacon, 2 eggs, beans, sausages, tinned tomatoes, and fried bread, his 2 slices of toast on a side plate.

The tap on his shoulder was light but insistent, 'sorry Sarge but you are wanted at the gatehouse.'

'He looked up, tell em–I'll be there soon!' He went back to his breakfast.

Two minutes later, again the tap on the shoulder, 'Sarge you must go now Corporal Hemming says you have an incident.'

'Incident, I'll give him bloody incident when I see him', he picked up his breakfast and took it back to the counter, 'keep this hot for me please Doris.' She slid it under the heated lamps. It was to remain there for over an hour when it would be disposed of.

Sergeant Ellis briskly marched down the corridors, out and across the open parking spaces, failing to notice the nice new dark blue Range Rover now correctly and precisely parked between the lines in a bay.

He shoved open the outer door of the guardroom, seeing no corporal Hemming slammed through the inner door and confronted the bemused looking Hemming.

You know better than to call me during my breakfast only on fear of fucking death do you do that laddie, his Scottish ancestry coming out in his speech now. What fucking problem have we got he said with heavy sarcasm!!

He saw Hemming glance over his shoulder, and became aware of the man stood behind the door he had thrown open.

'You could say I am your problem Sergeant Ellis.' He identified himself to Ellis, who looked at first a little sheepish, and then gathering courage said, 'well not good I admit, but lesson learnt we sergeants have to stick together, otherwise the bastards will grind us down.' He smiled at Brook.

'Its Staff Sergeant Brook to you Sergeant Ellis, and this bastard will grind you down, you are relieved of duty as of, he looked at his watch 0840. Do not bother to go back in to collect anything it will be sent on later this morning to Warminster. ----Your Transport is outside.'

A Land Rover with Army marking for number 3 Parachute Regiment sat outside with the engine running, an impassive 3 Para corporal at the wheel.

Staff Sergeant Brook turned to Corporal Hemming, 'you are also relieved of duty at 0840, and the same applies to you, your kit will be sent on to Warminster.'

'You will both be met at Warminster by a Senior Officer who will decide what to do with you. Goodbye Gentlemen.'

He strode past them, acknowledging the two members of 3 Para now manning the guardhouse with a nod as he walked past them and towards the main offices.

## 0830 hours Westbury Mod Facility. Outside the office of Duty Officer.

Sergeant Major Dale Turner knocked on the door!!
'Come' came from inside.
Sergeant Major Turner walked in put two fingers together like an imaginary gun and said 'bang bang you're dead'. And handed Rees-Jones an envelope took one step back and stood to attention. His eyes focused on the wall eight feet away and some six-foot up.

Rees-Jones read the letter and rang the number; it went straight through to Colonel Lanes office. 'Could I have Colonel Lane please, this is lieutenant Rees-Jones Westbury Detachment.'

*The President Is Down*

He was put through immediately, 'This is one call Robin I was hoping I wouldn't get; remember a chain is only as strong as its weakest link, your chair snapped on the first pull.'

'You will stay in place, take advice from Staff Sergeant Brook and Sergeant Major Turner they are both top men and know their stuff. You should learn something out of this all mighty cock up.'

'Put Turner on', he spent a couple of minutes talking to Sgt Major Turner. 'Yes of course Sir, not a problem.'

There was a knock on the door and in marched Staff Sergeant Brook, He came to attention and Rees-Jones said, 'We had better drop the formalities in view of the circumstances, where do we go from here.'

'Well Sir, firstly there are 10 other ranks from 3 Para on site apart from myself and Sgt Turner, this gives us 4 x 2 man teams, and two singletons, they are both highly effective NCOs. The two of them are currently doing a recce of the site and assessing risk on 1 – 10 ratios 1- 6 we will cover with active units and patrols, 7 to 10 with passive defences and 3 dog handlers. They arrive this afternoon Sir from Aldershot.'

'We need now Sir to get all your Army staff on duty, and all your Army staff who are off duty BUT on site in your conference room at 0930. Those off base need to be contacted and unless they have doctors certificate, or away on holiday, need to report for 1400 today and we will run the briefing again at 1410. Anybody who does not attend outside of these criteria will be AWOL. Please make that clear.'

'We will leave you to organise that Sir and I shall see you at 0925. Staff Sergeant Turner will no doubt join us when appropriate'. Both men saluted smartly, turned and marched out. For a minute Rees-Jones held his head in his hands, and wondered what he had done to deserve this?' Then he realised this was for real, he could be dead now, and his heart missed a beat.

0925 the conference room held 150 people; it was set out in theatre style with a raised platform at the far end. Rees-Jones and Staff Sgt Brook sat on two chairs, with a table in front of them.

The first person walked through the door and hesitated and would have gone back out if Staff Sgt Brook had not stood up and said, 'Ah good man, would you stay at the back on the door for a few minutes, and send everybody down to the front' The corporal replied, 'Yes Sergeant' and wondered whom hell he was.

As people came in the corporal sent them down to the front, and Staff Sgt Brook stood at ease but very erect at the front of the platform.

At precisely 1005 he nodded to the Para Corporal who had taken over from the other Corporal. Nobody was to be let in with the exception of one individual. There were now some 26 people in the room in total.

He coughed and cleared his throat; the burble of voices died away, 'Good Morning, to those of you who have been dragged in on your day off, my apologies. I am Staff Sergeant Brook of Number 3 Parachute Regiment, over the next few hours you will get the meet my Parachute Regiment colleagues and me more intimately. Before I start, I would like to just ask two questions, and please answer truthfully.'

1. 'Put your hand up if you have served in a theatre of War and in that I include Northern Ireland.' 9 people put their hand up.
2. 'Put your hand up if you have ever been in a fire fight, or discharged your weapon at live enemy targets, and been shot at in return.' 3 put their hand up, and he noticed 2 wore Sergeants chevrons. He nodded to the Para at the back who whispered something to each of them.

'That's about what I expected,' (bloody worse than I thought he said to himself)

'Why are we here, well there have been rumours about a guest we have here in our midst, you may also be aware that a gentleman who came to visit him tragically was killed shortly after he left here. The Newspapers will tell you that this was a terrorist attack on that man, and again the newspapers will have informed you that his wife was also killed later the same day.'

'All of this is true', he waited for that to sink in, 'you are in danger, but don't worry we all have had the training, they can't get in here not with our armed guards in place, camera's, razor wire or can they?' He nodded the door opened and in came Sergeant Major Turner, in full camouflage battle dress, and complete with a self-loading rifle and a side arm.

He marched down to the front and stood at ease. ' This is Sergeant Major Turner number 3 Para, now unlike you and I, who dutifully signed in, I take we all did?'---- nervous laughter.

'Well he bloody well didn't, what he did was drive in through the front gate with all his kit and rifle, and side arm and six grenades, right under the nose of our armed guard, remember the one keeping us, all of us safe!!.'

'What's worse he walked into Lieutenant Rees-Jones office and shot him!! He persuaded a young lady who works here to bring him in on the back seat of her car. In Lt Rees-Jones you are seeing apparition, -- a ghost, and a dead man.' To a one --- he now had their undivided attention.

'We are we here, at the request of lieutenant Rees-Jones we have come in to tighten things up, and ensure you are all safe, and chummy is also,---- until that is the powers that be decide what to do with him.'

He looked at Rees-Jones who nodded a thank you!

'The enemy, has already made a recce of Westbury, we don't know what he will do, or when, but we have to believe HE WILL.'

'So what else do we know about these particularly bad men, we know they don't think the same of human life as we do, they believe that when they die/killed in a jihad which is a holy war, they become martyrs and go to heaven, none have come back to dispute that,' again a titter of laughter.

'All of you are in the Army, you have avowed to serve the Queen God Bless her, and keep her realm safe from this sort of thing, you have all signed the official secrets act at least once. And you are now going to meet and beat this threat. But *Not* by doing what you do *NOW* and in the manner you do it *NOW.*'

'We have to think outside the 'Box' as they say, the knowledge they have now of this place and *YOU* will be *useless, meaningless, of no value what so ever to him.* Why'? 'Everything is going to change overnight, right now, as of 1400 today in fact.'

He turned to the large presentation white board, and pulled down an over-size plan of the site. 'You will all recognise this, you are here, --- here is the main gate, ---- this is the rear gate for emergency vehicles etc.'

'This area here is the current barbed and razor wiring. This is the no mans area, between the inner and out wires. This is the open field at the back and a housing estate of 30 houses or so.'

'Currently you work 12 hour shifts, you will work 8 hour shifts but more frequently, and your shift will be overlapped during first four hour with two other men, and last four hours with two other men.'

'Each over lapping patrol will contain at least I Para, between these wired area's, 3 army police dogs will patrol on 8 hour shifts, one will within the wire and one outside. Should you come across a dog, DON'T go to pet it you CAN'T! --- Stand very still and the dog handler will be with you in seconds.'

'You will all wear one of these, he held out a small radio with an ear and mouthpiece a bit like a switchboard operator would have. It picks up all speech, you just talk, and you will hear every other conversation around you, so don't go telling us all what you got up to behind the bike sheds. That's unless you want to. Seriously, this is not yet standard issue you can whisper, you can shout, all will hear every word as you say it. So do not say anything unless YOU NEED TO.'

'During the day a state of Orange will exist i.e. High alert. After the civilians are gone at night, that means after 1800 and this will include regular cleaner's etc. A state of Red alert will exist until 0800 the following day.'

'Between 1800 and 0800, every person without exception will have to obtain permission from the duty movement sergeant to move from premises to premises, or out on the town etc.'

'You will hear those arrangements and that permission being given, or NOT given as the case may be.'

'Should you come upon any person moving who has NOT got permission, you will tell them to stop, do not approach them, give your colour code location, remember we all can hear. If they do not stop, SHOOT THEM.

Shoot them in the legs. If they go for what you think is a weapon or devise, shoot them in the body and shoot to kill.'

'Those are the stated and agreed rules of engagement; you cannot be prosecuted if you carry out these orders to the letter.'

'At all times there will be 24 hours a day 2 loose Para's on patrol they will wear these identification flashes they measured about 10cm x 10cm or 4 inches by 4 inches. At night time this band through the centre will glow. If you come across a Para without these showing SHOOT him, before he shoots you.'

'Finally the field and its approaches, if you are pursuing a suspect, and he makes to go across the field DO NOT follow beyond the exit/ entrance gate. There is a very nasty surprise in store in that area.'

A voice piped up, 'Sir there are family houses down there and sometimes children go to play in the field.'

'Let me just say they won't get in there, however what's in there will not kill you, but you will have trouble standing up or walking for 4 to 6 hours.'

'Now nearly finished, for the time being no heroics leave that to the Para's we need the medals.' A genuine ripple of laughter followed.

'This is the last item, think of a name particular to YOU and you alone, remember it and give it to the movement sergeant, he will log it. It could be your wife's name, a child, dog etc. If you get into trouble and need help quickly think of a sentence and incorporate your special word in it.'

'Our software monitoring all speech will pick it up. Help will be with you in a flash. That's what the 2 loose Para's are for.'

A lot to absorb there, but simple if you think about it though.'

'Keep what you have heard to yourself; see the Sergeants at the rear for your new shift duties. Good Luck.' He remained standing whilst the hall emptied. He had just 10 people to cover on the next briefing at 1400.

Lieutenant Rees-Jones stood up, 'a stunning performance Staff Sergeant; very impressive but I couldn't help noticing you never mentioned the front entrance and guardhouse and what we would be doing there.'

'No Sir, right now as we speak, a chicane with rocks is being installed, plus raised speed bumps, 1 Para is standing 25m from the vehicle shall we say being examined in full view and obviously threatening, the other Para, does the vehicle, briefcase, in car and under car checks, and books the person in.'

'Unless we have prior knowledge and expecting the person/s they are turned away by another Para. I wanted them all to see for themselves as they left tonight, those that are not leaving the site will be advised accordingly.'

'I regret having asked Staff Sergeant,' said Rees-Jones feeling a little deflated and not for the first time that day...

At 1755 that night the last of the civilian staff were leaving site at Westbury, they included 3 men who left together in a Ford Mondeo; they arrived at the main London line station in Westbury at 1810.

They caught the 18.22 to Paddington, getting off before the trains final destination. Only two men returned later that evening, returning to Westbury by 0015 supposedly after sampling the delights of Westbury and its nightclub on the trading estate. The booking Sergeant had booked two out, and now two were booking back in.

The system worked. Abdullah Sugama was no longer at Westbury. Although no one would be told that.

# Chapter three

**Connaughts Gentlemen's Club, London.   Wednesday 23rd October 2003**

   Sir John Wilkinson formerly an MP and now a Senior Civil Servant heading the Home Office team. Sat opposite Sir Bernard in a leather wing back and sipped his Islay malt savouring the peaty aroma and the highland heather. Sir Bernard favoured his Bushmills, Sir John's club 'Winsley Gentlemans Club' provided the intimate setting.
   Sir John was first to speak,' you rattled Stern-Price today at the Joint Security meeting; he has made a couple comments to the Home Secretary about non-co-operation.'
   'Don't know why Sir Bernard said, He was bloody un-helpful over the 'Matice' business you will re-call.'
   'Yes I do actually, as did the Home Sec, I think he said, 'Tit for Tat', Stern-Price has really no sense of humour, that or the home sec's is a bit beyond him.'
   'Anyway, enough of all that, we have given some thought to Abdullah what's his name, here's the package we envisage.'
   He pushed a single sheet of paper across the table to Sir Bernard who picked it up.
   Quickly skipping past the verbiage at the beginning he read the detail.

1. Lump sum of £100,000 banked and only accessible in small agreed units.
2. Pension of £15,000 per annum indexed linked

3. Provision of a house to the value of £200,000 in an agreed location in the UK or abroad somewhere again by agreement.
4. Assistance with learning the English language, he already spoke some.

Sir John spoke.

'The true cost of course is likely to be much less; we expect he will be dead within 2 years at the most. We can give him a new identity and documentation, which we will do. But you know what will happen he will go looking for his own people wherever he is living at some point, which will be his downfall, he will get turned in for a 'hand-full of gold..

'May I keep this said Sir Bernard'?

'Yes of course you may, I will have it put together properly as an offer from the Foreign Office for services rendered. You I believe have promised to meet with him again? I can have it round to your office by 9.00am tomorrow if that will help'.

'Yes, I shall have him seen by Superintendent Gardner as soon as possible now I have this, thank you.'

'Now Bernard, on to much more important things, how about dinner? I've assumed you will join me. Teddy Johnson your ex-no two should be joining us about 7.15 if that's alright with you. They do a very good Dover sole. Personally I prefer the steak and kidney pie, absolutely superb and Sue say's it's the only reason I come here.'

"I would be delighted John, I need to make a phone call first,' he said pocketing the document, and putting his glass down".

Sir Bernard went out into the lobby and entered one of the telephone booths, within seconds he was speaking to Chief Superintendent Gardner. 'Bill I have the package you want for chummy, yes that's right he said listening to Gardner's comments. I think tomorrow say about 1100 hours. You can pick up the letter and documents to sign at 0915.

'See you then,' and with that he rang of and returned to Sir John and his Bushmills

## River Thames Wapping, London. Wednesday 23rd October 2003

Two metropolitan police officers stood looking at a dredger very close to the bank, its mechanical grab had half lifted a white Ford Transit out of the water, a barge going down river four hours earlier had hit it, and reported it to the River Police.

The transit looked in good condition, not the type you would dump. The dredger crew were allowing water to come out through the side windows, and one of the rear doors. The vehicle was half out of the water, when one of the PC's saw the wording Price Construction Ltd on the side. He reached for his radio.

The semi-drunk who wandered across to get a better view, belched and with a can of lager in hand remarked to the PC not on the radio, 'inconsiderate bastard he was dumping it in the river, and all to save a few quid.'

'You said inconsiderate bastard, did you see who dumped it?'

'Of course I did, I said so didn't I, and what ever was in them two parcels as well, 'he said making to walk away.

'Hang on there, said the PC, don't go away yet, somebody will want to talk to you.' He said now reaching for his radio.

'Normally can't bloody wait to move me on, now you want to talk to me! It'll cost you'. He said thinking of few more cans of lager, maybe even a case.'

# Chapter four

**A4 London, close to Heathrow.  4.00pm Wednesday 23rd October 2003**

The man and women entered the Palace hotel, and she immediately began to enthuse.
'Yes darling it's just right, and Jamie can watch his precious aeroplanes till his hearts content.' She said in loud voice.
They approached the desk, the receptionist listening to their conversation but pretending not to. 'No, I think two rooms, she said hugging her husband after all it is supposed to be a romantic holiday isn't it, and he is a little old now to share with us,' she said blushing slightly.
'How can I help you, Madam/Sir?' She said.
'We are going on holiday to the Seychelles for two weeks, not exactly a honeymoon, but special nonetheless'; the women said speaking quite forcibly. She wore the trousers for all to see. 'We are taking our 16 year old son, he's bit of an aeroplane nut, a bit like you were john with your trains,' she said turning to her husband.
'He didn't want to come, can't imagine why. John do stop fidgeting!! And pay attention.'
I can, thought the girl a week of you and I would be round the bloody twist.
John's eyes were fully occupied by the two young women in their early 20's stood near a luggage trolley; they were waiting to be picked up to go on to the airport. Bending down and checking their luggage the women revealed an excess of cleavage seemingly appreciated by John.
'John!!'-- John turned.' yes sorry dear, you were saying?'

'I was saying we need a room for Jamie at the front so he can watch the planes dear, we shall have a room at the back, and I don't want to hear them.'

'When is this for ?' Asked the receptionist.

'Tuesday night 4th November,' said the women,

John said 'err yes I think that's right.'

She looked at the receptionist and raised her eyebrows, as if to say 'men '.

At least you have got one, thought the receptionist, and one that can afford two weeks in the Seychelles, I had to make do with a girlie week-end in Brighton and copped off with that horrible nerd from Nottingham. The thought of his hands all over her again made her shudder.

'Now we shall be arriving at, she looked at her husband, you are finishing early aren't you,' she said?

'I may not go in at all,' he said.

'Let's say we will be here for 6.00pm is that all right?'

'Yes that's fine madam, how do you intend to pay for the rooms? We shall of course need a deposit.'

'John pay the lady, it will be cash, John does not have a credit card now do you dear,' she said looking at him.

'A credit card is normal madam, we won't charge against it if you cancel by the previous day.'

'As I said dear, she said looking at the receptionist, and lowering her voice. John isn't allowed one he's a bankrupt so he has to pay with cash.'

'Sorry, said the receptionist, I quite understand that will be perfectly alright.'

'£90 for the double and £70 for the single VAT Inc, and of course there is a full breakfast included. £160 in all, oh do you wish to leave you car for the duration of the holiday, if so that will be a further £65'.

'I told you to check that out John you have wasted yet another £35!! She was most annoyed'.

John filled out the form, and paid over £160 for which he received a receipt.

'Now John, go and look at a room for Jamie. And don't take all day over it it's only a bedroom with a view'.

The receptionist handed three keys to the porter who said, 'walk this way sir please.'

**The porter opened room 306.**

A typical standard good quality hotel room, private bathroom, double bed, desk and drawer arrangement, colour TV and video, two comfortable armchairs and a large double window covering the whole of the wall at the front of the room looking out over the A4 and directly at the main Heathrow runway, the one that runs over the twin tunnel entrance and exit to Heathrow terminals 1/2/3.

A British Airways 747 jumbo was landing it was about 100 foot up in the air, and seemed to be standing still as it went past 100 yards away. Two perimeter 2 storey buildings blocked the view of the Jumbo at two points.

**Room 308** had virtually the same view.

**Room 310** The room was built on a bias, and the corner was chopped off it provided a perfect uninterrupted view of the runway from both the front and the angled window, of the United Airlines Boeing 757 landing on it.

'Well done said John, he will love this,' and gave the porter a £5 note.

An hour later the couple arrived home at their squalid rented back to back terrace house on the outskirts of Oxford. The Browns, as they were known to the milkman and the next door neighbours Pam and Jim Dudley, Gave each other a little hug. 'That's that then', said John suddenly wearing the trousers, and now displaying a slight American accent.

# Chapter five

**SIS Headquarters London. Friday 25th October 2003**

Sir Bernard Hills was sat at his desk, when the intercom went.

'Sir Bernard I have a Captain Pat Harrison on the line wishing to speak with you regarding Mr Henderson, he's not sure but feels he has something that might interest you.'

'Very well Mary put him on. Captain Harrison I understand you wish to speak to me.'

'Yes Sir Bernard, I briefly bumped into Peter and Martine Henderson recently at Kefalonia airport I thought I should tell you about it in view of recent events.'

'They were going back home to the UK, and my wife and myself were waiting for our transport to our hotel. We spent about 10 minutes with them as you do, and then a couple of days later in the local Kefalonia newspaper there was an article about Peter saving a young boy from drowning in the sea.'

'There was a photograph of the boy and his father on the deck of a luxury yacht. But what has made me phone you is the fact that the man nearly out of shot in the photograph I know from my time in the Royal Military Police in Germany and Iraq. He was suspected of; can I say things openly on this line Sir Bernard?'

'Yes you may,' replied Sir Bernard.

'The individual concerned we believed in the RMP to be Russian by birth although we also believed he had spent a lot of time in Afghanistan, possibly with the Taliban. I know him as Petor Milcovic; he is most certainly Russian Mafia what ever else he is.

He tried to acquire anti-tank weapons, and surface to air weapons from UK and US sources whilst in Germany, we set up a "Sting" operation and caught the lot, except Milcovic.'

'One of the other pieces of intelligence to come out of our three-month operation in Germany was the fact that he has had some training in Iran and the USA in viruses and microbiology, although not medically qualified

'Captain Harrison, can I stop you there, where are these photographs, and how soon could you be here to look at this in more depth? Also are you a serving officer?'

'Yes I am currently on detachment to the Sultan of Oman's Army, in Oman. I do have some leave due; I could be with you within 24 hours I would have thought. And the photographs are with me there are no copies, and I have not said a word to anybody else at this stage.'

'I am going to put you back to Mary my secretary, she will take some contact details and get back to you within the hour, that's with a view to you coming over here. Is that OK?'

'Yes that's fine Sir Bernard; I will speak with, and then await her return call.'

Sir Bernard put the call back to Mary, and rang Chief Superintendent Gardner.

Superintendent Gardner's mobile rang and when he answered it he found he was talking to Sir Bernard Hills.

'Bill, there's been an interesting development! Did you know Peter Henderson had been on holiday to Kefalonia recently, but then again there is no reason why you should?'

'Whilst he was there, and possibly unwittingly, he was on the Island at about the same time as a major player. Can you ring me back with a slot for late tomorrow p.m.? We have a chap coming in from Oman, and it could prove to be relevant to your enquiries.'

**Some 90 minutes later Mary rang Pat Harrison. In Oman.**

'Captain Harrison? This is Mary Bishop again; I have you booked on British Airways BA72, Boeing 777 or 747. Departing Muscat International Airport at 2355 your time today. That's in 3 hours can you make it?'

'Yes that's fine, I am only ½ hour from the airport,' he said.

'Would you make a note of the following, you drop into Abu Dhabi at Nadia International, departing there at 0055 your flight time to Heathrow is then around 7 hours 40 minutes, you should arrive at Heathrow at 0650 tomorrow our time.'

'Your tickets are Club Class sleeper seats, so you can get some rest during the flight they are at the BA desk in the name of Dr Carl Anderson. There will also be a passport with that name on it in a separate envelope. Please do not open this until you are on your own. Not the best of photographs I'm afraid due to the time we had available, but you shouldn't need it.'

'The tickets are open-ended so you can make your own return arrangement if you wish. Would you ensure you bring the photographs with you? There will also be a small brown envelope with some expenses in it should you need anything.'

'About half an hour before landing at Heathrow, give the stewardess the small card in your envelope, stay in your seat and somebody will come on board take you straight through customs your luggage will be brought on if you have any. If you don't mind Sir Bernard would like to see you as soon after you land as possible if that's all right'?

'Yes that will be perfectly OK Mary; may I call you Mary?'

'You may Captain Harrison,' she replied.

'You are booked into The Cavendish hotel; the bill merely needs checking and signing. Both the air tickets and the hotel are showing a Dr Carl Anderson'.

'Sir Bernard thought technically it might be as well if you were still in Oman whilst you are here so to speak. You never know who is watching the ticket issues.'

'Do you need to inform anybody of your visit/ or were you thinking of bringing your wife? If you did wish to bring her that's not a problem, although she would need to use her own passport and "Bump" into on the aircraft, which might be fun'.

'No she is staying in Oman with our youngster. She will not take him out of school until the school, holidays. There is nobody else to tell.'

**British Airways desk, Oman International Airport 1 hour later.**

Hello there, my name is Dr Carl Anderson; I understand you have some tickets for me?

The young women at the desk gave him a strange look, and handed him, two envelopes one large and bulky and the other small and slim. "Thank you" he said as he pocketed them.

As soon as he left the desk the attendant picked up the phone and spoke for a couple of minutes to somebody in Farsi. He approached Club Class check in desk, and completed the formalities without a hitch, the check in clerk said, ' you are in seat 2a Dr Anderson, you will be boarding through gate 3 in about 20 minutes, have a nice flight.' His single case suit-bag he kept with him as cabin luggage and took a seat in the first class holding area to await the call for boarding.

Thirty minutes later he was comfortably seated, and stretching his legs whilst speaking to the cabin attendant.

Is anybody going to sit next to me?' He asked. Acknowledging the very evident empty seat next to him.

'No Sir, we were asked to keep it clear for you.'

I could get used to this thought Harrison/Anderson.

Pre dinner drinks were being served in the upper deck bar of the 747, and Harrison was enjoying canapés and a very large Gin and Tonic. Mindful of the fact that he wasn't Harrison but somebody else he was careful as to what he said, and to whom.

The bar steward spoke to him for the second time calling him Dr Anderson before he answered him, he quickly pointed to his ears and taking out his handkerchief blew his nose hard. The steward nodded sympathetically.

The photographs were safely in his jacket and that was where they would remain throughout the flight.

He began to think about his forthcoming meeting with Sir Bernard, the old boy seemed OK, a bit of a stickler for correctness by the sound of him. But that wouldn't be a problem. What had Henderson got himself involved in that had caused him to be killed and then poor Martine murdered as they obviously had been?

Was he himself being a bit of a 'pratt' by getting involved when he didn't have to? His wife Jennie had thought so. What if the same fate awaited them both? No more Gin and Tonics if this is what they did to him. He was beginning to feel more than a little maudlin, and sorry for himself.

He went back down the stairs and ordered dinner, and decided on the Chablis.

The aircraft landed at Nadia International, a tall distinguished Arab gentleman came into the forward cabin looked around and went to sit in the seat next to him, 'You don't mind if I sit here do you, I do so dislike window seats?'

'No that's fine I don't mind at all.'

The stranger settled himself in, and introduced himself.

'My name is Dr Abu Narunda,' and held out his hand.

'Carl ---!! Carl Anderson pleased to meet you.'

The stewardess came into the cabin, and was obviously distressed to see the seat next to Anderson now occupied, her instructions were very specific, and NOBODY was to be seated next to Dr Carl Anderson.

She approached Dr Narunda, and said 'I am so sorry Sir but could I have a quite word with you?'

'Yes by all means,' he got out of his seat and followed the stewardess to the rear of the club class cabin.

'Its very embarrassing Sir, but I have very specific instructions not to let anybody sit in the seat next to Dr Anderson, he has had a very traumatic time recently and his Company paid for the seat you were sat in so he wouldn't be disturbed. This should have been explained to you when you bought the 'stand by' that your allocated seat was the only one available.'

'No, don't feel embarrassed my dear you are quite right, and I do apologise, I shall of course use my allocated seat. He said returning to the seat next to 'Anderson'.

He leant over and spoke to 'Anderson', 'I am so sorry I hadn't realised that the seat was vacant for a reason, you should have said and I wouldn't have bothered you, once again please accept my apologies.'

Anderson was so taken aback, he hadn't got the faintest idea what he was on about, and he could see his non-reaction was taken for aloofness. Still never mind he had got his peace and quiet back, and hopefully could get some sleep.

The 'Jumbo' took off on time, and an hour later and the Boeing 747 had reached its cruising speed over just over 600 mph and height of 40,000ft (the 747 jumbo has a ceiling of 45,100ft) and was over the Persian Gulf.

After a very pleasant 'Dinner' by aircraft standards he changed into his slippers, dropped the seat into slumber mode, having first secreted the photographs under his body, and fell asleep within seconds.

Five hours later he was awaked by the stewardess gently shaking him, and asking if he would like breakfast before landing, they were due to land at Heathrow in just under an hour and a half. It was now 0530.

As he went to the washroom to freshen up before breakfast he passed Dr. Narunda, who asked him if he had had a good flight and managed to get some sleep? They passed a few pleasantries and he carried on to the washroom. He suddenly remembered the photographs that were under the blanket on the couchette, and turned on his heel to go back.

Ahead of him he saw Dr Narunda close to his seat 2A; within seconds he was behind him and said, 'can I help you?' A very startled Narunda turned and replied.

'I was looking for the stewardess, have you seen her?'

'She is on the upper deck at the moment.' He said sitting back down in his seat.

'Thank you I will speak to her later then,' said Narunda turning round and going back to his own seat.

*The President Is Down*

Harrison gave it ten minutes, and then went again to the washroom this time taking the photographs, and displaying his electric razor in his left hand as he passed Narunda. 'Forgot my electric razor,' he said as he passed by with a smile.

Narunda smiled back at him, but it was a cold hard look and he did not reply.

Having breakfasted, washed and changed, he read a book on the approach to Heathrow, remembering to give the small card to the stewardess who took it to the Captain, she came back few minutes later, with a new look of respect on her face.

'Captain Woods compliments Sir; it will be all right for you to remain aboard.'

'Thank you, and thanks for looking after me during the flight,' he said.

She blushed and turned away.

Ten minutes later, and after the last of Club Class passengers had left he was approached in his seat by a small bespectacled man who introduced himself as, George Smith from the MOD, and showed him a security pass to support it. 'I have a car waiting he said. On the airway outside there will be a customs chap, just show him your passport, and then follow me. I have been told to take you for breakfast if you wish, other than we go straight to SIS at Century house 'Let's get straight off; I have had breakfast on the aircraft.'

The M4 and then the A4 into London was beginning to get busy it now being 0715, never the less the MOD driver got them there in less than thirty minutes.

# Chapter six

**SIS Headquarters, London 7.50am, Saturday 26th October 2003**

There were four people sat around the conference table in Sir Bernard's office.

Sir Bernard, Chief Superintendent Gardner, Sergeant Tucker, and Captain Harrison.

The introductions completed, Sir Bernard spoke directly to Harrison.

'Firstly, thank you for coming over it is much appreciated, and I hope your flight was alright.'

'Yes Sir, very comfortable, but before we start, it could be nothing but an Arab gentleman came and sat in the seat next to me, making the excuse that he did not like window seat and had moved for that reason, the stewardess actually moved him back and he didn't seem at all pleased. The reason I mention it is because I caught him a little later again near my seat, he said he was looking for the stewardess yet he must have seen her go upstairs. His name was Dr Abu Narunda.'

'We will get him checked out, now if you could tell us n your own words what you started to tell me on the phone,' said Sir Bernard.

'It was this summer last month in fact during late September, my wife and I had just landed at Kefalonia airport, we had picked up our luggage and were waiting to be collected by taxi, and standing just inside the airport doors. I then noticed Peter and Martine Henderson pushing their luggage towards us and coming in to the airport .'

'It's about two years since I last saw Peter. We spent about 10 minutes talking and then our taxi arrived. We promised to keep in touch as you do, and parted company.'

'A couple of days later we bought he local newspaper, which they also print in English, on the front page, was a photo of the local boy made good and now a multi-millionaire I think he is in olive oil and petroleum products. He had his son with him and the article mentioned an Englishman on holiday that had saved the boy from drowning. That Englishman was Peter Henderson.'

He pushed the newspaper clipping across table to Sir Bernard.

Sir Bernard was looking at a grainy black and white photograph of a short dark stocky Greek looking man probably in his early fifties, he had his hand resting on the shoulder of a young boy who looked to be about ten or twelve years of age, and both were smiling at the camera. They were all on the deck of a luxury yacht. The name *'Joyce 11* 'inscribed in letters across the stern

'To the right upper part of the photograph, just going out of shot on that is a man whom I know to be Petor Milcovic.' Said Harrison.

'He is very bad news as I said previously,' and he repeated what he had said to Sir Bernard the day before.

Captain Harrison reached into a folder he had brought with him, a produced some excellent shots of the same photograph, now showing much more of Milcovic. 'I took the trouble to get these from the press photographer saying I wanted to give them to Peter Henderson, which was why I rang Peter in the first place. In view of events I have taken the liberty to bring these photographs of Milcovic in various locations and mode of dress. My CO gave permission when I told him why I wanted them. He handed them to Sir Bernard. I also brought these with me,' he pushed across a file about 10 pages thick, and it detailed what the RMP had been able to get on Milcovic.

'Captain Harrison I am more than impressed, you have brought a lot more to the party than I envisaged, would you do me a favour I want to discuss something with Superintendent Gardner if you don't mind.'

'Not at all Sir,' he got up and left the room.

Five minutes later he was back in the room.

'Captain Harrison, we are going to take you into our confidence, but before I do so can I ask you if we could get leave of absence from your unit for a few weeks if necessary would you be prepared to stay on and help?'

'I would be pleased to Sir; I want these bastards that did that to Peter and Martine.'

'Right here's the deal, currently you are a Captain in the Royal Military Police, that's about Chief Inspector in the civilian police. We propose to give you an acting rank of Detective Chief Inspector, the reason for that is

Superintendent Gardner is going out to Kefalonia to see if we could glean anything useful to the enquiry. Particularly from Mr Astinikis.'

'We both feel you should go with him, and to keep things a little low key, we propose that you become a member of The Metropolitan Police, as a DCI. If anybody is watching it just might make them think this is just a police investigation and that the Army and Intelligence forces are not involved. You are also going to need to be armed when you get back from Kefalonia.'

'We will get you booked in to your hotel on an extended stay basis, we will meet back here a 1400 in the meantime somebody will take your photograph now, for a warrant card. Your card will be back dated about 10 years so its fits your legend.'

**1400 Sir Bernard's Office that same day.**

'Mary would you do the honours please,' said Sir Bernard.

Mary who by now was getting used to Sir Bernard and his building habit of delegation, sat down with a folder of documents.

'Right gentlemen, you will be flying Britannia Airways flight BY340A from Birmingham at 0830 tomorrow, this is quicker than going out to Athens and then on from there by scheduled airline. You have seat 'Bumped 'two people; you may have to do the same on the way back, this is a holiday charter flight.'

'Tonight you are booked into the Metropole hotel just outside the airport, on the Birmingham Exhibition site a taxi is booked for 0630 tomorrow morning to take you to the airport which is only 3 minutes away. It been arranged that you leave your car at the hotel.'

'When you get to Kefalonia, look out for a Colonel George Aristostis, he will walk you through customs and help you as much as you need. He has also offered a car and driver if you would prefer it.'

'I think we will accept his offer to Skala and then hire a car, it will us more flexibility as long as Patrick here is going to drive it, I'm bad enough on these roads so what I would be like on those on Kefalonia I have no idea,' said Gardner.

'When you get to Skala you will be staying initially at the San Georgia hotel, its about a mile out of Skala on the coast road, it's the hotel that the Henderson's stayed at, its also nearly opposite where the near drowning took place.'

'Colonel Aristostis says Aristo Astinikis and his young son Peter live in the Villa right on the coast about 200 metres from the San Georgio, he has a small inlet cove/harbour, for his yacht, when he is not in Athens or on his yacht.'

Late evening they arrived at the Metropole hotel Birmingham near the airport had a good dinner a got to know each other a little better. They mutually agreed that the plan of action was simply tracing the Hendersons last few weeks to see if they were any lines of enquiry worth pursuing, this was to be the line to take with everybody there was to be no mention of terrorists or the US president etc.

The next morning saw them in line with 220 holidaymakers looking for the sun, and awaiting their baggage checking in. They both looked vaguely like holidaymakers but didn't quite make it.

Superintendent Gardner looked like a policeman trying to look like a holidaymaker, or so thought Harrison. On the other hand Harrison thought his son would think he looked 'Cool' dressed in pale blue open necked Sea Island shirt, dark blue chinos and brown loafers. With a casual jacket slung over his shoulder.

Their two bags were retained as cabin luggage and went on the aircraft with them.

They arrived at 1350 local time and on time, and were met the air side of customs by a short jolly figure of a man with a dark bushy moustache and a full head of black wavy hair, Colonel George Aristostis looked the part.

Beaming broadly he introduced himself, and said,'good just in time for lunch I suggest a little restaurant close to the beach at Lourdas it's just off the main road and half way to Skala. We can sit under the vines out of the sun and eat whilst you tell me what help you would like.' Put like that they could hardly refuse.

The colonel took them through customs with a hardly perceptible nod to the customs man. Colonel Aristostis's car was an old, immaculate, and very shiny dark grey e-class diesel Mercedes, his driver was a good looking police corporal about 25 years of age, Harrison could only imagine his success with the girls. His immaculate uniform and highly polished black belt and holster contrasted starkly with the crumpled but expensive suit that 'George' was wearing.

The driver sat at a separate table near the entrance to the open air restaurant, a canopy of mature vines now almost devoid of fruit was above, shading them from the afternoon sun, the restaurateur seemed know 'George' as he insisted on being called and treated him with some reverence.

The food when it came was a mixture of pasta-seafood and roasted vegetables, with a huge green salad, and a big carafe of white wine to follow the first one, which they had sipped gratefully. It's near icy coldness refreshing and seemingly not very alcoholic, which was a myth in itself.

'My driver Yanis is available for you if you wish'. 'That's very kind and generous of you, but it would be less inconvenient I am sure if we simply hired a car.' Said Gardner, who was now 'Bill', as Harrison was now 'Pat'.

'Let me tell you about Yanis, he is one of the top pistol and light machine gun shots in Greece, he could have been a top rally driver, but he has one problem. It is between his legs, and will bring him much trouble in years to come, and break many hearts he's like a 'Rabbit' do you say,' and bellowed with laughter.

# Chapter seven

**Andrews Air Force Base, Md 89th Presidential Airlift Group Friday 25th October 2003**

2 Star General David 'Traffic' Bloomberg stood looking at the love of his life: 231 feet 10 inches long, 63 feet 5 inches high, a wing span of 195 feet 8 inches, her immaculate blue and white livery shimmered in the lights of the massive hanger housing it Boeing 747-200B tail number 28000 and its partner identical in every way apart from its tail number of 29000. Either was call signed **AIR FORCE ONE.** When the President of the United States was on board

He loved these two aircraft with a passion only ever reserved for his late wife Jennie, and now solely lavished on them. He had looked after them both from the day they were delivered in 1990; he remembered the first flight of AIR FORCE ONE 28000 as though it were yesterday it carried George Bush Snr to Kansas, Florida and back to Washington.

29000 delivered in December 1990 transported Presidents Clinton, Carter and Bush to Israel for the funeral of Prime Minister Yitzhak Rabin. Now he was just one month from his retirement and losing yet again the loves of his life. He reflected on when they were first delivered, no they would ever replace his two beautiful C-137C Boeing 707's tail plane 26000 and 27000. Or would they? Over time they had done so.

26000 probably the most widely known ever of the Presidential Flight. It carried the President Kennedy to Dallas on November 22nd 1963, and returned his body to Washington DC following his assassination.

Lyndon B. Johnson was sworn into office as the 36th President on board it at Love Field in Dallas. This fateful aircraft was used to return President Johnson's body to Texas following his state funeral on January 24th 1973.

In 1972 President Richard Nixon made historic visits on board 26000 to Peoples Republic of China and to the former USSR. 26000 was retired in May 1998 and is on display at Wright-Patterson AFB, Ohio.

27000 replaced 26000 and carved its own history when it was used to fly Presidents Nixon, Ford and Carter to Cairo, Egypt, 19th Oct 1981 to represent the United States of America at the funeral of President Nasser of Egypt.

The 747 did change his affection and his life, some twenty plus years now of Presidential service and forty years in the Air Force coming to an end. He still wondered just how Boeing had made the aircraft what it was, truly unique; it carried state of the art navigation, twice the wiring of a 'normal' 747 shielded from the effects of atomic blast. Mission communications, 85 telephone, as well as multi-frequency radios for air to air, air to ground, and satellite communications. Capable of being refuelled mid-air.

A 4,000 sq. ft 'Oval Office', conference and dining rooms, quarters for the President and the First Lady, and offices for senior staff. Two galleys each capable of providing food for 50 people. A food storage facility for 2,000 meals, a medical facility. Automated loading. And its own counter attack equipment and measures.

He was aware of somebody behind him.' Excuse me Sir, are you alright?'

'Yes why wouldn't I be sergeant?'

'I am sorry Sir, but you have been stood in the same spot for the last ten minutes, I just wondered if everything was OK.'

'Yep, I'm getting sentimental in my old age, but don't tell anybody, he winked, it's our secret.' (Not bad for a black man from the boon docks, as he surely was).

'Yes Sir' replied the sergeant saluted smartly and continued his patrol.

**The White House, Washington DC Later that day.**

The President of the United States of America, sat behind his huge desk in the 'Oval Office' And looked at his chief of staff Henry Painter.

'OK Henry what's the plan of action and the proposed date/s we now have for the visits to London and Brussels?'

Henry Painter had given up a senior partnership in the top legal practice in Washington to become the current Presidents Chief of Staff. He ran the 'Oval Office', love him or hate him he was the best there had been at this, and he knew it.

Cross him, and you got the run around or nowhere as many had found to their deepest regret, go along with him and you were made.

The Presidents phenomenal work load was only completed because of his 'filtering and fine tuning'.

He enjoyed the power it gave him to an extent that he was more powerful than the Vice President Morgan Price Stanley. Who was an overweight ex-football star, very popular with the electorate and who carried the black vote that was so necessary? He had a thought on that which he intended to put to the President this very day.

Henry Painter looked at the President and answered, 'Yes Mr President I think we should run through my proposals to see if you would like to amend them, at the moment they are just that, proposals. However, I have had to firm up on a couple of points such as the dates involved, and who should accompany you etc.'

'We need to meet with Tony Salter as you have agreed, and preferably in London, I suggest that we make that the first meeting, and then go on to Brussels. There is no possibility of you and the first Lady stopping with the Prime Minister as 10, Downing Street is pretty small.'

'I suggest you stay over at our Embassy in Grosvenor Square, we can make that very secure and the CIA and I would feel much happier with that arrangement. Ambassador Henry would also be delighted. As to travel arrangements, we have agreed to keep this 'low key' and the numbers down. We can accommodate all within AIR FORCE ONE and her sister plane.'

'Speaking of AIR FORCE ONE Mr President, I have a thought, the presidential elections are only 12 months away, and I thought as General Bloomberg is retiring at the end of the month. We might take him on the trip and make some mileage out of it when we get back. We need the black vote more than ever and this alone would help.'

'Yes, I like the idea Henry, General Bloomberg has overseen the Presidential Flight for god knows how many years, I always feel I should ask permission to use AIR FORCE ONE, he said laughing. Yep, a great idea, and never mind the vote aspect the man deserves nothing less. You know they are throwing one hell of a party for him at Andrews Air Force Base he isn't supposed to know, being the guy he is I expect he suspects something.'

'Moving on to air cover, Mr President 4 National Guard Strike Eagles of will escort AIR FORCE ONE from Andrews AFB till mid-Atlantic, 4 other Strike Eagles takeover from them having taken off from RAF in southern England, they will have flown in from their base in Germany the day before. They will stay with AIR FORCE ONE until it lands and then return to the RAF base to refuel, and then cover the Brussels stage the next day.'

'The return is somewhat easier as we don't have to visit with Tony Salter or stop off in London. We will simply repeat the security arrangements in reverse.'

'Air traffic control on our side of the Atlantic can impose a no fly zone around AIR FORCE ONE at about 50 nautical miles, we shall also have an AWACS with you, he gets to go the whole distance. He has got the range and won't need to refuel. Coming out from England we have a KC135 to refuel the fighters that need it. The only problem area is within Europe itself, the Brits can control their air space, even though it's pretty crowded air traffic wise.'

'They have a new air traffic control centre in Hampshire, England, but your flight will be handled from RAF Uxbridge. That used to be the main ATC centre in the UK prior to the new one. Those guys know what they are doing and are pretty discreet.'

'As I have said it's when ATC gets handed on to the French that potential problems could arise at the moment they are being a little difficult but it should be OK. Its only minutes before you enter Belgium airspace and they are OK.'

'As an additional security measure your pilot Colonel Masters has the choice of multi-landing sites, you can choose one of them or he can for landing, we only need to choose and advise RAF Uxbridge one hour before landing of the choice. This we think is a pretty good arrangement, one of the Brit intelligence guys came up with this idea.'

'Unfortunately we can't copy it in Brussels.'

He handed the President a short list headed **Confidential** and showing only three names on the circulation list:

The President
The Vice President
The Joint Chief of Staff.
**The alternate landing sites are:**

**RAF Northolt,** this is just outside of London its about 30 minutes from Downing Street, by automobile currently it handles VIP Flights, the British Queens Flight is based there, and it now some distance from the main road, the runway used to be directly alongside it.

**For it:**  Runway protected from view.
Close to London Central by road, 30 minutes.
**Easy to chopper into Central London and fast, we**

**could set down In Buckingham Palace grounds in 10 minutes. Tea in the Palace And onto the our embassy**

Against: Nothing we can see.

**RAF Lakenheath** in Suffolk, this is about 45/60 minutes out by chopper, it's a big US Base built for heavies.
B52's were based there in the recent past.

For it: Large runway screened and secure.
Can come in from the east coast of England, thus avoiding a lot of air Traffic.
**Easy to chopper in, landing arrangements as before.**

Against: Pretty far out and a long time expose en-route, thus a Higher level of danger.

We have three others, Luton, London-Gatwick, and London-Heathrow.

Luton, an entirely civilian airport.
This first one Luton we have dismissed, simply because it's too small, and your flight would stand out like a sore thumb and attract too much attention, road travel is not easy from there, and could get hold ups along the motorway system.

**London-Gatwick**, again a solely civilian airport.

For it: Good runways some of it screened.
Motorway link from the airport straight into London.
Subject to massive delays at times, particularly on the M25
**Straight chopper in from here 35 / 40 minutes tops.**
Good approach from the sea without significant over flying of land.

Against: Road link lengthy journey with a very significant danger level, and a motorway prone to delays and stoppages.

**London-Heathrow**, civilian airport, Britains biggest.

For it: Good choice of runways Aircraft landing every minute, making it possible **'Hide'** in the stack and approach traffic.
Motorway link good, but can get very busy,
30 minutes to central London.
Security excellent as a norm, easy to beef up.
Has a separate VIP area round the other side of the airport
Many exits on to the main road, without using normal roads.

*C. G. Poplett*

|  | **Fast straight chopper in to London 15 mins.** |
|---|---|
| **Against:** | Very open on most sides, perimeter roads are all used by the public and very close to the main runways. |
|  | Over flies many potential danger points, particularly if the approach is over central London |

'The analysis at the end of the day seems to rule out automobiles, and come firmly down in favour of a helicopter, the only problem with a chopper is vulnerability during its flight to potential missile attack during its take off, approach on landing, and of course whilst on the ground immediately AFTER landing, the exposure in time to a potential threat is the shortest, so one could outweigh the othe".

'Well you have done your homework Henry as usual, as you say lets think about over the next couple of days. By the way does Colonel Masters know of these options yet?' Asked the President.

'Not at the moment Mr President. But as you know he will need to know at least when we are mid-Atlantic. Said Painter. I have a problem with not telling him sooner Sir it looks as though we don't trust him.'

'You are right of course, we tell him prior to take off, and I will leave that to you Henry.'

'Lets talk about General Bloomberg, what do we know about him Henry, I seem to remember something about his wife dying a couple of years ago,' said the President.

'Well Mr President, where do we start? General Bloomberg is one of our top 2 star generals, he got where he is on pure ability, and he has been in the Air Force 40 years at the end of this month. He served in Viet Nam, and he was a helicopter pilot then, he was shot up pretty badly three times in all, twice whilst picking up marines. In each case they came out OK he would always make the pick up.'

'His 'Nickname' is 'Traffic' as the last time he was shot down in Nam, and walked for 20 clicks, then for six days he lay in hiding alongside a major Viet Cong supply route that we didn't know of, and called in air strikes over and over again. The VC tried to find him, and thank god they didn't. They would have hacked him into little bits if they had found him.'

'He just calmly called in the strikes, cooling saying, I have some 'traffic' for you hence the nickname. A couple of F4's kept the Viet Cong busy when we eventually choppered him out. That's when he started moving up the ladder. He's quite a hero. Purple Heart an all !!'

'I think he has been involved in the Presidential Flight since the early 80's, so some time now. He came as number three and is now number one. He's a very hard man by all accounts 100% is the norm in all things and if people can't perform they go. However, the men think the World of him; he is 'God' to them.'

'OK Henry thanks for that, I am going to speak to General Bloomberg personally, I will catch up with you later, and can you put back my Joint Chief of Staff meeting an hour?'

The President picked up his telephone and spoke with his secretary, 'Wilma would you get me General Bloomberg, Andrews Air Force Base please.'

## Andrews Air Force Base Md 89th Presidential Airlift Group a few minutes later.

'General Bloomberg Mr President what can I do for you Sir?'

'General nice to speak to you again, how are you keeping?'

'I'm fine Mr President.' Wondering why the hell the President was ringing him and asking how was he!

'General, I will cut to the chase I know what a busy man you are, you will be advised by the Chief of Staff of a trip to London, England, and Brussels Belgium, at the moment it to those that need to know only.'

'Of course Mr President, until I get my official orders I know nothing.'

'Excellent General, on to something more personal, I understand you will be retiring at the end of this month, had enough of us have you?' Said the President with a chuckle.

'Yes Mr President that is correct I am retiring, although it's not something I am looking forward to at all Sir.'

'General I would deem it and honour if you flew with me in AIR FORCE ONE as senior Air Force officer, and were in charge of all arrangements and the flight itself on this trip, can you manage that alright General?'

There was a stunned silence which lasted about 10 seconds, but felt like an eternity.

'Mr President I am deeply humbled and honoured, and I am delighted to accept your kind offer Sir.'

'Good, well that's settled then, I was hoping you would say yes, you do most of it anyway, so could be a bit of a bus mans holiday eh General, ---- Henry Painter will be in touch later today or tomorrow to clarify a few dates and times with you, I look forward very much to your company on board General.'

And just one final thing, Walter Sternham the C.E.O. at Boeing, he and I were chatting a couple of weeks ago, he has rather an interesting position he needs to fill, I suggested you might be interested, so don't be surprised if you get a call later this week. He's in the Bahamas on holiday at the moment. Oh, and screw him down he can afford it, see you soon General .'

General David ' Traffic' Bloomberg, had tears in his eye's when he realised exactly what had just happened, they were the first tears he had shed since the parting from his beloved

Jennie 3 years ago.  She would understand.

# Chapter eight

**Kefalonia, Sunday 27th October 2003**

The drive on to Skala was stunning; the road not very wide in places passing through small pretty roadside villages, usually with a side road dropping down the Aegean Sea and some quite spectacular beaches.

One such when in a mountainous section looked down from a good height onto a semi-circular deserted golden beach within a superbly picturesque bay? Yanis had stopped the car and pointed to the treacherous and difficult road down to it; this served only to protect its privacy and rewarded those who ventured down.

The shallows a jewelled light green-blue, with dark deeper shoals, melded into a solid dark blue sea far out into the distance. A sea mist had sprung up and on the horizon a cruise ship; ethereal and white could be seen emerging out of the mist and into the failing sunlight. No doubt on its way to berth for the night and allow its passengers a night ashore to savour the islands delights.

Coming down out of the mountains and moving closer again to the sea, past the small fishing village of Katelios famous for its fresh fish, sardines, squid and lobster. 'George' glanced at Gardner and said, 'we will eat there one evening I have many friends there, the food is excellent.'

Back up into the high ground for a short distance before the drop down into Skala, and the rugged pebbly beached coastline and the sea.

'Yanis, please go into Skala past the roman mosaics and down the main road, not the coast road, I would like them to see Skala before night falls.'

They entered Skala near the top of the main road, a road bustling with people, the colourful shops some with old fashioned canopies, others with modern chrome and glazing mixed in with open fronted restaurants and bars, motorcycles and cars aged and new were parked haphazardly alongside the storm drained pavements.

In spite of all the activity an air of peace and timelessness seemed to exist. Harrison determined to come back at some later point for a holiday here and simply fell in love with the place there and then, he felt at home, something he had not really done for years.

The drove the short distance to the bottom of the road and turned left, wending their way through the pine trees and down on to the coast road proper. The sea paralleled the road at a very short distance of 20 to 30 metres for some 15 kilometres to the next village-port. The narrow twisting poorly surfaced road undulating and occasionally pot holed along its length.

Immediately on their left across the road from the beach and were a number of good and expensive looking hotels, interspersed with typical Greek shuttered housing, and a smaller number of smallholdings, goats, sheep and cattle were all to be seen in the fields or alongside the road in a short distance of a couple of kilometres.

Breasting a small hill they came upon a 20 foot fishing boat, firmly beached on the left hand side of the road and actually on the grass verge, the derelict boat freshly painted was the typically Greek Restaurateurs way of advertising his fresh caught fish and the restaurants speciality, the elevated restaurant tables all looked out to sea.

A few minutes later Yanis pulled over to the entrance driveway to a large white villa on his right. The villa was impressive in its size and architecture, a columned entrance porch terrace, led to a massive wood and glazed double door entrance. The covered terrace extended around the whole of the front of the building and disappeared around to the back.

The two storey terracotta roofed building featured a partially exposed terrace seeming to again go from front to back, down the right hand of the villa there was road within the grounds dropping down to a small harbour and wooden and stone walled jetty, a luxurious white yacht could be seen nestling up to the harbour wall, and two people a man and a woman turned when they heard the car stop and the colonel and party had got out.

'George' waved to the man some 100 metres away, whom returned his wave and set out to meet them, George made no effort to open the gates, the reason became immediately apparent when two Doberman pinchers tore round the corner of the villa and flew at the gates, snarling and barking as they did so.

The main entrance door to the Villa opened, and a young boy shouted something in Greek at the dogs, which fell to ground silenced for the

## The President Is Down

moment, but watchful. The young boy waved and yelled 'Uncle George', 'Uncle George', and ran towards them; he stopped for a few seconds to fondle the dogs that rolled around in obvious delight. He opened the gate and all four of them entered to be greeted by Aristo Astinikis and his wife Joyce. The introductions over him led the way up the marble staircase and on to the terrace overlooking the sea.

'Gentlemen welcome to my home, may I offer you some refreshment, a drink perhaps of my own chilled white wine, the vines are some my father planted some years ago and produce delicious wine, dry but with a fruity elegance as 'George' will confirm.' He said glancing at 'George' who nodded his agreement.

'Ari, you are very naughty, the Superintendent and Chief Inspector may wish to check into their hotel, it must have been a long day already for them.'

'Ari, was shocked and chastened, 'how inconsiderate of me of course you must go and check in if you wish, or Joyce can show you to two of our guest rooms if you prefer to freshen up, and then perhaps we can have that drink?' He said glancing at his wife.

'That seems an excellent suggestion' said Gardner not wishing to break up the rapport that seemed to be building.'

Ten minutes later they both emerged on to the rear terrace, set out on gleaming white table cloths was a superb selection of crab, lobster, sardines and an array of other fish, olive bread, salads, dips and iced water.

On the adjacent table cut glass crystal glasses glittered and shone in the sinking sunlight, casting myriad flecks of brilliant coloured light across the tablecloth. White wine in a tall crystal decanter misted with the cold chill, dark ruby red wine in a shorter plumper one, and a tall thin crystal decanter of 7 Star Metaxa brandy completed the array.

'Just a little something as you must be a little peckish by now. Said Ari. Please help yourself.'

It was only around two hours ago that they had last eaten, but not wishing to offend 'Ari' they tucked in to the wonderful selection of fresh seafood.

When all of them had some food on a plate and a glass in their hands, 'Ari ' spoke.

'I need to say something Superintendent, firstly I feel we ought to start tomorrow morning lets say 8.00am, the reason I am suggesting this is because I do not want your first night on my beautiful Island spoilt by vicious and sadistic killers. These people must be caught. And when they are I will punish them, they have taken the lives of two people I hold most dear to my heart. I am Greek; we do not forget or forgive such violence and treachery as many have found over the years.'

'You will find them and lock them up, I would have them killed,' and his tone hard and cold and Gardner felt that he was losing control of the meeting.

'Ari', I quite understand your feelings, I share them in many ways I promise you, but you must not talk of punishing them, that is the domain of law,' which sounded inadequate and pompous.

Enough of this talk tonight said 'Ari' lightening his voice and smiling, tonight we dine together at the San Georgio; I would like to introduce you to my great friends who own it. They are looking forward to meeting you, if they get back from Athens.'

They took their leave of the Astinikis couple and were driven the short distance to their hotel.

The San Georgio has a long sweeping steep drive to the main building and reception. A large swimming pool and a popular outside bar and small shop are on the same level, and form a continuation of the main building. The first floor dining room is split into a covered indoor section, and a superb terrace area with uninterrupted view over the Aegean Sea.

Overlooking the pool and continuing up the hillside are apartments to a maximum of two floors, all well appointed and with their own spacious balconies. The owners are a middle aged Greek couple, he is an Architect and she runs the hotel, it's a combination that works, the place looked immaculate and quite unique, cool and inviting.

The Astinikis couple arrived on time at 9.00pm and met Gardner and Harrison in the bar near the pool; both were obviously well known. Joyce wore a lovely red off the shoulder sheath long dress, tight fitting and showing off her superb figure and pale golden tan to perfection, she wore a single piece of jewellery around her neck, it was a fine gold chain, with a solitaire diamond pendant. Her long blonde hair fell naturally over one shoulder, she looked stunning.

His superbly tailored off white linen suit and open necked dark blue silk shirt and black highly polished Italian shoes were the perfect companions.

They looked a complete couple relaxed, sophisticated and in control. The body language and gentle casual touching showing a deep and genuine affection for each other. Joyce sat on a high stool at the bar; her legs crossed revealing very shapely long legs, and elegant high-heeled delicate sling back, red shoes.

Gardner and Harrison felt decidedly under dressed in slacks, and blazers, and very formal ties around their necks.

They all had a drink and then went upstairs in the main building to the restaurant. A table on the terrace had been reserved for them, ' Ari ' explained that this was their usual table, it overlooked the superb sea view.

The full moon shone from a clear sky reflecting off the surface of the gently rippling sea, in the distance they could see a cruise liner lit up, and a ferry on the horizon which in minutes disappeared.

On the hillside behind them and now in darkness, they could hear the gentle tinkerling of the bells around the goat's necks as they foraged for food. Harrison reflected how could there ever be bad in such an idyllic world as this? After an excellent dinner they parted company and agreed to meet up at the villa the next morning at 8.00am.

## Monday 28th October 2003 the Villa of Aristo Astinikis Skala Kefalonia Greece.

Chief Superintendent Gardner and Chief Inspector Harrison were seated at a breakfast table on the terrace drinking coffee and awaiting 'Ari' who had been called away to the phone, he came back on to the terrace.

'Sorry about that one of my tanker captains was having some problems in Malta.'

'Do you have many tankers?' Asked Gardner.

'I have 6 what you would call super tankers, or VLCC, Very Large Crude Carriers these carry 200,000 plus tons of oil, liquefied gas, or liquefied petroleum gas, and 2 ULCC or Ultra Large Crude Carriers can manage over 300,000 tons, the ship can weigh empty 200,000 to 400,000 tons, they can travel at 18mph or nearly 31km/h,

3 smaller ones, at 100,000 tons and 2 - 20,000 ton freighters, and 1 - 12,000 tonne freighter. And a 35,000 ton Cruise liner. It's the second largest fleet outside of the main oil companies with their own or leased ones.'

Gardner was very impressed.

'It might be helpful Bill if I told you how I came to meet Peter and Martine Henderson'? It was four weeks ago when I nearly lost my only son Peter, his voice dropped and he had to clear his throat, Peter has been told before not to swim off the rocks unless an adult is with him.'

'He swims like a fish and we have difficulty keeping him out of the water, usually our swimming in the sea is very safe, we had just had lunch. Peter was catching sardines off the back of the yacht. He does this often, the sardines swim around under the stern in the clear water and he catches sometimes too many. He likes to grill them for us occasionally!!'

'The two dogs were with him as they usually are they follow him everywhere, they even sleep on the rear terrace at night outside of his open window/sliding doors. He had slipped into the water using the stern ladder and diving board, again nothing unusual as the boat was firmly tied up and secured it would seem he had seen a school of dolphins about 100 metres out, they follow the small fishing boats and take the sardines on the edges of shoals.'

"He says he got close to the dolphins that came towards him, and he played with them for five or so minutes, he then realised he had gone out a bit far, at turned towards the shore. The effort gave his stomach cramp, and he couldn't swim properly, he got in to difficulties and began to panic.'

'He did not have his body buoyancy aid, which would have kept him above the surface; he started to go under, again and again. The dogs had been watching and started to run up and down the yacht deck side, the bitch jumped into the water and started to swim out to him but couldn't make much headway.'

'Joyce and I heard the dog going absolutely mad on the yacht, and at first couldn't see what was wrong. We started to shout and look for Peter at the same time. There was a man and a woman walking along the little pebbled cove a few metres from our boundary. He looked up, I suppose because Joyce and I were shouting the name 'Peter', he then realised we didn't mean him and looked out to sea and saw the dog.'

'At first he thought we were shouting for the dog, until he saw the dolphins, and between the dolphins and the shore a figure which kept going under the surface. Peter must have got really worked up as he shot out of the water, and Peter Henderson realised it was a child in trouble.'

'He just took his sandals off an dived in, he is, -- was, he corrected himself, a strong swimmer thank god, and quickly reached our son, he brought him back very quickly, and up onto the deck of the yacht. We thought Peter was dead, he wasn't moving and did not appear to be breathing.'

'Peter Henderson knew what to do, he put him on his back, tilted his head back and pinching his nose breathed twice into his lungs we saw his little chest inflate, he then put his hands on his chest and pumped it. He kept doing this; we were too stunned to do anything and could only watch.'

'Suddenly, Peter coughed, and water shot out of his mouth, he was rolled on to his side and he kept vomiting up seawater. His eyes opened and he put his hand up for Joyce. I realised that tears were flooding down my face; Peter Henderson said we should get him to hospital, we have a small town one in Skala, and we took him there. He stayed in overnight and the next afternoon we were allowed to bring him home. There were and are no problems that we know of, other than he won't go in the water without one of us with him, and he always wears his lifejacket now.'

'Later that afternoon we all went over to the San Georgio to thank Peter Henderson, the following day was my 55th birthday and Joyce had planned a party in celebration at the villa and on board the yacht.'

'We were to have a large buffet and barbecue, from mid-day on the terrace, water sports off the yacht, and clay pigeon shooting out to sea off the jetty. I wanted to put it off or cancel it, but young Peter can be a loving and stubborn child when he likes. He gets that from his mother, he said glancing at her with obvious affection. He absolutely insisted that we go ahead, and also invite the Henderson, which of course we did.'

'We had a lovely party the following day, and Peter and Martine Henderson became one of the family. Peter organised the clay pigeon shoot, and some of the water sports. Martine very unobtrusively helped Joyce, she took the niggling things off her and it allowed Joyce to host the party that much better, they were like sisters it was good to see'. 'The Henderson's at that point had been at the San Georgio just under a week, and therefore had another week to go, I am afraid I took over their holiday.'

'We cruised up to Fiskardo at the top of the Island, it's the prettiest village and harbour on Kefalonia, we went by Joyce 11 the yacht and stayed on board. The dogs as usual came with us as it was a short trip.'

'It took us 3 days to get to Fiskardo; we called in at Argostoli, and saw the turtles swimming in the bay right alongside our tied up yacht. Peter Henderson was interested in Argostoli the Capital of Kefalonia, as it was totally destroyed in by an earthquake; it was completely rebuilt losing much of its old Greek charm, being rebuilt with streets in straight lines and parallel to each other. A modern marble pedestrianised centre, but retaining its Greekness in other ways. The Cruise ships come in here and whilst the tourists love it, it is not the real Greece, it's far too new.'

'We then did a bit of proper sailing around the western side of the Island and up to Spiridon and to one of our many monasteries on Kefalonia, we went around the cape of Kakata, and into Myrtos Bay, we lunched on the beach it's the finest in Kefalonia and at the bottom of a cliff, very secluded and the most photographed bay on Kefalonia, but always from the cliff tops.'

'We called in at Assos, and stayed the night there as my uncle Tomas lives there we dined at his home that night. The next morning we set sail early and cruised round the top of the Island and arrived at Fiskardo for lunch.'

'The small harbour at Fiskardo, its lovely waterside shops and restaurants in their blue and white and the side streets with their Greek homes, immaculate cool and pretty, make you want to stay forever, but you have seen it all in a day. We stayed overnight on board, and enjoyed our meals ashore.'

'The next day the weather was not very good, it was cold, and misty until lunchtime when the sun broke through, we sailed down the Ithiki's Straits and into Sámi Bay and the port of Sámi. This is where the film Captain Correli's mandolin was filmed. Some of the top Hollywood actors Nicolas Cage, Penelope Cruz and John Hurt stayed there for months. You can still see the square concrete filled holes where the false town fronts were erected in the port on the road. And then destroyed in the fierce fire fight in the film.'

'There is a restaurant/bar now called Captains Correli's, there are photographs on all the walls, and pillars of the filming and the stars, Nicolas Cage as Captain Correli's being one. It now costs nearly twice as much to eat drink and stay in Sámi, due to the money the Hollywood stars splashed around.'

'We stayed to explore Sámi for a couple of hours and then headed down to Poros arriving in time for a late dinner.

We sat and watched the ferry to Killini coming in and going out, and as it was a bright moonlit night so we cruised back down the inshore coast to home and Skala, we tied up in time for breakfast.'

'I know it seems as though we are always eating, but that what you do, you go here and arrive in time for dinner, you go there and arrive in time for lunch.'

'We had cruised around the whole of the Island, and both Peters at one point had played 'Captain' for the day, Joyce and Martine hit it off, and enjoyed each others company, and would have done so for years to come, we had planned to do it properly next year, but not now,---- his voice was sad, and low.'

'The strange thing about the dogs, normally people can't get too close to young Peter without they seem to want to protect him. They didn't do anything they just watched and keep close to him, Peter Henderson, stroked them, fed them and even played with them, something I can't do, and when young Peter was within reach of Peter Henderson they just ignored it. It's as though they knew he alone wished young Peter no harm.'

'This was their last night so we drove into Katelios for a lobster dinner, by the way Colonel Aristostis said to tell you he will pick you up tonight at 8.00pm to take you to dinner at Katelios for 'lobster' if that's what you would like.'

'The following morning we went over to say our goodbyes, and they both promised to write which they did within a few days of getting back home'. 'That was the last we heard of them, until your office rang, we haven't even seen the newspapers or television over here mention their deaths.'

The whole interview to that point had taken just over an hour it seemed longer.

'Thank you for that very descriptive narrative of the time spent with the Henderson's. I would like to cover another avenue of enquiry if I may?' said Gardner.

He nodded to Harrison, who reached into his jacket pocket and took out a photograph.

'Can you tell me who this man is?' He pointed to the man just going out of shot from the local newspaper photograph of himself and his son on the deck of Joyce 11.

'Ari' looked at it and said, 'that's Mr Bradley, 'I can make you an offer you can't refuse!' He said smiling.

'He is a Russian/American businessman, who wished to lease three of my V.L.C.C's and one of my U.L.C.C.'s for a 2-year period. He had an initial certified cheque from Credit Suisse for $25,000,000 the cheque was made out to Appolonikis Shipping Line. This of course is my Company.'

'I turned him down, we do not lease ships to others, and we contract to our clients, the major petroleum, and gas companies to move their products.'

'He was very annoyed, and said he would be back with an offer I could not refuse. I assumed he meant a bigger 'Bond'. All of my Captains have been with me over five years; some were with my father, which means 25 years at least, my crews stay with Appolonikis because we pay the best wages and salaries. My cruise liner staff is paid nearly twice normal cruise pay. I never have a problem, and always fulfil my contracts. I do not need to impress my shareholders; I, Joyce, and one other are the shareholders.'

'My accountants have long since stopped advising me to be more competitive with wages, pay less, increase profits, reduce operating costs, slim down be lean and mean, reduce pension payments and death benefits etc, etc. Why should I? They would save me cents and cost me dollars.'

'If a crew member dies or is killed at any time whilst in my employ, within 24 hours we are talking to his family and making sure they have enough money, and all the help they need. They then get 3 times his or her annual salary within 7 days. Then we look after their family for life.'

'This is why my crews stay, my ships have the best maintenance record of any I know, and they do not break down, why, because they 'belong' to the crew who take a pride in them. This is not me, but my father who said, 'Always remember a ship is no good without a crew, and to be a good ship it has to have a good crew, employ the best, train them and look after them, and you will have a good crew.'

'We have prospered where other has failed, and I believe it is all down to our way of doing things. So even if I wanted to I could never let somebody else run and crew my ships.'

'Now I have answered your question, please answer me, who is this man Bill?'

Gardner, decided to take a chance, he believed that Astinikis was a hard businessman in spite of his philanthropic attitude, and that he was telling the truth, and that he did think the man in the photograph was a businessman who merely wanted to lease his ships.

'We have reason to believe that the man you spoke to and call Bradley, is in fact a terrorist called Petor Milcovic. At this time we can't imagine why he would have made you the offer he did. Has he been in touch since your meeting, what was it four five weeks ago?'

'No he hasn't, said Ari. If he does I shall let you know immediately.'

'Please be careful Ari, this man is very dangerous, he may or may not be involved in the deaths of Peter and Martine Henderson, at this stage I can't honestly see the link 'said Gardner.

'We need to be getting back to London as soon as possible, tomorrow if we can get a flight.'

'You came in on a holiday charter they do not arrive every day; I shall take you to Athens in my 'King Air' tomorrow. I will have my secretary book you on the first Olympic airways tomorrow if that would suit you. We can leave at around 6.00am and you can get the 9.00am flight to London.'

They said their goodbyes and drove back to the San Georgio.

8.00pm saw them in Colonel Aristostis's Mercedes on the way to Katelios. They pulled on to the rough ground near the bus stop, and walked along the seafront. The restaurants all had covered areas right up to the beach.

They picked a lobster each from the tank and enjoyed a bottle of local white wine whilst it was being cooked. 'George' introduced them to the restaurant owner who came and sat with them and drank the wine with them; they were on the third bottle as the lobster arrived.

Gardner went to pay for the meal, and the restaurant owner Costa, declined payment.

'We know why you are here Bill, go and catch the bastards,' he shook hands with them all, and they returned to the San Georgio.

They had a last nightcap drink in the San Georgio bar.

Gardner felt the need to thank the colonel. 'George, I would like to thank you for all you have done to help, without you smoothing the way, and your introductions, things would have been very different. I am very grateful. Naturally we will keep in touch. And if there is anything that comes to light from this end I would appreciate you telling us.'

With that they parted company, and watched the tail lights of the car as it went out of sight along the coast road and back to Argostoli.

**0615 Tuesday 29th October 2003 7,000 ft over the Aegean Sea**

Aristo Astinikis true to his word was piloting his twin engined 'King Air' 10 seat aircraft with Chief Superintendent Gardner and Chief Inspector Harrison on board and en-route to Athens airport. Gardner and Harrison were booked on the 11.00 Olympic Airways flight to London Heathrow.

After landing 'Ari' took them through from airside back into the terminal, and waited with them until they had booked in, all three then went for a coffee before saying their goodbyes.

'Ari' promised to contact them should 'Mr Bradley' get in touch with him, and to report his conversation, he also promised to be careful, now he knew exactly who Bradley was, and what he was. He was to be in touch quicker then he had thought.

# Chapter nine

**3.00pm later that day, M4 London.**

Superintendent Gardner was on the secure car phone to Sir Bernard Hills. He and Chief Inspector Harrison were on the M4 and approaching Central London.

' We should be with you in about 20 minutes Sir Bernard,' said Gardner, little knowing that a mere 300 yards from him at that very moment an Arab man about 35 years of age with a deep scar on his left cheek, was viewing a small bed-sit with his new landlady.

' Yes this will do fine, I will need to bring some of my video and sound equipment in from my car on an evening if that's alright with you, it cost a lot of money and I would hate to have it stolen out of my car during the night.'

' No Mr Rashid, that's fine, I quite understand, you have to very careful these days its such shame really, this area used to be lovely 20 years ago, and look at it now, full of Bla---,' she started to say 'Blacks' and realising Mr Rashid colour changed her mind and instead became embarrassed and very red faced.

Rashid smiled at her seeming not to notice the insult, ' Yes I am sure it was, some of the properties are quite nice even now, yours for instance, such style and cleanliness, a picture of good housekeeping Mrs Symonds, if I may say so?'

Mrs Symonds was not used to such compliments from her gentlemen lodgers, and failed to realise he was simply telling her what she wanted to hear, the place was in fact a dump. But he had won her over; she would not present him with any problems during his brief stay of a few days. He could park his car under the front room window on the concreted area her 'Albert' had laid some years before for a car they never did get.

Mrs Symonds three storey inner terrace house in Hounslow, central in a block of 10 similar ones, was just a little to the left of the flight path for the main Heathrow runway, and about 1 minute from touch down, as the

British Airways 747 Jumbo passing overhead and a little to the right and about 150-foot up in the air was demonstrating. She was so pleased that Mr Rashid seemed not to care about the noise as they both looked out of the window and watched it seemingly very slowly fly past.

Later that evening Mr Rashid brought in his 'sound' equipment whilst Mrs Symonds was watching her favourite TV programme Coronation Street, he timed it so that the programme was just starting, guaranteeing Mrs Symonds was otherwise occupied, and able to truthfully say to the Police some 4 days later that she had never actually saw him bring anything in, and certainly not the two wooden boxes that would be found in the room.

## 4.30pm Tuesday 29th October 2004 SIS Headquarters, Sir Bernard's Office.

Chief Superintendent Gardner and Chief Inspector Harrison had spent about an hour briefing Sir Bernard on the Kefalonia visit, and being updated them selves. George W was coming to the UK that was confirmed and the probable date was the 4th November, possibly early am, so George W could get good nights sleep over the Atlantic.

US Strike Eagle fighters based in Germany were going to fly in to RAF Waddington in Lincolnshire, this was the home of number 8 and 23 squadron RAF flying Boeing E3D AWAC's and 51 Squadron flying Nimrod R1's these being the UK equivalent. 26 Squadron RAF Regiment, complete with Rapier surface to air missiles were also based there. The RAF Regiment would cover all four possible landing sites with Rapier missiles.

The US Strike Eagles would fly out from Waddington into mid Atlantic and take over from the four Strike Eagles that had flown with AIR FORCE ONE from Andrews Air Force base.

Sea Harriers from HMS Ark Royal would also supply a box support 40 miles around AIR FORCE ONE whilst some 250 miles out, and up to landing. The Harriers would close up to ½ a mile whilst over London and coming in to land. Their unique capabilities allowed them to slow right down and come to a stop in mid air, and hover if need be something the Strike Eagles could not do.

Tactical support for the air operation would lay with the US Air force AWAC's, whilst over the Atlantic; this would be handed over to RAF Uxbridge at 100 miles from the UK coast.

RAF Uxbridge was designated UK and European Tactical Support. 4 star US Air force General Hal Berber would head up the team. He was a close friend of General Bloomberg who would be on board AIR FORCE ONE as senior Air Force Officer and Mission Commander whilst airborne.

Mary, Sir Bernard's secretary brought in another fresh pot of coffee, and a pot of tea for Chief Superintendent Gardner who disliked coffee, he smiled his thanks. A couple of minutes later she was back with plates of sandwiches.

Sir Bernard spoke, 'well Bill I hate to say this but how about going to see Sugama this evening he hasn't had a visit and I think we need to know all his has to offer whilst we have the chance, the American President will be here before we know it. You have had another long day already so I quite understand if you wish to do it tomorrow.'

'No we'll go tonight Sir, said Gardner looking at Harrison, who smiled and nodded his acceptance, I had better give Sergeant Lowe a ring.'

'Oh Blast said Sir Bernard, I clean forgot to tell you, sergeant Lowe is off today and tomorrow, he is attending his brothers funeral in Scotland, he died last Thursday. You will need a MOD pool driver; I'll get Mary to sort it for you. There is no way either of you two should be driving.'

At exactly 5.30pm a metallic red Rover 800 drew up, to take them to Northamptonshire, Gardner got in the back and Harrison got in the front seat next to the driver. Harrison was tired and even if he had not have been he would have been hard pressed to spot the tail they had on their car, not only was it the worst time of day to be exiting London, but superb cover for those following.

The people tailing them knew what they were doing; they used four cars and 2 fake courier motorcycles, all in touch with mobile phones. In the heavy traffic it wasn't necessary to 'swap' places as regularly.

As the traffic thinned out the cars swapped places irregularly and one dropped out that had been the initial lead car after 25 miles altogether, the two motor bikes had panniers for luggage fitted after all they were courier bikes and needed them. In the panniers were three changes of brightly coloured and totally different jackets. This allowed the riders to change identity, nobody sees a 'courier bike' only the jacket. They each changed jackets twice.

Sergeant Lowe may have spotted something, Michael, the pool driver didn't. He was too intent on getting there and back without denting or scratching the Rover, the paperwork was horrendous if you did. And at £5.50 an hour he wasn't exactly paid to do anything else. The traffic on the M1 helped the group tailing them, only when they came of at junction 14 did the danger of being spotted increase.

They pulled up outside the safe house in Olney and Harrison leant over the seat to wake Gardner, He shook his shoulder gently. 'We are here Sir' he said. He barely noticed the motorcycle that cruised past and turned round the corner at the end of the road.

With Michael and the car safely parked outside in the horse shoe shaped gravel driveway, Gardner and Harrison approached the substantial heavy oak door, knowing they were on camera and had been since the end of the road.

As Gardner reached for the bell push the door opened, and a smart middle aged military gentleman stood with a broad grin on his face said,' Chief how nice to seen you again.'

Gardner went forward and shook the others hand, 'Harry Benson how are you old devil, I thought you had retired at least a couple of years ago? At least that's what I heard. Gardner turned to Harrison, Pat meet Harry Benson, Harry was with me for 10 years in Special Branch from the late eighties, best Sergeant I had. But watch your pockets.'

They quickly moved from the hall and into the large sitting room.

'How's Mr Sugama behaving himself'?' Asked Gardner.

'A couple of days ago when he first came here, he was a mild as a mouse, now he is full of his own importance, a bit of an arrogant sod to be truthful.' Said Benson.

'Is he now, well that will not help him one bit when he gets to leave here, we have to impress upon him that he has to literally disappear. Unless he wants others to recognise him, where is he now?'

'He is in his room watching television, I will go and get him 'said Benson.

Three minutes later Sugama stood in front of them, with a big smile on his face.

'You have come to tell me good news Superintendent?'

'Yes I have, let's go and sit at the dining room table, Harry could you organise some tea or something please?'

When everybody was seated, Gardner took a single sheet of paper out of his briefcase and handed it to Sugama, it was the British Governments proposals for his re-settlement. Sugama read it carefully, and said:

'Its not as generous as I was told it would be Chief Superintendent.'

Regrettably Mr Sugama it is not negotiable, that's it and I have to say by today's standard it's very good.'

'Very well I accept said Sugama, what happens now?'

'Within the next few days somebody will come and see you, they will go through all this with you, they will show you some properties that can be bought, and if you find something you like they will buy it for you. You need to have what we call a legend, that is to say some credible story as to why you are here. They will help with that.

If you wanted to buy something elsewhere outside of England they can help with that. Now I wish to ask you a few more questions.'

'I have told you everything I know,' said Sugama.

'Well lets see shall we, for instance you said your uncles friend in Baghdad had said that Ali Halakim had told them at the meeting in the Palace that you witnessed, the President of the United States plane was going to be shot down in England. Where is it going to be shot down and how do they intend to do it, and when?'

'They have some shoulder missiles, we used them to shoot down Russian helicopters in Afghanistan, and they were American made', said Sugama.

Harrison stepped in, 'he probably means a 'Stinger', that's what the CIA supplied the rebels with, they could even take out a fully armoured Russian Hind Gun-ship. They are shoulder launched and can be used by one man, whether they would knock down a Jumbo 747 is another thing. It's quite a tough bird and would take a fair bit of damage before it came down. But having said that a strike in the right place could do it.'

'However, we have to assume the aircraft would be at low level and therefore at its worst flight configuration, i.e. going slow on fully extended wings to maintain the necessary lift and just comfortably above stall speed. It could climb back out from that situation but not manoeuvre too well.'

'Where is it going to be shot down?' Gardner said.

'I do not know, I cannot know I was never told', said Sugama. I do not know anything else to tell you, does this mean I will be sent back to Baghdad?'

'No, everything I have said will happen, do not worry. If you think of anything please let me know,' he passed a business card across the table to Sugama.

A few minutes later having finished their tea and said goodbye to Harry Benson they were on their way back to London.

In the car they were both sat in the back and mulling over what had been said, and what they now though the weapon would be if an attempt was made on the Presidents plane.

# Chapter ten

**Tuesday 29th October 2003 Larne, Northern Ireland.**

At about the same time and in 'Murphy's bar' in Larne Tom O'Leary was on his fifth pint of Guinness and treating the other six people in the bar for the second time.

'Sure he's won the lottery, said Mick O'Donnell, raising his now full glass to Tom, your very good health, slange.'

During his three hours in the pub, and knowing some of the 'Boys' were in he had made a vague reference to missiles rotting and unused but now going to be put to good use at last. It made him feel big, and in his Guinness befuddled brain he knew he had maybe said too much. He also incorrectly believed it had gone unnoticed.

2 hours later Tom had staggered home, fallen over the dog in the kitchen whilst trying to feed it and gone upstairs to bed on his hands and knees, eventually falling onto the bed fully dressed but minus one shoe. At about the same time, the unlit public phone box outside the grocery store was used to make a 30-second phone call to a Belfast number.

The person making call would be £250 better off within the next few days, and would not be buying drinks for all in Murphy's bar or indeed any other.

The Special Branch collator in Belfast entered up his log for the night, included in the 26 items of credible intelligence was the fact that Tom O'Leary a known IRA supporter and suspected gun runner had suddenly come into 'Money', there had been a vague reference to missiles of some sort.

Within 3 hours an Irish Army Captain was having a known weapons cache on a farm 20 miles from Larne checked. They found that 6 Stinger missiles and launchers missing. They decided to remove the cache and discontinue observations.

Within a further hour this a information was flashed to all security units in Ireland and the mainland, it was also flashed to the Provisional I.R.A Chief of Staff, who despatched 2 men to have a 'word' with Tom O'Leary.

As dawn was breaking Tom O'Leary fell out of bed, he wanted a piss, groping his way to the bathroom he unfastened his trousers and started to urinate, the relief showing on his face. He became aware of somebody alongside him in the semi-darkness, and turned his head to the right.

The hazy figure of a man spoke, 'now don't you go wetting your pants Tom me boyo, I just want a few wee words with you'. The voice was hard, Northern Ireland Belfast and very cold. Tom, lost control and direction and urinated over the side of the toilet bowl for a few seconds wetting the cheap vinyl floor covering. The man noticed and laughed quietly as he stepped back onto the small landing and clicked the light on.

Tom O'Leary sat on the edge of the bed absolutely terrified, his eyes moving rapidly from one of the men to the other, the one who had spoken to him was stood about 5 feet away from him and looking down on him. An automatic pistol, black, huge and menacing dangled from his right hand.

The other younger man was going through the bedside table drawer, he tipped it out on the bed, and bottles of tablets, a couple of wristwatches, a box of matches, a penknife and other accumulated junk were piled up.

He went to the wardrobe and opened the doors, Tom O'Leary knew at that second he was lost, the man reached in and pulled out a shoe box, the shoebox had a pair of well looked after black oxford shoes in it, these were the ones Tom kept for weddings and funerals. Inside the right shoe was a bank cash bag.

The man casually tossed it on to the bed alongside O'Leary,

'That's my life savings,' said O'Leary with a nervous smile.

'Of course it is, said the elder of the two, picking up the bundle of notes, and how long have you been saving this money, what's here then a five thousand or what?'

Not content with finding the first cache of money the bastard was looking for more which he found a minute later.

Tom O'Leary knew he was doing the wrong thing when he tried to bluff it out.

'It's what I have been saving for years now,' said O'Leary.

## The President Is Down

The elder of the two picked up the second bundle which was considerably larger, and nodded to the young fair haired one who casually strolled round the end of the bed, and struck O'Leary a vicious blow across his face with the back of his hand, as O'Leary fell forward off the bed, he body was met by a well aimed solid kick to his crotch.

He screamed and doubled up holding himself and rolling around on the bedroom floor in pure agony.

The elder man slammed his right foot onto O'Leary's neck and stopped him rolling, but couldn't stop O'Leary sobbing and crying out in pain.

The fair haired man spent 15 minutes checking the remainder of the house, whilst the elder sat on a chair in the bedroom and watched O'Leary trying to surface from the excruciating pain and agony he was enduring.

The two men exchanged a few words and unceremoniously half carried and dragged O'Leary down the stairs and out into the street outside. They bundled him into a dark blue Ford Sierra saloon car and leaving the front door of the house open drove away.

The dog went to the front door, sniffed the cold night air, cocked his leg up on the rose bush outside which was already on its last legs, turned and went back in doors to once again guard his owner and his property, oblivious to the fact that the former was no longer there.

An hour later and the pain was a little less, more of a deep throbbing, O'Leary had stopped sobbing and was beginning to feel a little better until the car stopped at the end of a long rough and rutted driveway, and the rear doors opened and he was dragged out. He could not stand upright, and could only hobble as they forced him to walk and shuffle towards a large old farmhouse.

There was just one window to the right of the main door that was lit and uncurtained, a face could be seen briefly at the window before the door was thrown open spilling a wedge of light across the last few yards to the door, a voice said ' hurry up and bring him in.'

O'Leary was pushed through the door which he heard slam behind him; he stumbled and fell on his knees to the floor. A pair of rough brown corduroy trousers and a pair of muddied brown boots were all he could see 2 feet away and directly in front of him. He raised his head and found himself looking into the bright blue eyes of

Martin Carmichael the Provisional I.R.A.'s chief of staff.

'Get yourself up man, what the hell have you done to him, I said ask him to come and see me?' Carmichael helped him to his feet, and gently guided him to a large rough wooden carver chair, one of four around a big kitchen table and close to the open log fire.

O'Leary knew now he could talk his way out of this if he was careful, he was as clever as any of these people, what had they achieved, nothing absolutely nothing, hanging on to the myth of the IRA and playing toy soldiers. He didn't see the look that passed between Carmichael and the other two, had he have done so he would have had different thoughts.

'You look like you could do with a drink, bring the Bushmills over here John, and I will speak to you two later.'

He dismissed them with a curt nod of the head.

O'Leary took the large glass of Bushmills and drank deeply, the warm glow hit him immediately and spread through his chest and warmed him through. It took a little of the pain away, and gave him a sense of false security.

Carmichael was sat at the other side of the table around 3 feet from him, and looking directly into his eyes, he looked a little distressed at what they had done to him. He said, 'we had a wee report of you spending a lot of money now the lads don't have much to do nowadays so we keep the on their toes and let them check a round for people being a bit silly. They got a bit carried away.'

'Tell me where did you get this, he pushed the smaller of the two packets of notes across?'

O'Leary looked at it, and didn't touch it, 'its part of my life saving, what you have got there is all I own in the World, even the house is council rented. Mary dead these two years and you can't take it with you'. He said with a little more bravado than he felt.

Carmichael picked up the Bushmills and half filled O'Leary's tumbler with neat whiskey, 'Indeed you can't that is for sure,' he said putting the bottle back down. O'Leary didn't notice that he failed to top up his own drink.

'You see the problem I have Tom is this, I know you from the troubles there was no finer man, risking his life, and his freedom for the cause, running guns and missiles and things in for the lads. Avoiding the Royal navy and the Army, as I say a real supporter and one to be relied on. Of course now we have the peace process and its working thank God, no more internment, no more knocks on the doors in the middle of the night, no more kids losing their 'Da' for months or years on end.'

O'Leary was listening; he could see a way out of this perhaps!

Carmichael continued, 'you see the problem we have is when Martin signed the peace process and we declared how much we had of weapons and ammunition, missiles and grenades etc. Well ------- we kept a bit back. Just in case things didn't go the way they should. Also bear in mind how carefully we had hidden them in the first place, some are now a severe embarrassment, in a dangerous condition in some cases and we have to try to dispose of them, for cash if we can' or the dangerous ones we 'leak' to the Brits they dispose of them for us. It's a bit of a game. '

'Some of the lads have had weapons secreted on their property for years, and need to get rid; the more knowledgeable ones have quietly disposed of some already, and given the cause its cut. We have to look after the families of those still in prison as you know, and need money to do that. Now I have to be honest with you I thought this money was he said looking down at the two packets of notes. Something like that and that you would be contacting your old divisional commander, but then of course you can't he died of cancer last year.'

O'Leary's befuddled brain knew what to do, he was away free!!

'You are right; it's from some of the cache we had on 'Blackberry Farm '. I thought we had forgotten all about, I needed some cash to go to Australia to visit my daughter and family, they want me to move out there, but it takes money, I have the boat that I can sell and £14,000 here. I was going to give half to the cause, but I couldn't contact anybody.'

'Well that's all right then, all well that ends well, I am glad we sorted that out Tom, I'll get John and Michael to take you home, have a few painkillers or aspirin and get to bed, you'll feel better tomorrow.'

I'll keep this and you keep that. He held back the bigger package and passed the smaller one to O'Leary.

Oh, just before I ask the lads back in, Carmichael lowered his voice and leant towards O'Leary in a conspirator manner, who did you sell the missiles to, was it back to the French?'

O'Leary found himself answering,' no John Thompson of Frystone' before he knew it.

That's all right then said Carmichael, he's one of us, he shouted 'John—Michael', both came into the kitchen, take Tom home now we have sorted out this little problem. He gently squeezed O'Leary's shoulder as he stood up and hobbled towards the door.

They helped O'Leary into the front seat of the Sierra, Carmichael stood watching from the door waiting to wave goodbye or so O'Leary thought. Suddenly Carmichael shouted, 'John you have left your phone,' waving something in his left hand, he walked towards John who took the phone off him, and exchanged a few words with him before returning to the car.

John drove very carefully, and O'Leary was soon fast asleep, he was totally drunk and the heater going full blast in front of the car simply deepened his sleep, within minutes he was snoring loudly.

He came to partial consciousness to find himself swaying gently to the motion of his fishing boat which was heading out to sea and about ½ mile off shore. Michael was sat next to him holding him upright.

'John and I thought a nice swim would help you get sorted, didn't we John?' Said Michael grinning. He was still grinning when he half pushed O'Leary over the side of the boat, and hanging on to his legs held his head under the water. With the boat rocking from side to side it took a little longer for the violent leg movements to cease. He waited another 2 minutes and then pulled O'Leary back on board.

It took them 10 minutes before they were satisfied that he was now dressed to go fishing, they eased him over the side, complete with his wedding and funeral shoes on, and watched him slip below the surface. Carefully checking that they had got all his normal clothing, they got into the Gemini started the outboard and headed back a mile up the coast away from Larne.

4 hours later the tide change had grounded the fishing boat on the breakwater rocks, when the coastguards went aboard some hours later they found it abandoned.

2 days later O'Leary's bloated body was found, the post mortem results indicated he had died from drowning as a result of falling overboard whilst fishing and being totally intoxicated at the time. Like most fishermen O'Leary was known to be a non-swimmer. But in his state it would not have made any difference. He clearly had no money worries as his pockets contained over a £1,000 in notes. The Coroner recorded a verdict of 'misadventure'.

# Chapter eleven

**11.30am Wednesday 30<sup>th</sup> October 2003 Manchester International Airport, England.**

The 11.30am flight into Manchester Airport from Aldergrove Ireland had 4 passengers of interest to Special Branch, when the 4 men left the airport one of then rented an Avis Rent A Car Ford Mondeo, all four got into the car and drove into central Manchester. They parked in the Piccadilly hotel car park and all four went inside.

2 Special Branch Officers had followed them from Manchester Airport, a very experienced Sergeant Dowle and a very in-experienced Detective Constable Strange.

Dowle thinking there was just the off chance that he had recognised one of the men, and that he in turn may have recognised himself, sent DC Strange in to observe, he was very specific in the few seconds he had to brief DC Strange. ' Don't get too near, don't be seen to be writing anything down, turn your radio off, if you think you have been spotted quietly leave. Come back here in 15 minutes and tell me what's happening, now GO.'

Strange walked in and casually looked around, all four men were sat a low table near to the bar and close to the toilets. He walked up to the bar and ordered a tomato juice, in the bar mirrors he could see the 4 men very clearly. 2 had very distinctive jackets on which he wouldn't be seen dead in, the jackets looked a few years old, and from another era.

The waitress brought a round of drinks to their table, and they all shared a bit of banter with her, their friendly Irish brogue being disarming and easy to go along with. One of the men with a bright plaid green jacket on went to the toilet; the chap sat near the revolving doors had got up and also went to the toilet. A couple of minutes later both came out within a minute of each other, Mr Bright jacket sat down, the other man left.

10 minutes later a gentleman with a walking stick came in and went straight to the toilet, the second Mr bright jacket which was light blue got up and went to the toilet, joking with the others as he did. He stopped to pick up a leaflet and said something to the others.

Shortly afterwards, the gentleman with the walking stick walked past Strange, and said 'excuse me' as he did so, Strange said sorry automatically and moved to let him pass between his stool and the table next to him. Bright blue jacket came out and sat down, throwing the leaflet on to the table and saying something as he did. They all laughed at his comment. One of the group ordered more sandwiches, and having opened a briefcase and a laptop computer, they all took off their jackets and made themselves comfortable. Why not they would be there for as long as it took.

The gentleman who had sat near the door, and the one with the walking stick had now switched with two others and John and Michael as there were known to the others were currently renting a car at the Grand Hotel across the road.

Less than an hour later they were driving at a steady 60mph on the M6 heading north.

DC Strange went outside and reported to Sergeant Dowle that all was well and the men were having a business meeting. All four were present and could just be seen from the position Dowle occupied.

**3.00pm a Lay-bye just off junction 36 M6 on the A65.**

There were three cars in the lay-bye all were 'Rep' type cars, Avencis, Mondeo, and Astra, the drivers had one thing in common they were all eating ' Maggie's' monster bacon sandwiches and drinking pots of tea, either in or close to their cars. The two men feeding their faces with a bacon sandwich each appeared to point something to the Avencis driver on the other side of his car. One of them said something to him and appeared to touch the wing showing him what they had seen. He nodded his thanks and reached into the car through the rear door.

One of the men from the Mondeo walked back to his car finishing his sandwich, the browning automatic now safely tucked in his trousers behind his back, the silencer concealed up his jacket sleeve. The Mondeo with the two men in started up and turned, and drove back towards the motorway. The Avencis driver was still messing about with something on the nearside of the car. He had however delivered his 'package'.

## 5.30pm Frystone -on-Sea, England.

The Mondeo, cruised into Frystone and stopped outside the post-office general store, 'John' now using a very upper class English accent. He wondered if they could help him, he was hoping to drop in on a friend John Thompson?,' no problem', said the shopkeeper and proceeded to direct him,' slightly out of town, take the left fork, and the big white house on the left was John's.'

Thanking the shopkeeper he got back in the car, and followed directions, they drove past the house and went up a short but steep hill to a car park on the cliffs, the sort favoured by courting couples. Getting out of the car and going to the extreme left corner, the front door of 'The White House' came in to view. He was just in time to see the door open, a well dressed middle aged women came out kissing the man in the doorway on the cheek, and the man watched her get into a white Mercedes saloon car and drive off down the road.

They waited ten minutes, it was now totally dark, they left the car where it was and locked it. It took them less than 5 minutes to walk back unobserved to the house. John knocked on the door with the big black knocker, he had a large A4 scratch pad in his hands, and Michael stood to one side of the door out of sight. He had something a little more lethal in his; the Browning now fitted with the silencer.

Looking through the 'Spy hole' in the door John Thompson was inclined to ignore the rather ordinary looking individual standing here and smiling. Probably selling double bloody glazing or something, soon get rid of him. He opened the door and started to speak, and was taken completely by surprise when he was violently pushed in the chest, falling over backwards he fell to the floor, and starting to get up felt the silencer on the Browning pressed hard against his head.

The door was now shut and two men not one was now in the hall. The one he had originally seen said, and one other he hadn't. His immediate thought was they were after the valuables in the house.

'Is there anybody else in the house?'

'No, just me said John Thompson; my wife's gone out why?'

'When is she coming back?'

'Around 10.00pm said Thompson? What is this all about?'

'I'll ask the questions', said John pushing Thompson towards the sitting room. He went to the other side of the room and closed the curtains. 'Sit down ,' he said indicating one of the armchairs furthest from the door.

'Now we have had a lovely wee trip, he said dropping into a strong Belfast brogue, just to see you, haven't we Michael?' The other man merely nodded his head and continued to point the Browning directly at Thompson's crotch, which Thompson found unnerving.

The elected spokesman continued, 'you see you have been a naughty boy, buying Stingers and shipping them to --------- well you tell us John?'

'I bought 3 stingers from the 'Boys'. I don't know who will be using them, but I know who bought them.'

said Thompson.

'Now which 'Boys' would that be John?'

'The IRA 'said Thompson beginning to get a little annoyed at this game whatever it was, the Browning coughed and simultaneously his wife Dorothy's favourite piece of Lladro on the shelf above the open fire exploded.

'Now let's start again shall we said John, who sold you the stingers?'

'I arranged to pick up 3 stingers from Tom O'Leary of Larne, I paid the cause good money £15,000 just ask

him, 'said Thompson.

'I can't do that ------ he went swimming, and ------ well let's say he got out of his depth.'

Thompson began to sweat, this was going the wrong way, and he had to do something. `

He poured out the whole story, they both listened, and then John went into the hallway, they could hear him talking to someone; there were long gaps whilst the other person spoke, and which they could not hear.

John came back in; he whispered something to Michael, who began to unscrew the silencer off the Browning.

'Now you are a very lucky lad, the chief says you have one last chance. Go upstairs and pack a bag you could be away for week, we have to find those 'stingers'. Michael will go upstairs with you, well go on then get a move on.'

15 minutes later Michael and Thompson came down stairs to find John had dug the bullet out of the wall and filled the hole with polyfilla that he had found in the garage. He had painted the hole with magnolia emulsion he had also found in the garage, and picked up the pieces of Lladro.' It's all wet at the moment but should be dry by the time your wife gets back. She won't know quite what's happened, and will think you have done something stupid.' He said.

'Now write your wife a short note, tell you will be away a couple of days on business, and that you will ring her tonight on your mobile around 10.30pm.'

5 minutes later, they were picking up the Mondeo from the car park on the cliff top, and Michael remained with John Thompson who was now driving his Toyota land cruiser. John followed in the Mondeo. Just over an hour later they stopped at the lay bye at junction 36 on the M6 and left a small parcel. It was collected five minutes after they had dropped it.

John came to an agreement with Avis that they could leave the Mondeo's at Lancaster at the THF hotel, and at the Piccadilly in Manchester. ¾ of an hour later they dropped the one car off at Lancaster. All three were now in the Land cruiser. 'I have booked us in at the Holiday Inn at Great Bar that's the hotel you did the change with the stingers at. You will be sharing with one of us'.

**10.00pm Piccadilly Hotel, Manchester, England.**

Dowle and Strange were getting fed up with waiting and observing the 4 men, apart from drinking and eating at the table, and the now more frequent visits to the toilet the seemed to be set for the night.

One of them was taking a mobile phone call. He said something to the others they all got up donned their jackets and picked up their belongings prior to leaving or so it seemed. 2 or 3 minutes later all four were stood in the doorways shaking hands and saying goodbye to each other, they left

The 4 men ignored the Avis rental car and walked down the ramp and into Piccadilly itself. The men nodded to Dowle and Strange in passing and said goodnight. There was something about them that had Sergeant Dowle worried apart from the obvious fact there were 'four of them', and two of the good guys, if they split up he and Strange would have a job following. He couldn't help thinking they were taking the piss!!

2 hours later he was sat at home with a can of beer, when it hit him, 'Strange you bloody incompetent, thick ignorant, stupid bastard. The green jacket on the man was too long, it had previously been a perfect fit ,they had been well and truly fitted up. So where the bloody hell were the other one or even two original men, and what had they been up to all day?

# Chapter twelve

**9.30pm Wednesday 30th October 2003. Craigavon, Northern Ireland.**

The Provisional Chief if Staff for the IRA rang a certain number in London.

'How can I help you? said a cultured voice'

'I would like to speak with Sir Bernard Hills please; you will need to say 'Raven' would like a word.'

'Just one moment Sir, I will see if we have a number listed for that name.'

30 seconds later Sir Bernard was on the line.

'Don't try tracing it Bernard I am ringing from home and you know where that is,' said the C.O.S.

Sir Bernard Chuckled, 'yes I imagine I do, so why are you ringing me Martin?' Nobody called the PIRA Chief of Staff Martin, they wouldn't dare.

'We have a problem, a few days ago, one of our members strayed, he dug up shall we say some items we had forgotten about, 3 stingers to be precise, apparently your special branch over here know of it. To the best of my knowledge they have been buried at least 3 years, unless somebody knows precisely what they are doing, they are unlikely to function.'

'At this moment I have a team of 3 in England looking for them. The object being to tell you where you can find them. I emphasise, we will not use them or recover them for our use.'

'If we locate them you will be told where to find them. The person who strayed 'swims with the fishes' as the Italians say. This should be a clear warning to others. We want no more such incidents. What I would like from you Sir Bernard is an undertaking that you will not hamper our efforts. I give you my word this is a genuine request.'

The C.O.S. fell silent.

'Well Martin that the most I have ever heard you say, you have my word we will not get in the way intentionally, but you must not to carry out any 'disposals' in the UK. And to keep me abreast of progress daily or the deal is off, I will do the same from this end, I will use the mobile number you gave me, is that OK?'

'Yes that's all right Bernard, and thanks for your understanding, goodnight.'

At about the same time, the two IRA men and John Thompson were booking in at the Holiday Inn, and Thompson was making the phone call to his wife. He then made a phone call to the plump man who had picked up the stingers, his brother who had called to pick up the dog and who was taking it home with him the following day answered the phone. He was on holiday for the next three weeks. Somewhere abroad and in Europe, he and his wife was touring in their new car. Regrettably they was uncontactable.

This was reported to the PIRA, Chief Of Staff. Who immediately rang Sir Bernard Hills? Both men now knew where the man who had picked up the Stingers lived, and that he and wife were abroad.

Sir Bernard rang Chief Superintendent Gardner, they spoke for some 15 minutes, and when Gardner came off the phone, he made four phone calls, one to Paris, one to Madrid, and two in the UK.

Within minutes, one of the UK contacts was able to establish that a Mr and Mrs Henry Peters, were travelling in a dark blue Mercedes 'C' Coupe, they had been booked on the ferry to Bilboa Spain, which had arrived six hours ago. All police patrols in Spain were now on the lookout for the Mercedes. The car had filled up with fuel after leaving the ferry. The police were circulating all petrol station and garages and hotels, from a radius of 250 miles to 400 miles with a complete description. The occupants were to be detained but not questioned.

At 11.30pm that same night a young police motorcyclist who had come on duty at 10.00pm local time came upon a dark blue Mercedes Coupe parked too near to a fire hydrant in the main street of Cantabria some 2 kilometres from the main Bilbo – Barcelona road. He was stood close to the car awaiting the return of the obviously British owner.

When he rang the number in he was told they had just received notification that the driver and occupants were to be detained and that they could be dangerous. He was told to back off and observe the vehicle from a distance until assistance arrived. Before assistance could arrive, a man and woman approached the car and got in; the policeman walked across and knocked on the window.

'Please get out of the car sir, I wish to show you something' he said in broken English.

The man got out and the policeman took him round to the front of the car and showed him the yellow line, and the fire hydrant, he had just started to explain, when 2 police cars slid to a halt alongside, within seconds 4 pistols were pointing at the man and woman who both looked totally shocked.

They were both handcuffed without a word being said and bundled into the two cars, which sped of. A third car pulled up and the duty inspector got out, he patted the young policeman on the shoulder and said 'well done.'

The young police officer still didn't exactly know what he had done.

# Chapter thirteen

**11.45pm GMT Wednesday 30th October 2003, Special Branch New Scotland Yard.**

Superintendent Gardner was elated, he had just been speaking the chief of police in Cantabria, they had detained two people who had been driving the blue Mercedes, and he was holding them for 48 hours pending enquiries regarding the ownership of the vehicle. He would take matters slowly; a court case due for next week had been brought forward to ensure the court time was occupied for the next 48 hours at least. He was assuming a British police officer would wish to interview the two detainees. And this would give them time to obtain the necessary warrants.

Things were moving fast, Chief Inspector Harrison and Sergeant Tucker were on their way to RAF Lynham, near Chippenham, Wiltshire. RAF transport command had identified a C130 Hercules that was due to take spare parts for a NATO base some 40 miles from Cantagari in Spain, the plane would hold for their arrival.

Shortly before 0200 the 'Fat Albert' as the Hercules was affectionately known took of for Spain, four and a half-hour later it was landing at the NATO-Spanish airbase at base in Pamplona. A Sergeant Major from British Military police on the base and a Spanish Major also a Military police officer who would act as liaison with the civil force were standing by to assist.

Whilst the Hercules was in the air, a search warrant had been obtained for 138; Stretton Street, Kingston upon Thames, in the garage attached to the house and under a concealed vehicle inspection pit was found a wooden box with a US Army Stinger complete with 2 missiles. The two detained people were now to be treated as suspected terrorists.

## 8. 00 am local time, the Police Barracks, Cantagari Northern Spain.

The two Military policemen and the two British police officers were shown into the office of the Commandant

Jose Carrera. A tall, smart very precise and friendly officer. He welcomed them warmly, ordered coffee and sandwiches and bade them sit down.

Commandant Carrera was used to getting his own way, something he now demonstrated; 'I received this e-mail whilst you were driving here from the NATO base', he gave them each a copy. It was from Superintendent Gardner and detailed the result of the search of the detainee's house. There was a stunned silence.

You are now clearly dealing with a terrorist matter, I have cancelled the previous holding charge in favour or our Spanish Terrorist and Security Protocol, and this simply means we have cut the red tape for you. When you have completed your interview with Mr and Mrs Peters, you will have to arrest them under the new European Anti-Terrorist legislation, they will be immediately taken to the Court room attached to the Barracks. I have a Supreme Court Judge waiting for me to declare these people non-desirables and wanted for suspected Terrorist activities in the UK. He will immediately grant extradition for both people back to UK.

There is an Iberia (Spanish National Airline) flight from Bilbao International Airport to Heathrow four times a day you are on whichever one you choose. There will be no objection to you using handcuffs throughout the flight if you wish all Spanish airliners were fitted with handcuff seat secure points. The 'Ball' as you say is in your court Chief Inspector, with that he sat back in his chair and awaited a reaction.

Chief Inspector Harrison stood up, 'I can't thank you enough for your help, with your permission Sir, and I would like to get started.'

'Yes of course follow me,' said Carrera and the led the way. They passed through five sets of steel doors before reaching the holding area, they passed through the last door and into a bright and airy court room. They walked straight through the deserted courtroom, along a corridor and into an interview room.

2 people were seated the far side of the table next to each other, an armed policeman guarded the door.

Harrison went straight up to them and said. 'I am Chief Inspector Harrison, and this is Sergeant Tucker we are both Metropolitan policemen'.

## The President Is Down

'About time too, I can't imagine how you are involved in a bloody parking problem, are you here for the football drunks? However, now you are here you can get us out of this place,' with that Mr Peters stood up.

'Sit down, and speak when you are spoken to,' said Harrison. He glanced at Mrs Peters, who looked tired, shocked and worn out. He felt sorry for her; she probably knew little of this.

Peters sat down heavily.

'I am going to read you your rights, and caution you, said Harrison and he did so. There was no reaction from either. Harrison carried on. A short time ago an American 'Stinger' Missile was found in a box in the inspection pit of your garage, how did it get there?'

'I wish to see a lawyer before I answer any more questions,' said Peters and sat back with a smile.

Harrison said very quietly, 'Henry James Peters, I am arresting you under the European Anti Terrorist Act 2002, he then cautioned him again. You will be taken before a Spanish High Court Judge, and I shall make an application for your extradition to the United Kingdom.'

'Rose Peters, I am arresting you under the European Anti Terrorist Act 2002, he then cautioned her, you too will be taken before a Spanish High Court judge, and I shall make an application for your extradition to the United Kingdom.'

Both of them looked totally stunned.

'You can't do this, I have a right to see a lawyer, I know my rights, you bastards are in Spain now not fucking London, you have no jurisdiction here whatsoever, get me our Embassy, and do it now.'

A male and female Spanish police officer stepped forward at a nod from Commandant Carrera; they handcuffed the Peters to them, and pulled both the Peters towards the door and the Court room down the corridor.

The group entered the Court Room from the back of the Court. The Courtroom was empty apart from an armed policeman on the main door, and at the front of the Court and sitting quite alone, was a Judge in cap and gown.

Commandant Carrera stepped forward, he removed his cap and bowed to the Judge, he spoke in English.

'May it please your Honour, I am Commandant Carrera of the Garde Civille, I am making an application for the Immediate extradition of Mr Henry James Peters and Mrs Rose Peters to the United Kingdom, they have been arrested by an officer of the Metropolitan Police, Chief Inspector Harrison.

My application is made on the grounds that they are undesirable persons, and are wanted in connection with suspected terrorist activities in the United Kingdom. They have been arrested on Spanish soil under The European Anti Terrorist Act 2002. And I am satisfied that they have charges to answer in the United Kingdom.

I am not aware of any criminal activity being committed or planned in Spain, enquiries will continue, if subsequently we find there are charges to answer, we stand behind the United Kingdom in wishing those charges to be dealt with, and reserve the right to extradite one or both individuals back to Spain to be dealt with under Spanish law.

The Judge leant forward, he said. 'Would the defendants come forward'?

The Peters together with the police officers handcuffed to them moved forward and stood in front and below the judge.

'You have heard the application by Commandant Carrera, and I have heard that you have been quite properly arrested on suspicion of Terrorist Activity in The United Kingdom. I am satisfied that the application to extradite you both is legal and just, consequently you are to be extradited within the next 24 hours from Spain at the cost of the British Government'.

However, enquiries will continue into your activities whilst you were on Sovereign Spanish soil, should it be found that you have been engaged in any activity prejudicial to Spain, an application will be made for your extradition back to Spain when you have been dealt with by the British Courts. There is no time limit to this process.'

'This means that if you are found guilty by a British Court of Law, and you serve your sentence, when you are released if you have committed any offences as stated in Spain you are liable to be re-arrested and extradited to Spain to answer those charges, Do you understand?'

Neither answered, they were too shaken.

'I also have to inform you that you are no longer welcome on Sovereign Spanish soil. This applies to mainland Spain, and any and all Islands governed by Sovereign Spain.'

He then looked at Chief Inspector Harrison and Said. 'You are free to remove the accused from this Court, and to arrange for them to be transported to the United Kingdom to face charges. The Spanish Government will assist you to do this. Thank you Chief Inspector.'

Harrison said, 'I am obliged to your honour,' and bowed his head to the judge, all turned to leave the Courtroom.

He looked at his wristwatch; the whole proceedings from Commandant Carrera starting to make the application to them walking out of the Court had taken exactly 5 minutes.

Waiting outside in the Barracks yard was an armoured prison van, and 2 motor cycle outriders. The Peters were put into separate cages within the van, and an armed police officer accompanied them.

Commandant Carrera turned to Harrison and said, 'my Brother and his wife were killed by a bomb 3 years ago whilst shopping in Madrid, ETA claimed responsibility, so make this stick Chief Inspector, you make sure you nail them, and those behind your Mr and Mrs Peters.'

He shook hands with Harrison and Tucker, and said,' the van will take you right up to the aircraft, an immigration official will stamp the exit visa on their passports, and will also stamp an official declaration that they are prohibited on Sovereign Spanish at any time in the future, unless the Spanish High Court waive the prohibition.'

'They will be put on the aircraft, and handcuffed to the seats, this is usually the one in the back rows, and there should 3 banks of seating for your party, so they do not mix with other passengers. The aircraft Captain will advise you.'

**Thursday 31st October 2003 11.00am (local time) Bilbao International Airport Spain, Iberia Flight 26a to Heathrow.**

Just over an hour later, the Peters were safely installed at the back of the aircraft, the Captain had allocated three rows of seat, and the gangway was taped off to stop the other passengers using the toilets at the rear.

Rose Peters sat close to Sergeant Tucker on one side of the aircraft, and Harrison sat close to Henry Tucker on the other side.

Henry Peters at last spoke to Harrison.

'So Mr smart arse policeman when are they bringing my car back, I wonder if they will be as bloody quick to do that?' He said in a sarcastic voice.

'They aren't, in fact nobody is, you have to make an application to the Spanish High Court and then go and collect it personally, which you could find somewhat difficult. It's a bit like smuggling, only worse they can keep your car and sell it. Just like that' clicking his fingers, said Harrison with a grin. He felt quite elated for the first time in 3 or 4 days.

# Chapter fourteen

**Thursday 31st October 2003 4.30pm Paddington Green Police Station Metropolitan Police.**

Upon Landing at Heathrow the Peters were taken by separate cars to Paddington Green Police station.

Apart from giving them food, nobody went anywhere near them for the next few hours, at 8.00pm exactly Henry Peters was taken to an interview room, at a table sat Chief Superintendent Gardner and Sergeant Tucker, Gardner did the honours and told Henry Peters to sit down.

On the table was a tape machine, a pack of cigarettes and a box of matches and an ashtray. Gardner also had a slim A4 file.

Henry Peter's eyes went to the cigarettes, which Tucker casually picked and put in his jacket pocket. Peters was dying for a cigarette it had been hours since his last one. As Tucker knew only too well.

Superintendent Gardner opened the file and said, 'before I turn this thing on, he nodded at the tape recorder, we need to establish, if you are a complete cretin or a reasonably intelligent person, who understands the seriousness of what we are looking at here'.

He extracted three photographs, the first was of the front of Henry Peters house, the second was the open trap door over the inspection pit, and the third showed the two open wooden boxes in the pit, and a stinger missile launcher and two missiles. Gardner never said a word; he waited for Peters to speak. It took over two minutes before Peters broke the silence.

'I am not a terrorist, I just supply things, a middle man if you like, I have no idea who would be buying that stinger as I said, and I just buy them or the odd gun. But I never use them and I don't know who does, I have the contacts from my army days, I make a few grand a year that's all.'

'Oh well that's all right then we can all go home can't we?' Said Superintendent Gardner.

Superintendent Gardner leant across and turned on the tape, 'this interview is recorded at 2005 hours Thursday 31st October at Paddington Green Police Station. Present are Chief Superintendent Gardner and Sergeant Tucker special branch, the accused Henry James Peters has been cautioned.'

'Now Mr Peters I have just shown you 3 photographs, do you recognise your house at 138, Stretton Street, Kingston upon Thames, and do you further recognise the inspection pit in the garage of said property?'

'That's my house, but I don't how that got there.'

'What's that on your right hand Mr Peters, for the benefit of the tape I am pointing to a sticking plaster on the heel of Mr Peter's right hand?'

'I cut myself in the garden whilst pruning the roses; it has taken a bit of healing.'

'It's probably the same blood group that's on the edge of the box containing the stinger,' said Gardner to Peter's

'No it couldn't be', ----- said Peters.

'Is that because you were wearing these heavy industrial gardening gloves, he said pushing across the table a pair of grey and green striped heavy gauge gardening gloves, they were blood stained on the inside, and some of the blood had just seeped through the lighter weight part of the glove near the wrist? For the benefit of the tape I am showing Mr Peters a pair of blood stained gardening gloves.'

'Right lets start again Mr Peters, where are the other two stinger launchers and missiles that accompanied this one, he said pointing to the photograph? Before you answer let me tell you there are people still in prison, after many months that have still not been tried in a court of law, where terrorism is concerned You are running with the big boys now Peters, not some stupid little petty thug wanting an untraceable gun.'

'This carries a life sentence or possibly the death sentence if the others get used, are you ready for that,-------- yes I did say the death sentence, for you, ----- and even your wife!!'

There was a long pause,-----------' I honestly don't know I delivered two to a building site in Peckham, we just moved them from my van to a Mercedes white van, the driver was probably Australian or American, there was an Arabic looking guy with him. I couldn't pin down his accent. They just gave me my money and took them, I was supposed to deliver the other to the back of a pub in Uxbridge but the guy never turned up. He still hadn't done when I went on holiday, and he bloody well knew I was going away yesterday.'

Gardner stood up abruptly, 'Superintendent Gardner and Sergeant Tucker are leaving the room interview terminated at 2020 hours.'

'Constable return Mr Peters to his cell please.'

As soon as they were outside Superintendent Gardner turned to Sergeant Tucker and said, 'Tommy get on your mobile to the Inspector at Stretton Street, tell him to get out now and leave as much like it was as is possible, tell him to clear his blokes from the area and no radio traffic, it all has to be done by word of mouth and right now.'

'I will speak to Wayne and Roberts, they can carry out observations tonight, we will pick a team for tomorrow when you get back. Now get on with it.'

# Chapter fifteen

**3.00 am Friday 1ˢᵗ November 2003, Stretton street, Kingston upon Thames, London, England.**

Sergeants Wayne and Roberts were sat in the back of an old Ford Granada with smoked glass windows, 50 yards from the home of the Peters family. It was now 3.00am the London taxi had gone past twice in the last 10 minutes slowly as though looking for an address. The first time they had thought nothing of it the second time, Wayne said, 'what does a London taxi drivers have to do that no others in the UK do?'

Roberts said, 'that's easy he has to pass the 'Knowledge,' (potential drivers work for years sometimes to obtain the knowledge, without it they CANNOT drive a London cab).

'So why is this driver on his second time round said Wayne, if he comes again we clock him properly. Check his number anyway.'

**'DS Wayne to Alpha control,'**

'Alpha control to DS Wayne, go ahead.'

**'DS Wayne, vehicle check Sierra-Alpha- 52- November -Bravo – Delta.'   (SA 52 NBD)**

2 minutes later, 'Sierra-Alpha-52 November-Bravo-Delta. Is a Black London cab, it is registered to Malik Alssad,

Do you wish the address DS Wayne?'

**'DS Wayne to Alpha control, yes please.'**

'Alpha control the address is 298, Braybrook Street, Shepherds Bush, that's near Wormwood Scrubs Prison.'

**'Many thanks Alpha control.'**

The cab never came back but 15 minutes later a dark blue Ford Transit, came straight down the road, and quietly reversed into the driveway of 138. The van door opened on the near side and a dark shadowy figure got out.

Through the open window of the police vehicle they thought they heard a wrenching sound as though the lock hasp was being forced off the wooden door.

'**DS Wayne to Alpha control,** we need that armed backup urgently, we have two targets, both believed to be male, and one is still sat in the driver's seat of a dark blue transit in the driveway, index number Kilo-237-echo-tango-hotel. Silent approach please.'

'**Alpha control to DS Wayne**, assistance on its way 2 armed response unit's one 5 mins maximum the other 15 minutes.'

'**DS Wayne to Alpha control,** advice back up units there are two armed plain clothed officers on site, both will wear narrow florescent wrist bands on the right wrist.'

'**Alpha control**, message received and understood.'

'**Alpha control,** both armed response units have been informed 2 plain clothed officers on site, both will wear narrow florescent wristbands on the right wrist, good luck!!'

DS Roberts said, 'I've got to get a bit nearer, I'll go back down the street and come up the other side in shadow, no heroics Ted you are getting married next week. 'With that he slipped out of the back seat and using the vehicle for cover hurried away from the scene, he got to the bottom of the road, and worked his way back up the street using the gardens of the other houses for cover. One of them had a lighted streetlamp which didn't help and for a couple of seconds he was exposed. He didn't think he had been seen.

Wayne was advised that the first armed response unit was closing off the top of the road, and that it would then block the bottom of the road, two officers were coming down the road towards the house, and approaching DS Roberts from his front. The other unit was still 5 to 8 minutes away.

The garage door opened and a figure was seen to open the rear doors of the Transit, and put something in the back of van. He went back and brought out another box or parcel and put that in the back of the van.

The driver of the van started the engine, DS Roberts was 30 yards away and the back up team a little further, the van started to move it was not showing lights.

DS Wayne started his engine, knowing it was unlikely the men in the van would hear it, he pulled out of his parking space between three other cars, and accelerated rapidly up the road towards the van, and he was not showing any lights and his fast manoeuvre had caught them by surprise.

The van was turning away from him and had emerged onto the road, the passenger in the transit opened fire with an automatic pistol and four shots were fired one bullet went through the windscreen and took DS Wayne in the shoulder, another ploughed into the offside head light, and finished up under the dash board narrowly avoiding his right leg, the others missed.

DS Wayne's car swung violently to the left and hit a lamppost, he was thrown forward towards the broken windscreen and his head hit the car roof just above the top edge of the windscreen. He fell back and his head came to rest on the steering wheel, the horn blew continuously.

DS Roberts leaped out into the road, he went into a crouching stance and fired 8 shots rapidly at the van from around 10 yards, and the van wobbled and came to a dribbling halt up against the pavement.

Three armed police officers were running towards the van, an arm shot out of the drivers side, and a voice shouted 'don't shoot—don't shoot please I am unarmed.'

The officers levelled their weapons at the man and told him to get out, with his hands on his head. One officer approached from the near side, the man sat in the passenger seat had half of his head shot away there was little doubt he was dead.

DS Roberts had run back to the Ford Granada and DS Wayne, at first he thought he was dead until Wayne muttered, 'It hurts like fucking hell,' Roberts nearly cried. He would make bloody sure Wayne walked down the isle at his forthcoming wedding. As his best man he was supposed to look after him, not get him shot. He could see a bollocking coming from Patricia, Wayne's fiancée, and found himself grinning.

One of the armed response team was speaking on the phone and getting an ambulance, another came to assist DS Wayne, he was trained in the treatment of gunshot wounds, and the bullet was still in the shoulder but seemed to be reasonably OK. He dry sterile padded the shoulder wound and was cleaning up the head wound.

The section leader approached DS Roberts, and said 'are you OK,----- that's good, well I take it by the wristband you are one of the two good guys. Remind me not to take a shot at you. Chummy got his just deserts for what its worth. I was a bit concerned as we had not had time to take up ideal positions, our shots might have gone astray and that's not good news in a residential area such as this, well done.'

In the back of the van was 2 wooden boxes containing the 2 Stinger missiles and launcher?

They could hear an ambulance coming in the distance, and two minutes later it drew up, the ambulance crew treated DS Wayne in the car initially, giving him an injection for the pain, they then transferred him to the ambulance and took him to hospital.

Other officers had arrived on the scene and a uniformed Inspector took over, residents were asked to remain inside their homes for the time being whilst the crime scene was photographed and examined.

# Chapter sixteen

**8.00 am Friday 1st November 2003. 10, Downing Street, London, England.**
**The office and home of the British Prime Minister Tony Salter.**

It was a grim gathering of people in the PM's 1st Floor conference room, and the rear of the building and overlooking the garden.

Sir Bernard Hills, looked around the table whilst the group settled and shuffled their papers. His friend the PM Tony Salter had visibly aged in the last few days, he face looked grey, drawn and tired, his eyes lacked their usual sparkle and his step seemed to have lost its bounce. The warm smile when it came was genuine.

' Well gentlemen thank you for coming, I hope I will not entirely wasted your weekend, with a bit of luck we should have finished the meeting by lunch time, whilst that may mean some of us can go home, it will probably be the start of a busy few days for the rest.'

'You have in front of you a briefing from Sir Bernard Hills, whom you all know,' he nodded towards Sir Bernard.

'This covers the whole picture as we know it up to 5 hours ago, when one of our special branch officers was shot in the line of duty, his assailant was shot dead by the first officer's partner as I understand it. One suspect was arrested at the scene and an American manufactured 'Stinger' and 2 missiles were recovered from a vehicle that both the suspects were in at the time.'

'I am very happy to report that the special branch officer who was shot, has had a bullet removed from his shoulder there will be no long term damage, and he should be fit to return to duty in about a month or so should he wish. As he is to be married within the next two weeks, a little longer time might be appropriate.'

'Metropolitan police armed response units also attended the incident; the shootings were witnessed by five independent and fully trained firearms officers. They were lead by Chief Inspector Williams of the Armed Response Unit.'

'Following the submission of statements by all, I together with the Home Secretary have reviewed the incident in detail.'

'We have concluded that other officers were at risk from this gunman who had shown no hesitation in using the weapon to attempt escape. Therefore the use of a firearm by DS Roberts to protect him and other officers who had just come upon the scene was totally justified. Justifiable homicide is our conclusion. I have little doubt the inquest will confirm it. The inquest is being held this afternoon in camera.'

'Now onto the broader picture!!'

'We have as I have said one 'Stinger' and 2 missiles, accounted for, that according to intelligence leaves a further two stringers and possibly 4 missiles, the source we know to be ex-IRA stock as it were from Northern Ireland. We also have an unusual situation, the Provisional IRA's chief of staff has been in touch with Sir Bernard, they have an active service unit here on the mainland looking for the other two stingers and missiles, we are told with a view to handing them over to us.'

'They do not want them used on the mainland, or indeed anywhere. Sir Bernard assures me this is a done deal, and they will not renege on it. If they locate the weapons they will, sit on them and tell us where they are. They have asked that we co-operate in this matter. What they don't know of course is that our concern is the pending visit of the US President on the 4$^{th}$ November. So whilst we can I believe on this occasion trust them, we cannot afford to back-pedal ourselves. So it's maximum effort until we find them, and the people acquiring them.'

'We have confirmation that the President will be leaving the States at around 7.00pm Washington time on Sunday 3$^{rd}$ November, in other words in 2 days time, the arrival time here is around 6.30am on 4$^{th}$. This gives him the chance to sleep over the Atlantic. I have tried to re-schedule but he won't, he says he will not let terrorists run his life.'

'You have a short agenda, which I would like you all to take on board; we will go through the items very briefly at this stage so you all get a flavour of your colleague's involvement. Naturally we will take each item again in more depth with those directly involved. Time is of the essence.'

1. Transit over the Atlantic:

## The President Is Down

'As you all now know, AIR FORCE ONE will be escorted by US air force Strike eagles from the US side to mid-Atlantic, he will have an AWAC's with him, and this will come the whole way. US air force Strike eagles from Germany will take over from the others who will refuel and turn for home. There will be an exclusion zone around AF One, monitored by, and policed by the eagles.'

'Around 250 miles from our shores, 4 Harriers from HMS Ark Royal, will supply additional support and I believe will form a box formation at some distance from AF One, they will continue up to and including the landing stage.'

2. 'Landing site, ------at this stage I cannot quite honestly say the President has a choice of 4/5 such sites and

his pilot as I understand it will make a choice about an hour out.'

3. 'The threat, -------we believe that 'Stingers' are the SAM that are likely to be used, we know that

3/6 missiles and 3 launchers. You will recall we have recovered 2 missiles and 1 launcher. This was the incident that the special branch officer became injured. We have also arrested a man directly involved in that incident. And in addition we have arrested a man and woman in Northern Spain, who were also involved with the purchase and supply of all 3 launchers and missiles.'

4. 'The missing Stingers: We need to find these today or tomorrow latest, I don't say it will be easy, we have to find them. Jeremy Paxman is interviewing me this afternoon; I do not want to be on the back-foot with him.'

5. 'After landing the president will be helicopter'd to Buckingham Palace, a reception at the Foreign Office will follow and then on to the American Embassy where he and the First Lady will stay during their 2-day visit.'

6. 'In this room today we have the best brains and physical organisations in the Country, MI5 and MI6, Special Branch, the Anti Terrorist Squad, Scotland Yard, you are all are working flat out to find out who is behind this threat and neutralise them, but apart from what we have gleaned already there seems to be nothing happening in the background, none of our informants, political or otherwise are aware of any specifics. But then few

people are in the know regarding his visit. However, that can't last, there is far too much going on.'

'I am going to hand the meeting over to Sir Bernard Hills, SIS, his team and Special Branch have been closest to the situation, and he above any knows the current situation. I have promised any and all resources to help you.

Please consider all options, and report back with a clear and detailed action plan to:'

   a) 'Detect and detain those involved.

   b) Contain the situation should an incident occur with the President and or his Aircraft.

   c) Options for damage limitation for the British Government.

   d) And if (c) occurs, a follow up plan.'

'Finally, you may not be aware, but it is the Presidents intention to go from here to Brussels to visit the European Parliament. Again as he wanted this visit to be low key, he has not made public his visit. The CIA have of course being going the rounds, and tied up as much as they can in Belgium, but again to a certain extent he has made life difficult for them. Tom Franks, whom most of you will know is here, he nodded to Franks, Tom is officially White House Liaison with the CIA, he therefore represents the CIA, with his CIA colleague Eric Benson, he nodded to the tall black American sat next to Franks.'

The Prime Minister stood up, picked up his papers and said, ' Gentlemen—Sir Bernard, I will leave you now and good luck.'

The PM left the room, and Sir Bernard took over the meeting.

'Right here's what we have as of 5.00am this morning,' and he spent 40 minutes briefing them all. From time to time an individual member ask a question to clarify a specific point.

Lunch came and went and took the form of tea/coffee and sandwiches, and at 4.00pm a clear action plan had been formulated with specific areas of responsibility. Sir Bernard reflected that he had never seen such co-operation inter-service, or determination to crack this one.

The meeting broke up at 4.45pm, and at 5.15pm Sir Bernard laid out the plan of action.

**Later that same day.**

In the background, certain Territorial Army units were put on full alert, and a notional 'Terrorist scenario training exercise' was under way.

*The President Is Down*

All 4 viable landing sites were covered, the RAF Regiment, provided Rapier SAM to all site. The police identified all roads close to runways and landing sites, and developed a plane for diversions on the day that would be put in place one hour prior to a possible landing of AIR FORCE ONE. All Hotels were visited and staff interviewed regarding guests booked in over the next few days.

It was significant that when the two Metropolitan Police officers called at the Palace hotel, on the A4 and opposite the main runway at Heathrow, the receptionist who might have remembered a couple booking a room for themselves, and room 310 for their plane-spotter son, wasn't on duty and was suffering from flu. The porter who would have remembered was having his coffee break and was never asked.

The ITV News and BBC News on Television both carried a photo-fit of the Arab with a scar down the left side of his face. The 20 year old, taking over at an Esso petrol station in Ealing did not see the 6.00pm news on either, however he did see the 10.00pm ITV news and listened to Sir Trevor Macdonald presenting the news and when he spoke about the man wanted in connection with a shooting a few days ago, he knew he had seen the man with the scar.

Terry French was a young black and constantly being pulled up for 'Stop and Search'; it was 4.30am the next morning and close to the end of his night shift, when he reluctantly decided to phone the police. Some 10 minutes later a young white police constable drew up, entered the shop, and said.

'Did you ring in about an Arab who had a scar down his cheek?'

# Chapter seventeen

**11. 00 am Friday 31st October 2003, the Jolly Miller public house, Braintree, Essex.**

The two IRA men Michael and John were sat with John Thompson awaiting an IRA contact who felt he had heard something of interest on the Stingers, Michael got a round of drinks in and was on his way back from the bar when a scruffy looking individual in a cloth cap came in to the lounge and approached the table. He took his cap of and looked from one to the other, 'Would I be looking at Michael Docherty?' He said.

'I'm Docherty and you are? '

'I'm Flynn sir, Patrick Flynn.'

'Sit down Patrick, will you take a drink? He nodded to the barman who pulled another Guinness and brought it over to the table. John had joined them by now, and having put the drinks on the table he sat back and looked at Flynn.'

'Now where do I know you from Mr Flynn?' Said John. There was a stony silence, Patrick Flynn's face reddened he stammered.

'I don't know sir, I was one of the active service units that mortar bombed Downing Street, and I was on the St. Pancras job. It may have been from there.'

Michael, intervened, 'now this information you have what is it?'

Flynn was relieved to be getting back to his reason for his being there and it showed, his brow was damp with beads of sweat even though it was quite chilly in the pub, his complexion was returning to normal, and he smiled his nervous but grateful thanks to Michael for stepping in.

'I work at Heathrow airport on week ends, last week end I heard a loader talking about an Arab he had seen in the street he lives in carrying some boxes and things into a bed and breakfast, he lives in Hounslow. He said he thought they were similar to the ones he used to move around on a US army base some years ago. They had 'Stinger' missiles in them. I heard today that we were looking for Stingers so I rang my old area commander. He rang me back and told me to meet you here.'

'What's the name and address of this 'loader?' Said John.

'I don't know, I tried to find out this morning but couldn't. I only know its in Hounslow, on the flight path, I know that because he complains about the big aeroplanes, and say's he can nearly reach out and touch them.'

'What kind of car does he have?'

'I think he has one of the new minis, it's a dark red colour, but I don't know the number.'

'Just sit there a minute Patrick I want a quick word with Michael,' said John and stood up, and moved over to the bar area with Michael.

' I don't trust the bastard, said John, for Christ sake, I only said where did I know him from and he spills the beans on two jobs, we could be anybody, the 'Brits', special branch, the bloody SAS, any bugger.'

'He did come to meet us, after speaking with Martin O'Toole now didn't him? I agree we use him but don't trust him.' With that both men went back to the other two at the table.

'Now do you think Patrick my man you would recognise the loaders car if you saw it?'

'I think so, what do you want me to do?'

'It's very simple, all four of us together with another two will search along the flight path at Hounslow for the mini'. When and if we find it, you will identify it for us. You can leave the rest to us, is that all right with you Patrick'? He didn't wait for a reply, and said; Right before we set up the local search in Hounslow, lets take a look at the staff car park at Heathrow, he could be there and it would save us a lot of time.'

An hour and a half later, there being no sign of the red mini in the staff car park at Heathrow, they took the two cars the short distance to Hounslow, and started watching the aircraft coming in.

When John was confident that they were in the right area they all split up and took the two main roads, and all the side streets, there were more side streets than he had thought.

Patrick was half way down Somerville road when he spotted the Heathrow loader going into a terrace house, the mini was not to be seen, almost immediately he noticed a small sign in one of the windows of the houses to his right. The sign read VACANCIES; he had found a Bed and Breakfast hotel. He walked the length of the street and could not see another.

There was a concreted area in front of the front room window for parking a single car, it was empty. He decided to enquire after a vacant room, Patrick rang the doorbell. There was no answer. He rang it again and tired looking elderly women answered the door.

Patrick put on his best smile and decided to ask if there were still vacancies.

Mrs Symonds, said, can I help you?'

'I would like a room for a couple of days if you have one.'

Patrick's accent was very strong Belfast and Mrs Symonds didn't like the Irish, she didn't like a lot of other people either, Blacks, Asians, Chinese, Indians, and Arabs even. In fact she was a bit of a snob, but couldn't afford to be, she needed the business nowadays from whatever source. So she showed him the room on the first floor and explained how everything worked. He paid his two days in advance, and Mrs Symonds gave him a front door key. If he had a car he couldn't park on the concrete strip under the window as her nice Mr Rashid put his car there.

'Is Mr Rashid in,' he asked.

'No Mrs Symonds replied he usually came in around 5.00pm.' It was now 3.30pm.

Mrs Symonds footfalls faded as she descended worn the carpeted staircase to the ground floor, Patrick waited a couple of minutes and quietly opened his bedroom door, he stood in the doorway listening for a further two or three minutes, but the house was silent.

He tried the doorknob to Rashid's room, the door was locked. He slid his hand into his inside jacket pocket and pulled out a thin leather wallet, selecting a thin piece of semi rigid plastic he slipped it into the thin gap between the doorframe and the door, and gently eased it down across the Yale lock, there was a click and the door swung open silently. He entered the room, checking for any obvious traps, there were none, or at least none that showed.

He had not noticed the single long hair that had been wetted and place across the gap between the door and its frame at the top of the door.

Under the bed was a large wooden case about six feet long, he gently pulled it out from under the bed, the lid was held down by two screws which he could see were loose and a small brass lock. He inserted his lock pick into the lock and within seconds it too was open. He withdrew the two screws and removed the heavy wooden lid off the box, there as large as life itself was a Stinger launcher. There was a smaller wooden box beside it.

He pulled his jacket open, and felt for his mobile phone, he pressed the digits to call Michael, who answered on the third ring.

'I have found a stinger and two missiles;' before he could give the address, he felt a slight draught and turned round. He was looking at the wrong end of a Colt automatic complete with silencer.

The colt was very steadily held by a well dressed middle height Arab.

'Turn the phone off and put it down on the floor to your left side.' Patrick did exactly as he was told, he was absolutely terrified, his hands were shaking, and Rashid in that second knew he wasn't looking at a hero.

Rashid ground his heel into the mobile phone shattering it completely. Patrick looked at it and began to bodily shake, he felt a warm glow around his groin and realised he had wet himself, more from frustration, and humiliation than from courage he saw red and launched himself at Rashid.

Rashid was looking in disgust at the huge stain on Patrick's trousers and was nearly caught out by the swiftness of Patrick's actions, Patrick's head caught Rashid in the stomach and he bent over slightly winded, he felt a hand trying to pull the colt out of his hand, with his left hand he grabbed Patrick's hair and tore out a large chunk.

Patrick in great pain released his grip on the colt, and Rashid brought it round viciously and dealt him two violent blows to the head with the heavy gun. Patrick fell to his knees with the force of the blows, Rashid levelled the unbalanced silenced gun and fired once the bullet entered Patrick's head just below his left ear and exited through his right eye, smashing his jaw on the way through, he was still alive and holding his bloodied head in his hands as he staggered to his feet.

Rashid his chest heaving and beginning to panic as Patrick turned towards him once again, he shot him twice more in the chest. Patrick fell over backwards, hit the wall behind him heavily and crashed down onto the bedside table, it was a flimsy cheap self assembly chipboard affair, his weight demolished it completely and he noisily slumped into death with a gurgling blood vomiting groan. The dark red blood from his head wound spread out across the cheap linoleum floor mixing with the still bright rapidly fading pumping blood oozing from his chest wound, and being soaked up by the cheap scatter rugs.

Rashid collapsed onto the bed, his chest heaving, his hands were shaking and he felt totally weak bodily and out of control mentally for the first time in his life. He dropped the colt onto the bed. In a matter of seconds two completely diverse religions would come into play, and found to be wanting.

The bedroom door was gently opened, and Mrs Symonds stood there looking at the broken and bloodied and now very dead body of Patrick. Her eyes quickly flicked to the colt now lying exposed and menacing facing her on the bed, and back to the dazed looking Rashid who now had a wild animal look in his eyes, she had started to say something, but now stood there in a state of shock for a second. She was the first to recover and slamming the bedroom shut she ran along the corridor towards the stairs as fast as her arthritic legs could carry her.

The worn and threadbare edge of the landing carpet at the top of the stairs had a small hole in it. Today the deeply religious Mrs Symonds God deserted her, Mrs Symonds heel caught the loose threads and held, her left leg hesitated for a split second her bodied didn't, she fell forward head first down the staircase.

The stairs had a bend in them, there was sharp dry crack as her neck broke when her whole body weight was thrown on to it against the wall, her limp body crumpled untidily, with her dress up over her head, exposing the upper part of her legs, and the voluminous and dirty underwear that covered them.

Rashid was revolted at what he saw his religion now kicking in, and making him aware he should not be viewing exposed female flesh in this manner. A situation he alone had created and would not be forgiven for. The broken body had now come to an abrupt halt in a strange and impossible angle.

What was he going to do now, in the space of less than three minutes his carefully laid plans had fallen apart------- or had they? Rashid went quickly to the door and looked out, all was normal nobody had heard anything. Why would they the colt was silenced and Mrs Symonds had not made a sound as she died.

He locked the front door, he went back into the sitting room and sat on the settee, he had to think this through.

His contact on Andrews Air force base had been very specific, air testing had taken place of AIR FORCE ONE and her sister aircraft, this always happened five days before a significant trip was made by the President. They did this in case air tests showed a problem, the five days allowed time to fix every situation, and was now a standard operating procedure, as was ordering the Presidents Texan steaks, and arranging delivery to the aircraft four hours before take-off.

The president was coming to England as planned on the 4th November it would be some time in the early hours.

He and the American had staked all on Heathrow, if he landed somewhere else they could and would wait.

Rashid covered Patrick's body in his room with a couple of bed sheets out of the airing cupboard, deciding to sleep in the room Mrs Symonds had rented to Patrick. He moved his belongings including the stinger and missiles.

He looked at his watch it was now 4.15pm, he knew Mrs Symonds did not have any other guests, just himself and the dead man, but had the dead man been on his own or was he with another or others.

15 minutes later having searched Mrs Symonds rooms, and the kitchen which she also used as her little office he knew there were no others. He also knew her husband had died some time ago, and she had not had any visitors in the few days he had been there. Should he risk it and stay until after he had taken his shot at AIRFORCE ONE or should he try and find some where else? He decided it would be better to stay where he was; after all it was now it less than 2 days before the US President arrived.

Rashid went into the kitchen and made himself a sandwich that was all he would eat for the next day and a half; he had no intention of going out of the house. He turned the television on and found himself looking at a photo-fit picture of himself. The bad news was it was a good likeness of him. By the time he found the right buttons to press on the remote the news item had passed on, he did not therefore know what the police knew about him.

# Chapter eighteen

Rashid locked the rear garden door and left the lights on downstairs, at 5.45pm he heard the doorbell sound, peeping round the curtains in his bedroom, he could see a woman about Mrs Symonds age stood on the front doorstep, and in her hand she had a shopping or similar sized bag.

Dorothy Smith rang the doorbell again; it wasn't like her friend to go out when she knew that every Saturday night they went to the 'Bingo' together in Uxbridge. Looking up at the front bedroom windows, and due to her poor eyesight she did not see Rashid examining her from the window of bedroom 3. Well maybe she had gone to the shops in which case she would pop back at the time they normally went at around 7.00pm she looked around before going, and noticed her friend's lodger's car on the 'car park' bit. Perhaps he had left it there and gone to work on the bus or something.

Dorothy hadn't really wanted to go to bingo that evening as her husband Bill wasn't well, and with his chest being as bad as it was she didn't like leaving him alone. ----- She would come back at 7.00pm. and tell Irene she wasn't going. Rashid watched her from behind the curtains as she slowly walked away down the street without a backward glance.

Dorothy and Bill lived in an immaculate 2 bedroom terrace house in the next street, they had bought the house nearly 30 years ago, and at their age didn't really feel like moving, they rather liked the different peoples that had come to live near them over the years. Certainly not a bother to them at all, in fact they enjoyed some of the new foods that they could now buy, and the 'take away's 'they could have. A bit different to fish and chips, pies, and jellied eels. The house wasn't worth as much as it had been now, with the Black people, Indians and Chinese

## The President Is Down

and others. But what would they do at their age with £300,000 any way?

Bill was watching the news on television and coughing and spluttering he was definitely not very well.

'I'll make you a nice cup of tea love,' she said as she passed him on the way to the kitchen. A few minutes later she brought the tea back in on a tray, and pulled out a little table from the nest of three that her son had bought them last Christmas.

She put the tray on the table, and pointed to Bills tea, 'I have put you a little drop of whisky in your tea, and there are some of your favourite biscuits there. I am not going to bingo, I'll pop back and tell Irene a little bit later, then I'll get you one of your curries if you like, we could share it, I don't want a lot tonight. It's going to rain anyway'.

She looked up at the TV screen, still talking as she did.' Remind me tomorrow morning I need to take your library books back otherwise you'll have another fine to pay, I can't see why you need four books at a time, if you only had three then they would never be overdue. Bill what they are saying about that man, turn it up please?'

'Wanted for questioning in relation to an incident involving a shooting of a woman in Ealing on the 15$^{th}$ October,

If you see this man, do not approach him, and inform any police officer, or telephone the number that will appear after this news broadcast.'

'The European Union appeared to have 'goofed' yet again according the Deputy Prime Minister John Tyndall, not content with interfering with our 'British Sausage', they now are going to set standards for our 'traditional' dish of Fish and Chips. Minimum weights for fish and portions of chips are to be recommended.'

'What's he saying Bill about that man with the scar down his cheek?'

'Something about a murder last week or something, why?'

For a few seconds Dorothy couldn't speak, 'I think that man is Irene's lodger. Bill she didn't answer the door when I knocked earlier, all the lights were on, I thought she had nipped to the corner shop. Bill what do we do?'

'Grab that pencil, they are going to give a phone number in a minute,' he pointed to the pencil lying across his newspaper on top of the television.

She picked up the pencil and started to go into the kitchen,' where are you going' said Bill, 'for a piece of paper,' she said,' write it on the bloody newspaper you'll miss it otherwise.'

'Now the telephone number you will need if you have any information that can be of help to the police regarding this man and a fatal shooting in Ealing on the 15$^{th}$ October, the number is 020 5678 999 Please do not approach this person he is believed to be armed and dangerous. 'The number will remain on screen for a further minute.'

Her hand was shaking as she finished writing, 'what do I do now Bill?'

'You've got to telephone the police, go to the box at the end of the road, or nip next door.'

Dorothy nipped next door, fifteen minutes later a tall plain clothes policeman knocked on the door and identified himself to Dorothy, she told him all she knew, and what she suspected.

'What's going to happen now 'asked Bill?

'It's already happened Sir, the street has been blocked off, and we have quietly empted the houses either side of your friend's house. There are some armed police now on site and we are checking if there is anybody in the house.'

## 6. 36pm Saturday 2<sup>nd</sup> November 2003 SIS Headquarters London

The phone on Sir Bernard's desk rang, the offices were just about empty of people for the weekend only people on shifts and overseas desks were still around.

He listened for a minute, 'bloody brilliant, if he is in there take him alive if possible, but please emphasize I do not want any more officers shot Commander'.' I should be with you in ½ hour all being well.' As Sir Bernard's driver had gone home for the night, he called on the Met to take him to Hounslow, a very competent Metropolitan police driver threaded his way through the London rush hour traffic and along the A40 and out to the incident.

Whilst on the way to Hounslow Sir Bernard's mobile rang, it was The IRA chief of staff, 'Raven'.

'I won't piss about Bernard; have your lot picked up one of my men in Hounslow?'

Sir Bernard paused,' no we haven't but I have bad feelings, if your chap was looking for a 'stinger', he may well have found it, I am currently in a police car, and about five or so,--- he glanced out of the window, the car was on the dual carriageway and passing the RAF Northolt turnoff, he finished---minutes away from Hounslow, we have a suspect murderer in a house we are laying siege to. It could be your man was a bit ahead of us. I'll let you know.'

The car cruised round the corner and into Caledonian way, a Chief Inspector Higgs greeted him with a salute.

'Good evening Sir, we think we have an Arab with a very deep scar down his left cheek and fully fitting the description of the security alert murder. He arrived a couple of days ago. The street is blocked off; he can't get out without us knowing, provided of course he is in there. The alarm was raised by a lady who is friends with the lady who owns and runs the bed and breakfast. She went round to arrange about not going to bingo tonight, the door was locked and there was no answer to the bell. She then went home, that's just round the corner, thinking her friend had gone to the local shop. And had intended going back later. She saw the 6.00pm news and phoned us.'

'When we arrived a few minutes ago, I informed New Scotland Yard, and their collator has just finished talking to me. Apparently at 3.00am this morning one of our officers took a statement from a young petrol station attendant.'

'He reckoned that he had seen an Arabic or Mediterranean looking gentleman with a very deep scar on his left cheek driving an old grey Volvo estate two days ago. The chap filled the tank and changed a sidelight bulb that's how he remembers him. That, he said pointing to a dark grey N registered Volvo estate, parked under a window of a house some 30 yards away, could be the car.'

'What have we got in place right now, and what's on its way?'

'We have already got one armed response unit on site; we nicked them from Heathrow it only took them five minutes to get here. There is another on its way, we have a dog and handler, and the police chopper is about ¼ mile away just tootling around until needed. At the moment I don't think whoever is in there knows we are here.'

'The plan at the moment is to get two of the four man ARU round the back unseen, we used the rear gardens and they are now in position. I intend using the bullhorn on the car, and try to get them to come out. If they don't I will bring in the chopper he will hover about 50 foot off the top of the roof, it should dis-orientate whoever is in there, under cover of the noise our lads will go in via the back door.'

'They have very specific orders to bring them out alive, whatever that means I do not honestly know, we have no actual knowledge of anybody being in there, the house could be empty. But I doubt it.'

'An excellent plan Chief Inspector, if somebody was watching the street from the front windows how many house do you think he might be able to see?'

'Just those eight on the other side because of the bend I would think, why?'

'Might I just run this past you?' They spoke for a few minutes and put Sir Bernard's plan into action.

The gas board van pulled up at number 32, the driver got out carrying his hand held devise for recording meter readings and a clip board, he knocked on the door, showed the clipboard to the person who opened it, and was invited in the door was closed. He repeated this for numbers 34, 38,42,44,46, and 50 just for good measure.

He took a 10 minute break and then apparently came back the other way, knocking at Mrs Symonds door quite vigorously. Rashid was watching from an upstairs window, he had seen the gas board man go into some of the houses opposite, why only some? Then he realised they were the ones that worked through the day he was obviously checking their meters or whatever he did.

He was ringing the bell now, looking up and pointing to the meter reader devise, and waving at the window, he's seen me thought Rashid. I will have to let him in then that will stop him coming back tomorrow.

He went down the staircase and into the hall and towards the front door, a 747 jumbo or something was passing overhead the noise was horrendous, it was in fact the police helicopter slowly passing overhead at fifty feet, he opened the door and tried to speak to the man, the gas board man accidentally dropped his meter reader on the carpet and slowly bent down to pick it up, as he straightened up, he pointed to something over Rashid's shoulder.

Rashid turned half round and found him looking down the muzzles of 2 Heckler Koch sub machine guns held by two people dressed completely in black. He made to turn round and run out of the front door and walked straight into the gas board man who was now holding a very large looking Browning automatic. They quickly handcuffed him and laid him face down on the hall way floor; one man searched him thoroughly and then stood with one foot on his back so he couldn't move.

The other searched the house and it was some ten minutes before he declared it safe to enter; they found the bodies of Mrs Symonds, and Patrick. They also found the 'stinger' and two missiles.

## 7.30pm Saturday 2nd November 2003    47, Caledonian way

Number 47 was a hive of controlled activity, the stinger had been removed, the two bodies were taken to Hounslow morgue after the scene of crimes officer, and the duty Police Doctor had finished.

Sir Bernard looked up as another large aircraft passed at very low level, it would be like shooting fish in a barrel, although he wondered if a stinger could bring down 747 Jumbo?

He took his mobile out and rang the PM. 'Somewhat better news Prime Minister,' and proceeded to tell him.

He finished by saying Chief Superintendent Gardner had been informed, and Rashid was on his way to Paddington Green, he would be held but not questioned. Gardner would do that.

# Chapter nineteen

**10.25pm Saturday 2nd November 2003 Paddington Green Police station, London.**

Rashid had been sat in the interview room for over 20 minutes, the armed policeman on the door and the one sat near him had not said a single word the whole of that time. They had just looked at him continuously. There was a knock on the door and two men entered, and sat the other side of the table facing Rashid.

The older one of the two spoke.

'I am Chief Superintendent Gardner of the anti-terrorist squad, this is Sergeant Tucker also of the anti-terrorist squad, we intend asking you some questions regarding four murders that we believe you have been involved in. Depending entirely on how you answer those questions will be the course we will take when formally charging you.'

'You have been cautioned already, however telling us nothing will not help you, assuming that you wish to be treated leniently.'

'We believe you are one of a small cell of people, some of whom are UK residents, who have carried out terrorist activities in the UK over the past two weeks, and probably even longer. We further believe that you personally shot and murdered Mrs Martine Henderson on the 15th October 2003, and that you together with one other man may have also murdered her husband Peter Henderson on the same day. You were detained following information received a short while ago at 47, Caledonian way, Hounslow, two dead persons were found in the house, we believe you murdered them both. We further believe that you had intended to shoot down the 747 aircraft of the President of the United States on the 4th November using the stinger SAM found in the said address. Your two colleagues in America

*The President Is Down*

who have been feeding you information have been arrested, one is now dead.'

Superintendent Gardner had spoken all of this without a pause, and whilst looking straight into the eyes of Rashid.

Rashid, had returned an indifferent gaze, seemingly uncaring, until Gardner had dropped the two colleagues in America into the picture.

Rashid spoke for the first time, 'I wish to speak to my embassy and to have a lawyer present before I say anything.'

Sergeant Tucker spoke, ' you are not getting a lawyer, and access to your embassy is denied. You will be dealt with under anti-terrorist legislation as you have chosen not to co-operate, which allows certain actions to be taken.

I must also inform you that the charges that will be laid against you carry the death sentence, in other words if found guilty you will be hanged by the neck until dead.'

Rashid for the first time looked uneasy, 'You can't hang me I will not permit it.'

'You won't have any say in it,' commented Tucker.

After an hour of questioning, they were not getting very far, Gardner looked at Tucker and nodded.

Tucker cautioned Rashid, and detailed the charges that would be initially laid against him, and advised him that further could follow. Under the circumstances as he was to be held under the Prevention of Terrorism Act, it was inappropriate to grant him contact with others that may at this time prejudice the investigation.

Rashid, looked totally stunned, and did not reply.

Tucker looked at Rashid, 'for the benefit of the tape, this interview is terminated at 11.30pm Saturday 2$^{nd}$ November 2003. Both men stood up and told Rashid to get up and follow them.'

Rashid was taken to the front desk, the desk sergeant looked up as they approached, Tucker identified himself and Superintendent Gardner.

He outlined the circumstances surrounding the arrest of Rashid, he them went on to detail the four charges of murder, and finally of suspicion of being involved in terrorist activities. The possession of the handgun and the surface to Air Missiles and launcher. The sergeant looked at Rashid.

'Do you understand the charges laid against you, and the severity of them?'

'You can't do this, I demand to speak to a legal representative right now.'

'Mr Rashid, you will not tell us your full name so the charge sheet will show you as simply 'Rashid', I am satisfied with the legality of the charges

145

laid against you, and will accept them. I will convene a special court to hear those charges in detail, the court will be set for 8.00am tomorrow morning. You are to be detained under the Prevention of Terrorism Act 1974 as amended, and will not be bailed.

Rashid began to shout in Arabic, he kicked out at Superintendent Gardner and then lunged towards the superintendent, but was brought to an abrupt halt by the police constable stood on his right, who hit him very hard with his clenched fist just the once.

He had heard about the bodies at Hounslow and was not feeling well disposed to Mr Rashid or whatever his name was. Rashid fell over backwards, and was dragged to his feet and taken away. Superintendent smiled his thanks to the police constable.

The following morning Rashid was taken before a special court, convened at Paddington Green Police Station.

He was remanded in custody on the holding charges of four counts of murder and being in possession of a SAM missile without due licence and authority and three other charges related to the SAM and the handgun, and finally of being suspected with others of engaging in Terrorist Activity in the UK.

He would be locked up for a very long time pending further enquiries.

That evening newspapers, and television and radio broadcasts, simply said a man had been detained and was helping police with their enquiries into the murder of Mrs Martine Henderson, who had been shot at her home in Ealing on the 15th October.

Two incidents were to take place later the same day which were deemed to be related but turned out not to be.

## 8.18am Sunday 3rd November 2003 Olney, England.

The safe house at Olney was fitted with an electronic response button, this was connected to the local police station some 4 miles away. It had to be pressed every 8 hours starting at 00.00 hours with one press, 0800 with two, and 1600 with 3, there was a 5 minute safety window.

At 8.06 officers were sent to the safe house at Olney where the informer Sugama was being held. They did not to break in as the front door was wide open, they found the body of Harry Benson in the large hallway half across the bottom two steps of the staircase, a search of the rest of the building revealed Sugama's body, he had been shot in the head twice, the strange thing was his body had been found in the cellar of the house.

## 10.46pm The Lion public house, Westbury Wiltshire, England.

Corporal Granger of No 3 Parachute Regiment had been in the pub for an hour now he had been going in there for the past few nights. By now the locals knew roughly who he was, and where he was based in Westbury. You didn't have to be a brain surgeon to understand why.

The previous night and again tonight a young Arab or Indian man about 20/25 years of age had struck up a relationship with him. They had played darts the night before, and tonight it seemed that 'Tony' wanted to do the same again. Tonight 'Tony' mentioned his friend that worked in the kitchens at the army establishment, and how she thought the man they had there ate a lot of food for a small man.

The comment had been very cleverly 'dropped' into conversation when Grainger and Tony were discussing the merits of the local talent, and takeaway food. Grainger agreed with him, and called him a greedy pig, but then has he had nothing else to do all day but eat, read, and sleep it was understandable.

He also now recalled that Tony had said that he lived in one of the houses at the back of the army establishment, and had told Grainger about some of the secure measures that had been taken to protect it recently, he had said his son had been used to playing on the land between the houses and the back of the base. Granger knew what was there, and had not disclosed anything merely nodding his head at the time to acknowledge that something was different.

Putting the two conversations together felt it was time to get back to base without too much fuss. It was approaching closing time anyway. Grainger left the pub, went casually back to his unit, stopping to grab a burger on the way, to anybody watching him, they would not realise he had clocked what had happened, Grainger's tours of Northern Ireland and the lessons learnt sometimes the hard way by his mates was too fresh. He should have gone out with a 'mate', then one of them could have followed 'Tony' home if possible.

He hadn't dared use the public phone in the square, or his mobile in case he was being observed, and they became suspicious.

He approached the guardhouse and booked himself back in and asked that the duty Sergeant and Officer see him immediately.

One thing was puzzling Lieutenant Rees-Jones and Sergeant Major Dale Turner, they had already heard that Sugama had been assassinated earlier that day, so why was anybody showing an interest in Westbury, was Grainger making it up, or seeing and reading things into the situation that were not there?

Grainger had been with the troop three years, he was solid, not prone to exaggeration or telling stories, he had to be believed. Things had been very quiet and it would not be unusual for peoples guard to be dropping a little at this stage, it was human nature.

Within the hour Sergeant Major Turner had spoken to everyone on duty that night, and warned them to be on the alert.

He had also looked through electoral roll for the area, and could not see a foreign sounding name other than a Mr & Mrs Polcheski who had been there for over 30 years and were of Polish extraction, they did not have a son living with them, who in turn could have had a small son. One of the civilian night staff manning the cameras lived on the estate, he confirmed there were no persons matching the description given to him of 'Tony' living on the estate, or in the immediate vicinity.

At 3.00am an elderly Vauxhall Omega came into Westbury a little too quickly, got out of control when approaching the MOD facility entrance and hit the wall. The nearside front wing was badly damaged and the front end would never be the same again. A middle aged man climbed unsteadily out of the car and then collapsed on the pavement. The Para Corporal, manning the gate moved towards the man speaking as he did so.

The man appeared to be in some pain with his left shoulder and leg, he said he had also bumped his head.

Corporal Woods, told him to stay as he was and put a blanket he found on the back seat under his head, he called for an ambulance.

Corporal Woods's colleague did not take any part, he just quietly observed and did not approach.

The ambulance was on its way from Warminster it would be about 10 minutes.

At 3.04am an indicator on the temporary switch board lit up, it indicated a low voltage wire intertwined into the barbed wire section at K175 had been cut. The area was on the side of the premises, and at the rear of a deserted pub, which was for sale. The inner section wire was cut exactly 1 minute later.

Staff Sergeant Pete Brook was stood behind the operator of the security camera's and watching what appeared to be 2 men on hand and knees, coming through the inner wire. He could see one was armed with some sort of pistol, he didn't know about the other. The colour cameras were superb, and the definition was great. It was just as though they were looking at it in daylight.

He was speaking calmly on his radio, 'There are 2 believed male intruders, both dressed totally in black, at least one is armed, I repeat at least one is armed. Points one and two put on your flash goggles and confirm, points three and four shut your eyes now, and turn away. On the count of 3 they will be caught in the middle ground and in the floodlights. You all know what to do. I want them alive but don't take chances.'

'ONE-TWO-THREE, on came the 2,000,000 candle power floodlights, they would be totally blinding to the intruders. *'PUT YOUR WEAPONS DOWN AND LIE FACE DOWN ON THE FLOOR NOW.'*

One of the men dropped a pistol on the ground and immediately lay down, the other made to do so and then fired two shots rapidly at a faint shadow on the other side of the lights. The sound of his shots had hardly died away when there were six sharp cracks, his body convulsed at it hit the ground.

The other man laid on the ground cried out in pain as a stray bullet hit him in the leg. He was unceremoniously dragged away and searched, plastic handcuffs were placed on him, then they looked to his wounds.

The two Para's at the gate turned when they heard the gun shots, they had obviously been listening anyway to Staff Sergeant Brook on the radio. When they turned back the car accident man, was running away down the road towards Westbury centre. Unfortunately for him a police patrol car was coming up the hill in response to the road accident and the high alert status at the base. He quite sensibly gave himself up, he wasn't going to get shot for a mere £50 fuck that for a game of soldiers!!.

The army took the injured motorist into custody, who continued to claim his innocence, saying he only ran because he had heard some shots, and didn't want to get involved. He had been for a night out with friends, and was going home to Bath. When it was not very politely pointed out that he was driving a stolen motor car, and that he was taking the long road to bath. He changed his mind and began to talk.

Corporal Grainger identified the dead man as the one he knew as 'Tony', the other man he had not seen before.

Both men would be detained pending further enquiries, Chief Inspector Harrison was on his way to speak to both men he would see them at around 8.00am.

# Chapter twenty

**8.00am Monday 3rd November 2003. Andrews Air Force Base Md 89th Presidential Airlift Group.**

The activity on the base was intense but controlled, technicians from Boeing and Rockwell had been carrying out final equipment checks since the early hours, the two 747 aircraft of the Presidential fleet, had both been air-tested and had required little doing to them. The catering company was due to deliver its supplies at around 11.00am, and the chef and his team where already on board.

General Bloomberg was in conversation with Colonel Masters who would command AIR FORCE ONE, General Bloomberg due to retire at the end of the month was also flying in AF One as mission commander and in overall command of the trip as far as the two aircraft were concerned. He was flying with AIR FORCE ONE at the specific request of the President George T Clayton in recognition of 20 plus years he had been involved with, and then in total charge of the Presidential Fleet.

General Bloomberg looked up at the four men polishing the fuselage of one of the 747's, two master sergeants and a Air Force Colonel were issuing orders, and meticulously checking and cross checking from a mass of documentation. A perimeter of marines was carefully checking everybody who wished to enter or exit the defined zone around AF One.

At 2.00pm the flight crew were to be briefed on the mission, the meteorologist was already collating his information for the briefing, which would be brought up to date 1 hour and then again 5 minutes from take off.

*The President Is Down*

The staffers going with the President and First Lady, would be on board by 6.00pm, the President was due to arrive at 6.15pm and inspect the Marine contingent, and award two marines with medals earned in Iraq.

The flight crew were due on board at 4.00pm, and the flight attendants at 5.00pm.

The take off slot for AIR FORCE ONE was 7.00pm that evening.

At 6.10 precisely the Presidential helicopter escorted by two Black hawks hove in to view and landed dead centre on the landing site. The door opened and the internal steps were let down, the rotor blades were coming to a halt as the 43rd President of the United States of America stood in the doorway and waved to everybody and nobody in particular. He descended the steps, and turned to hold the hand of the first lady as she followed him.

Both were greeted on the red carpet by the base Commander Brigadier General Walt Caldwell, who smartly saluted the President and first Lady, and led them down the carpet to the parading Marines. The President went slowly down the line, and spoke to all. Upon reaching the final two, he accepted medals from a Marines Major and pinned them on the chests of the two marines, he spoke to them both for a couple of minutes each, before standing back and saluting the parade.

The President and the first Lady, walked the short distance to AIR FORCE ONE and were introduced by General Caldwell to the Flight crew, and finally to General Bloomberg. The President shook the hand of General Bloomberg and put his other hand on his arm in a show of affection. He spoke for a minute to General Bloomberg, turned round to face all those in the hanger, and waved. He and the First Lady climbed the steps to AIR FORCE ONE, and with a brief further wave when they reached the top of the stairs went out of sight.

At 6.52pm the huge hanger doors were rolled back and AIR FORCE ONE tail number 29000 was towed out of the hanger, the engines had already been started, and AF One taxied onto the main huge runway at Andrews. It held for 2 minutes for final checks and then at precisely 7.00pm local time it thundered down the runway, and lifted off into darkened sky.

Boeing 747 United State of America tail plane 28000 had taken of nine hours ago, it carried the marine's contingent, staff members and other,. and would be landing at Northolt, England about now.

A call was made on a mobile telephone from a diner just down the road from Andrews A.F. base, the caller spoke to his cousin in England and told him they had posted his birthday present and in fact there was two.

The call meant that the Presidents aircraft had taken off, and that he believed the landing site was (2) i.e.

Heathrow, London.

Colonel Masters and his crew settled down for the long 9 hour flight to England, he would decide where to land a little nearer the time.

The President was in his mini 'oval office' quite alone, he was reading and trying to assimilate a report from the US Energy Information Administration on the Global situation regarding Oil.

The main points were;

1. It was undeniable that the price of oil was at its highest ever, and set to rise.
2. The Chinese demand for oil accounted more than 1/3$^{rd}$ of the Global increase for oil. This would only increase.
3. America consumes one-quarter of the world's oil production. This is rising
4. American oil was at its lowest production level since the 1950's
5. Since 1970 American reserves have fallen from **50bn barrels** to **20bn barrels.**
6. Saudi Arabia, possess 25% of the world's oil reserves.. killings of Oil officials, and bombs in Riyadh. and the vulnerability of the Saudi's oil infrastructure reduced throughput dramatically.
7. Iraq, sits on the second largest reserves in the World, killing oil executives, attacking pipelines etc, all meant lower production than when Saddam ruled before the embargo.

**Consumption.**

Demand for oil increases at 2% per annum we consume 78m barrels of oil a day, this is projected to rise 112m by 2020

**Supply.**

Major oil finds peaked in 1964. In 2000 there were 13 new oil fields discovered, 2001 only one and

in 2002 there were 2 and in 2003 NONE

It didn't make good reading, he expected during his talks to be touching on the subject of oil, and what it was felt could be done about. There was a whole raft of other documentation to wade through, but that would have to wait until after dinner. The President and the First Lady were hosting a small dinner party for General Bloomberg to thank him for all he had done for the various Presidents of the United States.

The 4 Strike Eagles were in position and the AWAC's was some distance ahead. AIR FORCE ONE now at 40,000ft flew on towards the rising sun, and the British Isles.

Some hours later the US Air Force AWAC's radioed ahead and squared his position for the British air traffic control he was still around 100 miles ahead of AF 1. And about some 300 miles from the English coast.

US Air Force AWAC's call sign Delta 60 be advised you will see four blips on your screen around now, these are the 4 Harriers from HMS Ark Royal, speak with red leader on Guard channel, I repeat Guard channel, he will fly the box to your advice. Acknowledge please.

US AF AWAC's call sign Delta 60 I acknowledge, we have your Harriers on radar, they are painted as friendly.

Lieutenant Commander Paul Preston was leading the four GR9 Harriers, and had positioned his flight as requested

Some 50 miles out from AF1 one in the front one behind, and one to each side, the Strike eagles had now closed up on the President's aircraft and each were one mile distance at 50,000 ft

Debs the flight attendant was young 20 yrs of age, bubbly and up for it, she had rubbed him up now four times in the flight. The first time he had thought he had imagined it. The second time whilst bringing him his coffee, in the crew resting bunk her left hand had settled on his crotch where you could just see the outline of his penis in his trousers, she had looked him in eyes, and rubbed it a couple of times and then squeezed it gently. It had the desired effect as he started to harden she equally quickly moved away, and waving a kiss at him moved back from the flight deck.

He followed her to the kitchen at the back of the flight deck it was 2.00am and all were asleep or trying to catch a few minutes whilst they could, the cabin lights were down and Debs was the only member of the flight service crew awake. He came up behind her and moved his hands gently from behind gently up her waist and to her firm but yielding breasts. He gently squeezed them and her hand came behind her and reached for his hardening penis, she eased down his zip gently worked it out of his trousers, he turned her round and pushed her head down but she pulled back, and lifted up her dress, she had nothing on underneath. She leant back against the kitchen wall, and lifting up her left leg he slid into her, with his trousers round his ankles she lifted up her right leg and wrapped them both round him. The vibration of the aircraft on her back, was transferred to him, it increased the pleasure and they came together with a satisfying shudder, and a little scream of pure pleasure from her.

One hundred miles out from the British coast and the Presidential Boeing started a gradual decent from 40,000 ft.

Colonel Masters now had to decide which of the five landing sites to use. In true democratic style he let his new 'Girl Friend', who his wife would kill if you got to find .out--- choose, she chose London Heathrow. Debs had now played her part. And just to make sure she gently teased and squeezed him another twice before landing.

Colonel Masters was already phantasizing, a quick dinner and show if he had to, back to the hotel, and screw that sweet little arse for all he was worth. He was in dreamland, 47 years of age and having sex with a 20/22 year old.

The aircraft was under close protection now, the Harriers were a mere two miles around him, and the four Strike Eagles at 25 miles, the original four had turned for home nearly four hours ago.

Colonel Masters informed General Bloomberg that he had selected London Heathrow. Would he please check with the President it was OK. ----- It was.

Now at 9,000 ft they crossed the coast near Brighton, they had flown short of the normal entry point to avoid the usual traffic coming in from Australia, Hong Kong, and Asia generally, plus the normal US traffic. They were now between the 'Box' over Kent that was stacking some traffic and letting others through. AIR FORCE ONE was coming straight in.

A BA flight from Singapore was put into the holding box, this allowed AF1 to come on final approach behind an Air India 757 from Delhi the Presidential flight was in the middle of a gap of six minutes which was not normally there. Aircraft come in at a single minute gap between each most of the day. The 3 minutes gap behind the Air India and the 3 minutes in front of the Air New Zealand flight 747 from New Zealand would allow AF1 to land and clear onto the Alcock and Brown VIP stand.

AF1 had lost its Strike Eagles they had pulled away whilst over Kent, and two of the harriers were escorting the 747, they were positioned ½ mile either side one slightly in front and one slightly behind. The flight of three passed over the city at 2,000 ft, and in and out of the low cloud base, the flight was largely unnoticed, however one individual at the top of the deserted post office tower watched with his powerful binoculars, and passed a short message on his open mobile, it had been open for some ten minutes, to ensure he was in contact at the vital time.

They were at 1,500 feet now and nearly directly overhead ' Kew ' gardens, the Jumbo's landing gear came down and the flaps were now fully extended, Colonel Masters was flying the aircraft, no auto-landings for the chief they were all 'greased' or there was hell to pay. A slight correction to the right, visual flight rules applied, he could see the end of the runway

## The President Is Down

just under 2 miles away. Rashid would have missed with his stinger, the aircraft was just a little too far over to the right..

AIR FORCE ONE was over the boundary marker and dropping down on to the main runway running parallel to the A4 Bath Road, the RAF Harrier in front was pealing away to his right and climbing out towards the M4 his intention was a low level flight into RAF Northolt just than a minute away. The other Harrier flown by Lt Commander Paul Preston he was at 500ft and 200 yards behind AF1 and to its left, putting him over the airfield.

AIR FORCE ONE was some 30ft off the ground when the Harrier pilot saw a flash from a hotel window on his right and seemingly instantaneously AIR FORCE ONE shook, the tail plane appeared to break in half, everything was in slow motion, Colonel Masters must have poured on the power as the nose came up and the aircraft started to gain height, it reached about 100ft and started a slow rotating roll to the right away from the runway and towards the busy A4 Bath road. The time was exactly 6.45am GMT

The right wingtip sliced through the top of a building housing an airport food preparation facility, 11 people were killed in the offices, and the debris falling through the floor would mean 8,000 aircraft meals would not get delivered that day or for the next week. A taxi driver seeing the jumbo coming at him turned hard left at 35mph into hatch lane, one of his passengers would later sue him for £100,000 for a broken arm

The jumbo hit the A4 at 120mph, the right wing broke off and the two engines on it detached and destroyed 2 multi story buildings and over 40 parked cars, also killing three people walking and two drivers of delivery vehicles.

A bus on its way to an off airport car park and carrying 30 people was met by the main body of the fuselage sliding towards it semi-sideways down the A4, all on board were killed, AIR FORCE ONE continued its flight of destruction, and was now sliding down the slight hill towards the roundabout at the air side of the tunnel under the main runway. It was nearly spent now and was finally stopped by a bread van waiting patiently with other traffic to go through the tunnel and into the airport. The driver dived out and ran across the road, he was hit a glancing blow by a Mercedes exiting the tunnel and broke his leg. His bread van was crushed.

There was a deathly silence, people looked unbelieving at what they saw, a 747, huge at the best of time but now totally overwhelming, there was no fire, and no sound from the aircraft, some recognised it for what it was, and would dine out for months and years telling the tale. Others grabbed cameras. The rear section of the fuselage had broken off and had spilled a number of bodies onto the A4 some were dead and some very seriously injured

The Harrier pilot had gone into a hover, just to the left of the scene and was acting as on site incident controller until the emergency services arrived. He had reported the flash from the hotel, and police officers were already there whilst others were now arriving at the scene.

# Chapter twenty-one

**6.50am 4th November 2003. The Palace Hotel, Bath Road, Heathrow, London.**

The receptionist was quite bright, she thought through the people occupying the front of the hotel, and came up with two couples and one child who could fit the bill.

Officers immediately got themselves invited in to the bedrooms of the two couples, as everybody in the hotel must have heard the aircraft crash, there was no problem in getting people up or waking them up. The two couples were cleared within seconds. The Police constable knocked on the door of the 16 year old boy in room 310, there was no answer, he could be down to breakfast with his parents, another knock. Then the PC smelt something,' unlock this door and stand back please' this to the chambermaid who had accompanied him. She did so, and he pushed past, the boy was not in the room, but a stinger SAM was, and one round of ammunition the wall and carpet was still smouldering from the backwash/flare of the missile.

The PC immediately radioed his findings, and ran downstairs to reception, 'what's the room number of the kid's parents?'

'257 at the back,' and handed him the key.

The PC shouted to one of the armed officers, 'come with me please,' and made for the stairs. Outside room 257 they both stood to one side, and the first PC knocked on the door, there was no reply, he knocked again there was no reply, he inserted the key in the door and carefully opened it. There was nobody in the room.

The room was immaculate, not a thing out of place, they would later find all evidence of the two people that had occupied the room had been removed.

After firing the Stinger, Mr Brown had left room 310 and calmly walked along the corridor and down the rear stairs to 257. His 'Wife', was awaiting him, she had a carrier bag with some clothing in it. Together they unhurriedly went down the back stairs and into the rear car park the got into their car and drove out onto the main A4 which was deserted and turning left headed to Hounslow West Tube station. On the way Mr Brown took the two cheek pads out of his mouth, and peeled off his ginger-red 'eyebrows. He then removed his ginger wig replacing it with a dark haired one with a side parting; it was similar to his own hair which would grow back eventually.

Whilst he went to get the parking ticket Mrs Brown removed her platinum blond wig and spectacles now revealing her naturally brown short hair style. Ten minutes later they were on the underground and heading for Waterloo rail terminal.

35 minutes later at Waterloo station Mr Brown took two suitcases from the left luggage office and linking arms Mr and Mrs Brown strolled to the Euro-star terminal for their journey to Paris. An hour later they were enjoying breakfast and watching the Kent countryside glide past.

Upon reaching the Gare-du-Nore rail station in Paris, Mrs Brown deposited in one of the rubbish bins the first of ten little cut up sections of white coveralls, they had worn these for the whole of their time in the hotel, with latex gloves, catering hairnets and duster disposable overshoes. There was little forensic material for the Police to examine in the Palace hotel.

The contact address they had given was false, and they had paid by cash, so there was no credit card link. The link would never be made to their rented home in Oxford. Their 16 year old boy Jamie was never seen, because he never existed. The car was bought for cash already taxed and tested, it was never insured and the ownership was never changed.

Their car would be found two days later and a sticky ticket put on the windscreen, the next day it would be removed to a council pound, 4 weeks later it would be crushed. A letter would inform the last registered owner that the car he had sold 2 months ago had been crushed. 'As if he cared'

Paris was the second home of 42 year old Derek John Reynolds, alias Mr Brown US citizen, ex-US marine, ex-foreign legion, one of a breed of men whose gun and expertise was for hire. He only took the occasional 'contract' this one was worth £200,000 and would see him OK for the next 3 years. Long enough for people to forget.

*The President Is Down*

He didn't know or care who had paid him for the job, he only knew he was possibly Russian, and paid well.

He had now built up a tidy sum in 11 bank accounts throughout France, Spain and Greece, and was worth £1.6m at the last count. Mrs Brown a 35 yr old ex-prostitute gave him fantastic sex, was devoted to him and was proving to be an able assistant. They would stay together for many years and would never get caught.

On the TV news at 6.00pm Arial pictures were shown of the Presidents Aircraft AIR FORCE ONE, it showed the
fuselage in two pieces, the larger section with most of the left wing intact was resting on a bus and a bread van, both of which were crushed, the tail section had broken off and was in a hotels front car park, the other wing lay on its own huge and blocking one of lanes of the dual carriageway, the two right engines had damaged buildings and many cars.

The death Toll was believed to be 63 and rising, 18 people were injured to a greater or lesser extent.

The President and the First Lady were in a private hospital, there was no news of their condition.

There was an interview with the youngest member of the flight crew Debs Henry, who was crying for the loss of life on board and that of the aircrafts captain Colonel Masters, she said she had served him coffee in the early hours, and even though he was very busy how he had taken time out to talk to her. Such a nice kind man, she would miss him. And knew his wife would.

# Chapter twenty-two

**11.05am Tuesday 4th November 2003. The Cabinet Office, Downing Street, London.**

The cabinet office is in fact a large board-room, this is where the British cabinet of MP's who hold high office such as The Prime Minister, The Chancellor of the Exchequer, etc all sit in 'Cabinet' and deliberate on the Nations problems and decide on Government strategy and policy. It is in fact a large board room, at the rear of number 10 and leads on to a superb garden.

The British Prime Minister Tony Salter, the Home Secretary Geoffrey Aspinall , and various involved Secretaries of State, also represented were the security forces, and intelligence services of both Britain and the United States.

Tony Salter started the meeting, 'some of you were here but hours ago, for others it is your first time, the briefing documents you have in front of you are comprehensive and common to all of you. If you have already seen some of it, then you can ignore it, I wanted your colleagues who were not previously here to have the exact same information you already have.'

'Firstly we should start by saying the President and first lady are injured but not dead. The American Ambassador to the United Kingdom Alfred Henry is here, he nodded to him. Ambassador Henry has just left the bedside of The President and the First Lady. He tells me he is advised they are gravely ill. They will remain here in the UK until stabilised and then will fly back to the States. Their personal physician was on board with the President unfortunately he was one of those killed as was the Mission Commander General Greenberg.'

*The President Is Down*

'Of the 88 people on board AIR FORCE ONE 34 were killed outright, 6 people have subsequently died of their injuries, and 8 are seriously ill, 4 have minor injuries not requiring hospitalisation 36 are uninjured most of them were towards to rear of the aircraft and some of them were in the tail section that broke away'.

'I am going to hand you over to the Home Secretary.'

The Home Secretary Geoffrey Aspinall commenced. 'Of the actual attack on AF 1 we know from the observations of the Harrier pilot, only one missile was used and that it was fired from the second floor window (three floors up) of a bedroom in the Palace Hotel, on Bath road, Heathrow. Another warhead was found in the room. The Missile and launcher were Stingers of American manufacture.'

'We know from the previous good work by Sir Bernard and his team, and the security services of the United Kingdom, America, Greece, Spain and France that we have all three Stinger Launchers and have recovered 5 of the six warheads if that's what we call them.'

'The consignment of missiles, had been removed from a cache of buried IRA stockpiled arms that we knew of in Northern Ireland, there will I am sure be others that we don't have intelligence on.'

'The weapons were transported by private sailing vessel across the Irish Sea, and to a port in Cumbria on the west coast of England, they were then taken to Birmingham by road, and delivered to the buyer at a hotel some few days ago. From there the stingers were split up.'

'One we recovered from a house in London. The second we recovered from a house in Uxbridge directly on the flight path of AF1 which would have been at a height of about 150ft I am advised when passing. The third as you know was used to devastating effect.'

'The person's using the Heathrow stinger would appear to be a white male, maybe American-Australian or even British, he is in his mid forties with vivid red hair, his wife is a little younger, she is a blonde, and they supposedly have a sixteen year old son, although nobody at the hotel ever saw him. They could be genuinely blonde and red head; it could also be one big dis-information act if they are the professionals I fear they are. Currently scene of crimes officers are pulling the two hotel rooms apart, although I have to say from first reports I am not hopeful.'

' However whilst Mr & Mrs Brown the two referred to may be professionals, others involved most certainly are not. We have in custody five people who are being detained under the Prevention of Terrorism Act 1974'.

1. **Rashid.** The only name we have at the moment, Arab- possibly British.

'We believe he murdered Martine Henderson the wife of one of our MI6 agents, we also believe he murdered her husband Peter Henderson about 3 hours before her. We know he shot and killed a man who was a member of a Provisional IRA active service unit, who were tracking down the arms, and would have told us where they were. He also caused the death of an elderly lady with whom he was lodging. He may also have caused the death of an informant Abdullah Sugama we had in protective custody, and of our man Harry Benson who was baby sitting him.'

'Not a pleasant man. Documents on him and a passport suggest 'Al Qaeda' His familiarity and ruthless use of weapons supports that theory.'

2. **Tony.** ' Arab/British. Believed from Bradford West Yorkshire.' (Shot dead in gun battle with No 3 Para).

3. **Peter Aziz** 'Father from Morocco, mother British from Halifax, West Yorkshire.'

' Peter lives with his father in Bradford now, and went to the same mosque as 'Tony', he surrendered in the shoot-out'.

'2 & 3 are a bit of a puzzle, they broke into a secure Army establishment to kill Abdullah Sugama, but he was no longer there and had not been for many days, Sugama's killers knew, and knew where to find him.'

*'I think that might be an easy one', someone piped up from the back.*

*'If it's a Jihad, and somebody has offended, remember Salman Rushdie, then he is fair game and many could come after him.'*

' Thank you for that's actually what Mr Groves of the CIA thought.'

4. **'Mr Henry James Peters and Mrs Rose Peters,** Both British'.

'He and his wife were picked up in Spain whilst on holiday, he sold the weapons on, and he bought them from as he thought from the IRA, in the event he was wrong a IRA minion of past decided on a bit of private enterprise, the IRA man has since been found drowned, we are told a 'fishing' accident.

**Peters** fancies himself as an un-licensed small time arms dealer, his wife we feel has nothing to do with it, although she might have inkling that all was not quite Kosher.'

    5.    **'Mr Michael Jessup,** British'.

' He stole a car and crashed it into a military establishment as a diversion so other could enter. without doubt he was just earning ' beer' money as far as he was concerned,

'Thank you gentlemen, we will take a break at this point, have some coffee, and then I will open the meeting up'.

# Chapter twenty-three

**6.30am Thursday 6th November 2003, RAF Northolt, London England.**

The BAe146 of the Queens flight lifted off for the continent taking with it The Prince Paul of Scotland. The nephew of Her Majesty the Queen of England.

He was to make a speech to the assembly of the European Parliament later that morning.

At 10.30am he stood at the rostrum, and was introduced by the current President of The European Union Michel Faber a German.

When the applause had died down, he started:

'I well remember talking with Ted Heath before we joined the EEC in 1973; at first I have to say I wasn't really convinced that we should, after all how would the people of the British Isles would feel about being taken over by the French and Germans, as assuredly they would? Remember two World Wars in the Century only 21 year apart.' There was shocked silence this was pretty direct stuff and typical Prince Paul.

'Then we came in, and had years of butter mountains, lakes of wine, -- although I can't remember being offered any, ----- wine that is. I think my wife bought some butter, 'they laughed at this, and they were now being to get his dry sense of humour.' Pigs and cattle at different compensation prices. ------Then to cap it all they wanted our bloody pound, again more laughter.'

'Now of course we still have our problems, as a huge and diverse family we always will, look at mine for a damn good example of what not to do. Again the laughter, they were enjoying him. The problems of today are integration, member countries increasing in number, a unified

Germany again, doing the balancing between different currencies, health care, housing, jobs, defence, illegal immigrants, and the new one to most of us ----- terrorism.'

'Why as this suddenly reared its head globally as it has? -- What can we do about it? -- Well together perhaps a lot more than single Countries and States on their own. Let us all pray that is the case. Only two days ago we had a major terrorist incident in London, tragically many were killed when the aircraft carrying the President of The United States, George T. Clayton with his wife was shot down whilst coming in to land at Heathrow.'

He paused for effect!!!!----' Why I am telling you about this latest terrorist incident when he can tell you himself.

Ladies Gentlemen, I give you Mr George T Clayton and his wife Amanda the President of the United States and the First Lady.'

There was a stunned silence and then the parliament erupted with cheering and hand clapping, as the familiar figure of George T and the First Lady walked together onto the platform hand in hand.

Prince Paul stood back and also clapped them, George T turned round and shook Prince Philips hand and said something to him, which brought a broad grin to the Princes face.

The first Lady stepped back and joined Prince Paul.

The President walked up to the rostrum;

'My Friends I thank you for allowing me to talk with you today, and for the Lord in making it possible'.

It was actually planned that I might drop in to see you whilst in England if it had been possible for you to accept me at short notice. I wanted to come and to personally thank you for your support over various matters in the last two or three years'. Albeit we have had differences of opinion on certain matters Iraq in particular. We always will have problems of some sort.'

'What you are doing, and achieving is unbelievable, integrating most of Europe into one big Union, bigger in fact than the USA. Keep at it the most difficult days are past, the rewards are coming!!!'

Again applause from the assembly.

'I had a speech, written for me by those well intentioned people, who only ever see an office and its four walls, this is that speech.' He drew an A4 folder from behind his back.

'Well I don't need it now, because when you have come that close, he pinched his fingers together to show about an inch gap. To losing your life, and seeing your loved one lose theirs, ------ when you have met evil face to face and had the good fortune to survive. ----My friends I tell you, ------ you change, for most of us there is no other life, we are here only once, we bicker we squabble, we fight and for what? Most of us have all that we need in life, some of us have more than we need, and half the World starves,---- that's right half the World has not got enough food, ---- or clean drinking water or shelter, ----- no medical aid,----- NOTHING !!! '

'And we continue to squabble because it's the survival of the fittest that's what we have always been told. But hey,--------sure we put our hands in our pockets and give the loose change to charity, and FEEL BETTER for it, we have done our bit. ---- Bull shit. We have done diddly-squat, that means in polite society,------ NOTHING.'

'I want to tell you about a report I read whilst flying over the Atlantic; It frightened me to death: He read the report on oil to the Parliament who listened in rapt attention.

'Know what that means, we gotta get our act together otherwise there ain't gonna be anything to fight and squabble over. ---We have to find alternate means of sustainable energy, energy that we can transfer to the third world. Affordable energy that will not run out, and in the meantime, and this is NOT a cop out we have to make better use of what we have got'.

'Throughout the World we have the brainiest people that ever walked this earth, put those specialists and experts TOGETHER, not working apart with this Company and that Company, --- but together. Do you think we would get there quicker? I do. A Truly International team, well funded could concentrate on Fuel cells, Solar energy, Hydrogen, Wave and Wind energy.------ They could do it.'

Applause to this which was spontaneous and lengthy.

'There are two other things I would like to touch on':

'The first is world poverty, there should not be ANY, ----- ANYWHERE we throw away more staple food stuffs every day that could reduce, or even eradicate starvation. Why do we throw it away?'

'Because it would COST too much, to get it where it's needed and here's the killer,------ NOBODY would make any money out of it. I won't upset the relief organizations as they do a wonderful job, but WE, ----WE POLITITIANS could do more. And again why don't we put the best brains on it Internationally,-- and fund it Internationally.---- Let's teach them how to feed themselves and provide the means to do it.--- Let's get to the real root of the problem, not the cosmetic bit as we do now.'

Again spontaneous and lengthy applause.

'And finally Terrorism;'

'It's always been amongst us Genghis Khan, more recently Hitler, and now Al-Qaeda, Osama Bin Laden and the Taliban, why would the Taliban destroy the beautiful city of Kabul in Afghanistan, destroy its museums and its history and cripple its people. How can these people be allowed to get away with it. And to spread their terror? No we have to fight all terrorism in all its forms,---- with every resource we have got 24 hours a day, --- 365 days a year until they realise they cannot touch us and get away with it. Most Moslem's World over do not support terrorism.'

'If we don't our children and our children's children, will reap those terrible rewards, ---the refugees, who had nothing to start with, --- and lose anything else they might have left, --- their homes,----- their families, even ultimately their lives,---everything. It will only increase. There is no evil that can't be beaten, lets beat it together!! Thank you'. And God Bless you all.'

To rapturous applause and a standing ovation he stood for a full two minutes, then with one last wave put his arm through Amanda's and walked off the stage to the rear.

# Chapter twenty-four

**9.30am Thursday 6th November 2003, Skala, Kefalonia, Greece.**

The two men had been fishing of the rocks for the last two hours they seemed content not to have caught anything other than a small octopus, which one had smashed against the rocks to kill it, perhaps it would be part of his dinner that night.

At just after 9.30am their patience was rewarded, when they saw the young boy come out of the double iron gates at the entrance to the luxury villa on the waters edge. Young Peter Astinikis wheeled his cycle out through the gates and waved goodbye to somebody the men could not see. Peter mounted his cycle and rode off towards Skala town along the winding coast road.

His journey should take him a little over ten minutes to reach his friends who would be playing football in the playground at the back of the school, just of the main street.-- He would not get there.

They got in the scruffy battered white van and gently set off after him, they were about 50m behind when he passed the fishing boat restaurant, and saw the two waiters shout something to him and wave, he waved back. They drove past him, and got out of the vehicle and opened one of the van doors at the rear, one of the men stood casually by the door whilst the other was looking at and feeling the nearside wheel, as though something was wrong with it.

As Peter approached, the man near the rear door shouted at him something Peter could not quite hear about a punctured tyre. Peter stopped near the man, the one that had been stood near the front wheel, came up behind Peter grabbed him very firmly, and threw him through the open rear door of the van. The other man jumped into the van and shut the doors.

## The President Is Down

The man who had been standing near the front, now picked up the cycle and threw it into ditch which had a few inches of water in it, and became nearly submerged. The whole thing had taken less then sixty seconds and had gone unobserved. Peter started to struggle and shout, the man in the back of the van hit him hard across his face and Peter stopped. His legs and arms were taped together with heavy duty industrial tape, He was pushed onto a dirty mattress and told he was not going be hurt if he behaved himself. He left arm was fastened to one of the van body uprights.

Two hours later the van turned off the main Argostoli – Fiskardo road, about two kilometres from the Assos

turn-off. They drove through the olive trees and pulled up outside an old farmhouse, the shutters were broken or missing on some of the windows on the first floor, all had been repaired on the ground floor. An old lady had heard them coming and opened the farmhouse door, a mangy looking dog shot out and ran into the olive grove before the man could kick it.

The man in the back dragged Peter out, he fell on the dusty ground as his legs had been folded under him for the bets part of two hours, and had lost sensation. The man dragged him to his feet picked him up and roughly put him over his shoulder. Peters head hit the doorframe a glancing blow as they went through, and the first man shouted at the second to be more careful.

Peter was taken to a rear bedroom and thrown on the floor. The room had a bed, a small table and chair an oil lamp and a bucket in the corner of the room. On the table was a large jug of water some soap and a towel. Everything was dirty and grubby. Peter was close to tears but wouldn't give in his father had always said he wasn't allowed to cry, he had to lead men later in life and had to be harder than them, but always compassionate. He tried very hard now to do as his father had said.

The door slammed shut, and he was left on his own, he looked at his wristwatch, it showed 11.45am the room was pretty dark as both shutters were shut and locked, light streamed through the two broken lattice sections of each single shutter, and when his eyes adjusted he found it was lighter than he had expected.

He looked in his pockets for anything that could help him get out, and found his old little broken bladed penknife not much good, and only used for sharpening pencils, and opening clam shells. They hadn't searched him yet, so he hid the knife in the edge the mattress and hoped it wouldn't be noticed.

At 12.30pm the driver of the van opened the door and let the old lady in, she had some bread, olives, some Stifado in an earthenware dish. He was ravenous, the rich Greek beef and sweet onion stew was hot and steaming, and tasted wonderful. The old lady was a good cook. The man sat on the bed close to the table a stroked Peters fair hair, he pulled away from the man and the old lady shouted at the man and hit him hard on his shoulder. He got up and left the room. The old lady said she was sorry and pulled the door shut behind her gently. Peter heard the key turn in the lock.

What would his father do now? Peter thought he would eat his food and shout a bit to see if they came, he would look for a way out. Peter would also pretend to be frightened he was a little boy to them and should be.

He had heard the floorboards creak when the old lady had left he hadn't noticed them when the man had left.

Now for a bit of shouting, he went to the door and pounded on it with his fists, and shouted at the top of his voice that he wanted to go to the toilet. He heard footsteps, the door was unlocked and the other man who had been in the back of the van with him came in. He raised his hand to Peter who shouted , 'you hit me again and my father will chop it off.' The man hesitated and dropped his hand. And then pushed him towards the bed.

The man pointed towards the bucket, 'that's your toilet.'

'I'm not using it,' said Peter.

' It's better than the alternative,' said the man.

'Why am I here?'

'Somebody wants something your father has and he only gets you back when he supplies it, now shut and I will bring you some books to read, and a radio if you make another noise like the last one, you get nothing, understand?'

Peter wasn't missed until around 3.00pm, when he hadn't come home at 1.30pm as he should have his mother Joyce thought he was having something to eat with his friends, by 3.00pm she was just a little worried. Ari was in Athens and wouldn't be back until mid-day tomorrow.

She decided to go into Skala. She got the Range Rover out of the garage and drove into town and up the main street. A lot of the shops were shut now as the tourist season was at an end. Those that would be open were mainly closed for siesta, the bars and restaurants had very few people sat around. The playground was deserted.

She went to one of the two houses where she knew Peter had friends, their boy had not seen Peter at all, and he had been in the playground with the others playing football and other games. It was the same story at the other home.

Peter had never got there.

One of the boy's grandparents was a retired policeman, he took charge, he went to the taxi-rank telephone and called the police in Argostoli, Joyce said her husband knew Colonel George Aristostis, and he immediately

## The President Is Down

asked to be put through to him. He spoke for two minutes, then handed the phone to Joyce.

'Joyce my dear, don't worry it's probably nothing, I shall be with you in a little over half an hour, in the meantime

Petros is very good, he used to be sergeant in the local police, he will organise things until I get there.'

Petros was very good, with ten minutes he had five teams of two men searching specific area's for Peter, he had another 4 men knocking on the doors of any of the children who Peter would have played and been with that day.

Joyce was told to stay at his house for the time being, which she did, it was a lovely stone built house one of three that the old man had built for his family some years ago. They formed a semi-circle with a large piece of land it had its own clean but battered swimming pool, and set amongst old olive trees, lemons, and fig trees, it was lovely but she couldn't appreciate its beauty.

Joyce's husband had quietly done much for the local people, without showing off his wealth and they now rallied round to help without reservation.

The colonel arrived, at around the time they found Peters cycle, at that point it became apparent that something serious had happened to Peter, the local hospital knew him, but had not admitted him in the last three weeks. He had not had an accident and been taken there, the local doctor also confirmed he had not been brought to his surgery.

George had a horrible feeling that somebody was holding Peter for some reason, and the only one he could think of was money, it was no secret that his father was the richest man by far on the island.

It was now 5.00pm and around thirty men were gathered in the large assembly room in the local school in Skala, the Colonel stood on table at the front of the room and spoke to the men waiting patiently for him to speak, Peters mother Joyce was also in the room.

'As you know we have found the boys cycle, we can assume that he was taken around that spot, sergeant Petros has covered the road from the boys home to where we found the cycle, he says that a small old white van with the drivers door painted a different colour was seen going in the same direction as the boy and about 100m behind him when he passed the fish restaurant, the fish restaurant is about 500m from where we found the cycle, and the spot where we found the cycle is out view from the fish restaurant'.

We do not know if the white van has anything to do with it but at the moment it is the only thing we have got.

Sergeant Petros has lived in Skala for 40 plus years, he does not know of anybody in Skala or the next villages who has such a van. I have been in touch with police headquarters in Argostoli, all police patrols on the Island have been advised of this incident and of the van. All ports have been contacted and a watch is being kept. Athens has been informed and an all points alert has been issued.

If he has been taken away by private boat, then we have a problem, the ferries less so as we have spoken with all ferry companies, and they have confirmed that none of the four ferries that left Kefalonia in the time frame of 10.00am to 4.30pm carried a small white van as described or a boy answering Peter's description. They are now on a look out for the van and the boy. However, that is not to say that he has not been taken off the Island in another vehicle altogether.

For the time being we are going to assume he is still on the Island, every policeman is now on the lookout for Peter and for the van. Before it gets dark I would like you all to visit every house in Skala and look in any sheds, outbuildings, anywhere in fact where Peter could be. Sergeant Petros has been joined by 11 other police officers please let Sergeant Petros organise you into groups for the search, each group should have a police officer with them, who will assist if you are denied entry anywhere, or you need to report something. In any case you must report in briefly every hour to within fifteen minutes. Please do not waste time making your report, please be brief.

Please meet back here at 10.00pm unless you are asked to come back sooner, good luck and thank you. With that the Colonel climbed down off the table, he took a phone call on the one of the policeman's mobile phones, the call was from Peters father Aristo Astinikis.

'George what is happening, and where are Peter and Joyce?'

George brought him fully up to date, and found that Aristo had chartered a light aircraft and was flying back that night to Kefalonia from Athens, he should be in Skala by midnight latest, George said he would have a car waiting for him at the airport; he gave the phone to Joyce.

6.30pm darkness was closing in on the farmhouse, and the old lady went round lighting the tall glass funnelled oil lamps in the kitchen, which was also the sitting room to the farmhouse. There was a washroom and store for outdoor clothes on the ground floor, and food storage room. The old lady slept on a small wooden bed near the open fire which was also used for cooking and was permanently lit. The two men had a bedroom each on the first floor and Peter now had one of the two brother's rooms.

Theodore Pannikos was the elder brother at 45 years of age and Constantine the younger by 7 years; he had been the driver of the van. He was busy in the lean to shed where they put the farm implements and the van. He was painting the driver's door white to match the rest of the van. When he had finished he put the paint tin in a box deciding to get rid of it the following day.

# Chapter twenty-five

Friday 7th November 2003, the Villa of the Astinikis family, Skala, Kefalonia, Greece.

Ari had arrived home in the early hours, after spending over an hour with the Colonel going over what was known and what was being done, he and Joyce finally went to bed and tried to get some rest, in the event it was not possible neither could sleep, they could only think about their beloved Peter. When the dawn came it found them both out on the terrace at the rear of the villa, drinking coffee and looking out to sea. The two dogs knew something wasn't quite right and kept going to Peter's bedroom door that led onto the terrace, and whimpering.

Ari broke the silence turned to Joyce, and spoke in a very chilling quiet voice, 'when we find these people and get Peter back I swear they will never touch a child again whoever they are I promise you, and we will find him my darling whatever it takes or costs'. Joyce went into the kitchen and made them both a light breakfast which they both picked at.

At 8.00am a local police Captain from Argostoli called.

'I am Captain Gramitica, Colonel Aristostis has asked me to co-ordinate the search and enquiry, I have to tell you that I have been involved in two ' kidnappings' over the past few years, there are some difficult questions to be put to you both, and others. The Colonel felt he was perhaps too involved and that his deep affection for the family and emotion might get in the way of his judgement, which is why I am here. He has made it perfectly clear to me that he is still in overall command'.

'We understand Captain, please do not be embarrassed, you may ask any questions you wish and we will answer them as truthfully as we can.'

*The President Is Down*

'Firstly Sir, Madam Do you know of any reason why somebody would do this, can you think of anybody that would do this?'

'We have tried all night to do just that, and neither of us can think why or who would want to do this.'

'Have you had a serious disagreement with somebody, personally or in your business in the past or recently?'

'No, on the business side I have managers who conduct most of it, we have regular meeting here in Kefalonia and in Athens, and Gibraltar, there are no dissatisfied clients, suppliers, or contractors that I am aware of. And I think I would be.'

'What about on a personal level, is there anybody either of you have upset or declined to do anything to help them or has Peter done so.'

'I can answer that Captain, replied Joyce, we know that money and wealth can be a problem, it can cause people to be uncomfortable in your company, and make them draw away from you, they don't want to mix if you understand.

Ari, has always been careful not to flash his money around, he has helped to do things for the community quietly and unobtrusively, he helped raise the money through the Church for the new small hospital we have in Skala, and things like that. People like and respect Ari'. All our shopping is done on the Island and not in Athens. The local people would not do this to our family.'

'I too can't think of anybody for the moment Captain, is there anything else we can help with?'

The Captain looked a little embarrassed, ' As a matter of course you understand nowadays we have to consider that he may have been abducted by------- well by a paedophile , we are therefore checking all known persons on Kefalonia, the other Islands, and the mainland, this will take some time I am afraid.'

Joyce looked at Ari, and broke into tears, 'Oh God no not that, ------- please not that.' He went to her and glared at the Captain, who looked away.

'I'm sorry but we have to consider all possible outcomes, usually things turn out all right' he ventured, although not very convincingly.

'The other thing that I need to clear with you is, I have two telephone engineers arriving about now, we wish to monitor the telephone, I'm sorry but I feel it is necessary, the people holding Peter should contact you, and usually that is by mail or telephone'. The equipment they will install is totally automatic; it will record their conversation with you, and start to trace the call. They will not know it is doing so, so be quite natural. If you want to express emotion or anger then please do so, but please do not antagonise them and finally try to keep them talking as long as you can.'

'I have no problem with that Captain and we will do as you say, I will try to contain my anger, both now and then,' Ari replied.

A short while later two men arrived by private car, and left one hour later, the equipment was now in place.

Peter had slept all night on the rough bed, and when he awoke he was covered in tiny bites on his exposed arms and legs, he didn't know what there were. He also didn't know that the dog usually slept at the foot of the bed hence the flees that had been feasting on Peters blood all night. The usual occupant Constantine had slept on a mattress on the floor outside the bedroom door.

Constantine must have heard Peter moving around, and unlocking the door entered the bedroom, he saw Peter dressed in just his underpants and tee-shirt and wanted to hug him, he approached and saw the bites on Peters arms and legs, and touched them, he spoke in a strange hoarse whisper to Peter, 'you have been bitten by flees, the dog must have brought them in, I will get something to put on them for you. He went out of the room and came back a few minutes later he had a small bowl in his hands, a cloth and a towel.' Peter wondered why he had suddenly only got a tee-shirt, and shorts on.

The man started to wash Peters arms with the wet cloth, the bowl of liquid was a light brown colour and was simply plain water and vinegar, it was however very soothing and stopped the itching. He started on the boys legs and the door suddenly opened the old woman stood there looking at him, she had a big wooden tray in her hands. Constantine got up, put the bowl on the bed and left the room. The old lady came in put the tray on the table, and finished what he had started. She said she was sorry that flees had bitten him but that the vinegar would help.

'I want to go home right now,' said Peter as forcibly as he could, the old lady ignored him completely, she looked a little bemused herself, and in truth didn't know what to say to him. She had no idea he was coming until the evening before he did. Her elder son Theodore had said it was a business arrangement and that he was being held for a friend for two or three days to teach somebody a lesson, he also said the boy would be returned unarmed.

Things had been very difficult since her husband had died ten years ago. The boys had taken over the farm as they were entitled, they could have thrown her out, but they didn't. They let her stay and cook and look after them. Neither had married, who would want them, one fancied young boys and the other smelled and was very ugly looking not at all like her late husband who all the girls had chased until she warned them off and none too politely either.

She brought in a small battery radio, some books and magazines. The latter were years old and from a time when her late husband Costa used to buy them for her. One of the magazines had an article in them about a Greek businessman who had recently moved to Kefalonia from Athens with his English wife, and Peter broke down in tears when he recognised his Father and Mother and saw their happy photograph on an inside page, he sobbed uncontrollably for some ten minutes and the old lady wondered what could have upset him so. If her boys had have been at home she would have gone to him, but dare not risk it as he might run away. Then she would be in trouble.

The two men had gone into Assos and stopped in the main square, they were having a coffee and Metaxa when they saw a police motorcycle pull up alongside their van. The rider got off and started to use his radiophone, they couldn't hear what he said or what was said to him. He got back on his BMW motorbike started the engine and rode off without a backward glance. The repaired/repainted door had been on the other side from the policeman. They finished their coffee and brandy, did their shopping and set off to return home to the farmhouse. Constantine had bought the boy two comics; they were the ones he had asked for.

As they emerged onto the main road some few minutes later, they saw two police motorcyclists parked in a short lay-bye, talking to a motorist, one of the policemen glanced at the van as it went past. The door on the driver's side was white.

The two policemen finished helping the tourist, and returned to their motorcycles, one of them suddenly leapt on his bike, shouted at the other who reached for his radio, and the first set off down the road at great speed. He rode for some ten minutes at over 150km per hour. He then stopped there was no way the van could have got this far.

He spoke on the radio, and was told to stay where he was, and stop and check any white vans, Ten minutes later he was joined by a police patrol car whose crew set up a road block. All side roads were now being systematically checked by police and army patrols. Two young army regulars turned their jeep off the main road and onto the side road where the farm was located they had driven around 100 m when a small off-white van bumped onto the road out of a field on their left, it them drove away from them at a leisurely pace. Because of the width of the road they were unable to get past it, and had to stay behind for around 2km.

They missed the turn off for the Pannikos farm and never went back. As they drove around the vehicle to pass it they could see the old man driving was completely taken aback that they were there. He was even more so when they dragged him out of his van, and made him lean up against it whilst they searched him. He was sharply reminded of 1944, when he nearly lost his life as a young boy whilst driving a donkey and cart and the Germans had treated him similarly. Then he was scared now he bloody mad. He turned round and hit the nearest one a hard sharp blow to his chin, which sat him firmly on his back side, the other drew back and levelled his rifle. 'No don't shoot the silly old sod,' said the one on the ground just in time. He stood up and spoke with the old man.

'We have stopped you as we are looking for an old white van seen somewhere around here within the last 3 hours.'

'Well you have got it wrong then the old man shouted, this van isn't old it was new last year, and its not white its off-white, grey even.' The old man knew where they could find the van they were looking for but he wasn't going to tell them. They looked at the doors neither had been damaged. They tried to apologise but the old man wouldn't have it. The Germans could get away with it nearly sixty years ago, but not his own, oh no. ---- They would hear more about this. He drove on to the next village, and sat down with his coffee and brandy, and over the next two hours of his board game he embroidered and exaggerated the whole incident to the point where nobody was taking any notice.

# Chapter twenty-six

**8.10am Saturday November 8<sup>th</sup>, the villa of the Astinikis family.**

The telephone was ringing, it was the first time it had in 24 hours, and Ari picked it up. 'Hello Aristo Astinikis speaking.'

'Mr Astinikis I am so sorry to trouble you at such a distressing time, but I need to talk with you about my proposals for hiring some of your 'tankers'.'

'I have told you already they are not for hire now or ever.'

'I quite understand Mr Astinikis, I would feel the same if my son was missing, perhaps I could help you find him.'

'The police and Army are already looking for him and will find him soon, I am sure of that thank you.'

'As you say eventually they probably will find him, but will it be too late, are they looking in the right place, what happens if they get too near and the kidnappers injure or even sadly kill him because they don't want to be identified? I am sure you follow me.'

'Ari's blood turned to ice, he could barely speak, 'are you saying you have Peter my son?'

'Good God no, I certainly don't, I merely mean that I have resources that might be able to help you, if you were to help me.'

Ari paused for moment, 'Lets assume I would re-think your proposition, when could these resources act?'

'Oh very quickly I should think, probably the day after our contract was signed.'

'How soon could you get the contract to me?'

'My dear Ari, may I call you Ari? without waiting for a reply he continued now in a less conciliatory tone.

My agent can be in Athens at Athens International airport in 4 hours from now, lets say 1.00pm.'

'I will be there, how will I know him?'

'Don't worry he will know you, as soon as you have signed the contracts he will advise me and I will get my people looking for you, they have the very best reputation, if they find the individuals do you wish them punishing?'

'What do you mean punishing?'

'Oh Ari, for such a high powered businessman you are very how shall I say, naive!'

'No let the police deal with them.'

'Well we both have some deadlines to meet, so lets say goodbye for now, and of course the police and army need to be kept out of this otherwise my contacts will not operate, you do understand I hope?'

'Yes I fully understand,' Ari put the phone down, for the first time in three days he felt elated, Joyce had listened to the conversation. She was more cautious, 'please be careful Ari, what if they take you too, what can I do then?'

The thought had never occurred to him.

The phone rang again, 'Ari its George here, we traced the phone call to a mobile being used in the Russian Federation, in fact in the centre of Moscow to be precise.' The number was withheld but every mobile is like a beacon for a GPS. We can locate any mobile to within feet because satellites are used for the signal.'

## 1.15pm Saturday 8th November 2003. Athens International Airport, Athens. Greece.

Ari had been sat for some ten minutes and apart from somebody asking him the time, nobody had approached him.

1.30pm came and went as did 2.00pm, at 2.05pm and elderly man came and sat next to him.

'Mr Astinikis, I am so sorry I am late, but my taxi got a puncture, and the driver would insist that I stay with him and not change taxis. I am so sorry. I understand that you have requested these documents for urgent signature. I have had then now for some days now, you millionaires take your time but when you come to a decision you act quickly, I'll give you that.' He would have carried on.

'How long have you had these documents prepared?'

'Let me see now, yes it would have been Tuesday the 4th November, as I say a few days ago now.'

'Let me have the contracts please,' he took the contracts off the old man and scanning them quickly, signed them and handed them back, the old man put them in his briefcase and got up the go.

'Wait, you are supposed to make a call before we part.'

'Silly of me I forgot, but in any case I intended waiting until I got home before making the call, it's so much more expensive on a mobile you know.'

'Yes I do know said Ari, please use mine I insist,' and he handed the old man his Nokia.

He put the number in from a little book and pressed the button. Within a minute he was talking to somebody and before Ari had chance to grab telephone the conversation had finished.

'What did he say?'

'Mr Milcovic sends his best wishes, and he told me to say he always keeps his word, his people have been looking and think they know where the item can be found, all very mysterious I am sure, but no doubt you know what its all about, good day to you Sir, I sorry I can't give you Mr Milcovic's number but he is very possessive of it.' With that he turned and walked away leaving Ari, with an envelope full of copy contracts.

Ari took his mobile out of his pocket, and spoke to Joyce, and then George, he told them he would be back around 7.00pm George agreed to meet him at the airport in Argostoli.

## 6.45pm Argostoli Airport.

The colonel met Ari at the entry gate, and walked back to his police Mercedes.

'We have covered all the side roads between the two points where the van would be, we have drawn a blank I am going back for a de-briefing in Argostoli when I have taken you home'.

'I would like to come to the de-briefing if that is acceptable please.'

'Of course you can, let's get a quick meal and then we should arrive in time for the de-brief.'

Having had a meal, which they both felt better for, they were now in the conference room of police headquarters in Argostoli. There were around one hundred people in the room; the Colonel was seated at table on the stage as was the local area Commander of the uniform branch and two army officers, Ari was sat immediately on George's right.

The colonel called the meeting to order. Firstly may I introduce you all to Mr Aristo Astinikis the boy Peters father, it is no secret that we have been close personal friends now for many years, I therefore feel his grief and concern for Peters safety with him. We have looked for some hours now and have exhausted all the avenues that we would normally investigate. Each group of you has a spokesperson (there were 5 officers to a group) through them I have asked for contributions, anything you think might help, anything we haven't done, anything at all.

Before we start Mr Astinikis has asked if he can say a few words, he smiled at Ari.

Ari stood up, they could see he was a smart, not very tall man who commanded attention and respect, his clear gentle eyes showed the pain he was in, and all were affected.

He cleared his voice,' firstly I would like to thank you all what you are doing to find Peter, he is our only child and we miss him dearly. I know most of you have now worked double shifts without a break, I thank you for that. If it were your child that was missing I only hope that I could help you in the same way.'

'I have racked my brain to try to find a reason, and this afternoon we may well have found a reason, on the other hand it may equally be a cruel joke by some person sick in the head, who simply wants to turn the situation to his advantage, I honestly do not know. It all sounds a bit mysterious I know, and perhaps a little unfair not to tell you but I can't unless it triggers a tragic end to the matter. We will know one way or the other within the next 24 hours, until then please help all you can, but don't forget you must not neglect your loved ones to do so. Thank you.' He sat down.

There followed an hour of reports one young army Corporal was having a hard time with his conscience, he decided to speak up as the debrief was coming to a close. He spoke to his Captain who went immediately to Colonel Aristostis.

The Corporal mentioned the incident with the van earlier and how they had not checked the entire side road or the properties off it and why. 'I would like to go and check them again sir,' he said.

The Colonel put together a team of six, four army and two police. The army would take night sights and automatic weapons field and mobile radio's they were allocated a call sign specific to the event, which was 'Night owl' base Was Eagle one?

It took them about 30 minutes to reach the turn off, the time was 9.30pm the two jeeps crawled along the rough side road and cruised past the field the van had driven off some hours earlier. Within 2 minutes they came upon the dirt road leading to a building they could just see in the darkness, it looked like an old two storey farmhouse. They pulled the vehicles off the road, and splitting into three groups of two approached from the left right and centre.

They hid amidst the olive grove, and watched for over 15 minutes, nothing moved. There were lights on downstairs which appeared to be oil lamps, and the light was not bright and flickered.

The Corporal and a Sergeant agreed to scout the outbuildings, they had got within 20m of them when the door was thrown open and a man came out, a large mangy looking dog ventured its head out and the man shouted at it as he urinated alongside the farmhouse. He was fastening his flies as the dog plucked up courage and made a dash for it, the mans foot caught it squarely on its rump and it yelped and shot off into the olive grove. The man laughed and re-entered the farmhouse.

The dog by now was aware it wasn't on its own and was in the middle of other people, his hackles went up, and he growled. One of the policemen spoke to it and called it over, after a little it went, he stroked it and gave it a piece of chocolate which it devoured with relish, and they all quietly laughed. The dog now lay on the ground near them, somehow knowing they were no danger to it.

The Corporal and Sergeant had continued their search of the outbuildings and found the van, the driver's door felt smoother somehow as though it had been painted recently. This looked like the place.

Back in the olive grove they decided to leave two at the entrance to the farmhouse, and remove the vehicles out of sight into a field some 50m away. They reported their findings to 'eagle one'. Who responded that Colonel Aristostis was on his way, and to meet him at the main road?

It was decided they would wait until just before dawn before going in. vehicles would be allowed to use the side road without knowing they were there. The farmhouse would be covered by an army sniper and three other, one carried stun grenades. All had night sight glasses these produced perfect daylight vision, but the images were slightly green in colour. The dog was now sleeping in one of the jeeps, and was perfectly happy to remain there.

At 1.00am one of the officers saw an upstairs shutter move, somebody was trying to open the shutter.

Peter had used his penknife during the day to loosen the screws holding the left shutter; he had already managed the window. The shutter was causing a problem, he couldn't get his penknife blade onto one of the crews, and had decided to dig out the wood around it instead, but this was taking time as the knife was not only broken but blunt as well.

The officer had called up the Colonel who was now watching the window and shutter, he caught a glimpse of a blonde head, --- a boy's blonde head and wanted to shout. Instead he said to the other police officer,' withdraw down to the bottom of the driveway, and send back that corporal and sergeant that searched the outbuildings, do it quickly.'

Within two minutes the two men were with him, 'can you remember seeing a ladder that might reach that window on the first floor?' They couldn't.

'Farmhouses usually have ladders they use them for all sorts of things, go and have another look please.' within five minutes they were back, there was a set of ladders and they would easily reach the windows upstairs.

Now to stop Peter doing anything for the next couple of hours if possible.

They weighed up the for's and against's:

1. Firstly he didn't know they were there and could kick something off himself with disastrous results.
2. There was no way of knowing if they were watching Peter, although the fact he had been seen trying to open the shutters indicated they were not watching him closely.
3. They didn't know if the people were armed, how many there were, or where they are in the building.

'I would like to think we could get him out of the bedroom window without then knowing, we could then surround the place and make them surrender, nobody has to take any risks them, we simply starve them out if necessary,' this from the Captain.

'I suppose the only alternative is get him out as we stun grenade the downstairs, but what if there is somebody upstairs.'

They were not to know that the only person downstairs would be the old lady, the two men were upstairs, one in bed in the other bedroom, and the other asleep on the mattress on the landing.

The boy was at the window again, this time he was trying a bit harder, and making a noise, a light came on in the room behind the shutter; there was the sound of slap, and a cry of pain. They heard noises of disagreement.

The colonel had his night sight glasses switched on and, he said 'give me two minutes then follow, two minutes not sooner, not later,' with that he ran towards the house with his silenced automatic in his right hand, he opened the door gently and entered the room and shut door quickly, he could see the old lady looking at him, and knew she had felt something but as yet probably didn't know what and couldn't see him.

The staircase was in the corner of the room, he saw the old lady reaching for an oil lamp her hand trying to find the matches, as he went past he snatched the box of matches just before she reached them, he went quickly up the stairs and saw three doors, two on his right, the first a small box room which was open and empty he went past, the old lady shouted a warnings and a man came out of one of the other two rooms,-----he had a shotgun in his hands and it was pointing down the partially lit landing directly at the Colonel, he fired two shots rapidly, the man was knocked over backwards, and as he fell over he pressed the triggers on the shotgun both barrels blew a big hole in the ceiling, dirt dust and bits of timber dropped down around him.

He reached the second semi-darkened bedroom and kicked the door open, and quickly glancing in saw another man holding Peter in front of him, he had a handgun in his right hand, the colonel shouted, 'Peters its uncle George how many are there,' 'just two' before he was slapped again. Peter had had enough, he had his penknife in his hand, and he drove it backwards into the man's groin as hard as he could, he felt the knife go into soft flesh, the man screamed in agony, Peter fell to the floor as the man let go of him, he looked up and saw a strange animal with huge eyes, the animal fired something in his hand which went phut-phut then he was smothered for a minute when something heavy fell on him.

Uncle George was holding him when he next looked up, the Captain shouted up the stairs,' all secure here Sir

are you all right?'

'Never better Captain --- never better.'

George took his mobile out of his pocket, and rang Ari and Joyce's villa, he simply said I have some good news, and gave the phone to Peter. 'I'm alright Dad Uncle George got them both, is Mum alright and did you find my bike, and what about my dogs?'

For a couple of seconds Ari could not talk, then he said 'Mums here, we found your bike and the dogs want a word, speak now,' Peter spoke to the two dogs who immediately barked and wags their short tail for the first time in days.

George took the phone back of Peter, 'we will be with you in an hour, he's thin and he smells, and I do mean smells,' he said hugging him.

They walked down the stairs and got into the Colonels car and set off back to Skala, within two minutes Peter was fast asleep lay down on the back seat with his head in Uncle George's lap.

**11.30am Sunday 9th November 2003, the Villa of the Astinikis family**

The telephone was ringing yet again with people telephoning to say how pleased and happy they were that Peter was back home, the local TV station wanted to interview the family and was refused.

This time it was Chief Superintendent Gardner ringing from Scotland Yard, 'Ari I am so pleased its all turned out all right do we know who was responsible?'

'Well we think so, but I can't tell you on this phone, although I would like to discuss it with you, will you be in your office all day?'

'I can be if it will help, we have enough problems here to keep me busy, so ring anytime.'

'I will ring within the hour,' and Ari rang off.

**12.30pm the same day.**

Ari, had rung Chief Superintendent Gardner, and was speaking with him from the public telephone in the San Georgio hotel just up the road from the villa.

They had been talking for about an hour, and had covered all the recent events involving them both the Superintendent thought there was a continuing connection with Petor Milcovic in Moscow; Gardner put some thoughts to Ari, who smiled.

'Would it work do you think Bill?'

'I am absolutely certain it will, leave it to me. I will be in touch.'

# Chapter twenty-seven

**4.26pm Saturday 1st November 2003, Sheremetyevo Airport, Moscow, Russian Federation.**

It took John Clarke exactly two hours to get through customs and immigration to enter Russia. He was met by a very attractive young lady, wearing a fur coat, and hat, and she had over her arm another fur coat which she told him was for him. The board had said John Clarke Jnr; the Russians must think all second generations Americans with the same first name must be juniors. He smiled.

'Mr Clarke, my name is Irina, and I shall be looking after you for the few days you are with us, Mr Milcovic is away today on business, and I shall entertain you. I have a car outside to take us to our hotel.'

The journey into the centre of Moscow was bewildering, at first gaunt roads with little traffic, and equally gaunt buildings, massive blocks of featureless apartments, and then gradually it came to life, beautiful old buildings, well lit, massive side roads, and squares, and then the ride parallel to the river Moskva to their hotel the SAS Radisson Slavyanskaya located on the banks on the River Moskva, with views of the Russian White House, the Foreign Ministry and Europe Square.

Irina was obviously well know at the hotel, and she booked him into his room, they took the lift up to the 7th floor and stepped out onto a luxurious carpeted and pictured corridor, he wondered how long the paintings would remain in an American hotel, minutes perhaps certainly no more than days.

Room 719 was more of a suite than a hotel room; the large picture windows overlooked the river which looked quite pretty at night time with lights along its banks and the gentle traffic going up and down river. Irina sat on one of the two double beds. She stroked the duvet cover. And asked, 'which one do you want the one near the window or the bathroom?' He felt himself blush.

'I am sorry I have offended you, I have been asked by Petor to look after you that can be anything you want, and it is quite common I assure you. And its so much more convenient, than my pokey little apartment, you see I have a two hour journey to go home at this time of night on the Metro which is not very safe, and a two and a half hour journey to come back in the morning. I live on my own so this would be a big favour, plus I get to eat well into the bargain. What do you say, shall I go?' She looked at him appealingly.

'No – No stay by all means, you choose which bed you want.'

She went across the room, brushed against in so doing and bounced onto the bed nearest the window. She laughed, 'we are going to have a great time Mr Clarke.'

'You had better call me John now that we are sharing a room, I think I need to unpack and shower.'

'Let me unpack for you whilst you have your shower.'

He took of his jacket and tossed it on the bed, removed his shoes, and tie loosened his shirt and picking up his toilet bag headed for the shower.

'Throw your trousers out and I will put them in the trouserpress,' he did as requested.

The bathroom was huge there was no lock on the door, he stripped off, turned on the shower and stood under it, the cares and pressures of the day seemed to melt away, here he was in a strange but beautiful City with and even more beautiful woman, whom he couldn't work out. He never felt the door open and the first he knew of her being there was when she gently stroked his back, whilst getting in the shower behind him. He didn't dare turn round; she squeezed shower gel from a large bottle onto his neck and shoulders and massaged gently downwards, he felt himself getting hard, and her nipples were pressing into his back, she reached round him and grasped his enlarged penis in her right hand, the shower gel and her stroking nearly made him come right there and then. He turned round her hair was all wet and now lay long over her shoulders and down her back, her breast were just right, not too heavy and turned up slightly, he wanted to suck them, she lifted them gently with a smile, as he bent forward and first one and then the other into his mouth, and ever so gently chewed them. She smiled and mewed with pleasure.

They soaped and washed each other, all down their bodies, every nook and fold, and eventually she knelt down and took him in her mouth. He had never had oral sex before, it was always 'dirty' something the low life did, he had never experienced such intense pleasure in all his life. Much to his surprise he found himself quite naturally doing the same to Irina under the shower. They towelled each other off, and lay on the one bed on a large open bath robe and he snuggled up to her back, and held her breast in his hand as they both fell into a relaxed sleep.

It was 8.45pm when he awoke, still fitted into Irina, and now holding her waist and not her breast. She was ever so gently snoring and it sounded lovely, quite beautiful in fact, he could stay here forever.

The telephone tinkled rather than rang, and he turned over to answer it, suddenly realising he didn't speak Russian.

'Hello' which sounded pretty original to him at least?'

'Mr Clarke this is the hotel restaurant manager you have a reservation for 9.30 for 10.00pm in either the Mediterranean, the Russian or Japanese restaurant, could you tell me which you have decided on and I will confirm your reservation?'

Irina turned round, 'could we try the Japanese please?'

'Sure we can, the Japanese please, and we will see you shortly, thank you for ringing.'

He looked at Irina who had turned round and was facing him and laid on her right side, she looked beautiful, the turned down lighting casting shadows in the curves of her hips, and around her slim waist, the light from the small table lamp on the bedside table behind filtered through her black hair, creating a slight halo effect on one side, he felt himself falling in love with her, how could that be he had only known her what was it, four hours?. He had never felt this way before. He knew now what the expression meant, 'To Die For', and he would have.

'What are you thinking?'

He kissed her gently on the end of her lovely nose, 'that would be telling my love, that would be telling.

Come on let's get dressed for dinner, I am starving.'

She looked concerned, 'you have not eaten for days, oh no, we should have eaten earlier I am so sorry.'

He grinned at her, 'no it's just an expression, I last ate on the aircraft about 6 hours ago, but I could do with eating again.' An hour later they were sat in the cocktail bar drinking whisky sours, and ordering their food.

He chose Sake (rice wine) with the meal, and they sat cross legged on cushions on the floor, the food was served on a low table by a Japanese waitress who had also prepared the food. There was a sushi chef and in great demand but he spent a lot of time looking after their table. Irina had only had sushi once before. A whole experience of Japanese food was laid before them and the meal took 3 hours. It was 1.00am before they ventured into the Casino for a while.

Irina won at Blackjack although she had never played it before. It was 2.30am before totally exhausted they fell into bed together and snuggled up close.

**9.00am Sunday 2nd November 2003**

They had breakfast in bed, and Irina thought he always did that, she laughed when he told here he had to get up and make his own every day.

'What do you do for a living John, are you in investments?'

'Good Lord no,' and he found himself telling her all about him, which came as a bit of a shock as he had never opened himself up in this way before.

He was born in Ohio in America, his fathers father had come across from Germany just before the last war in about 1928. His dad had been involved in the steel industry, and then moved to Texas in the 1940's to get involved in the oil industry that wanted workers to replace those that had gone to war. His two brothers were born in 1950 and 1952 they were both killed within a year of each other in Viet Nam, neither had any family.'

'I was born in 1960 and my mother died in 1978, when I was eighteen years of age. She never saw her one and only Grandchild.'

'My marriage lasted exactly four years to the day. My wife found somebody richer and lives in Florida now.

I was very angry about Viet Nam, when I was in college as a lot of us where, he saw the 'Vets' coming home limbless, blind, and deranged, unfit for life in a lot of cases, and sometimes even social outcasts, they were the lucky ones, they had some chance of survival, my family had none, just two inscriptions on the memorial in Washington.'

'Viet Nam slowly but surely killed my mother, she was no longer the happy person she had been, she suffered mental problems, became hooked on anti-depressants, and died in her sleep from an overdose, some say she killed herself. So I revolted and sat outside the White House, with thousands of others, peacefully at first, and then when the FBI starting taking photographs, some objected and the trouble started. I got busted and jailed overnight, it frightened me to death. From then on I only objected passively.'

'I followed dad into the oil industry, I've done about every job there is, and right now I am in charge of the maintenance of two major oil fields in west Texas. He went very quiet, I have a tumour on my brain they say I only have 6 to 12 months to live, and things are going to get worse in the next few months.'

'I have no savings, and all my spare cash is spent on Dad, I owe about $100,000 in medical bills for both me and him, what I am doing now is wrong I know that, but the money will pay the bills and give Dad a final chance when I go. I have worked for the Company for 22 years, I asked them for help from the Company benevolent fund, and having filled in masses of documents they granted me $2,000 as a one off payment.'

Irina, sat on the edge of the bed with the tears streaming down her face, she cried without sobbing for a full five minutes, her eyes were puffy and red. He held her close and kissed her hair gently, and caressed her shoulders and back as he did so. They sat like this unmoving for what seemed like an age.

'Come on this won't do, you said I had a meeting this morning, when and where is it?'

'We have to be outside the hotel at 11.00am, she looked at her wristwatch, you have half and hour to get ready,' she dived out of his arms, and laughing ran into the bathroom, he heard the shower running.

He set out his clothes on the bed, and went and had a quick shower when Irina had finished, when he came out a few minutes later towelling his hair he found Irina laid on the bed in her bathrobe. 'Come on get dressed you are going to make us late!'

'I'm not coming with you; Petor is meeting you in reception and taking you on a 3 hours tour of the City. He wants to talk business, so I won't be there, but I will be waiting for you when you get back. We are going to the Bolshoi theatre tonight to see the 'Nutcracker', I hope you like ballet?'

He was disappointed but knew at some point they had to get down to business, and to precisely what Petor wanted for his money.

Petor was waiting for him in reception, he was sat in a leather high back chair sipping a tall frosted glass of Vodka, and when he saw him approaching, he put the glass down on the silver tray, stood up, and extended his right hand.

'My Dear John how nice to meet you again, good flight I hope, and is my wife looking after you?'

He nearly collapsed there and then, 'your wife I -----didn't know.'

'Ah, you are wondering about her sexual favours no doubt. Don't worry this is the normal practice, I have a problem and others take care of it for me, shall we say. Would you like a little vodka?' He raised his right hand and a waiter appeared as if by magic with two more tall crystal glasses of iced Vodka.

Ten minutes later they boarded the luxury coach that was waiting outside and went immediately to the seat at the rear, the attendant followed them and four seats from the back placed a decorative thick rope from one seat to the other effectively blocking the aisle. They took off their top coats and made themselves comfortable and the coach set off.

'Welcome to Moscow, the Premier City of the Russian Federation, formerly the USSR. '

'Today we have a wonderful day for our 3 hour journey, we visit Red Square, and many of you will have seen the vast parades in the past when the Former Russia's military might was paraded for all to see.'

'We shall visit the Kremlin, the fortified heart of Ancient Russia, the Armoury, housing a magnificent collection of Imperial treasures, including the Tsars throne. There is also a small collection of the famous Faberge eggs, and jewellery.'

'We move on to St.Basil's Cathedral with its multi-coloured onion domes and spires, and GUM the biggest departmental store in the World.'

'Next the Bolshoi theatre the home of Russian Opera and Ballet, following which we shall take tea at a famous tea house, where more vodka is drunk than tea.'

'And if we have time, we shall visit the White House, where the Russian Parliament called the 'State Duma' sit. And finally before we return you to your hotels one of the magnificent and sumptuous Metro stations. I promise you will never have seen anything quite so beautiful in railway station, anywhere in the world,'

The coach moved off, it was significant that the man who had positioned the rope was sitting two seats the other side of it, and would stop anybody going past to get to the back. Petor turned down the speaker system but left it on.

'Any time you feel you would like to see the exhibits John just say so.' He opened his briefcase.

'You work for Trenton Oil, their 3 major oil fields abut each other, and a major pipeline to the Gulf of Mexico passes through the fields. In the past you have criticised the condition of that pipe work, below ground and the pipe work and its supports when above ground'.

'As I understand it, because there is none, or little investment taking place in the West Texas oil field, safety might be a concern. When oil reached what would you say $41 a barrel or above, this could engender renewed interest.'

'However, due to lack of activity around 15,000 oil field workers have left the townships and the industry, is that right?'

'Yes I think that's about right.'

# The President Is Down

'For the 30 Texas Counties USDA categorized as mining dependent in 1989, oil production has fallen from a high of 462.7 million barrels in 1972 to only 167.2 million barrels in 1999, a 64% decline. Twenty five of the mining dependent rural counties have seen oil production drop since 1972, some almost disappearing, with one fourth seeing county oil production fall by more than 80%.'

'Natural Gas also has similar problems, only this time its demand outstripping on and off-shore supplies, in 1999 Texas produced nearly one third of the **Nations** natural gas supply. You will gather by now, I understand the business.'

'My business interests need a massive injection of capitol over the next two/three years, I have access to oil, which needs to be at around $38 to make it worth my while in shipping it from the Ukraine, and I also need tankers at the right price.'

'OPEC is struggling, and Iraq- Iran – and the Gulf States have a problem, Venezuela is a major supplier to the US and the World with increasing stocks being found, however they too want as many dollars as they can get for it.

So they are not a problem to me. Basically I need to disrupt a major oil producing area, and make it look to be a natural disaster. Casings are having to be purchased from Eastern Europe, I will ensure that are faulty and will crack.'

'You will ensure the pipe-work we spoke about ruptures in the right places; this will be classed as a terrorist attack. Help will be given you in this project, and it will need careful planning on the ground. You must personally be above suspicion.'

'I want the price way up there at $47 -$50 a barrel to make my killing. You will help me as I have said by disrupting your oil field, and I will do the rest.'

'I have agreed to pay you around $200,000, I now intend to give you that as a down payment right now, as we speak I only have to make one phone call and your new account I have opened for you in the British Virgin Islands will be credited with the money. A further $800,000 will follow when you have done as I ask.'

'My contribution to the oil industry will be miniscule, and will go unnoticed, however with loads of oil at those prices buying a Super Tanker. I will soon have all the money I could ever need. Unfortunately due to your ill health you will not be able to participate for long which is why I have tried to treat you fairly, if you need more money just ask and you can have it.'

'I want all of this done in the next 8 weeks, my oil is ready, my tankers are just about ready, and he smiled to himself. I just need you to say yes.'

'I am totally stunned; of course the answer is yes, now let's get down to it, the sooner the better for me.'

Petor opened his briefcase took out a mobile phone and made a call, the transferred money would be in the account when the bank next opened for business. He then went through his plans in more detail.

John returned to the hotel, and to his room of Irina there was no sign. He looked in the wardrobe and found only his clothes. On the bedside table was a hand written note. His heart missed a beat when he read it.

> 'My darling John,
>
> You have no idea how much I feel for you. For the first time I have found somebody I could leave Petor for. We may only have a few short months together but I would like to spend them with you and know I can't.
>
> Tonight would have been our last night together, you go home tomorrow, I had planned a romantic evening at the Bolshoi with you, and a last evening of passion to keep my memories of you fresh in my mind as you leave me forever.
>
> A tour guide will call at 7.30pm to take my place.
>
> Farewell my love, my only true love.
>
> Yours forever  Irina

He asked the receptionist to cancel, the tour guide when she came, and having showered went downstairs to the restaurant to dine.

He had an excellent meal, and couldn't remember any of it, went to back to his room and packed, he had an early night.

## 9.00am Monday 3rd November 2003. Sheremetyevo International, Moscow, Russia.

The British Airways Boeing 747, lifted off with a half full passenger list for Washington Dulles USA.

It landed at Dulles International at 8.00am the same day (Moscow is 11 hours ahead in time).

## 1.00pm Monday 3rd November 2003, the Mayflower Hotel, Washington, USA.

He had caught a cab into Washington and booked into the Mayflower hotel. At 1.00pm there was a knock on the door and a hotel porter was stood looking at him as he opened it. The porter walked into the room, shutting the door behind him. 'How did it go then John, and what's he after, said Chris Meddleman Assistant Director FBI. John spent the next two hours telling him.

'It doesn't stack up, ok he needs cash, he's got the oil, and he thinks he's got access to tankers.'

'This is a major criminal who starts off by stating he wishes to finance his nefarious criminal activities, and then changes tack. No there is more to this than meets the eye. He has major terrorist contacts, I don't buy into what he's saying which is that this is all about oil and making a financial killing to finance his future business activity. However, we have to run with it at least for the time being.'

'No more contact from us, we will await your call, just simply say you would like to book an Altcar car for a couple of days. We will catch up with you within the hour, check the corridor will you.' Then he was gone.

# Chapter twenty-eight

10.30pm Wednesday 5th November 2003, the Radisson SAS Royal Hotel, Nevsky Prospekt,
St. Petersburg, Russia. Some 450 miles northwest of the Russian Capitol.

Petor Milcovic had just finished an excellent dinner, complimented by the presence of his beautiful 'wife' Irina, who was paying great attention to their guest. A rather run down little man, with wispy hair and a pair of spectacles that kept sliding down his nose. He was a nuclear fission officer, who had been for fifteen years attached to the Russian nuclear submarine fleet, and the Red Army. He like many had been pushed to one side, and his services dispensed with some twelve years ago. No pension worth speaking of, a damp flat, and a depressing wife who nagged him constantly.

He had something to sell, something that would take him away forever from that terrible woman he had married in a drunken stupor twenty five years ago, and regretted it every day since. If he could only pick up somebody just a bit like Irina, and money would do it, then fine, he would lead the life of a King.

He had agreed to 'find' and deliver three nuclear shells, he would make them safe for transportation by ship, and prepare them for use. In effect he was going to put together three nuclear weapons. Each would be 4 times the size of Hiroshima. One was to be installed in an American 4 wheel drive Jeep Grande Cherokee. And another in the engine compartment of a lift truck, and the last one on a ship. He was to be paid $1,000,000 US dollars.

To obtain the necessary materials, he had twelve ex-Russian special services at his disposal.

## The President Is Down

He had consumed a little too much brandy as well as copious amounts of good Vodka, not rubbish, and was having trouble standing. Irina took him to his room, she undressed him and put him to bed, she took a red bra out of her handbag and rumpling it up, put it beside him in the bed, and dented the other pillow alongside him as though somebody had slept there.

She carefully folded his clothes, messed the bathroom up a bit, she took a condom out of her handbag removed the wrapper, put a little shower gel in it, crumpled it and put it in the bin with the wrapper, and then smiling to herself, went back downstairs to the restaurant and her 'husband'. The next day the poor little man would find the 'bra', and used condom and relive his night of passion which if he thought really hard he could just remember.

The next morning Alexei Androvitch awoke at 10.30am, his left arm moved slowly to the other side of the bed, it was empty she had left, moving his hand downwards he touched the red bra and looking at and feeling it he relived the delicious night of passion in his mind at least. No longer was he the insignificant low level official, but a somebody of worth, a man going places. He picked up the bedside telephone and ordered breakfast in bed as he had seen the movie stars do with an authority he had not exercised in years, if ever. After breakfast he dressed in his shabby clothing for the last time. Today he would dress in clothes more in being with his new found status.

Androvitch rang the telephone number given him and agreed to meet a Major Kalinoff for 'lunch'. The major was in charge of Androvitch's hit squad.

The Major looked hard cold and unfeeling, and was to prove all of those plus a very efficient killer, in the last three days they had located and secured the three nuclear shells, triggers, dosimeters, lead lined boxes, and test equipment. Along the way 'Mother Russia' had of necessity lost five of her sons. Kalinoff had personally murdered three of the soldiers, the last one an elderly sergeant had fought back and had succeeded in cutting the major's forearm quite badly, the cut had required 15 stitches and the major had gone berserk. He had literally hacked the sergeant's head off his body. Androvitch brought his recently eaten 'blinis' back vomiting the contents over the unfortunate dead sergeants dead body. For some twisted reason this seemed to amuse the major.

The shells were now safely housed in the lead boxes, secured and ready for transportation by road to a certain oil tanker due to dock in the port of Gdansk Poland in 5 days time. Androvitch supervised the loading and securing of the shells in their protective boxes in the back of a 40 foot refrigerated articulated trailer, he connected the radiation monitors and coupled one to the cab of the unit. If that went over the top whoever went to reseal the lead lined box was a dead man, but he chose not to mention this.

Having loaded the shells it was now the turn of a new looking dark metallic blue Jeep Grande Cherokee, anybody looking in back of it might have wondered why it had a brand new driver's door in the same colour across the rear seats. The Jeep was followed by two pallets of bricks and a large gas powered heavy duty fork lift truck. Lashed to the side supports of the trailer were welder's bottles, there were a number of steel tool boxes on the floor. Apart from the driver there were two other men who had examined the Jeep and fork lift before they were loaded, they looked like mechanics or something similar.

Androvitch was to go home and spend a few days with his wife, whilst awaiting a call on his new mobile phone, he was told not to spend any money at the moment and be a little patient, he chose to ignore this advice; his actions would cause his wife a lot of grief sometime later because of it. His new found wealth and freedom did make him suddenly more attractive to the younger woman and he sated his hunger on three such 'ladies' a number of times over the next 5 days.

His wife would make do with a new washing machine and a used but good fur coat, matching hat and gloves, it was far less messy and much more satisfying than trying to establish any long lost love they had for each other. She on the other hand tried to treat him 'nicely', which they both found embarrassing and soon gave up. He would send her some money at some point. He did not intend to ever return to her or this squalid apartment, and equally squalid life.

Some two weeks had now elapsed since his night of bliss with Erina. The phone call when it came from her was short and to the point. If he looked on his doorstep right now he would find a brown envelope. Pack a bag with clothes for 2 weeks maximum. He would be away for around two weeks, much longer if he wished.

He opened the door and picked up the large brown envelope, he looked around just in time to see a tall figure disappearing around the end of the apartment block. He went back inside and into the bedroom locking the door after him. The envelope contained travel documents and cash, an ID folder, a visa for the USA for 6 months, some Roubles and a lot of Dollars, a Russian Federation passport dated from six months back in his name, and finally an Aeroflot ticket to Gdansk airport for the following morning. He would be met by Erina, the thought of that beautiful body that he had possessed but fleetingly, greeting him once more made him warm all over, he trembled in anticipation. This time he would drink less and enjoy her more.

# Chapter twenty-nine

**Monday 13th November 2003 the Pentagon, Washington USA.**

The US Chief of Staff Donald Fielding chaired the meeting; he was not in a good mood.

'Gentlemen before we get into this, I would like to introduce you to two of our colleagues from the UK, Sir Bernard Hills Chief of MI6, Chief Superintendent Bill Gardner of the British Special Branch, Bill is involved in anti-terrorist and 'other' things whatever that means, he smiled at Bill Gardner. We have these two gentlemen to thank for catching the terrorists involved in the UK end of the attack on our President two weeks ago, they also recovered the other two stinger launchers that could have been used and the warheads.' He paused for effect.

'We---- we on the other hand have spent $6,000,000 trying to get to grips with this whole situation and have achieved 'fuck all 'I will come back to the FBI in a minute, he looked at the CIA and NSA attendees, who looked decidedly uncomfortable. You gentlemen have spent hours briefing me over the past two weeks on absolutely nothing, you have given me profiles, you have told me how many different ethnic communities 'might' , you have given me as many again who 'could' do it, you have arrested dozens of people, and questioned thousands, and given me absolutely NOTHING, ZILCH,ZERO. And upset many more thousands.'

'The FBI, he glanced across the table, on the other hand have had some success, they have an asset in place whom we believe, he now glanced at Sir Bernard, who nodded his agreement, is locked into the very same people who were involved in the attack on the President. Because of the possibility of that information, either blowing the operation, or the cover of our asset that is all you are going to be told at this time about that person/s. Any further information about the asset is on a strictly need to know basis, and only five people do know and that's how its gonna stay.'

'You all have in front of you a numbered briefing document which you will now sign for, as you know any attempt to copy this document will show, so don't copy it and don't lose it or give it to anybody else. The briefing document was distributed two weeks ago in London by Sir Bernard to the British security services, again on a need to know basis. Our representatives in the UK were present and aware of it, and have also I am told contributed to it.'

'When you have read it, and following today's meeting get your people out there onto their contacts and informers, put the pressure on so pips squeak, make it absolutely crystal clear that they get NO MORE MONEY or PROTECTION from us unless they produce the goods, somebody somewhere knows something!!.'

'So what else can we positively say we know that is highly likely to be linked to the incident in London and the President?'

1. We have a link to a known American/Russian suspected terrorist, whom we think may have, and I stress the may, links to Al Qaeda of some sort. Since September 11$^{th}$ every damn happening gets laid at the door of the Taliban and Al Qaeda and that clearly can't be correct. Whatever happened to the Red Brigade or Black September etc. You know what I am saying.

2. A positive link between the above and a Greek shipping magnate, WHO IS NOT a crook, but is working under duress and with our knowledge.

3. A probable attack on West Texas oilfields, this I can't say too much on at the moment.

4. The leasing of three super tankers for a twelve month period, the first happening about right now on the 16$^{th}$ November. The destination we will know shortly.

5. The asset we have in place, when I can I promise I will reveal more on this, and looking ahead it will probably be at about the same time I am going to need some pretty swift help from you gentlemen.

A further hour of interchange took place before the meeting broke up, it had been agreed that MI6 and Special Branch would work with the FBI, and would be given facilities in Washington for the next two weeks. This being considered the period of greatest danger.

Sir Bernard and Superintendent Gardner booked into the Mayflower hotel, just round the corner from the White House. The Mayflower is one of the finest hotels in Washington, deceptively large with superb conference rooms, and an excellent choice of accommodation, first class food and facilities and used by various Government departments and agencies for meetings both formal and informal.

That same evening they met with the British Ambassador Sir Terence Strong and briefed him on their visit, he was surprisingly up to date, and provided them with a confidential list of contacts they could call upon throughout the USA for help if they required it. He gave them a name of an individual in the Embassy who would confirm at any time of night or day their 'credentials', should somebody enquire. The list of both the people and the 'skills' they offered surprised Sir Bernard.

# Chapter thirty

**1300 hours 14th November 2003, Gdansk Oil Storage and Refinery Poland.
On board the ULCC 'Athonikis'**

The Appolonikis ULCC tanker was 7 years old, and in superb condition, it was as though she had just come out of the shipbuilder's yard for the first time. Its Greek Captain had been her master from the day she was released from the builder's and down the slip into the mighty Ocean for her sea trials. He was finding it difficult to hand his ship on to a new master and crew for two months as he had been instructed. He had told Mr Astinikis when he spoken to him on the ships telephone that he could not fault the Russian Captain or crew. He was as happy to leave the ship in the Russians hands as anybody's.

In the few days prior to arriving at Gdansk the 'Athonikis had been a hive of covert activity; she now sported a 24 hours GPS device which was transmitting the ships position every hour by fast radio burst. The pulse or burst lasted 1/100th of a second and could not be detected by anything known in current technology. There was no way the new crew would be aware of its existence.

She also had micro eye-lens camera's similar to those used in the new mobile camera phones, these were hidden amongst the wiring, cabling and pipe work, they too were transmitting colour pictures 24 hours a day, there was even one in the Captains toilet or john as the Americans called it.

Modern tankers are luxury vessels to travel in, the accommodation for the crew is equal to a good class of hotel, the Captains suite and day cabin are sumptuous, and in the case of the 'Athonikis' she also had a stateroom suite for the owner if he/she were ever on board. The stateroom had a large outside balcony, a huge sitting room with satellite television, radio, and telephone. A dining room and conference room/study. A full size bathroom with sunken bath and Jacuzzi, a dressing room, and a double bedroom with picture window, and balcony.

Petor Milcovic and Erina Ludmilla Ronofskia were stood out on the main balcony about 100 foot up in the air looking down onto the massive deck stretched out before them, bemused by the two men cycling along the deck checking the valves and hatch covers. In the far distance and near the bows over a quarter of a mile away they could see the Jeep Grande Cherokee covered up and sheeted down with tarpaulins, as was the huge forklift truck.

The air was chilly and the light fading as they took their drinks back into the centrally heated and air conditioned suite closing the electrically operated curtains behind them. Dinner would be in an hour's time and some two hours before they sailed. Alexei Androvitch had a smaller suite down the corridor. Erina had greeted him at the airport, and when he had come on board she had begged him not to tell Petor of their lovemaking, or he would have them both killed and tossed overboard. The ploy had worked he now kept his distance from both of them and would not be bothering her.

Dinner was a rather grand affair hosted by the Russian Captain and three senior officers. The six-course meal could well have come from the kitchens of a top notch 5 star hotel, which in fact was where the chef came from.

The selection of wines was superb, the cellar having been chosen by Ari Astinikis the ships owner. None of the crew drank any alcohol; Captain Deraukia ran a 'dry' ship.

The vessel was moored half a mile out to sea alongside a fuelling point, she slipped her anchors and got under way at 22.30 it took her nearly an hour to work up to her cruising speed of 15 knots. If she ever had to stop 'quickly' from this speed it would take over 30 minutes to do so and five miles. She would need 5 to 9 miles to turn a complete circle without damaging her multi-section hull whilst under way. The journey was planned to take 12 days.

Petor Milcovic and Erina watched the final moments through the stateroom window as the ship slipped her anchors and moved out into clear waters. Half an hour later they were in bed together, there was no sex there never would be she laid her head on his shoulder they often lay like this for ages before falling asleep. Milcovic had a problem

One he had learned to live with. He didn't like sex with women and the thought of it with men disgusted him, so he remained celibate. Fully recognising he had to at least give the appearance of being 'normal' in society and business, even if in today's society that meant same sex partners, he took beautiful women under his wing and paid the well for their time with him. Erina had been with him for three out of the last ten years.

The rules were simple, she could discreetly go with whom she wanted, and she would help him make targets more 'amenable', John Clarke being one such person. But only if she agreed, he would never force her to have sex with anybody she didn't wish to. This had meant just two men in those three years. John Clarke being one of them.

They were enjoying each other's company listening to a Rachmaninoff piano concerto on the superb sound system when she broke the silence.

'Petor, you always said when I met somebody I really liked I could leave you and move on, did you mean it?'

He stiffened alongside her, and at first didn't say anything, it seemed like an age to her before he said, ' I always say what I mean, I know that you would eventually want something more permanent, naturally I will miss you terribly, you mean more to me than anything else in the World. I have dreaded this moment but knew it had to come.'

He gently squeezed her hand under the duvet cover; neither spoke for some minutes, when they did it was Petor first.

' Tell me is it John Clarke?' before she answered he spoke again, I suppose I knew a few days ago that you felt a lot for him, you do know that he hasn't got long to live?'

'You don't have to give me an answer right now, please go to him for as long as he has got, then if you think you can, please come back to me.'

She turned and looking into his eyes, kissed him gently on the cheek, 'let's talk about it tomorrow. '

They both fell into a fitful sleep.

The following evening saw the huge Super tanker passing through the Skaggerak narrows, and out into the Denmark Straits and the North Sea. The North Sea was not as placid as the Baltic Sea had been and the weather was miserable, certainly not an enjoyable experience on deck with the waves coming over the bows and drenching the fore section of the ship from forward facing window and balcony the view was spectacular and distant.

# Chapter thirty-one

**12th November 2003 Washington Dulles Airport**

John Clarke was booking in on the Delta Airlines flight 1138 departing Dulles 2.00pm when he heard the call for him on the tannoy; he completed check in, and asked at the help desk for the details. He was to ring a Mr Al Burton on a Houston number before departing, something about his Altcar car rental.

Picking a booth that had one either side empty he rang the number, Chris Meddleman of the FBI answered.

' Mr Clarke, my name is Al Burton of Altcar, just to let you know we have delivered your rental car to the Sofitel hotel, that's just a few minutes from the Galleria shopping mall, just in case you needed to shop, there's also a complimentary voucher in the car for root beer or coffee and doughnuts in 'Starbucks.'

'Thanks Al I appreciate that, goodbye now.'

'You have a nice day Sir'.

Something had obviously come up for Meddleman to contact him on an open line, he looked at his watch, 40 minutes to take off, and then a 3 hours and 20 minutes flight, 30 minutes to clear, 30 minutes to hotel, plus 1 hour time difference, round up to nearest hour, he should be with Meddleman 8.00pm local time.

Delta Airlines flight 1138 took off and landed on time, Clarke picked up his bags and was crossing the airport concourse when he heard his name being called, he went back to the help desk, and was given a small brown envelope. He opened it, 'I do hope you enjoyed your time with Irina, when you get to your hotel, please telephone Clive Reynard on 768-3456-1000

Petor'. How the hell did Petor know which flight he was on? Was he being followed?

He approached the taxi rank and stood in line, carefully but he hoped inconspicuously checking around him, he was looking for somebody obviously watching him, somebody doing something unusual, or a cab being too eager, anything, he wasn't a spook and had only read what to watch for in novels. When it came to his turn he stood back and said to the young woman behind him, 'Please, you have this cab I have to make a call.' She accepted with a grateful smile and nod.

As he moved off the rank he noticed that one cab on the feeder rank had not joined onto the line of waiting cabs, he pretended to make a call on his mobile, a casual look in the cabs direction; it again did not join with the others who were passing it by. He finished his 'call' and went back to the rank. He got into the fifth cab, as it pulled away he leant back and put his right arm across the back of the rear seat, the other 'cab' was following.

He leaned forward and spoke to the driver, 'Could you drop me at the Galleria, I have to do a bit of shopping before I go on to the hotel?'

That's no problem sir, shall I wait for you?

'No, I don't know how long I am going to be, but thanks anyway.

As he got out of the cab and paid the driver, the other cab with only the driver in it, stopped and spoke to a Galleria Security guard. The guard gestured to the right, and he knew then he was going to be followed by the driver. As soon as he got through the doors he walked very quickly, quicker he hoped than the guy following, and ducked into the first shop that he could, which just happened to be card and gift shop, getting himself in position near to the window but not in sight from outside of the shop, he picked up a birthday card without looking at it, and watched the window, he saw a medium sized dark haired man around 45-50 years of age hurrying past.

He waited until he had turned the corner about 50 yards away and turned to go, dropping the card back in its place. He quickly went back outside and got into the second taxi on the rank. 'Sorry I am superstitious, I never get into the first cab, first carriage on a railway train, could you take me to the Sofitel hotel?'

Fifteen minutes later he had booked in to the hotel, having changed the room because he was superstitious of that particular number. He began to feel like a spy, or at least how he thought a spy would be acting and feeling. He smiled to himself. Looking at his watch he had less than 30 minutes to get back to the Galleria for 8.00pm

The rental Altcar was a dark blue sedan and was driven round to the front of the hotel for him; tipping the car park attendant he slowly looked

## The President Is Down

around for the 'cab' or its driver. Neither was to be seen. He slipped into drive and eased out of the car park and onto the main drag, around ½ mile down the road he came off the main highway, went over the top of it, and turned left into the Galleria complex.

Parking on the second level he started to walk towards the entrance proper, he had just reached it when he suddenly remembered something he left in the car and turned. There was nobody following. He re-opened the car door reached in and took out a newspaper folded it under his arm and walked back towards the Galleria.

Starbucks was on the first floor in the Mall, and he soon found it the time was 8.02pm he looked in through the open frontage and saw Chris Meddleman sitting at a table at the back, he ignored him completely and went up to the counter, 'could I trouble you for a glass of water, I need to take some tablets?'

The young blonde behind the counter looked most concerned and gave him a glass of water, 'can I get you anything else? She said with a big smile.

'No that's fine thanks; I'll take you up on a cup of coffee in a few minutes. I am expecting a call on my mobile and I'll take it outside he replied loud enough for Meddleman to hear.

He left Starbucks and almost immediately his mobile rang, ----- 'Chris here what's the problem? He very quickly told him.

'OK now listen carefully, go on into the Mall after 2 minutes or so you will see Wall-Mart on your right, go in, go to the men's clothes department and pick up a shirt, then go into the electrical section, browse around for say five minutes, I'll be watching you. If all is clear I will walk away and wait for you in Starbucks.

He had always wanted an 'English' check shirt for casual ware and as some were on offer a picked up a blue and white, and red and white fine line check shirt. He walked through to the electrical section and saw Meddleman already there; he had a kettle in his hand. Both went to the check out and paid, Clarke turned to the left towards Starbucks and Meddleman turned to the right.

Ten minutes later Meddleman joined him in Starbucks.

'To the best of my knowledge you were not followed here, so let's get on with it. I have some news for you so I'll go first.

'The Athonikis is due to sail from Gdansk on the evening tide of 14$^{th}$ November it would seem that its destination is the USA, but where we have no idea. Two days ago 3 nuclear shells were stolen from 2 armouries in Russia; the people who took them were pretty callous they murdered five soldiers, hacking off the head of one of them.

We don't know yet if the shells are coming here, but we do know that Petor Milcovic is involved, so at the moment we are putting 2 and 2 together, that's all we can do until they surface or we get to hear more.'

There is also a nuclear physicist on the loose and has been spending some money, a CIA contact says his wife has some pretty expensive new clothes, and so does he. It may be pure coincidence but this guy actually worked on one of the sites that the shells were stolen from. His name is Alexei Androvitch; we are being sent a photograph and a description. Now unless you have anything more to tell me, then I think you ought to go just in case you are under observation and they lost you.

Before you do put this lighter in your pocket. He gave John Clarke a gold Dunhill lighter, 'here just flick it like this, and it's a normal lighter, compress it like this and it's a GPSI its accurate to within one metre, if you activate we will assume your are in trouble and come and get you.

Ten minutes later Clarke was back at his hotel and collecting his key from reception, he decided to ring the number he had been asked to by Petor.

The room was on the third floor facing out towards the main highway that was very busy at this time of night, he went out onto the balcony and dialled the number, and 'Clive Reynard' answered it almost immediately.

'Hi John nice to speak to you,' was the immediate response. We need to meet up and discuss the business you spoke about with Petor!!'

'Yes, how about tomorrow morning first thing, say around 8 to 8.30am?'

'I suggest we meet in reception, we can go to my office and discuss matters if that's alright with you John?'

The following morning John Clarke met up with Clive Reynard in the lobby of the Sofitel hotel, after the introductions they went outside and were immediately ushered into a stretch limo.

'This is my office said Clive waving his left arm to cover the whole of the interior: Fax-phone, computer and internet link, drinks he said pointing to a fridge, and most important of all coffee, leaning forward to remove the coffee pot from the electric holder. How do you take it, black or with cream? I prefer mine like my women black and hot!!.

Clarke smiled, 'black with one sugar please.'

A slight nod to the driver and the limo glided away as though on a cushion of air.

'I suggest we go for a short drive to a nearby lake, we can have a civilised meeting overlooking the water without any danger of being overheard, I love it there and I think you will too.'

*The President Is Down*

Within ten minutes they were at the lake and parked up, the driver went for a walk.

Reynard leant forward,' we are looking to you to create a bit of mayhem he said smiling, what we would like to achieve is a sizeable chunk of the West Texas oilfields out of action for say 4-6 months if possible. The 3 fields that you are responsible for would constitute about 50% of the area we would like affected. Naturally other oil wells and fields have to be sabotaged so the blame doesn't come too readily to your door. Have you any thoughts on how we can do this?'

Clarke looked pensive, 'Knocking down and setting fire to individual well heads would be one way, but security is pretty tight these days and I don't think you would destroy many before the helicopters would be on to you.'

'What's this "you" John we are talking about you doing it, ----- or at least organising it not me. Let me tell you how I think we should do it.

'The pipeline you look after is 86 miles long, 14 mile runs underground the remainder is on the surface, it spans two rivers, and three gorges, and follows the riverbed at one point for a mile. The pipeline is an average of 30 years old, and has been maintained to industry standards, however as far as most of the pipeline is concerned this is to the bare minimum, how am I doing?'

How the hell did he know so much about Trenton Oil Inc?

'There are three booster pumping stations along the line to maintain pressure and flow, the holding tanks total around 200 in number and these service the refineries. Our feelings are that if we were to hit the pipeline at say a dozen strategic points both above and below ground, take out the three main well head area's, and hit the well heads of say four or five other smaller companies we would have seriously effected the ability of West Texas to produce meaningful levels of oil.'

Clarke looked at him, 'you are utterly mad, how on earth can that are done?'

Clive smiled, 'we have already over 30 land mines along your pipeline, and it took about two months to do it.'

'Now I know you are mad there is no way you could wander onto Trenton oilfields at will and lay mines without being spotted.'

'Oh but we were spotted John, as we intended to be, remember the insurance hike you had last year, and you complaining the cost had gone up too much? Remember the insurance company survey in June of this year?

'Lets just say the insurance company have yet to carry out a survey, and before they advise Trenton Oil I can tell you off the record the new insurance price still stands, the good news is the 'Hike' was to cover the cost of a percentage of any possible terrorist attack on yours or any other companies fields.'

'You see as far as the insurance Company is concerned Trenton Oil commissioned an independent survey of the total pipeline, and pumping stations. The survey report is genuine, the company that carried it out did so they think on your instructions, and they even think they met you personally, in their offices. When they reported they again reported to you personally in Texas City.'

'You then spoke to, and sent the report to the insurance company. They in turn are having it checked out, and are re-assessing the risk, and at the end of November they will be writing to you at Trenton and the other two smaller companies who also had their rigs, holding tanks, and service piping surveyed. And as I said the new premium will stand.'

The colour had drained from Clarke's face. In a strained and low voice he said.

'What exactly do you want from me?'

Clive had now lost all of his 'niceness', and was very businesslike, cold and indifferent.

'My Dear John, you will provide us with the access codes for these security gates along the pipeline,' he took a large map out of his briefcase and laid it on the small table in the limo. He opened it and indicated the security fencing and the numbered gates. There were 7 gates marked out of the 38 total numbers.

'The gates as you know are all fitted with electronic lock pads, the combination of each is randomly changed twice a day around ten people get to know those combinations as of right, and four others have access when needed. You are one of the ten. So there are plenty of other people who would know them at any given time, which makes it more secure for you.'

He handed Clarke a mobile phone, 'from around 8.00pm on Thursday 4th December, you must remember to be in circulation and in view of others at all times, apart from at 8.45 when you will visit the 'John' and make one phone call on this mobile phone, simply dial the only number stored like this, he pressed the number 1 key, which brought up a number. Read aloud slowly and once only the gate combinations in this order. He handed a list with gate numbers on to Clarke. Tear up the piece of paper and flush it away then go back and mix with your colleagues, at around 9.15 up to 9.45pm you will be getting reports of explosions etc.' As soon as you are able destroy and get rid of the mobile phone.

## The President Is Down

Clarke took the mobile phone in a daze, 'I don't know what to say, it sounds like utter madness, but equally it sounds as though it could work.'

It will work, you see to get a re-action you first have to have an action, and until we start to blow things up, there has not been a 'visible' action so to speak. I repeat it will work. Now one final thing before we part Petor is very, shall we say careful with his money, I would suggest that you are equally 'careful' with the $200,000 you currently have in your account.

Clive knocked on the glass partition and the limo started up and drove away.

'We shall not meet again unless it's by accident, if we do I would appreciate you totally ignoring me.'

The 'limo' dropped Clarke off at his hotel ten minutes later.

Clarke picked up his key from reception, and went upstairs in the lift to his room; he had just taken off his jacket when the telephone rang.

'Mr Clarke good morning Sir, this Charles the head waiter here, did you still wish for lunch in your room Sir?'

Clarke immediately recognised Meddleman's voice, 'yes that would be fine, around ½ an hour?'

'If I might just check the order Sir, last night you ordered clam chowder, a 16ozs porterhouse rare, a green salad and a bottle of shiraz, would you still like that Sir?'

'Yes that's exactly right'.

Half an hour later there was a knock on the door, Clarke looked through the viewer and saw Meddleman looking back at him, he opened the door, and stood aside to let him and the trolley he was pushing in.

'Would you like it on the balcony as usual Sir, it's very pleasant out there today?'

'Yes that's exactly what I was going to ask you to do, thank you.

When they were both on the balcony Meddleman said very quietly, 'your room has been bugged whilst you were out and very professionally too. 'When you have finished your lunch walk downstairs to room 666,don't bother about the tall slim black guy in a dark grey suit and carrying a newspaper under his arm, he's watching your back and playing interference for you.'

Meddleman left and Clarke was left to eat a superb steak he had never even ordered.

Clarke finished his steak, changed into a pair of slacks, blue sea island shirt, and brown loafers; he carried a jacket over his arm. As he emerged from the room he saw a tall smartly dressed black man strolling towards him, he had on a dark grey suit and was carrying a newspaper under his arm.

He nodded to Clarke as he went past him.

Room 666 was at the far end of the 6$^{th}$ floor, Clarke spent just five minutes talking to Meddleman, he told him all he knew and was surprised at Meddleman's calmness.

Clarke was to carry out his instructions to the letter, Meddleman would not tell him what they were going to do, and he was only to get in touch if the date or time changed. As he left the room the same black man was coming down the corridor towards him. The black man set off down the stairs and Clarke followed him to the bar, he needed a drink and some different, normal company.

# Chapter thirty-two

**15th November 2003, Liverpool Docks, England.**

**MV Deanboy** is a Container ship. Built by Odense Steel Shipyard, Odense, Denmark. She has a powerful 23,030 SHP Sulzer power plant, has a single shaft, a length of 652 feet (198.86 meters) Beam of 106 feet (32.33 meters). She displaces 48,000 long Tons (48,768 metric Tonnes) fully loaded. She has a top speed of 19 knots (21.87 mph). And carries a crew of 21. She is special in two ways.

Firstly she features climate controlled cocoons on her weather deck that allow the ship to carry approximately 45% more cargo, whilst protecting the additional cargo from marine environment, and:

Secondly, one of the cocoons is double ended; it allows entry from both ends. It had been used for various illegal activities in the past and would be again. The man who built the 'special' cocoon was greedy, and went on the cocoons maiden voyage, he was never seen again. The cocoon is loaded from one end just like the others and customs sealed. But if you know how, you can remove the other end and alter the load, put back the end and the cocoon looks just like the rest on deck, complete with its still intact customs seals. On this occasion cocoon number 16 was carrying motor parts for the Del Rio Manufacturing Inc, of Galveston, Texas. From The Ford motors plant at Halewood, Liverpool.

Five days later she came up behind the ULCC Athonikis in mid Atlantic, the Athonikis had dropped its speed to 8 knots, this gave it a steady head and way, and she maintained station.

A strange thing could be observed on the deck of the tanker, the spare door of the Grande Cherokee, was lashed to one of the pallets of bricks on deck, the fork truck on deck pushed the door and pallet of bricks into the side rails, breaking them in the process, the fork truck driver continued to push until the door and bricks fell over the side of the ship and disappeared into the Atlantic Ocean.

The side rails were now scuffed with dark blue metallic paint, bent and broken.

The Captain of the Container ship took nearly two hours to get the approach right to the Athonikis, when he had matched the Athonikis and was finally running parallel and some 100 feet away he skilfully used his bow and stern thrusters to inch the ships closer together, when they were 40 feet apart he began the transfer.

The boom of the massive deck crane loomed over the deck of the tanker, a large vehicle transfer net was laid on the tanker deck, and protective side sections put in place, the Grande Cherokee was quickly lifted off the tanker deck and onto the deck of the container, the large fork truck followed. The two vessels slowly moved apart and continued on their way. The engine parts in cocoon number 16 went over the side of the container ship. The weight matched exactly that of the Grande Cherokee and the forklift that now took their place. The customs seals were still intact.

700 feet down in the Atlantic Ocean beneath the Athonikis and the Deanboy, an 'Ohio' Class USN Submarine was drifting on a layer of air bubbles, and playing tag with a British Trafalgar Class, they were testing a new sonar array. The chief sonar operator recorded the signatures of two large vessels that had run very close and parallel to each other for over half an hour. He thought it worthy of message to the US Coast Guard at the first opportunity. (In the event that would be some 2 days later).

Four hours later the captain of the Tanker notified a possible hazard to shipping, a Grande Cherokee, motor vehicle had fallen over the side of the ship, when it was being re-positioned on deck. Nobody was hurt, and the vehicle appeared to have sunk, he gave the co-ordinates.

On board the Athonikis Petor Milcovic was talking to Alexei Androvitch in his stateroom, Irina was elsewhere.

'Have you installed the shell in the in the hold yet Alexei?'

'The shell has been in position for five hours now, the trigger has been fitted and the timing mechanism is in place but not connected, I shall brick it all in tomorrow solidly up against shaft in the bottom of the ships hold. The blast will go downwards for maximum effect. The timer has a maximum of twelve hours.'

'The timers on the Jeep and fork truck I will set for 6 hours and 20 hours respectively, that will give me time to be miles away when they go off.' They will detonate within 15 minutes of each other.

'I want you to know I am very pleased with you, although I wasn't too happy about your antics with Irina, fortunately I know what a little tease she can be, so I have forgiven you.'

Androvitch looked absolutely terrified, he wasn't a brave man and he knew what Petor Milcovic was capable of.

You will be taken off in a Gemini with one of the crew who will handle the boat, the Gemini will not show up on radar so when you have fallen behind by about 10 miles, you will be picked up by our contact fishing boat, and the Gemini will be sunk, you will meet up with the Jeep and the Fork Truck again in Galveston,

The fork truck gets left in Galveston, and the Jeep goes to Dallas. Before you set the timers make sure that the Jeep is already in Dallas and you have your flight booked and transport laid on for your flight, you can't afford a slip up in timing.

I will see you for dinner at 7.30pm, he looked at his watch it was now approaching 6.15pm and he had things to do.

Realising he had been dismissed Alexei got up and left, having reached his suite he remembered that he had planned on asking Petor Milcovic if he had contacts that would help him stay in the USA, so he turned around and made his way back, he reached out to knock on the door, and heard Milcovic talking to somebody on the satellite phone, what he heard sent a chill through his body, he felt numb.

'When he has started the second timer, he will set out for the airport just make sure he doesn't get there. He knows far too much I have put $30,000 in your account.' There was a silence; Milcovic had finished on the phone.

Alexei turned around and hurried back to his suite, he threw himself on the bed, what could he do now?

Over the next hour he began to develop a plan, he was surprisingly calm about it, one thing he knew for certain was that he now knew when they planned to kill him, therefore he had a good chance of turning that knowledge to his advantage. His scientific brain took over, and he actually enjoyed pitting his brains against the utterly ruthless Milcovic.

At 7.30pm they were gathered in the dining suite enjoying pre dinner drinks, Milcovic was the perfect host looking after Alexei with warmth he had not displayed up to now, so much so the Alexei began to have a niggling doubt as to what he had actually heard.

Having enjoyed a superb meal Milcovic, Irina, Alexei and the Captain were sat in comfortable chairs on the owners lounge enjoying Cognac and cigars in the case of Milcovic and Alexei, Irina was sipping at a Grand Marnier liquor,

The Captain true to form was enjoying a mineral water and a Monte Christo cigar.

'I have been giving some thought my dear to what we were talking about the other day, your desire to meet up with John again, what if you were to go ashore with Alexei in the fishing boat, he has to pick up the Cherokee in Galveston and drive it on to Dallas for me, you could go with him and arrange for John to meet you in Dallas, you could have the use of the Cherokee until I need it next month, 'he finished by looking at her in an affectionate manner, and awaited her thanks.

She ran to him and threw her arms around him, kissing him on both cheeks, 'thank you Petor, you are so thoughtful.' She clung on to him for a few more seconds before he gently pushed her away smiling, 'careful darling you are embarrassing the Captain and Alexei'.

Alexei was stunned, Milcovic intended that they both should die, he being shot perhaps, and her in a nuclear explosion. The man was totally devoid of feelings of any kind. He saw Milcovic looking at him and realised his face must be displaying some form of emotion, he spoke, 'that's a good idea Petor, I am sure we can arrange that.'

Later in his suite Alexei, began to develop his plan, by the time he fell asleep he felt he had a way forward that would possibly allow him to hide away in the USA, after all it is a huge country and he would have money.

# Chapter thirty-three

**9.30am 15th November 2003 Sofitel Hotel, Houston, Texas.**

John Clarke picked up his rental car from the underground garage, and set off for downtown, at the second set of lights on the highway the car hesitated and began jumping forward, it then smoothed out and progressed normally to the next set, the lights were at red and he stopped, the lights changed to green and the car just sat there not moving. Auto horns began to sound their strident angry noises just as he set off the lights turned again to red, he was now just under half way over the junction when the car stopped again.

Autos were now going from right to left across bonnet/hood and boot/trunk. He heard a siren coming from the rear and saw a police cruiser approaching, it slowed alongside him, the officer next to the driver shouted at him. 'Stay where you are we will be back in a minute'.

One officer stopped the traffic whilst the other and two other drivers pushed the hire car across the junction and on to the sidewalk. Clarke explained to the policeman that his rental car had been a pain in the butt for the last two days. The officer used his mobile to call Altcar, and gave them a verbal tongue lashing for issuing a defective automobile to a client. They said they would have liked to have waited until Altcar arrived but didn't have the time. He thanked them and they left.

The rental car was up on the sidewalk with the hood locked up, when the replacement rental car arrived driven by Meddleman; he looked under the hood with Clarke. 'What's wrong?' said Meddleman.

'He is a fucking lunatic that Milcovic, its all in a report under the back seat, give me a quick call or let me know what to do, I am out of my depth on this, to date as far as I can see you have done fuck all. Twelve months of working for the bureau internally on oil related projected terrorist activity, has hardly equipped me for this.'

'I don't even know if my legend will stand scrutiny, because believe me this guy Milcovic is on the ball, he may even know that I am not what I seem.'

'Calm down John, there is a mobile phone in the glove box use it whenever you want, it is totally secure. Speed dial your day of birth for me, and the last two digits of your year of birth for the bureau. I will read your report and speak with you at 8.00am tomorrow or sooner if need be, the charger is with the phone.

He then grabbed a clipboard, and went all round the auto he was taking back making notes as he did so. He then shook hands apologised for the vehicle letting Clarke down, left the replacement car and drove away, the breakdown truck followed him.

## 16th November 2003 2.20pm Houston International.

Continental Airlines Flight 1079 lifted off for its non-stop flight to San Antonio, arriving 3.15pm local time. Clarke picked up his car that had been dropped off for him at the airport, and drove in to his office in downtown San Antonio. He had a lot of catching up to do. At 7.00pm he drove out to the Companies 'alpha' field and spoke on his bureau mobile to Meddleman.

By the next morning all 7 gates were to be covertly covered 24 hours a day by special forces units, they would be hidden from view and required no assistance, nobody was to come looking for them, and he (Clarke) was not to mention their existence to anybody. The only other person in the know was Big John 'Wayne' Trenton the CEO.

Their brief was to identify and detain any persons acting suspiciously at or near the gates. Force was to be used only as a last resort. Sophisticated microwave communications were being used. Clarke's vehicle number and that of his three line checkers were known to the 'Delta' force units. Clarke would inform Meddleman of any changes to vehicles or staff.

For the first time in days Clarke felt relaxed, he no longer felt as though he was on his own. His thoughts wandered briefly to Irina and he at once felt sad and unhappy. He realised he loved her with all his heart and she was thousands of miles away, and in any case was committed to another. She would never know that there was nothing wrong with him, and that hopefully he had many years of good health ahead of him. Years he could have spent with her.

# Chapter thirty-four

**Monday 24th November 2003, the Pentagon, Washington.**

The US Chief of Staff Donald Fielding again chaired the meeting.

Present were representatives of the FBI, CIA, and the Homeland Defence Force, USCG, US Army and US Navy and Air Force. The SIS and Special branch from the UK were also present.

'Well gentlemen since we last met a lot would appear to have happened, you all have the briefing notes collated from each department. Some of that which was pure guesswork on the part of certain members is wide of the mark, whilst some is surprisingly accurate.

'We now firmly belief that the tanker Athonikis is involved, and having checked its manifest we know that Petor Milcovic is on board. The Captain is ex-Russian Navy as are I suspect most of the crew. Nothing wrong with that nor should we necessarily read anything in to it. A lot of professional sailors and airmen switched to civilian jobs when they lost their service ones, probably much better paid now too.'

'Lets return to Milcovic, ones of ours, he holds joint American and Russian passports very unusual but true. He is a bad penny, known to be involved in illegal arms deals, suspected of extortion and murder. Not the kind of person you would wish to be associated with. On board is a young woman possibly his girl friend, and a male nuclear scientist. '

The scientist is called Alexei Androvitch who within this last month has obtained a six month US visitors visa, stated object tourism. Normally one would fly if going on holiday, he chooses a tanker, again nothing wrong with that just unusual.

'Now to two reports regarding the tanker and a mysterious other vessel. Captain Chuck Henderson US Navy is going to enlighten us, over to you Chuck!.'

'Thank you Sir, two days ago one of our subs and a British sub were testing a new sonar array out in the Atlantic our sub was 'hiding' under a thermal layer of bubbles, the sonar chief thought he heard something strange on the surface so he recorded the sound. It's pretty faint but you can just make out two types of shaft and screw's.

'The British submarine also recorded the incident. Theirs is clearer because they are above the thermal layer. Here's where we have had a bit of luck. The British have been taking vessels signatures in the English Channel now for a few years and have an extensive library. They cross referenced both shafts and screws, the very large vessel is a ULCC probably the Athonikis as she reported losing a vehicle overboard 60 nautical miles from this sighting, the other is positively a container ship Deanboy. There was a stunned silence.

'How sure are you Captain?' this from Superintendent Gardner.

'There is no doubt Sir, the two vessels that were a mere 30 meters apart and travelling at the same speed for at least ten minutes, were the Athonikis and the Deanboy, it could have been much longer in time we simply don't know. The sonar tests were at a crucial point and it wasn't really practical to break off.

'So something or somebody or both were transferred maybe more, but from which vessel, and why?' said Fielding.

Captain Chuck Henderson spoke again, 'we have a USCG Hamilton Class cutter in the immediate vicinity, the

'President Romero 'if I recall, he glanced at the two British policemen, the Hamilton class is a 378-foot Ocean going craft, armed and with a helicopter on board, she's about the size of a destroyer. She could quite legitimately visit the tanker regarding them losing the vehicle overboard, we might be able to get a feel for things what do you think?'

Captain, I think that's a brilliant idea, but lets go one better, all sea traffic knows they are liable to stop and search in the Gulf of Mexico, and the tanker should be entering the Gulf within the next 5 or so hours, how soon can the Coast Guard cutter intercept the 'Athonikis?' This from Fielding again.

Chuck Henderson, took a sea chart out of his briefcase and spread it on the table, 'at the moment she is about here', he pointed to a position well past the Bahamas and approaching the 'Gulf'. The President Romero is in the Gulf and heading towards the Athonikis, my last check put her about

2 hours from interception should we wish. Mere minutes of course with the helicopter.

The Coast Guard Captain who had remained silent up to now spoke, Captain Flannery Sir, might I make a suggestion?'

'Please do Captain,' said Fielding.

Five minutes later Fielding with a big grin on his face said, 'lets do it gentlemen', he looked at Captain's Flannery and Henderson, 'do not let us detain you two.'

FBI Special Investigator Perry briefed everybody regarding the actions being taken to safeguard the Texas oilfields, but declined to identify their asset in place. Perry mentioned the 'Delta' force involvement but again was non-committal.

He then went on to ask for specific help, the army agreed to provide four choppers and crews, as fast reaction forces to back the delta units on the ground, the Air force would provide AWAC's coverage of the whole of West Texas during the period at risk. A command centre would be established in Fredericksburg at the National Guard Headquarters. Colonel John James Hogwaters would co-ordinate the joints forces efforts. Delta force would not strictly speaking be under his command. He was not happy with this.

## 1320 hours Monday 24th November 2003, Gulf of Mexico. US Coast Guard Cutter, President Romero

Commander Bill Nicholson the cutters Captain was bending over the radar display with his number one and the ships helicopter pilot. A large blip could be seen on the display west of the Bahamas and approaching the gulf and the President Romero. This was the Greek ULCC tanker the Athonikis. The tanker was making 15 knots and the President Romero a comfortable 30 Knots. The estimated time to interception was 65 minutes if both craft maintained the same speed and heading.

It was agreed that the helicopter would fly towards Key West off the Florida coast and to starboard of the tanker it would by pass the tanker with a 15 miles separation, fly 10 miles past the tanker, turn and approach it from the stern.

When the helicopter was 3 minutes out from the Athonikis, the pilot would advice the cutter. The cutters Captain would inform the tanker that they were about to get a visit from the cutters helicopter who had been searching for the vehicle that went over board, and would be requiring further information regarding the incident. The helicopter would be putting 1 coastguard and 1 customs officer aboard to facilitate enquiries.

'This is US Coastguard cutter President Romero to Motor Vessel Athonikis do you read'.

A minute later the Athonikis responded.-----'ULCC Tanker Athonikis to US Coastguard go ahead.'

US Coastguard cutter President Romero to ULCC Athonikis, this is the Captain speaking, my ships helicopter is approaching you from the stern, maintain heading and speed please, we shall be putting 2 officers on board to follow up on the vehicle that was lost overboard. Please have the ships full manifest available for inspection. This is your lucky day Sir, you have been chosen for a full on board customs inspection and examination, as you are aware we are now routinely carrying these out as an anti-terrorist exercise prior to docking, I thank you in advance for you co-operation. We shall be with you in around 20 minutes Sir.'

On the bridge of the Athonikis Petor Milcovic was livid, the Russian Captain was more composed, and it was he who spoke to the Coastguards.

'Us Coast Guard President Romero, this is Captain Deraukia I copy and will do as requested, please advise your helicopter of radio mast on the bridge and satellite antennae on the deck behind the bridge. We will guide him in for landing on deck if you wish, do you copy?'

'US Coastguard President Romero to Athonikis,--- thank you but the helo will not land he will come in to a hover 20 feet above the deck, the officers will abseil on to the deck a steadying hand on the ropes would be appreciated. We will try and get the inspection over as quickly as possible for you, and of course you will not need a port inspection. Once again thank you for your co-operation.'

The white and red helicopter was now flying alongside the tanker some 20 or so feet to starboard, very slowly and in a nose up position, the pilot gradually matched the tankers speed, and then began slowly moving over the deck, the side door was open and two men were sat in the doorway with their feet on the skids, hands on abseiling ropes.

Both men came down the ropes with ease, a point noted by the tankers Captain who greeted both men on deck.

He saluted them, and shook hands, 'welcome aboard gentlemen, come up onto the bridge,' they followed the Captain up the external and internal stairs to the massive bridge. The view from which was spectacular. Taking off their helmets, they replaced them with peaked caps.

'If we could start Captain with the vehicle you lost overboard.' This from the USCG lieutenant Groves.

'Yes of course, before leaving Liverpool the Jeep was positioned towards the foredeck between two of the major run off pipes, it was secured and tarpaulin'd, during the crossing of the Atlantic the rough weather loosened the tarpaulin, and salt water had got onto the vehicle.'

'It was decided to reposition it on deck, wash it down and then replace the tarpaulin, the man moving the vehicle is a fool, he left the engine running with the brake on but in gear, the Jeep was an automatic and it crept on choke, he didn't notice until it had run into the guard rail, he panicked and the vehicle went over the side. The vehicle appeared to float for a couple of minutes then sank. You can see the damaged rails on the port side, we have had to use ropes as a temporary measure until we reach port.'

Groves glanced down the massive deck, just in the distance he could some bright orange rope work on the port side. 'Yes we noticed it as we came in, we will have look at the point it went over a little later, can we now take a look at the ships manifest please?'

They spent the next hour checking the load details via the ships computer with the manifest; a further two hours were spent in checking valves and meters. The propulsion chambers and the engine room were quickly inspected or so it appeared, nothing was found.

Back on the bridge, Groves spoke to Captain Deraukia, 'all appears to be in order Sir, we now just need to see all the people on the manifest that we have not met, and I believe that to be a Mr Milcovic, a Miss Irina Ludmilla Ronofskia and a Mr Androvitch. Please have them bring their passports and visa's with them.'

Milcovic was not pleased at being summoned to the bridge, and it showed although he did his best to hide it. Groves was checking the passports of Milcovic and Irena, and US Customs Officer Garcia was looking at Androvitch's passport and visa, Garcia looked at Androvitch and said, 'thank you Sir, all appears to be in order enjoy your stay.'

Half an hour later both 'Coastguard/Customs' and the tanker Captain were stood looking at the broken guard rails, there were very clearly scuffed with dark blue metallic paint, the exact same colour as that of the Jeep. So the jeep had gone overboard as they had been told.

The Coastguard helicopter had been called some minutes before, and having said their goodbyes to the tankers Captain they were winched back onto the chopper and flew back to the President Romero.

Both men were back in the wardroom in less than twenty minutes.

Captain Bill Nicholson was the first to speak,' let me tell you what we have from this end its quite enlightening, firstly we were right to fit you with Geiger counters and vibration monitors, from the information they sent back to here it would seem there is a low level of radiation somewhere close to a revolving vibration, which would indicate the prop shaft at a point close to the engine room. It's a good job they were silent monitors. You have no need to worry the level is perfectly safe, less than that coming of an 'Ohio' nuclear sub power plant. However, it does indicate the likelihood of one of the 'shells' being on board.'

Inspector Garcia US Customs laid a piece of notepaper on the wardroom table, 'the guy who is down as being a nuclear physicist handed me this in his passport, he pushed the notepaper across.

*Urgent I contact you in next 24 hours to stop a disaster.*
*Androvitch.*

'Also it look's like the Jeep went overboard like he said, we have no idea why the Athonikis and the Deanboy ran along side each other. It could be drugs, it could be anything. But it's definitely not 'Kosher'.'

2 hours after the departure of the coastguard/customs, a grey Gemini pulled alongside the Athonikis, within five minutes Irena, and Androvitch had transferred to the Gemini, and 20 minutes later they were on board a fishing boat stood on the flying bridge and looking at the Athonikis some five miles away. They changed into casual gear and prepared to be part of the people who had been fishing for the day.

The Gemini had not showed up on the radar covering the 'Gulf', and the fishing boat was one of a dozen or so in the gulf at that time and on one of its regular trips out of 'Key West', Miami. It would tie up at its berth at 8.30pm that night and the 'fishing' party would have a few beers, talk about the one that got away, and go home to their families, all but two who would take an internal flight to Galveston Texas that night.

Unaware of the fact that two of the three passengers of the Athonikis were no longer aboard, the joint operation to board the Athonikis was started.

# Chapter thirty-five

**Tuesday November 25th 2003, The Gulf of Mexico 0230 hours.**

The two Huey helicopters with their 16 marines on board were coming in fast and low, surprise would be of essence and when they popped up over the side of the tanker one at either side, they discharged their full compliment of marines in just over sixty seconds. The first two were on the bridge before the officer of the watch knew what had hit him. He had been watching a portable television now the Captain had gone to bed. Faced with two fully armed Marines he co-operated without hesitation, he called the Captain to the bridge as requested not giving a reason as he had been instructed.

Four marines and a civilian had already reached the engine room, a quick look around and they found the bricked in area around the prop shaft. The civilian was in fact a bomb disposal expert; it took him fifteen minutes to establish that the bricks were not booby trapped, and a further fifteen to do the same with the bomb casing/box.

He spoke to Donald Fielding the Chief of Staff, 'You may inform the President that the information from the Russian Androvitch was correct, we found a medium grade nuclear shell adapted to act as a bomb, the timer had been activated at midnight but the line connecting it to the bomb had been broken and then spliced back together at first sight it would look as though the bomb was set to go at 12.00noon our time.'

'It would not have exploded which is a bloody good job as it is powerful enough to blow out the bottom of the tanker, vaporise the rear section and discharge the entire contents into the gulf, over 250,000 tons of crude would cause an ecological disaster in the gulf of immense proportions.

The oil and the nuclear fission together would have made the Gulf barren of any sea life for many years.'

There was a stunned silence from Fielding who was visibly shaken could the bomb disposal man have seen him.

The Captain in charge of the marines was speaking to Milcovic, who had adopted an attitude of complete indifference

' I am not quite sure Captain why you fail to understand, they tell me my English is excellent, that being the case let me say it again, I have absolutely no knowledge whatsoever of any bomb on board or drugs or whatever. I am simply a businessman, I am on board as I have leased this ship and others and intend visiting a number of clients in the USA, my helicopter will be picking me up at 8.00am, I have a meeting at 11.00am with the President of Trenton Oil.'

The Marines Captain glanced up from the paperwork he was reading. 'Sorry Sir, nobody leaves this ship until we dock tomorrow morning.' With that he turned away.

Milcovic flew across the deck at him and grabbed the Captains arm, 'Captain you can't do this I demand that you let me off this ship at 8.00am when my helicopter arrives. I have been cleared by the US Coastguard and US Customs, these are International waters you have no right to detain me.'

The Marines Captain, shrugged off Milcovic's hand, 'Don't do that Sir, you must understand this ship has been seized by the Government of The United States of America, it has a bomb on board that we have defused, there are no communications possible from the ship, only secure military traffic. All other means of communication has been cut.'

Milcovic paled, 'what kind of bomb was it?'

'There's no need to worry Sir, we found it in time and its been defused, it was only a small bomb and wouldn't have done much damage, it was fitted with a booby trap but we found it, so as I say don't worry about it.' The Captain looked at his watch it was exactly 3.10am

They had only found the device that looked like the bomb; it was some kind of back up trigger he knew that Androvitch had set up 2 two booby traps not one, the bomb was still live!!! He walked dazed to his stateroom and sat on the massive bed. It was all going wrong; he was going to be blown to bits together with everybody else on this nuclear time bomb.

He lay back on the bed, for the first time ever Petor Milcovic's mind was blank, he could not think of one single thing to do, other than declare his hand. Maybe if he told the Captain about the other two bombs and the plan to blow up the West Texas oilfields he could 'buy' himself some kind of amnesty.---------. He wasn't to know that Androvitch had already done that, and that 'they' already knew most of what was planned.

Milcovic had decided, he had to get off this ship, he tried the cabin door, it was unlocked and the corridor was empty they were not watching him. He gently closed the door again, if he could get out of his cabin and down the deck to where the jeep had gone over, there was a lifeboat to the starboard side of the deck, it had an electric winch and could carry ten men, with a bit of luck he could get off the Athonikis unseen, set up the outboard and head back towards Key West which would be about 35 miles back.

He opened the bedside table drawer and took out the colt automatic, he checked the clip and pushed it back into the butt, and finally he attached the slim but effective silencer and put the gun on the bed. He gathered all his black clothing together and put on a couple of wool jumpers with long sleeves, black pants and socks and shoes. He had now made himself as invisible in the dark as possible. The problem with the deck of a super tanker is that the area around the bridge it very brightly lit, along the deck there are strategically sited lights pointing downwards towards the sea, this makes the deck visible if you are looking at it.

But the fact is you tend not to be looking directly at the deck but into the distance beyond. As the bow of the ship is a quarter of a mile away from the bridge the crew depend upon radar and its very size to warn them and others of danger. It was this that Milcovic was banking on when he exited the stateroom some ten minutes later.

He checked the corridor, it was empty, he quickly ran to the end, and opened the bulkhead door carefully onto the external stairs to the deck. This side of the bridge was in semi-darkness, he then realised that it wasn't the tanker crew that was conning the ship it was the US Coastguard or US Navy, they being unfamiliar with the deck lighting and the length of the ship had turned most of the deck lights off. Probably so they could see better.

He quickly moved into the shadows and ran along the deck towards the bows, he had been running for about 200 yards when somebody shouted and shone a torch on him, he instinctively raised the silenced colt and fired three times, the shadow behind the torch lurched fell to the left and collapsed on the deck, and the torch went out. The whole incident had taken 4 or 5 seconds. Oh God this was not what he wanted, he looked towards the bridge, there had been no reaction. He felt the body and knew the marine at his feet was dead.

How long had he got before they came looking for, the marine had been at his post just 10 minutes of a 4 hour watch, the bad news for Milcovic was that he was due to report in at 1 hour intervals, there were 50 minutes before his next check in, and probably 1 hour before they found him. --- None of which Milcovic knew.

He found the starboard lifeboat, and kicked of the safety lock, and started the electric motors driving the twin winches, he got in the lifeboat and swung it out, the lifeboat gently descended to the surface of the Gulf of Mexico.

He stopped the lifeboat about 3 foot off the wave tops, now what did he do?

The ship was making 10 knots, he furiously thought, that was about 12 MPH it was too much, far too fast the lifeboat would hit the water and probably turn over if it didn't get crushed by the side of the tanker. He had to do something, he dropped the lifeboat until it was just going in and out of the water, he the chopped the rear davit holding the stern out of the water. The rear of the lifeboat dropped into sea and immediately began to sway quite alarmingly from side to side even though it was calm water this far down the hull. He reached forward and started the lifeboat motor and ran the engine, he dropped it into gear and trying to match the forward speed of the tanker he dropped the bow davit.

The lifeboat hit the water and lurched towards the tanker, the bow of the life boat bounced off the side of the tanker and a chunk of the lifeboat upper deck came away, Milcovic was thrown first forward and then to the right, and nearly fell over the side, he fell forward again and his head struck the combing in front of him with a sickening thud. Milcovic fell to the bottom of the life boat in daze, he couldn't see properly out of his left eye and knew he had badly injured it, the pain was intense. Blood poured out of the socket.

The lifeboat was about 20 feet from the side of the tanker and heading back towards it when he grabbed the wheel and turned it away from the side of the tanker. The lifeboat was making just a little less speed than the Athonikis and he was able to distance himself. The Athonikis began to pull away from the lifeboat and very soon was dipping up and down in the spreading wash left by the tanker.

Milcovic was not a sailor, but he could see the line the tanker had been taking and headed well to the left of it, and noted the compass reading, he knew if he kept that heading he would finish up somewhere on the Florida coast, he also knew that he only had about seven and a half hours before the bomb went off, he should be well clear of any problems, the Athonikis would be around 150 miles away when it went up. He found the colt in the cocoon cabin sliding around on the floor.

Milcovic eye was causing him considerable pain, turning on the cabin lighting he looked for the first aid kit, broke it open and found an eye dressing and a phial of morphine it was preloaded in a needle and only needed to be pushed into his arm. It took about five minutes for the pain to dull and become bearable.

**Tuesday 25th November 2003. MV Athonikis, Gulf of Mexico. 4.10am**

'Go and find him, how the hell you can fall asleep on the deck of a tanker I don't know,' secretly the Marine Captain was a bit concerned it wasn't like Kowalski to be a problem, he was a bit of a thinker and should make sergeant in time.

They found the body of Private First Class Matt Kowalski aged 22 years and 4 days, in a pool of blood between two inspection hatches, he was difficult to see, and it was evident that he had been sheltering from the wind coming off the bow when he had run into trouble. Somebody had shot him at close range, in the breaking dawn his young crumpled body was twisted and somehow aged in death, and didn't seem to belong to the youngster who only four days ago had been dancing on the tables in the Rococo club, Clearwater Miami.

An inspection of the Tankers deck quickly showed the starboard bow lifeboat was missing. The marines Sergeant radioed their findings. A cabin inspection quickly showed all three passengers also missing. It hadn't been realised that Irina and Androvitch had already left the ship some hours prior. It was assumed that all three were on the lifeboat, and could have been away from the Athonikis for up to one hour that gave them 10 miles plus 12 to 14 the ship had made steaming in the opposite direction, so they were around 25 miles away maximum.

The Coastguard cutter President Romero sent its helicopter to look for the lifeboat, it was now daylight and the Gulf was quiet in the early morning with the sun still low and a freshness in the air, the clear blue waters, and peacefulness belied the tragedy that had recently taken place and the terrible revenge that was about to be played out.

The President Romero received a ship to shore message with the co-ordinates of an orange lifeboat that some nutter was cruising around in. A former American Airlines Captain sailing his 45ft yacht in the Gulf and heading for Key West was not impressed to see a ships lifeboat being handled by some idiot who had no idea that his boat had right of way over a motor vessel. And felt it was worth the Coastguard checking it out.

The helicopter over flew to starboard of the lifeboat and then tuned back on it, the load hailer was used by the helicopter crew to tell the lifeboat to heave to. The lifeboat ignored it. The helicopter came round again and a coastguard rating was sat in the doorway about to be winched down. He was about 30 foot away from the lifeboat and just about the drop into space when the man piloting the lifeboat fired a handgun at him, he felt the bullet hit his thigh and shouted for the helo to peal away.

The pilot of helicopter turned hard and fast, dropped the nose and hammered at the lifeboat, he thundered over the top at over a 100 miles per hour, the lifeboat rocked violently, the helicopter turned and repeated the manoeuvre, the lifeboat now rocking left to right, and dipping in and out of the waves virtually turning turtle as it did so. The rating who had been shot was having his wound dressed, and was replaced by another coastguard, now sat in the doorway, he was holding a high rate of fire M60 which was permanently fixed to the fuselage of the helicopter. The coastguard looked very angry. He shouted through the loudhailer to the lifeboat to heave to and stop. It didn't.

The man piloting the lifeboat again turned and fired the hand gun at both the pilot of the helicopter and the coastguard sat in the doorway. Jonnie Lee-Field was the great-great-grandson of a Pawnee Indian Chief and proud of it, he also happened to be the best shot with an M60 on the Coastguard base. His instructions were clear give two warnings and then take them out; they had just had the second warning.

The twenty second burst from the M60 tore through the back of the lifeboat chewing it up as it went, it continued over the man with the gun his, body appeared to split in two, and his head exploded leaving a stump where the head had been, the shells continued to stitch a line over the lifeboat to its bow, the lifeboat fell apart as the helicopter passed overhead. Jonnie Lee-Field was as sick as a dog, and sat there mesmerised until he was pulled back into the aircraft. It was not the same as firing at targets that couldn't fire back and were inhuman ones that popped up again for the next man to try his luck.

As the helicopter turned to fly back over the remains of the lifeboat two slim dark dorsal fins cleaved through the water and dived under the remains of the lifeboat. Bits of the lifeboat were tossed in the air as the sharks fought to get the bigger pieces of meat for themselves, soon there was complete inactivity and the helicopter returned to its mother ship to look after its injured and make its report, as the sharks lazily swam away.

The camera's onboard the Coastguard helicopter would later confirm that the man visible on the lifeboat, had ignored warnings, and had opened fire twice on the helicopter injuring one man in the process. It was likely that this was the same man who had murdered the marine on board the tanker some short time before. There was no sympathy for him, but some for the other two people presumed to have died with him.

The tanker was brought to a halt a hundred miles of shore and in the middle of the gulf, US Navy destroyers and two Coastguard cutters kept the public their boats and light aircraft away from the Athonikis until the 'devise' was safely removed, and a complete search was made of the tanker. The MV Athonikis then went on to dock at Galveston and discharge its cargo of oil. The ship was impounded and the owners informed of events. It was now 8.00pm Wednesday November 26th.

# Chapter thirty-six

**Wednesday 26th November 2.45pm. FBI Texas Regional office, Galveston, Texas.**

Special Agent Chris Meddleman was sat with Alexei Androvitch in the smaller of the conference rooms; their conversation was being secretly video-taped.

'Well Alexei the information you gave us was absolutely spot on, right down the how to disarm the bomb, the ship is now on its way into port here in Galveston.'

'In view of what you have told us already and the additional information you have for us I am empowered to offer you a deal:'

'We will give you a new identity, immunity from prosecution for the offences you have admitted committing in the USA. Help to relocate you, and provide you with a government pension of $70,000 a year, you have some monies of your own, and the IRS will not be touching them so you start with a clean slate. All this however depends on you locating the other two bombs. By the way where is the woman?'

'Irena is booked in with me in the downtown Holiday Inn,----- he blushed we are not sharing a room, she is in room 277 next door to mine. She knows nothing of the bombs, she doesn't even know that Petor Milcovic intended for her to die in the explosion when the bomb in the Jeep went off, he didn't care where it was when it exploded anywhere would have suited his purpose.'

Meddleman was tired and loosing it. 'Lets not forget in all of this that *you* actually, watched while 5 men were killed, murdered in fact, *you* supervised the making safe of the nuclear shells, *you* turned them into individual bombs, and *you* installed those bombs, one on board ship, and the other two onto vehicles. I personally have no time for you whatsoever Mr Androvitch; in fact I only have utter contempt for you. Milcovic, by the way is dead!!, in my opinion you are as guilty as those that killed the Russian soldiers.'

There was a lengthy silence, which Androvitch broke, 'I can see why you would think that way, but it was always my intention to sabotage Milcovic's efforts and build a new life for myself in the United States.'

'Bollocks, we are wasting time, where are the other two bombs now, right now?'

Androvitch knew that whatever he said Meddleman was too 'near' to the situation he would never believe him about the bombs. He pulled a piece of note paper out of the top pocket on his jacket, 'the second bomb is on a large forklift/dumper vehicle in the heavy goods section in dockyard parking, the name Tracey Construction Equipment in all over it, it's located alongside the Pacific Package Company, right here in Galveston docks. The third one I will tell you about when I have my agreement in writing. I no longer trust you Mr Meddleman' he said with typical Russian bluntness.

It was Meddleman's turn to feel a little uncomfortable, he wouldn't get any prizes for upsetting Androvitch, they had already had the best result ever. If he blew it by being stroppy with Androvitch he would never survive it.

'I am sorry, please understand this would be the second major disaster to strike us in the USA in two years, maybe even worse than 911, I don't know. What I do know is that you personally can have anything you want at this time, this bomb or bombs must not go off, I am sorry if I offended you please accept my apologies.' He looked at though he meant it.

Androvitch looked at Meddleman for what seemed an age, 'your apology is accepted, I too apologise for my actions and for saying I didn't trust you. He paused.

'The other bomb is in the Grande Cherokee Jeep, it didn't go over the side of the tanker, that was a pile of bricks and a car door the same colour as the Jeep. The jeep was transferred to another ship; a container ship called the 'Deanboy', the container was to be delivered to Del Rio Manufacturing Inc here in Galveston. It should be there now.

Meddleman picked up the telephone and spoke for a couple of minutes, the Fork lift was to be located and very quietly the immediate area evacuated, police units were already on the way to Del Rio Manufacturing, the owner was known to be a bit of a shady character and was being picked up by other units right now.

There was to be no radio traffic, it was not Meddleman's intention to alert the media, the last thing he wanted until after the bombs had been located and neutralised was TV news vans descending on them. The raid on Del Rio Company premises was supposedly raided by the IRS, all the computers were taken out, filing cabinets were seized, and all managers were detained pending being questioned. When the TV camera's arrived courtesy of a certain sergeant making a phone call on his mobile, and being $500 better off as a result it was far too late, the show was over.

Androvitch had insisted on showing the US Army bomb disposal unit how to make safe the two bombs, they were subsequently take by air to Fort Bragg and safely stored in the underground bunkers.

Although Androvitch and Irena had entered the US somewhat illegally, they both had current passports and visas, Meddleman arranged for immigration to visit them at the hotel. Their 'Stay' was now official and legitimate.

They were both being held for their own protection until the witness protection programme could be put in place for Androvitch at the very least. Meddleman had something else in mind for Irena he needed to check out a couple of things yet. At the moment Meddleman was Mr Golden Balls, he could do no wrong, and the FBI were riding on the crest of a wave, which glittered with success the like of which they hadn't had in years. Making up somewhat for the Waco disaster right here in Texas. He intended to make use of that success as much as he could right now.

Meddleman took Irena to dinner that night; they dined on fabulous seafood, lobster and sea bass, superb salads and good wine. Meddleman told Irena all about the death of Petor Milcovic, and she shed a few tears, he had always treated her like a lady, given her anything she wanted and never made demands, whilst she did not love him, she never the less had affection for him akin to that of a treasured brother or sister. Then Meddleman told her about the three bombs and how Milcovic had intended her to die, she was stunned.

She told him of her role and in particular her feeling for the man she knew as John Clarke, he merely mentioned that he knew him slightly. Meddleman took Irena back to the hotel, kissed her lightly on both cheeks, and arranged to pick her up the following morning. He had to take her somewhere away from Androvitch where she would be safe until it was decided where she could relocate to.

# Chapter thirty-seven

**Friday 28ᵗʰ November 2003, the Pentagon, Washington.**

Sir Bernard Hills and Superintendent Gardner were being briefed by Donald Fielding the US Chief of Staff.

' Well Sir Bernard we had a near miss with the bomb on the Athonikis and the other two bombs, I dread to think what might have happened without the input from yourselves, he nodded to Gardner, and the British Government. The Greek guy Ari, what's his name has been terrific in going along with us. As you know the tanker has been impounded, however following our discussion this morning the ship will be released back to its owners. And I believe that Ari has sent its usual Captain and crew to take over the ship. They should arrive on Sunday next.'

'The unknown quantity at the moment is this planned attack on the Trenton group pipeline, that may still go ahead, we have no way of knowing other than it was originally dated and time as: Thursday 4ᵗʰ December at 8.00pm.'

'Now we have closed off the nuclear weapons side of things I had thought of simply locating the 'mines' that had been laid along the pipeline, digging them up, and waiting for the guys who are going to activate them turning up, that way we have a chance of picking up the complete cell of terrorists in one hit. The downside to that is that they could be watching, see what we are doing and abort. We lose the lot then.'

Gardner chipped in, ' how do we actually know that they are going to penetrate the security again to set the mines off, why not simply drive past and do it electronically? It could be a bluff, just because they have gone through this charade of obtaining electronic pad numbers for gates, and telling Clarke all about it doesn't mean to say that's what will happen, its been worrying me how open with information they have been.'

Fielding looked at Gardner, ' Shit, --- that's exactly what the Delta force Captain said, he said he would have laid mines or explosives with either timers on, or ones that could be set off by a radio signal. He would not have risked assets by having to go back in again, we overruled him.'

I will speak with Perry FBI, and get hold of Colonel Hogwaters who you will recall is co-ordinating our joint forces efforts in Texas. Let's hope we are not too late.

# Chapter thirty-eight

**Sunday 30th November 2003, Glenville, San Antonio, Texas**

Today was the 55th birthday of Lee 'Lucky' Ballinger, it was 6.30am Lee had showered and dressed in his lightweight flying suit, i.e. jeans, tee-shirt and an ex- 191st Assault Helicopter Company blouson. He was lucky in many respects, lucky in his marriage, his children and his 5 grand children, his health and his job. Not only was he celebrating his birthday today but 32 years with Trenton oil.

He well remembered the 30th November 1968, that was the day after which they named him 'lucky'. The day had started a little like this the sun had risen at 0553 over the Mekong Delta, Viet Nam, he was a young sergeant helicopter pilot and it was his 20th birthday. The sortie today was to insert the 'Longknives' into a LZ. His was one of four ships they had been given a number of area's along the canal to check out. He had completed his insertion and was returning to re-fuel and await the pick up, when he and another Huey were told to vector onto a map reference near a village 16 miles north and deeper into the delta.

Two boats of the River Patrol Force had come under heavy fire, in the daytime patrols consisted of just two boats which operated within radar range of each other, the patrols had a duration of around twelve hours the VC had let the first PBR go past and waited for the second, they had caught it just as it came round a bend and was frontal on to some of the VC and broadside to other VC. They had coned their fire which was devastating, and literally cut the PBR in two taking out the forward deck gun and killing most of the crew members.

The River Assault squadron now had 2 brigades shore based at Vung Tau and Mytho, the third brigade was river based and thus totally mobile.

The floating base was always in a hostile zone; it was from this base that the two PBR had come.

The cry for help when it came was very weak, air support in the shape of two F4 Phantoms was 10 minutes away, he banked, pushed the nose down on the Huey and set off, he did not take evasive action as every second counted, the lead PBR was turning back to help, it ran into another ambush exactly the same, and was under heavy fire with engines out and drifting. The two air gunners hung out with their M60 ready to blast anything that even looked like VC. The other Huey was tailing him at a regulation 100 yards.

He came upon the first PBR it was listing badly and making a little way, towards it partner, the foredeck gun had gone, the main rear deck gun was still returning fire, there were two bodies on the deck around the gun. He swept in weaving from side to side, and the two side gunners let rip, he wheeled around and came back again, and this time was able to bring his pilot operated 4000 rounds a minute mini gun to bear the effect was devastating, the canal bank erupted and bodies spilled into the water like nine pins, their black outfitted bodies looking strangely surreal and puppet like.

One of the door gunners was hit badly and fell out of the door, he dangled there unable to pull himself back in, the crew chief grabbed his harness and pulled him back in, only to be shot himself, he was dead within seconds. Most of the VC was retreating and he went into a hover trying to push the Patrol boat to the other bank with the rotor wash to where there were fewer VC. He felt a sharp pain in his left leg and knew he had been hit.

There was only one man visible on the PB now he was firing his assault rifle and trying to pick off the VC, who had now started to come back knowing they could finish the job. That was when Lee lost his cool for the first and only time in his life. If he was going to die in this God Forsaken Hole he was gonna take the bastards with him. He swung the Huey round and sat looking at them whilst he poured thousands of rounds at them. The Huey was taking multiple hits, mainly from the side and these were whipping through the fuselage or in one door and out the other, he calmly pivoted to the left and took the VC out, and then to the right.

His left leg was going numb, and he was having problems controlling the side slip. There was only very sporadic firing now, he turned back to the PB which had now wedged itself into the canal bank and was listing heavily. He dropped the skid nearly onto the deck; the soldier on the PB pushed another wounded man on board, and heaved himself up, then waved them off. The other PBR was to sink with no survivors.

Lee spun the Huey round, and set of back to safety, he remembered little of the landing apart from telling a medivac chopper to get the hell out as he was coming in hot. It was the worst landing of his life, the Huey hit the ground hard, skidded, and side slipped into a water filled ditch, he and the rest on board were carefully lifted out, then he fainted.

He came to 24 hours later, very weak and dehydrated; they had managed to save his leg. The cooks were using the Huey as a 'colander' for draining vegetables, there were so many holes in it. It was estimated by intelligence and from what Lieutenant John 'Wayne' Trenton told them that Lee had personally wiped out forty plus VC.

Two months later he was presented with a Purple Heart for being wounded and displaying conspicuous gallantry in the face of intense enemy fire, and for rescuing his fellow soldiers with little thought for his own safety. And for killing so many of the enemy. General George Jackman also presented him with an invoice for a new Huey, ---- he still had the invoice.

Two years later he had been bumming around New York, not settling after Viet Nam, few could. When he decided to take a short holiday in New Mexico, he had seen a familiar face at a bar. Two days later; he was buying an Army surplus Huey for Trenton oil, and flying the pipeline. He had been with them ever since. Meeting his wife at the Trenton Christmas party that same year she was soft enough to accept his hand in marriage later the following April, and they had been happy and lucky ever since.

Today his luck was going to be challenged yet again, the company now had two Huey choppers, 'Trenton One' configured for passengers and light equipment and luggage, and 'Trenton Two' stripped out as a heavy work horse. He was to fly 'Trenton Two' the heavier work horse today; sections 1 to 11 of the pipeline were to be visually inspected today by the Vice President of Trenton Oil, Lee Lucky Ballinger. He was also going to deliver a one ton wellhead valve to section 14.

Wayne Trenton had told him of the threat to the pipeline, and of the troops somewhere out there looking after the pipeline, John Clarke had been informed by Wayne of the fact that he had told Lee Ballinger, it was his business and neither the Government nor President of the United States were going to tell him what he could or could not say about Trenton Oil. John Clarke had to accept that.

# Chapter thirty-nine

**Sunday 30<sup>th</sup> November 2003 0740 hours, Trenton oil headquarters heli-port.**

The Trenton Heliport was a shared runway and hanger facility with another local Texan Company, it worked well there was always somebody on site 24 hours a day 7 days a weeks all year round, security was good. The huey was parked on the pad outside the hanger, with the rotor blades tied down, it took around 15 minutes to check the aircraft out and release the blades.

He ran up the engine and signalled his intention to move over to the freight side of the area. Lifting a mere 25 feet off the ground he carefully flew the aircraft to where the wellhead valve was awaiting him, he landed alongside it and shut the engine down. Don Robinson his flight engineer approached. Don was a jolly giant of a man, black as coal utterly reliable, he had been with Trenton for 15 years now, this had been Lees doing. Lee thought he was the best Huey helicopter engineer ever, even Huey admitted if he didn't know the answer to a Huey aircrafts problem, they would be hard pressed.

'She's on top line Lee, maximum power available through the whole range, the radio has been changed and is the latest Marconi, this one has a GPS 24 hour hook up. In other words if you squawk this here, -- he pressed a button, then it relays your exact position to here at Trenton and the local ATC'.

The top section of the well head was firmly encased in a wooden packing case that had been centrally placed on a cargo net; eight nylon straps with adjustable fixing cleats were attached to the corners and sides. Lee would lift off and go into a hover, his nylon straps would be attached to the ones on the net. The straps would be adjusted to ensure the load was level and evenly distributed.

Ten minutes later with his load securely in place and suspended some 10 feet below the Huey Lee turned on to a heading that would taker him cross the main highway and to airspace over Trenton land, the time was now 0855 hours, radio checks complete Lee settled down to flying the now slightly cumbersome helicopter. The plan was to follow the pipeline at a height of 100 feet and visually inspect the pipe for damage or seepage. He settled on a forward speed of 65 Knots.

The time was now 0945 and Lee had completed sections 1 to 5, it was a clear day and visual flight rules applied, the sun was over his left shoulder and beginning to develop some autumnal strength through the side windows.

Around a mile ahead of him he could see the first of the in line booster stations. Suddenly there was a huge explosion and the booster station was clouded in smoke and dust, within seconds it had burst into flames which were shooting some 150 foot skywards.

Within 2 minutes or so he was close enough to observe the damage, and was already calling it in to the Trenton emergency control. As a turned the chopper round the far side of the booster station out of the corner of his left eye he noticed a flash, a reflected light, it was followed almost immediately by another explosion on the pipeline. Lee knew that he had seen the sun reflecting off an aircraft wing or fuselage; he completed his turn and was now facing directly at the site of the latest explosion. Dropping the nose and cursing the wellhead hung beneath the helicopter he headed as fast as he could towards the position he had last seen the aircraft.

'This is Lee Ballinger, Trenton Two calling in an emergency on Guard channel, I am flying the Trenton pipeline south, my position is, just a sec I am going to press the squawk button', he pressed the button, has that shown my position?'

'Lee this is Sergeant Winnow National Guard Salina AFB; we have your position what is the emergency?'

'Some bastard is blowing up the Trenton pipeline, maybe bombing it I don't know, you need to advise Trenton direct that we have one booster station number D Delta destroyed and on fire, and wellhead 34 also destroyed and on fire.' I am following a Cessna single engined aircraft, it's about 1 mile distant, my airspeed is 110 knots.'

Also you should be aware a situation exists with the FBI, you need to contact their San Antonio office immediately that's why I called in on 'Guard '.

Lee was beginning to catch up with the Cessna, he moved over to his left to try to get the rising sun behind if he could as he made his approach, the pilot of the Cessna hadn't noticed him, but that wouldn't last long.

What the hell was he going to do? Another explosion and a section of pipeline was no more, it didn't catch fire but began discharging thousands of gallons an hour of crude oil over the landscape. The booster station further up the line was doing its job very efficiently.

He knew what he had to do!

'Lee, this is Salina AFB, fire fighting units are on their way, we have an F16 Strike Eagle being prepped right now he will be airborne and over your location in 15 minutes over.'

'Trenton two to Salina AFB, another section of pipe has gone, what are the F16's rules of engagement over?'

'Hold Trenton Two'.

'Trenton two, he will over fly the Cessna as close as possible, and scare the shit out of him, then direct him to Salina, there is a chopper on its way to intercept and escort him to Salina AFB over.'

Another section of pipeline went up, with the same spillage, this caught fire.

'Trenton two, to Salina another section of pipeline has gone up, south of the last one, my position is, ---- he squawked again, this guy is crazy I am going to try to get him to land, or at least frighten him off!!'

Lee was now some ¼ of a mile away a closing fast, what happened next seemed to be in slow motion but in reality only took 5 seconds; they were the longest of Lee's life.

Lee moved up to run parallel on the left of the Cessna and slightly higher he wanted to turn the Cessna pilot away from the pipeline and to the west of the pipeline over rough scrubland, the Cessna pilot started to turn to his left and towards the helicopter now some 100 feet away, he saw the wellhead dangling under the Huey and was too late to avoid it entirely, but managed to fly under it, the wellhead just caught the top of the Cessna's tail plane, and it seemed to stop in midair for a split second, bits flew off and hit the huey, the Cessna continued its very low level flight to the east , it was now at about 250 foot in the air wobbling slightly and gaining height when the tail plane fell of, the Cessna dived straight into the ground, turning over twice before exploding, and coming to rest in pieces.

The cabin and engine remained together. As Lee flew over the remains of the Cessna he could see the pilot still strapped into his seat and not moving.

## The President Is Down

'Trenton two to Salina AFB, there has been an accident, the Cessna collided with the wellhead I am transporting, its crashed the pilot appears to be dead.'

'Trenton two, be advised ground units will be on site within 2 minutes, they were close to guarding one of the entrances to the pipeline, they report full vision of the incident. Please confirm that the Cessna pilot flew into you over?'

'Trenton two to Salina AFB, yes he turned into me, the pilot can't of seen me until it was too late the last thing he would have expected would be a helicopter with a huge well head suspended underneath. I can see the ground based units now, I shall have to fly on to unload the well head, and I can't land until the well head is taken off.'

The Huey was now at 150 feet and flying at 85 knots, there was little warning when it came just a slight shake from side to side, then the tail rotor started to break up, ' Jesus Christ, Mayday-Mayday, this is Trenton two going down, Lee started to descend rapidly whilst bleeding off forward speed as he did so, the tail rotor disintegrated whilst he was still airborne and at around 100 feet, the chopper immediately started to rotate and spin, the well head below could not keep up the spin speed and rapidly rose up to meet the descending helicopter. There was one awful collision which shook the chopper, it hit the ground still spinning, turned over and cart wheeled leaving the wellhead behind as the straps broke away. Lee was thrown out of the chopper and into a ditch. The huey's fuel tank caught fire and the helicopter exploded with a loud whoosh.

The troops on the ground, found him some minutes later in the ditch, having believed at first that he had been trapped and burned in the fire,---- Lee' Lucky ' Ballinger had survived yet again, with a broken leg, and collar bone. The Huey was worse off than the last one he had crashed 35 years ago to the day.

# Chapter forty

**Monday 1st December 2003, San Antonio Memorial Hospital.**

Lee Ballinger, awoke to find his wife Maria sat at his bedside and gently holding his left hand as though it would break. He smiled a weak smile through his still drug befogged mind. His mouth was dry and he had trouble speaking, 'hello, hell of a place to go on a date', still holding his hand she bent over and kissed him, and hugged him till it hurt.

'Don't you ever do that to me again Lee Ballinger or I shall have to find me another man,' she said with mock severity.

'He ain't gonna get the chance, he's fired, wrecking a US Army Huey is OK, they can afford it, hell we left over 600 in Viet Nam when we left, but wrecking one of mine is decidedly not on, as I said he's fired'.

Lee's eyes focused on the lanky frame of John 'Wayne' Trenton, stood at the foot of the bed with a huge grin on his face.

'Yep. You are no longer Vice President of Trenton Oil as of this morning; I have a last woken up. As of one hour ago I submitted my resignation to the 'Board' and shall be retiring at the end of next month. You are now President of Trenton Oil as you are too dangerous to let loose with a helicopter.'

'John Clarke has agreed to accept the position of Vice President.' So stop malingering and let's have you up and about ASAP. Your first job is to check out a new 'Condo' for me that I have bought in Barbados for a couple of weeks over Christmas. Then you officially take over on February 1st 2004. He came round the side of the bed and shook Lee's hand. He left Maria and Lee to their happy thoughts.

## 4.30pm Tuesday 2nd December 2003 Beeville, BW Texas Inn

The BW Texas Inn, Beeville, is just over an hours drive from downtown San Antonio, John Clarke had spoken with Chris Meddleman of the FBI and requested a meeting to discuss 'certain matters', Meddleman has suggested the BW Texas Inn, it being away from the 'office', and close to hand.

Meddleman was waiting in the bar when Clarke arrived, they shook hands.

'I have booked a room for the night so we have somewhere to talk privately if that's OK?' said Meddleman.

He led the way to room 205 at the rear of the hotel, the room was in fact a suite overlooking the golf course and lake at the rear of the hotel. Meddleman got two glasses from the bar put some ice in them both and poured two generous measures of 'Wild Turkey' in to them, he gave one to Clarke and sat down. The gas fire flames twinkled on the two cut glass glasses.

'So what's this all about John?'

'I agreed to help the FBI just over two years ago on an informal basis, primarily to advice on the Texas oil fields in respect of potential terrorist activity, that tenuous link was formalised some months after. Somehow or other I have now got myself involved in area's that are just not me, --- by that I mean ones I am not suited to, ---nor trained for. This business of going to Moscow is such an incident.'

'I know it worked out well when we had the approach from Milcovic that the FBI already had somebody who knew the oil industry and could step in. But that's over now, so-----.'

'Stop at that John, you see I have to tell you that we are coming to an end of our relationship, I have to tell YOU that regrettably your services are no longer required. We have decided to set up a full time oil company liaison expert as of next year.'

Now as I have said we have decided to create this position, and knowing you would probably turn us down, we have to unfortunately to let you go.

The severance pack is 12 months FBI pay, a 40% pension entitlement at the age of 55 yrs. And we have arranged that as the $200,000 you have received from Milcovic cannot be returned to him or his Company which has had its bank accounts frozen, all payments out prior to the freezing are being ignored. Therefore the view is that this sum of money was an expense payment, which the IRS has decided not to pursue. You may keep it.

'Now if you were to submit your resignation, I am sorry to say the 12 months FBI pay would not apply, and the total package may well have to be reassessed, he leant back in his chair with a big grin on his face, sorry, you were about to say?'

Clarke looked at him, 'nothing, absolutely nothing, of course I am dis-appointed but accept the FBI's assessment and consideration.' He leant forward and shook Meddleman's hand. 'Thanks Chris, I appreciate it'.

You might like to know, that both Androvitch and Irina have been granted immunity from prosecution, the right to stay in the USA and annual salaries and pensions plus the benefit of US personal protection programme, seems a bit unfair but the girl would lose her annual salary if she married.

There was a knock on the door which Clarke had his back to, I'll get it said Meddleman getting up. He walked past Clarke and to the door of the suite; he signalled the waitress to come in and pointed to the small table alongside Clarke. 'Put it down there please'.

The waitress moved past Meddleman and placed the silver tray with two glasses and a bucket of ice on the table nestling in the ice was a bottle of Champagne.

'Shall I open it Sir? The waitress moved the white napkin over the top of the bottle in anticipation.

Clarke in a daze stood up and turned round, facing him not three feet away was Irina, she looked at him with a mixture of anticipation, love and mild terror. He threw himself at her and enveloped her in his arms, kissing her gently and passionately for what seemed an age.

'Don't you ever leave me again,' he said gently pulling her down onto the rug in front of the flickering open fire.

An hour later he found the key to the suite on the bed, the note attached to it simply said, 'Enjoy'. Chris.

**0115 hours Thursday 4th December 2003 British Airways 777 flight to Heathrow, England.**
**High above the Atlantic Ocean.**

The two gentlemen sat in row two Club Class had had a good dinner, and had turned down the lights to try to get some sleep, the cabin attendant was reluctant to wake up the more elderly military looking gentleman he had seemed so tired. She gently shook his right shoulder and he was awake within a second.

'There's a call for you on the radio Sir Bernard, I am so sorry to have to wake you up.'

## The President Is Down

'That's all right my dear, lead on'.

Sir Bernard Hills accepted the headset from the first officer and put it to his ear, the message was being relayed from an AWAC's over the Atlantic on a secure channel direct from Downing Street.

'Sir Bernard Hills here'.

'I have the Prime Minister for you Sir Bernard, ----- go ahead Sir'.

Sir Bernard listened for a couple of minutes in shocked silence and simply said, 'Yes Prime Minister, we shall be with a soon as we can after landing, I have a car already arranged.'--- Thank you Captain, he went back to his seat.

He looked at Gardner fast asleep and turned on his side,------he would tell him later when he awoke that two bombs placed in the European Parliament building in Brussels had exploded, 125 people were known to be dead, many more were missing in the now huge demolition site.

# About the author.

Colin G Poplett Born in Yorkshire, England during the middle of the last war .CG Poplett is a former British police officer, and a former C.E.O. of a number of British businesses. He is happily married, with two long since grown up daughters, and lives with his wife of some 40 years in his now beloved West Country.

This is his first novel, and will not be his last. More are envisaged depicting World events, and MI6 (SIS) and Sir Bernard Hills and his team.

Printed in the United Kingdom
by Lightning Source UK Ltd.
106738UKS00001B/296